THE BEAUTIFUL STRANG__

When Jim McGowan brings  is
small mill town, no one kno
With her dark hair and flaw
most beautiful woman any oᵣ ᴜᴇ.ᴜ ʜᴀᴠᴇ ᴇᴠᴇᴜ ꜱᴇᴇᴜ. ɪt
is as if Elizabeth Taylor had moved to town. So
naturally, Lester Coleman, the town wolf, has to make
his play. But Terese only has eyes for Jim, and doesn't
give Lester a moment's thought. Which doesn't stop
the tongues from wagging—the jealous wives are
quick to assume the worst about Terese. And while
they worry about the new woman in town, the men
debate the possibility of the union coming in. Everyone
knows that Lester is a snitch for management. The
situation is primed for disaster. And that is just what
happens.

THE MISSING HEIRESS

Seventeen-year-old heiress, Virginia Forester, has gone
missing. Has she been kidnapped, or is she just hiding
out? The hunt is on, and all the newspapers run the
story. So when a new couple show up at the Shady
Dell trailer park, Mrs. Camarilla is suspicious. There's
a reward for Virginia's return, and Mrs. Camarilla
would like to be the one to receive it. But first she
must deal with the problem of an old nemesis who
pulls into the park with a new husband and a new
identity. There may be a quick profit to be made here
as well. When Mrs. Camarilla is found murdered in
her trailer, the cops find their missing heiress. But the
coincidence is more than Inspector Granger can allow.
Only Virginia had something to gain by the death of
Mrs. Camarilla—and that is exactly who he suspects.

Bernice Carey Bibliography (1910-1990)

Novels:

The Reluctant Murderer (1949)

The Body on the Sidewalk (1950)

The Man Who Got Away With It (1950)

The Beautiful Stranger (1951)

The Three Widows (1952)

The Missing Heiress (1952)

Their Nearest and Dearest (1953;
   abridged as *The Frightened Widow*, 1954)

The Fatal Picnic (1955)

Stories:

Wanted: Wealthy Husband (McClure Newspapers, 1935;
   as Bernice Carey Fitch)

Columbine Street (*Story*, Nov-Dec 1939; as by Bernice Carey Fitch)

Just Jerry (*Breezy Stories*, December 1949; as Bernice Carey Fitch)

He Got What He Deserved (*The Lethal Sex*, 1959)

THE BEAUTIFUL STRANGER

THE MISSING HEIRESS

TWO NOVELS BY

BERNICE CAREY

INTRODUCTION BY CURTIS EVANS

STARK
HOUSE

Stark House Press • Eureka California

THE BEAUTIFUL STRANGER / THE MISSING HEIRESS

Published by Stark House Press
1315 H Street
Eureka, CA 95501, USA
griffinskye3@sbcglobal.net
www.starkhousepress.com

THE BEAUTIFUL STRANGER
Originally published and copyright © 1951 by Doubleday & Company, Inc.,
New York. Copyright renewed January 5, 1979, by Bernice Carey Martin.

THE MISSING HEIRESS
Originally published and copyright © 1952 by Doubleday & Company, Inc.,
New York. Reprinted in digest format by Mercury Publications, New York,
1954. Copyright renewed January 10, 1980, by Bernice Carey Martin.

"He Got What He Deserved" originally published in The Lethal Sex edited
by John D. MacDonald, published by Dell Books, New York, 1959, and
copyright © 1959 by Mystery Writers of America by arrangement with the
author.

Reprinted by permission of the Bernice Carey estate. All rights reserved
under International and Pan-American Copyright Conventions.

"Women Alone: Bernice Carey, The Missing Heiress and The Beautiful
Stranger" copyright © 2022 by Curtis Evans.

ISBN: 978-1-951473-79-2

Book design by Mark Shepard, shepgraphics.com
Proofreading by Bill Kelly

First Stark House Press Edition: July 2022

Women Alone:
Bernice Carey, The Missing Heiress and The Beautiful Stranger

By Curtis Evans

Crime writer Bernice Carey was born, and lived for the first sixteen years of her life, in Chetek, a little town nestled by lakes in northwestern Wisconsin that derived its name from the Ojibwa Native American tribe's word *zhedeg*, meaning pelican. Caucasian settlers variously spelled the name, to them strange, as Sheetak, Shetak and Chetack before finally settling upon Chetek when the small community's first post office opened in 1872. When Bernice Carey was born in Chetek on June 27, 1910, the town had, according to the federal census conducted that year, a population of but 829 individuals, including the newborn Bernice and her parents, Charles Carey, a realtor and farmer, and Caroline (Hansen) Carey, the eldest daughter of Danish immigrant farmers Hans and Dorothea Hansen, who had originally settled out on the plains of Nebraska around 1880. When, sixteen years later in 1926, Bernice left home for what she hoped would be bigger, brighter things in California, Chetek's population had increased by less than a couple of hundred people.

In August 1949, after the publication of her debut novel, the inverted crime tale *The Reluctant Murderer*, a newspaper in the town of Bruce, near the town of Thornapple, where the widowed Charley Carey then lived, interviewed both Carey and his writer daughter for an article, in which Bernice talked about her happy early years in Chetek, some twenty-five miles from Bruce. "It was during my childhood in Chetek that I first became an ardent reader," she recalled. The family subscribed to the *Superior Evening Telegram*, published in the city of Duluth, Minnesota, about 120 miles to the north, and for Bernice the *Telegram* had been as much a part of childhood "as the hammock hanging between towering elms in front of my Grandmother Hansen's farmhouse ... where I used to spend the summer afternoons catching up with [the comic strip] 'Freckles and His Friends.'" She noted proudly that her late mother Lena had served as the *Telegram*'s local correspondent in their little corner of rural Wisconsin.

While living in Los Angeles between 1926 and 1928 Bernice Carey, a tall, tomboyish-looking girl with a shaggy bobbed haircut, attended Long Beach Polytechnic High School, the largest high school, in terms of student population, west of the Mississippi, where she served, following in her mother's footsteps, as a reporter on the school newspaper, *High Life*. (The paper also published a parody paper, called, naturally enough, *Low Life*.) But the immediate question in this context is: how did Bernice, then but sixteen years old, end up living in Los Angles, while her parents remained behind in Chetek? No one in her family seems to have any idea. My conclusion is that Bernice must have gone to live with relations, presumably her Aunts Lois and Lucy Carey, younger sisters of her father Charley and twins who became nurses and moved out to California and married sometime in the 1910s—although Lois and Lucy lived in the San Francisco area and Bernice attended school in Los Angeles. In any event, on June 25, 1928, just a few weeks after her graduation from high school, Bernice, then two days shy of her eighteenth birthday, and a certain Walter Haynes Fitch, a young man of twenty-three originally from Arizona who was also the offspring of a farmer, filed in the *LA Times* a notice of intention to marry, which they did a week later on July 2. Their marriage would last fourteen years, with Bernice giving birth to sons in 1938 and 1940 before the couple permanently parted not long afterward.

Two years after her marriage in 1930, twenty-year-old Bernice Fitch, as she was now known, resided with her twenty-five-year-old husband Walter some seventy miles northwest of Los Angeles at a small rented house with no radio set in the small city of Ventura, then undergoing an economic boom due to the heavy drilling in the Ventura Oil Field that had commenced a decade earlier. Between 1920 and 1930 Ventura's population nearly tripled, from around 4000 to about 12,000. A fit five foot nine and 155 pounds with blond hair and blue eyes, Walter Fitch worked in the oil field as a rotary helper, or "roughneck," i.e., worker on a drilling rig, subordinate to the driller, whose primary station is on the rig floor.

After three years of marriage the Fitches moved upstate to the family-owned company town of Spreckels in Monterey County, then home to the Spreckels Sugar Company, the largest sugar beet factory in the world, and later Alisal, a working class neighborhood of Salinas, the county seat of Monterey, then populated heavily by Latinos and Midwestern Okies displaced by the calamitous Dust Bowl. By this time Walter was a foreman with the Salinas Valley Wax Paper Company. The couple had migrated politically as well, or at least Walter had, he having started out as a registered Republican in Ventura. Possibly Bernice had always had leftist inclinations.

For a list of party registrations taken when Bernice and Walter lived in Spreckels, in which their occupations were given as housewife and laborer, the Fitches together declined to provide any political their party affiliation. They were two of only three households of the over 370 people to so decline. (Another individual declared no party affiliation, while everyone else declared themselves either Republicans or Democrats.) Since Bernice subscribed to, and published review articles and other pieces in, the Communist newspaper the *Daily Worker*, which at its peak in the Thirties attained a circulation in the United States of 35,000, it is not difficult to surmise where her, and presumably her husband's, political sympathies lay.

Bernice's journey from housewife to professional writer was a long one, with her first novel not appearing until 1949, when she was nearly forty years old and several years into her second marriage, to like-minded high school history teacher Dick Martin. In 1933, after five years of marriage with Walter, she began publishing poems, under the name Bernice Carey Fitch, in the *Oakland Tribune*, where they appeared regularly for the next three years. Poetry often is an intensely personal literary form, so we can perhaps infer certain autobiographical details from Bernice's poems. Some of the details are anodyne, like the revelation from "Worshipper" (1936) that Bernice likely owned a cat (or was owned by a cat, as the case may be):

Cat,
With golden, half-shut eyes
Purring,
Rubbing sleekly at my feet,
Why do you follow me,
Trembling as in ecstasy,
Like one before an idol's shrine?

Is it because I deign to smile at you?
Is it adoration?
No,
You only want
Another can
Of salmon.

Other poems, like "Housewives" (1936), hint at other, profounder dissatisfactions in Bernice's life than the presence of a mercenary, salmon-devouring feline, anticipating the feminist thought of Betty Friedan, who similarly had been discontented with her lot and attracted to

Marxism in the 1930s and '40s:

> "I got this pattern from Suzanne—
> Cunning, isn't it?
> I don't think she looks good in tan.
> Yes, I've just learned to knit."

> "Pork chops for dinner, that sounds
> good.
> I baked a cake today.
> Our bridge club meets, I under-
> stood
> With Grace, or is it May?"

> The world may sweat in pangs of
> death
> From economic ills,
> Ready to draw the faithful breath
> Which either saves or kills;

> Philosophies may change the
> thought
> Of millions by their force,
> Science fresh wonder may have
> wrought,
> Art flow in some new course;

> But, sunk in triviality,
> Of food, and clothes, and games,
> They sit and chatter endlessly,
> Engrossed by trifling aims.

Another poem, "The Dark Day" (1936), deals not with global economic depression, but the author's mental depression:

> The skies are pressing down with
> heavy, grey
> Restlessness, and there is nothing
> bright
> To pierce the dreary pall of rain
> this day
> Has worn to hide its mournful face
> from sight.

I shall control my melancholy fear,
This sick despair I'll suffer till
again
The sun returns. Perhaps when skies
are clear
New strength will come. If not—
if not—what then?

One can surmise that in her writing Bernice Carey found some measure of personal satisfaction which she was not finding in her marriage and housewifery. In 1936 she found a new literary outlet when a play which she had written, a three-act comedy-romance titled *The Young Folks at Home*, was staged by the newly organized drama club in Spreckels. Bernice, who was vice-president of the club, also directed the play, the eight-member cast of which included her husband, Walter. In 1939, not long after Bernice had given birth to her first son, William Carey Fitch, she published a short story, "Columbine Street," in the prestigious literary magazine *Story*, which then enjoyed a circulation of 21,000. Motherhood and marital crisis disrupted her writing during the war, however, and in 1948 she even found herself publicly denounced as a Communist in the California Legislature's Fourth Report of the Senate Fact-Finding Committee on Un-American Activities (Communist Front Organizations), based on her having published subversive pieces in the *Daily Worker* like "Two Good Books for Youngsters."

However, with the steadfast encouragement of her second husband, Bernice, who claimed never actually to have read a mystery story when she started writing her first one, found her footing precisely as a writer of crime fiction with a social conscience, which attracted an audience and won critical praise even in the Frightened Fifties.

The eponymous character of *The Missing Heiress*, Bernice Carey's sixth of eight crime novels and the second that she published in 1952, to some extent reflects the author's own youthful personal experience. When seventeen-year-old schoolgirl heiress Virginia Wilkins Forester becomes smitten with handsome male gas station attendant Bill Morgan, she runs off and marries him, albeit illicitly, being at age seventeen legally underage to marry without her widowed father's permission. The pair hide out, Virginia incognito under the name Marge, in Shady Dell trailer park, located near San Jose. There she tries to avoid the persistent inquisitions of the nosy local hoi polloi, like Josie MacLaren, "self-appointed arbiter of the manners and morals of Shady Dell," and her more reserved and perceptive friend, Stella Camarilla, who suspects their new tenant might be the missing heiress in all the newspapers and hopes to cash in on the $10,000 reward for information leading to her recovery. When Stella ends up shot dead in her trailer and the police tumble to Marge Morgan's true identity, Virginia becomes their prime suspect. Can she and Bill find Mrs. Camarilla's true killer, all the while fending off the plaints over her perfidy from her wealthy family?

Crime writer and reviewer Frances Crane pronounced *The Missing Heiress* the "best story this reader has read by Miss Carey," with a "wind-up [that] is very well-handled." In my estimation *Heiress* is indeed a quite entertaining and suspenseful crime tale, benefitting from its convincing setting and characters that are decidedly out of the norm for many vintage mysteries (especially those by women authors), where even in the Fifties the crime milieus tended to be more suburban and middle class (if not upper) than is the case with Shady Dell. In terms of the novel's trailer park setting, readers might have to look back a decade to find something similar, to *Mother Finds a Body*, the 1942 detective novel by a decidedly unorthodox mystery writer, stripper Gypsy Rose Lee.

It seems likely that, like Gypsy Rose, Bernice Carey wrote of what she knew, by which I mean that she likely had experienced trailer park life as the young, lonely bride of a roughneck. In 1936 she published a poem, "Trailer House," that is quite suggestive in this context. Moreover, Bernice also is able to place herself very convincingly into the mind of her seventeen-year-old runaway bride, which is not surprising, given that Bernice herself married just a week after her eighteenth-birthday to a blond and blue-eyed boy who was five years her elder and worked ruggedly in the oil fields. Surely this act came, at the least, as something of an unpleasant surprise to her family, just as Virginia's decidedly does to her wealthy relations in *Heiress*. Bernice limns both the development of her young couple's relationship and Virginia's personality with admirable economy and firm strokes.

Indeed, *The Missing Heiress* is a quietly superb crime novel, refreshingly far removed from both the high and low life of typical mid-century murder. Critic Anthony Boucher, who observed that the crime novel was really an affecting tale of "the heiress' attempt to integrate herself with a life she never suspected existed," was moved to reflect how Bernice Carey had remarkably managed to discover murder's sweet spot, if you will, between classic mystery's "glamorous and ostentatiously overwealthy upper classes" and the hoods and gangsters of the hard-boiled school, which had "abandoned the penthouse for the gutter."

□ □ □

Remarkable as well is *The Beautiful Stranger*, which appeared the previous year in 1951. The novel, for which Bernice drew on the few years she resided with Walter in Spreckels, is as much a study of a community as it is a story of a crime. Here the murder is not so important in and of itself, but in how it impacts the people of the California mill town of Conway, named for the fabulously wealthy San Francisco family who own it, for whom Bernice drew inspiration from the real life Spreckels family. Among the plain people of Conway we find the eponymous lovely stranger, Terese, mill worker Jim McGowan's beauteous new bride, a former San Francisco shopgirl deemed even more of a knockout than that big film star Elizabeth Taylor. To her dismay Terese finds that the women of Conway view her with reflexive suspicion, because of her great beauty and seeming remoteness. Why would someone who looks that gorgeous ever be content to live in little Conway, so the prevailing view runs. What is she hiding in her past?

The author digs deep into the company town's social attitudes, and what she unearths makes very interesting reading, brimming with insight. "In Conway people never really expected to get the Best, in women or in anything else about life," she observes. "Somehow in Conway you just accepted the fact—without even thinking about it—that there were all kinds of things that were too good for you, things that only people like [mill boss] Mr. Faber and the almost mythical Conway family could have."

When the would-be town wolf, Les Coleman, starts flirting (futilely) with Terese, rumor alights from the idle tongues of housewives, who often find themselves with altogether too much time on their hands, that Terese must be something akin to a floozy. When Les is found beaten to death in an alley, suspicion focuses on Jim, although blame for Les' death is placed firmly on the putative woman in the case, Terese. If Jim killed Les, so the view runs, it must have been Terese, clearly no better than she should be, who drove him to do it.

But is there an alternative explanation for Les's death, one having to do with the recent drive to expand union membership? The labor group known as the CIO (Congress of Industrial Organizations) has come to town, we learn, wanting to unionize every worker at the mill, and the owners and management are not happy about this development at all. In addition to being a wolf, it seems, Les had also been something of a company stool-pigeon....

Anthony Boucher praised *The Beautiful Stranger* for achieving "an unusually successful blend of a study of union difficulties with a purely personal plot" and concluded that it "makes a movingly real novel." He argued that Bernice Carey's realistic and socially conscious novel offered welcome relief from the great bulk of complacent American crime fiction, which was hardly representative of the real American scene:

> There's a belief among publishers and editors that American readers prefer, in their escape entertainment, a "nicer" sort of life than that which they themselves lead. I'm not sure how justified this belief is; but it results in the fact that the lower middle class and the working man are almost completely absent from the detective story, save for incidental witnesses, comedy-relief bit-parts and an occasional Pegler-type labor racketeer. [This is a reference to right-wing curmudgeon journalist Westbrook Pegler, who won a Pulitzer Prize in 1941 for his work exposing racketeering in Hollywood labor unions.]
>
> The man from Mars, reading a year's crop of whodunits, would wind up with some strange ideas as to the prevalence of penthouses and country estates, and would never learn even of the existence of trade unions. (Which is particularly odd since most writers belong to a trade organization of some sort, the Mystery Writers of America or the Authors Guild.)

I agree with Anthony Boucher that Carey does a wonderful job of bringing the company town of Conway and its citizens to life in what constitutes a fascinating variant on the English village mystery, one however that happily sheds classic mystery's often condescending attitude toward the working class. The labor issues could not be timelier for readers these days, with the attitudes of the white blue collar workers having become a much discussed political topic. Conway seemingly is almost an all-white town, although the well-off Fabers bring in a black maid from San Francisco, Dora, and there is a major second-generation Mexican-American character, Johnny Rodriguez. How much, readers may ask themselves, have popular attitudes changed since the 1950s, as portrayed in the novel?

The author does not neglect the Conway's "better half," however—far from it. Terese is an extremely well-rendered portrait, as are several lesser female characters in the novel, and the social observation of these women is on the level which we find in the best of Golden Age British mystery, although the author as mentioned evinces genuine interest in all social classes and refrains from reducing the workers to the level of caricature.

This 1951 novel provides a crisp, clear snapshot of the postwar years in the United States, when women were being urged to shed wartime jobs, get married, keep house and raise kids. Most of the women of Conway have fallen in with this way of thinking, in stark contrast, as we have seen, with the author herself, who clearly felt constrained in the twinset roles of housewife and mother.

Conway wives tend to be more cautious about pushing the union issue, being fearful of jeopardizing their economic security and their tidy homes filled with "automatic" appliances and labor-saving devices. ("You men. Always taking things so seriously," chides Jim's mother about the union squabbles.) Yet they often are bored too. ("There was only so much housework one could find to do.") Jim McGowan's younger sister, Florence, idling away her life after high school, is addicted to trashy romance magazines, her mother reflects.

Here is an example of some of the social observation which accompanies the murder, as the author discusses film-star-beautiful Terese's touchingly modest dreams for her life in Conway:

> Terese was wearing a yellow sun-back dress with only straps over her shoulders, and even at ten in the morning she looked fresh as a daffodil. Lorraine noticed that, and it fretted her a little.
>
> Somehow, even when they wore clean, starched house dresses, most wives seemed to look slightly bedraggled until early afternoon. During the course of dishwashing and bedmaking and scrubbing out the bathroom washbowl, your lipstick faded and face powder mysteriously vanished and your hair separated and the starchiness departed from your skirt.
>
> Lorraine did not stay long, but Terese went back to her ironing with a new buoyancy, thinking already of what she would wear the next evening and dreaming ahead of the days to come, when the rigidity would relax between her and Lorraine, and Lorraine would come and sit in the kitchen while she went right on with the ironing and they talked over all kinds of intimate things, like how soon they wanted to have babies and how much they had paid for their washing machines and whether an automatic was really the best....

This really is the essence of a crime novel—i.e., a study of how a murder impacts people's lives—and, as such, it is a very good one indeed. Crime fiction had broadened enough by the Fifties to give scope to ambitious writers like Bernice Carey, who wanted to use violent death to reflect on passionate life, in the manner of the mainstream novel. In this sense, one might argue, *The Beautiful Stranger* is the author's finest achievement, and a fitting finish to Stark House's welcome series of Bernice Carey reissues.

—April 2022
Germantown, TN

Curtis Evans received a PhD in American history in 1998. He is the author of *Masters of the "Humdrum" Mystery: Cecil John Charles Street, Freeman Wills Crofts, Alfred Walter Stewart and British Detective Fiction, 1920-1961* (2012) and most recently the editor of the Edgar nominated *Murder in the Closet: Essays on Queer Clues in Crime Fiction Before Stonewall* (2017) and, with Douglas G. Greene, the Richard Webb and Hugh Wheeler short crime fiction collection, *The Cases of Lieutenant Timothy Trant* (2019). He blogs on vintage crime fiction at The Passing Tramp.

THE BEAUTIFUL STRANGER

BERNICE CAREY

To Richard

CHAPTER 1

Most of the streets in Conway had no sidewalks. Between the tall white oaks with their charmingly uneven bough spread and the modest lawns bound sometimes by low privet hedges, sometimes by picket fences, sometimes by no separating markers at all, ran smooth dirt paths as hard-packed as asphalt.

Lorraine Bowen stood shielded by the casement-cloth draperies of her living-room window and watched Terese McGowan walk past on the path. Lorraine had not been married a full year as yet, and people still thought of her as what in an older day they would have called "the village belle." Although a new bevy of high-school lassies was emerging into delectable maturity, Lorraine was still remembered as the prettiest girl in Conway.

But now Jim McGowan had brought Terese onto the scene.

Any young woman who was suddenly introduced into Conway as a bride and whom no one in the village had seen before would have aroused interest and curiosity, but in this case people began to look at Jim as if he himself were a stranger.

His father, Tom McGowan, had been a maintenance foreman in the mill almost as long as anyone could remember. Jim and his brothers Ned and George and his sister Florence had all been born in the same house facing the road that led to town. Jim had done nothing remarkable in his life. He had gone through the eight grades of the Conway elementary school and graduated from the high school in town ten miles away and gone around some with Lorraine Miller who was Bowen now (with quite a few people thinking they might make a match of it) and taken a job in the maintenance crew in the mill and gone on living with his folks.

Somehow, people said, it was so *unexpected*.

As Terese passed the house next to Lorraine's, Mrs. Fraser lifted her head from where it had been bent over the pansy bed under her front-room window and said, "Good morning."

Terese started, but returned the "good morning" politely. It was a new experience, this being greeted by strangers. In the city you ignored people you didn't know. But already she was getting used to it.

Looking ahead, Terese raised her eyes to the irregular lines of the oak tree limb that straggled out heavily from the parent trunk to cast its drooping shadow over the Hansons' graveled walk and yellow frame walls.

The people she knew in the city had viewed with some misgiving her going so far away and to such an out-of-the-way place—and such a little one. They had hinted to her that she would die. What did people *do* in Conway—population, Jim said, about six hundred?

She had wondered herself, but she had been ready for a change—any change. And now she was not sorry. Actually it was fun. Almost like living in the middle of Golden Gate Park. Anywhere you looked you saw leaves and flowers and grass, and in three directions, when you raised your eyes above the housetops, you saw the crest of hills with more trees growing down the depressions in their sides.

The meditations of Emily Fraser as she regarded Terese's retreating back were almost identical to those of Mrs. Hanson, who was sitting in an awninged canvas chair on her own side lawn, keeping an eye on the baby in its play pen and sewing buttonholes into the new play suit she was making for herself.

You had to admit the girl was beautiful. You admitted it, but you could hardly believe it—accept it, that is, deep down. Somehow you felt like denying it. But you couldn't.

This morning the bride wore navy blue gabardine slacks that *fit*—and I do mean fit, Gloria Hanson thought to herself—and a closely woven white sweater, with a wide red leather belt concealing the meeting place of slacks and sweater. Her hair gleamed black and silky and thick. It was straight and cut in bangs, curving in a gentle swell where it almost turned under all the way around. Her mouth was as red as the belt and shaped with as generous yet controlled precision as her figure. Already there had been comprehensive discussion among the women of Conway about Terese McGowan's eyes, with particular reference to their lashes. Gloria Hanson, in fact, was sure that, even at the distance of twenty feet from which she saw the woman now, she had been able to detect the sweeping spread of those lashes. Talking about it, she and Lorraine had decided that Terese's eyes really were brown; it was the shadowing lashes that made them look black.

Instinctively the women on the East Side of the park had recoiled in distrust from Jim McGowan's bride. There was something wrong. They just felt it in their bones. A woman who looked like that—there was something funny about her marrying a nice but unremarkable boy like Jim McGowan and moving prosaically into Mr. Cantoni's little house which had been providentially vacant for several months. A woman that beautiful—why, she could have been a movie actress, or at least an advertising model. So what was she doing here?

Only Marge Vale, the school principal's wife, had pursed her lips doubtfully over these views. The Vales, although their status as professional people might have admitted them to the north of the park crowd, were a part of the East Side, and not only because their house happened to face the park from the east. It was partly that when Byron Vale came in as principal twenty years before, he had married Marge Swanson, whose father was a carpenter on the mill staff, and that all Marge's friends and relatives were East Side people. It was partly also from choice on Mr. Vale's part. He was a man who shied away from formal social contacts and didn't seem to mind being considered a part of what the office crowd probably called "the workers" (behind said "workers'" backs; *they* considered themselves middle class).

Marge Vale, even before she married Byron, had been considered the bright one of her generation in Conway. Since she was not pretty, her nose being too long and thin, her eyes a little too closely set, it had probably been natural that she cultivated intelligence, although she never became so intellectual that it showed and made her obnoxious to the rest of the hometown folks.

In regard to Terese, Marge had demurred at Mrs. Fraser's remarks, tapping a cigarette on one of her extra-long, maroon-colored nails and saying consideringly, "Just being beautiful doesn't automatically make a girl a candidate for Hollywood or the cover of the *Ladies' Home Journal.* You have to have ambition—drive—and you have to be smart—on your toes, I mean, quick to see and take an advantage. And naturally it helps to have a little pull. And from what Gladys McGowan says, Terese's people are just working folks, no connections to fall back on. Of course you can't tell just from looking at the girl on the street, but I have a hunch that inside she's just ordinary like the rest of us, too lazy probably to try to get out and really *do* something about herself."

"Well, if what Gladys McGowan says is true, she was working in Woolworth's in San Francisco before she got married, and—*if* it's true, mind you—I don't think that shows she was lazy. After all, you know, I worked in the Bon Marché in town for two years after I got out of high school. And believe *me*, working in any kind of a store is no job for a lazy person. You get tired *out*."

"I know, I know; it's hard work, but you don't have to figure and plan and push yourself to the front; that's what I mean. I just suspect Terese hasn't got that kind of gumption."

"Well, maybe," Emily Fraser conceded unwillingly, "but, I ask you, did you ever see a more beautiful woman—outside the movies, that is?"

"N-no, I don't believe I ever did."

"Look at Lorraine Bowen. She was always the prettiest girl in town. Beautiful, with that naturally curly golden-brown hair and such a lovely complexion. But what does she look like beside this Terese? And yet Terese married Jim McGowan."

"Well, Jim's a nice-looking fellow, and not stupid or anything. And he's decent, never been in any trouble or anything."

"Honestly now, Marge. You know there're all kinds of fellows you can say that about. But how many women can you say are beautiful, really beautiful?"

Marge laughed. "Not about me anyway."

CHAPTER 2

Technically, Terese was on her way to the post office to see if there was any mail, but actually she was sort of reviewing the town again. It fascinated her, probably mainly because Jim had lived here *all his life*. Of course she had lived in San Francisco all her life, but in a different neighborhood every year or so. Her folks rented, and they were always trying to "do better," and the trail had led from Army Street to Dolores in the Mission, from McAllister out Fillmore way to Green in North Beach, and finally back to the upper Mission district with a flat on Seventeenth Street.

For Jim to have known one little neighborhood so intimately all the years of his life was amazing and in some ways rather awe-inspiring. And the things he knew about everybody! How much money they made, how long and to whom they'd been married, and every operation and illness everybody had had—it fairly made you gasp to think of knowing so much about so many people.

If Terese had known of the reactions she had produced in Conway, she would have been self-conscious and a little unhappy. She was used to cattiness from other girls and to wolf calls from men, and she was not unconscious of the way the men here in Conway eyed her surreptitiously in the store and at the post office; but she had assumed, without deliberately thinking it out, that her married status would change the way other girls her own age regarded her. As far as the older women were concerned, she did not think about them at all.

Instead of going straight to the post office, which was housed in the same building as the general store, between the store and the County Library (open Monday and Thursday, 7:30 to 9:30 P.M.), Terese turned at the corner and walked north along the park to turn again at the next corner and walk west on the dirt path edging the park lawns.

The park covered an area the size of two city blocks, and Terese thought it was lovely with its magnolias and palm trees and cedars, and flowering shrubs, and eucalyptus in a tall, graceful row to the west.

When the company had laid out the town some fifty years before, the park had been a magnanimous attempt to give all the residents a beautiful central "grounds" for collective enjoyment. The people of Conway enjoyed it, all right, but not in the sense the company had intended. They seldom used it. When they sat out of doors they did so in their own yards, and when and if they took walks, it was on the cement sidewalk past the one-story frame clubhouse next to the little County Library building, and around the corner past the store and down past the service station and the hotel, which was actually a large dormitory for the single men who worked in the mill. People looked at the park as they drove past in their cars, and deemed it "nice," and the families on the North Side cut through on their way to the store; but except for an occasional young couple out for an evening stroll, that was the extent of its usefulness.

Terese contemplated the row of houses on the North Side as she strolled along. They were all alike—solid two-story brown bungalows with dormer windows above deep porches. The lawns were not much more extensive than those on the East Side, but the houses were heavier, bigger. The office people lived here—the bosses in the office, that is, the ones who had little private offices or desks with a sign indicating their title. A few of the office help lived on the East Side—Millard Ellis, one of the bookkeepers, and Dorothy Goodwin, who was on the switchboard—but most of the stenographers and secretaries and business-machine operators came out from town on the bus every morning. It was surprising how few girls from Conway, even when they graduated with a commercial course diploma from the high school in town, got jobs in the Conway office. And when the men from the East Side went to work they disappeared into the darker regions in the rear of the office building, into the impressive, somewhat forbidding realm of black overhead pipes and massive, groaning engines and relentless conveyor belts and spinning wheels. Terese did not as yet know all this, but she was to learn gradually.

Lolita Morgan was returning home from the store, having cut across the park as usual, and as she emerged onto the street from between two oleander bushes she came face to face with Terese, who met her eyes indifferently and continued on her way, alternately contemplating the residences across the street and the variety of the shrubs in the park, thinking her own thoughts about what an adventure it all was, being married and coming to live in such a strange place.

Lolita had not seen the girl before, and she hesitated before crossing the street, staring after the white-sweatered figure, definitely taken aback. It was not entirely the shock of the young woman's beauty. It was also the unconcerned, almost abstracted manner in which Terese had met her eyes. People in Conway did not ignore one another when they met on the street, even though one of them might be a visiting stranger.

When Lolita had put her groceries away on the cupboard shelves and in the refrigerator, she sat down by the breakfast table and picked up the telephone from its shelf on the papered wall to call Eleanor Combs at the west end of Office Row. After the usual amenities dealing with what they had "accomplished" that morning, Lolita volunteered, "Say, I just saw that girl Jim McGowan married—ran into her as I came out of the park. And is she stunning, absolutely stunning!"

"I haven't seen her yet," Eleanor replied, "but Fred says the fellows down at the mill are all dying to get a look at her. The ones that have seen her have nothing to say but—" Eleanor's voice went into a two-noted whistle.

"She really is something."

"Flashy, I suppose."

"Well, yes and no. The way she was dressed, it was a little obvious. No subtlety, you know. A lot of contrast. But not exactly cheap. That is, she seems to know what suits her. What got me was the way she looked at me as if I wasn't even there. I suppose, though, that's from living in the city. I heard she was born and raised in San Francisco."

"Kind of sophisticated, I suppose."

"Well, not exactly." There was a brief pause while each woman sat with her telephone curved around the meditative expression on her face, then Lolita continued: "It seems so odd. Jim McGowan. They're such ordinary people, and she's so—so extraordinary."

"Fred says the East Side is all agog. Bet there'll be some watchful wives over there." Eleanor giggled. "Maybe *we'd* better watch out."

"I guess we can be thankful we don't run around in the same crowd the McGowans do."

Before this conversation took place Terese had turned the northwest corner of the park and halted about midway of the block to stand with her hands in the pockets of her gabardine slacks, gazing unabashed at the superintendent's home across the street. It never occurred to her that in Conway you didn't stop to peer openly into other people's yards. In the city you stared at what you pleased: people coming out of the St. Francis in evening clothes, the winos on Skid Row, the intermission crowds in the lobbies of theaters on Geary Street.

A Japanese gardener was running a power-driven lawn mower over the green carpet of grass contained by the driveway that curved before the porticoed entrance of the square white house with its wide windows upstairs and down. To the rear on the south was a garage big enough for three cars, and to the north beyond a rose garden was a latticed structure overhung with bougainvillea.

Terese sighed appreciatively. It was really elegant. Except for the school grounds which adjoined it on the south beyond a eucalyptus grove, there was only this one big, clean white house on this side of town. The rest of Conway extended off to the east in front of it, while behind it the hills rose in gentle green waves against the sky.

This was where the Fabers lived. Terese had already heard about them. Miles Faber was The Boss at the mill. No one ever considered the fact that Mr. Faber was in actuality an employee too, for as far as anyone else in Conway was concerned he was the final authority in all mill matters. Of course they all knew, when they stopped to think about it, that there was a higher authority centered in an office on Montgomery Street in San Francisco, where presumably there were flesh-and-blood Conways sitting at mahogany desks Making Decisions. Some of the old-timers had actually seen one or more Conways, getting out of limousines at the steps of the front office, or flanked by worshipful attendants making inspection tours of the mill. Once, years before, Tom McGowan had actually had his hand shaken by old T.J. Now, of course, T.J. seldom left the seventeen-hundred-acre ranch in the Peninsula hills below San Francisco. But as far as the practical affairs of their lives went, the Conways might as well not have existed for all the apparent impact they had on the residents of the village which bore their name.

The people of Conway took a casual, friendly interest in the doings of the family who owned their mill. If they read in the paper that Felicia Conway was being sued for divorce by another of the scions of old European families whom she seemed to have a fancy for marrying, they would sometimes shake their heads in tolerant amazement at the size of the settlement reputedly made on the disillusioned ex-prince as the price of Felicia's freedom; but they didn't think much about it. Nor of how many of young Tyler Conway's race horses won prizes at Bay Meadows or Santa Anita. They were, in fact, strangely indifferent to the Conways, with neither resentment of nor pride in their own vague connection with the family. If word had come one day that the whole Conway tribe had been wiped out by an atomic explosion, the population of Conway would have thought, "That's too bad," and gone calmly ahead with its conveyor belts in the mill and its lawn mowing on the East Side.

The Fabers, however, they regarded differently. Nobody stood boldly staring at their residence as Terese now did, although every household was acutely aware of them. The men knew exactly what model Cadillac Miles was currently driving, could quote the gems of political or sociological wisdom which fell from his lips around the office, and would find excuses to repeat casual remarks they had exchanged with him on the grounds of the mill or on the sidewalk in front of the store. The women read avidly all the newspaper accounts of Mrs. Faber's bridge teas or her trips back East or the list of her house guests over holidays. Some of the ladies on Office Row got invited to her larger social affairs, but except for Marge and Byron Vale, almost no one on the East Side had ever set foot even in the big central hall with its open staircase and highly polished floors.

Terese was losing interest in the gardener and was about to move on when she saw a girl in white shorts come out of the front door with a tennis racket in her hand and cross to a convertible car parked in the driveway. Terese's interest immediately came back to life. She even took a step closer to the grassy curb. There was a white crepe ribbon in a band across the top of the girl's blond hair, tied at one side in the back with the two ends trailing on her shoulder. Terese made a mental note to do that to her own hair the next time she wore her white sun suit. Her hair being so black and with the bangs, it would really look neat.

She saw the girl glance at her as she stepped into the car. Terese's eyes never wavered as she watched admiringly while the engine started. It was some car, that sort of cocoa brown with gold lights in it.

Marguerite Faber thought little of it when she noticed the figure across the street. But as the car moved down the driveway she realized that the other woman was frankly watching her. Their eyes met as Marguerite swung into the street, and the stranger neither smiled with deferential friendliness nor dropped her eyes bashfully. Marguerite had come to expect one or the other from pedestrians in Conway. No, the girl just kept on gazing at her with undisguised curiosity. And then Marguerite saw how pretty she was—the perfect oval face, the wide-spaced eyes, the straight nose. Looking into the rearview mirror as she pulled away, Marguerite saw that the young woman had turned her head and was still watching the car. A slight annoyed frown passed over Marguerite's face. What nerve! Must be a stranger in town. (The Fabers had not heard of Jim McGowan's new wife. Mr. Faber might have, but his womenfolk did not keep up with across-the-park gossip.) Slowly Marguerite's frown returned and steadied on her face. What a really startling-looking person she was. It gave you the sort of surprised feeling you'd probably have if you ran into the actress Elizabeth Taylor on the street. Except—and the creases between Marguerite's eyes deepened with perplexity—this girl was, if anything, more beautiful than the actress, like something drawn or painted by an artist rather than constructed by clumsy nature. In Conway you didn't expect to be slapped across the face by Beauty. That girl Lorraine Miller (Bowen now, Marguerite believed) had always been considered the prettiest girl in town, and she was attractive, in an unsophisticated sort of way, but one didn't think of her as a beauty.

Marguerite raised her hand to tilt the rearview mirror and took a quick look at herself, as if for reassurance. Of course she knew that, strictly speaking, she herself was not beautiful. Her forehead was too high and broad and her chin, in contrast, too round and soft; and her eyes, with her blond coloring, should have been a clear blue, instead of which they were a greenish gray. But she had always been considered cute, had never really been dissatisfied with her looks. But there had been something about that girl—she almost made you feel insecure. No, not that, exactly. But somehow she gave you a feeling that something was wrong somewhere. Mentally Marguerite shrugged off these reflections. It was just, she guessed, that in dreary little old Conway it was disconcerting to come across anything so out of the ordinary.

CHAPTER 3

The Conway post office was as drearily brown inside as all the others that had been set up in the early days of the twentieth century, with narrow, worn boards in the floor and one wall of windowed boxes and another decorated by fading posters over the scarred ledges where one might stand to address envelopes.

When Terese walked in and went directly to the McGowan box—where she twirled the dial and extracted two circulars directed to Box Holder, a postcard in her mother's handwriting, and another of the square white envelopes she had received so bountifully lately, with their enclosed cards of congratulation—Miss Schweitzer looked up and out through the grilled window behind which she sat to dispense stamps and money orders. Whoever the patron of the United States postal system had turned out to be, Grace Schweitzer had been prepared to chirrup a good morning and to engage in a sprightly discussion of the lovely spring weather.

But Terese never turned her head. All she did was walk out reading the postcard from her mother.

Grace Schweitzer looked at the empty doorway with a souring expression. She had grown gray in the service of the United States Government right there behind the window of the Conway post office, and she was not used to being ignored by her clientele. No one but Terese would have dared to come in for mail without speaking to Grace. She knew too much about everybody: who was getting curt letters from collection agencies (re velour furniture sets and unpaid dental bills), which young man who had lived at the hotel and moved away was writing now to which young woman, who subscribed to what newspapers and magazines, and who received what kind of C.O.D. packages and why. She not only knew, but could be induced to tell—after hours. So everyone was particularly careful to stay on the good side of Grace; and since she loved to talk, shut up as she was alone behind the grilled window, the way to stay in her good graces was to give her a chance for a casual chat whenever you came into the office.

Terese, however, knew only about the main post office at Seventh and Mission in San Francisco and the branch offices in the neighborhoods where her family had briefly lived; and the clerks in those establishments expected nothing but that their customers state their needs succinctly and make way promptly for the next citizen in line, who was probably drooping under an armload of packages to be weighed and insured.

Passing the store, Terese decided to get a candy bar. She had everything she needed for lunch, which all the men came home at noon to eat, and she was not prepared to do her shopping for dinner yet. Another trip to the store later would give her something to do. It was really wonderful the way she had time to spend. She reveled in not being confined to Woolworth's from nine in the morning until six at night.

Mrs. Amatelli came up behind the candy counter, smiling broadly. "Good morning, Mrs. McGowan."

Terese lifted her eyes and slowly smiled. It was still exciting, being called "Mrs. McGowan." She picked up a Love Nest bar and said offhandedly, "Put this on my bill." She had never had a charge account before. The Beauregards had always paid cash. So this, too, was rather entrancing, the casual "Charge it."

Mr. Amatelli was waiting on another woman down by the cash register, and Mrs. Amatelli leaned her elbow on the edge of the candy counter.

"Well, you all settled now?" she inquired cozily.

Terese, who had already turned to go, smiled back over her shoulder in a friendly way but kept on walking. "Just about." Then, in a sudden burst of affability, "There wasn't much to do, getting settled."

Still looking back with a faint smile, she pushed the screen door open with her shoulder, both hands being occupied with unwrapping the candy bar.

Mrs. Amatelli looked after her with a rather rebuffed expression in her dark eyes. Angela and Joe had been running the store now for five years, since Joe's parents had retired. Joe had helped in the store since he was sixteen, and after he married Angela she too had helped out now and then, such as during the last two hours of the day, when they were busiest, and on Saturday mornings. Naturally the Amatellis were more than just merchants to their customers; they were friends, or social acquaintances at the very least. And people didn't walk away when a friend started to chat with them—not when you had passed out all-day suckers and popsicles to their husbands since the latter had been able to talk plain enough to ask for them.

The only really tolerant reflections which had followed Terese's progress that morning came now, however, from Angela. The girl was a stranger, didn't understand yet how things were in a small town. She probably looked at everybody else as if they were strangers. Once she got acquainted, she'd be as friendly as other people.

There were facts that perhaps influenced Angela's greater readiness to accept the beautiful stranger. She had heard, as had everyone else, that Terese's people were French, her parents born in the old country. This made an unspoken bond between them, for although Angela's father had gone to work in the mill when he was twenty, he too had come from the old country—from Italy. Because of this, unreasonably Angela wanted Terese to make good in Conway.

But she stood looking at the screen door with the metal Grape-Ade advertising placard tacked across the center bar, and there was an uncertain shadow on her round face with its eyes as dark as Terese's and its shading of dark hairs on the upper lip and along the cheeks in front of her ear lobes, from which hung modest gold hoops.

The girl was too damn good-looking. An irrational, fearful feeling wriggled at the bottom of Angela's thoughts. It was not so much that her looks would rouse defensive, jealous instincts in the other women, or that they might rouse immoral desires in the men, nor was it the thought of the single men who lived at the hotel and who—since they were human— would take notice of the beautiful woman they would be seeing frequently on the streets and at the store. It was a vaguer disturbance, a feeling that Terese did not belong here, that her presence might upset some delicate balance in all their lives.

Terese, meanwhile, strolled along on her circuit of the town, on past the barbershop and the beauty parlor and the service station which faced the school across the street, eating her candy bar and thinking her own placid thoughts.

Around the corner and down from the service station stood the hotel, with its back to the clubhouse. A long porch flanked the first floor of the white-painted, barnlike structure. It was almost flush with the sidewalk, which started in front of the clubhouse and made a cement U around the block. No one sat now in the round-backed wooden chairs lined up along the veranda, but as Terese approached, the cook, Eddie McGillicuddy, came out of the kitchen door at the end of the building carrying a package wrapped in newspaper, on his way to a large trash can at the side of the kitchen steps. Eddie wore a soiled white butcher's apron over a sleeveless undershirt and black-and-white-checked washable pants. He was somewhat bald, inclined to plumpness, and had a rather flat nose and a congenitally mischievous expression. Eddie was indulgently considered a "character" in Conway. He was slightly nearsighted, and in the bright sun, which was a little blinding after the dimness of his kitchen, Terese appeared to Eddie as just another young woman in slacks. She might have been any of the housewives or maidens of Conway, so he called out cheerfully, "Hiya, toots. What's the good word?"

He was banging the lid on the trash can and Terese was only a half-dozen feet away when Eddie realized that her eyes had raked him coldly before her chin went up another inch and, looking straight ahead, she marched on, giving him, as he remarked afterward, the old freezeroo.

Impudently Eddie stood with his hand on the trash-can lid and observed derisively after her retreating back, "What's a matter, baby, cat got your tongue?"

"Fresh," Terese thought, hearing the cook whistling a disjointed tune as he clumped back up the steps.

She was used to fellows trying to get smart, and didn't give the encounter a second thought until that evening when she was telling Jim about her walk and mentioned some dope at the hotel who had wisecracked at her.

"That must have been Eddie. He's a character," Jim chuckled comfortably.

"Wise guy," Terese sniffed. "I've run across the type before. Making remarks about every woman that goes by."

"Eddie isn't like that. He doesn't mean nothing. Just being friendly."

"Well, a girl has to be careful with these 'friendly' guys."

"Suits me, baby," Jim had laughed, clutching her in a playful bear hug. "I don't want you being 'friendly' with anybody but me."

At the same moment Eddie was relating his impressions of the new Mrs. McGowan to two or three of the fellows in the lobby of the hotel. "Stuck-up as hell. Kind of a dame that thinks her sweat don't stink. She may be a looker, but, confidentially, I feel sorry for poor old Jim. She'll lead him a merry chase; you wait and see. I don't trust them kind that think they're better'n other people."

"Well, maybe," said an older man in baggy black pants and suspenders, "you offended her, Eddie. You're a stranger to her, you know."

"Offended her?" Eddie looked pained. "Just tried to pass the time of day like I would with anybody, courchus and refined as you please—"

The older man grinned faintly to himself.

"And what do I get?" Eddie tossed his head, placed his hands on his hips, and waddled in parody of a female gait. "Nope, you mark my words, that dame'll cause trouble. Thinks she's better'n other people."

As she strolled on homeward Terese was unaware of having hurt Eddie's feelings. In the middle of the next block she passed the older McGowans' home. For some reason now forgotten, the company had scattered a few two-story frame houses with steep roofs among the more modest one-floor cottages on the East Side streets, and the McGowans lived in one of them.

Terese had a brief impulse to drop in on her mother-in-law and Florence, but it passed, and she went on around the corner to her own new home. It was a little different from most of the other one-story places. Instead of being square, with the porch cut in so that the front bedroom protruded to make an L-shaped wall around the porch, hers and Jim's house was long and low with a narrow veranda across the whole front. It was painted white and there was a Paul Scarlet rose climbing up the pillars at one end.

A good many years previously the company had apparently gone through a period of indecision about Conway, allowing employees to buy the houses if they liked and selling a few vacant lots to whatever customers could be found. Terese's cottage was a result of this era. Someone had exercised his own taste in building it, and it had changed hands several times until now Angela's father, Mr. Cantoni, who lived one street over and was retired from the mill, owned and rented the cottage. Most of the houses, however, were still company-owned and rented "dirt cheap" to employees. The older McGowans' seven-room residence was, in fact, such a one.

Terese stepped through her front door with a feeling of contentment. Everything in the living room was new, so new that the room looked rather stiff and unused; but Terese did not notice that. The square sofa and matching chair were covered with a green corded fabric, and the cloth background of the occasional chair was cream with large green leaves printed on it. The rug was beige with green designs in the corners, and the windows were hung with long unbleached muslin draperies which could be pulled closed and which were banded at the bottom with strips of rose-colored chenille to match the same trimming on the cream-colored lamp shades.

In the bedroom there was a three-piece "set" of blond oak, in the dinette were a chromium and blue plastic table and chairs, in the kitchen were a new gas stove and an electric refrigerator, and on the service porch was an automatic washing machine.

All of it had been picked out in town earlier in the week. The total cost, if you stopped to think of it, was breathtaking. But Terese didn't think of cost in terms of totals. She thought of it in terms of the ten-dollar-a-month payments for five years. All of the five hundred dollars Jim had saved had gone into the down payment. He was still paying thirty-five dollars a month on his secondhand Chevrolet coupé, and their rent was twenty-five a month, but Terese never bothered to add it all up. That was one beauty about working at the mill. You might not have any money in the bank, but every two weeks there would be more coming, and if you were a son of one of the old-timers you didn't worry about getting laid off. You had what the labor unions were always yelling about—security.

And when she walked into her house this was just what Terese felt without consciously naming it—security. She also felt triumph, the glow of achievement. Here she was only twenty-two and she had everything she wanted: a nice husband, a house full of new furniture, and a score of lovely electrical kitchen appliances, wedding presents.

If Terese had ever been forced to put it into words, she would have confessed that this—what she had right now—was what she had always intended to buy with the beauty that she was perfectly aware she possessed. This escape from Woolworth's into the freedom of long, leisurely hours which were hers to use as she pleased, this having a house all her own to fix up. Oh, she had dreamed nebulously of being a movie star, of marrying a rich man (and by rich she meant a man who made maybe five hundred a month and worked in an office); but the daughter of Pierre and Annette Beauregard, laundry workers in San Francisco, had been essentially realistic. She knew that if she actually set out to use her looks to those ends, it would be harder work in the long run than working as a salesgirl, which took nothing more out of you than the expenditure of a little physical energy. And since what she had right now was really what she liked, why bother to scheme and worry and fuss trying to "be somebody"?

And then the movies and the magazines all said Love was what really counted anyway; and she did love Jim, had almost from the first time her girl friend from the store, who was a distant cousin of Jim's, had made a blind date for her with Jim one time when he was visiting his brother Ned in the city.

CHAPTER 4

Gladys McGowan had been dusting in the living room when she saw her daughter-in-law walk past. She turned toward her daughter Florence, who was lounging on the plum-colored velour sofa with her feet on a newspaper, reading a *Real True Romances* magazine and eating a piece of cold toast covered with marmalade. Florence had her dun-colored hair up in tin curlers and her face covered with a perfumed grease recommended to improve the complexion.

Florence was nineteen, and she was not working at the moment, although any day, like Mr. Micawber, she expected "something to turn up."

Florence had not gone back to high school after her junior year because when September rolled around that year she'd had what she called a "neat" job ushering at one of the movie theaters in town. Since then she had been a waitress, a clerk in a candy store, and a carhop in a drive-in. But something was always happening. She got the flu, or the boss was too fresh, or she couldn't stand one of her fellow workers.

Tom McGowan would say jokingly every now and then, "The only reason Flo doesn't get married is because nobody's asked her."

This type of humor annoyed Florence, but it was just about the truth. At the moment there were no immediate prospects in the matrimonial line. There were several presumably eligible bachelors in Conway. Her own choice would have been Johnny Rodriguez, even though his ancestors were Mexican; but he never seemed to pay more than casual attention to any of the local girls. Les Coleman had been giving her a little rush lately, but nobody in their right mind would actually *marry* Les, even if he could be persuaded that marriage was a good idea.

Now Florence's mother said in a troubled, patient tone, "I suppose we ought to do *something*."

"About what?"

"About Terese. An evening party is too much—the house wouldn't hold them—and if you use the clubhouse you have to ask everybody, and I just don't feel up to it."

Her voice trailed off and she rubbed the oily polishing cloth along the edge of a long table set before the front window with a potted begonia standing in the middle of the hemstitched runner.

"She has to meet people," Mrs. McGowan went on with a fretful undertone in her voice.

Florence swallowed the last of her toast and folded the magazine back for more convenient following of her story. "She'll meet 'em at the dance next week. Jim said they'd go this time."

"Well, you're supposed to entertain for a bride. It won't look right if I don't do *anything*."

"Her own friends had a shower for her before they came down here."

"Oh, I wasn't thinking of a shower. I tell you what I think I'll do. Instead of just the bridge club next Wednesday—it's my turn to have them—I'll ask a few more and have Terese, and have a special cake and ice cream for refreshments. In her honor. We'll play bridge first, and I'll have prizes. That way I won't have to ask everybody, like Angela and old lady Hanson. I'll have it as an excuse that they don't play bridge."

"Be a lot of work," Florence commented.

"Not as much as a big affair."

Florence had let the magazine fall back against her knees, and with her eyes resting vacantly on the tapestry drapes she said, "What do you suppose she ever saw in Jim?"

"Any girl would be lucky to get Jim," his mother retorted stoutly.

"You know darn well you nearly dropped dead the same as anybody else when he brought her over to Aunt Lily's last month when we were there for the weekend."

Mrs. McGowan looked annoyed, but she didn't say anything.

Florence turned shrewd eyes on her mother. "D'you suppose she *had* to marry him?"

"Florence McGowan, you ought to be ashamed!" The words did not have the force they should have had, however, for there was an uneasy note in the woman's voice.

"Well, I don't care; I'll bet there's some other reason than just love." Florence directed an ominous look at her mother. "She's a deep one; you wait and see."

"Terese is a lovely girl," Mrs. McGowan said staunchly, "and I don't want any more of this kind of talk. There's enough of it going on already, or I miss my guess," she added bitterly, and then, defensively, "Can the poor kid help it because she's beautiful?"

"Well, all I've got to say is, catch me sticking myself off in this hole if I looked like that."

"Everybody isn't like you."

CHAPTER 5

Not long after this conversation lines of men began to pass singly and in twos and fours from the open gates of the mill, which lay across a wide field opposite the service station and the hotel, backed up against the south branch of the hills which cupped the village protectively at the end of a railroad spur that ran in from town, politely bypassing the residential part of Conway.

When Al opened the front door and came in, Lorraine Bowen had lunch set out on the kitchen table beside the window overlooking the side yard. He washed his hands in the bathroom and sat down, helping himself from the pot of baked beans on the table. Lorraine kissed his forehead as she poured coffee from a glass pot, and Al pressed his head against her arm affectionately. He was several years older than Lorraine, and before their marriage had been the best-looking single fellow in *his* crowd. People had thought they were a good match, although a rather unexpected one. Al had been considered a little wild, drank quite a bit, and was never home, always careering off with a gang for dance halls twenty-five or thirty miles away, swaggering a bit when he walked the streets of Conway, addicted to tight pullover sweaters and highly polished, elaborately stitched shoes. His dark hair was always highly polished too, even now after a morning spent superintending an oil-consuming machine. The tight sweaters had been calculated to show off the development of heavy shoulders and chest.

When he first began to pay attention to Lorraine she had not thought she was in love with him. There were quickly rejected moments even yet when from subterranean depths unformed doubts rose up. Originally she had accepted his overtures and taken to dating Al as a matter of course. For him to notice a hometown girl—he never had before—had been too much of a triumph to reject. And then—well, things kept getting more involved, and there had been two dreadful weeks when she feared they *had* to get married, during which time they hurriedly did so, only to find it was a false alarm. But neither of them was sorry. They were, in fact, quite happy.

This day they had little to say over lunch, and finally, to save the meal from silence, Lorraine spoke. She hadn't meant to mention Terese. She felt it would be bad policy to emphasize the newcomer too much in Al's mind. Not that she had doubts of Al's fidelity. But just the same ... The woman had filled her thoughts all morning, though.

"I saw Jim's wife go by this morning," she remarked idly. "On this side of the street. She must have crossed over. I wonder why, if she was going to the store."

Al buttered a roll. "That so? Maybe she was just out walking."

"I think she was. She looked that way, as if she wasn't going anywhere special."

"I suppose she's lonesome. You oughta go see her. Invite 'em over. We could play canasta."

"I suppose I should." It was on the tip of her tongue to make a joking remark along the lines of Al being awful anxious to get better acquainted, but she repressed it. Somehow she couldn't joke about Terese.

"I still can't figure out," Al said indifferently, "how Jim happened to get her."

It was a remark made out of politeness, to keep Lorraine's conversational effort alive. He had been as interested as anyone else in Jim's bride, had done his full share of kidding the groom, kidding that included various ribald comments and questions of an intimate nature; but down at the mill lately another subject was circulating quietly and disturbingly, dominating the men's thoughts. It had not come out too openly yet to the women. The men themselves had wisely kept it under their hats. They knew that once a subject emerged for airing in their separate homes it would not be an under-the-surface topic much longer, but would soon be spoken of openly in the store and on the street.

Lorraine sensed her husband's abstraction and, centered as her mind was on Jim's new wife, she felt obscurely that Al's manner must be connected with Terese in some way.

"You got something on your mind?" she demanded with unintentional sharpness.

He glanced at her, surprised. "Yeah, in a way." He hadn't meant to discuss it with Lorraine. But they were pretty close. He had found since their marriage that it was kind of nice to have a woman to talk to. It surprised him a little the things he *had* talked to her about, religion and stuff like that.

"The boys are all talking the last couple of weeks or so— Now I don't want you to run down gabbling to Gloria about it the first thing this afternoon. It's all been pretty much on the q.t."

Lorraine shook her head, her eyes intent upon him, in her interest neglecting to feel injured over the insult implied in his reference to Gloria and gabbling.

"There's been some CIO organizers around talking up an election, and some of the guys have fell for it. Johnny Rodriguez and George McGowan and even"—he jerked his head toward the house next door—"Bill Fraser. Everybody's kind of uneasy one way or another, don't know how to take it."

"Well, for heaven's sake," Lorraine said, "we've got unions."

"That's the angle. We got too many—and yet not enough. The carpenters and machinists belong to the local in town, but these CIO fellows say we oughta drop our AF of L affiliations and have one big union representing everybody."

"But why? Nobody wants anything more than they've got, do they?"

"N-no. Of course our pensions aren't very big, and there is some unfairness about advancement and seniority. That is, us young guys that our family's been in the mill a long time, we do get jobs sometimes ahead of older guys that've only been here five or ten years and that're maybe in line for 'em."

"That's only fair. After all!"

"And then there is a point, we do kind of work at cross-purposes sometimes—about grievances and things, being in different locals." Al went on with an air of painful soul-searching. "And the wages. There is kind of no rhyme or reason to some of it. Guys in the shipping and loading rooms, for instance, doing just as important jobs as carpenters that're getting twice the money. I dunno. And foremen all over the place not belonging to nothing and us in the Machinists getting as much pay as they do. And then the guys in the lab and the testing department, not organized at all. Might as well be up in the office. I dunno. It's kind of patchy. Be more efficient if we all belonged to the same thing."

Lorraine gave an annoyed sigh. "Be a lot of trouble getting it, too. What do Mr. Faber and Mr. Combs and the rest of them on Office Row think of it?"

"They're not supposed to know yet." He paused and looked thoughtful. "But I suppose they do. If Les Coleman has heard about it, they do. You can count on that."

"Well, I bet they don't like it."

"I don't suppose they do."

Lorraine rose and brought two milk puddings out of the refrigerator. As Al dug into his he said slowly, "The company probably wouldn't be actually paying any more wages if we went CIO. But it's like Johnny Rodriguez says—they'll fight it because it would give us more power, all being in one big union. They couldn't deal separate with different groups and maybe play one off against another."

"Who wants power?" Lorraine sniffed. "We all got steady jobs and making good money. What more do we want?"

Al glanced around the bright little kitchen with its purring refrigerator and its old-fashioned painted sink boards. "I don't know," he said uneasily.

It was something you couldn't explain to a woman, that all belonging to something together would make a man feel easier in his mind somehow, give him more of a feeling of all pulling together instead of against each other.

"How does Jim McGowan stand on it?" Lorraine asked.

"Nobody's really taken a 'stand' yet. That is, most of us haven't—just the ringleaders on each side. And I guess Jim has other things on his mind right now, only being married two weeks."

Lorraine had lighted a cigarette too, and she squinted through the smoke. "I don't think I will go see her. After all, we've never been introduced. I'll wait till we have."

When Al started back to the mill he was thinking about Terese instead of the union. Lorraine's change of subject had been a sort of a relief. She was something to think about all right, Jim's wife. Even aside from her looks, the way she dressed and walked was enough to make anybody sit up and take notice. Her clothes seemed to set her off. They weren't just clothes, the way most women's were. And she moved with a sort of oblivious air. Like a queen, Al thought suddenly, surprised and pleased with the simile.

It gave you sort of a funny feeling, a fellow like Jim McGowan winning something like Terese for himself, something so unattainable, something you really felt a common workingman in Conway shouldn't expect to have, something almost too good for folks in Conway.

Of course you couldn't tell; she might turn out to be a regular hellion to live with; but the time he had passed her coming out of the post office she didn't look like it. There was something calm in the expression of her eyes, as if she had a cheerful disposition.

The men were all conjecturing about her morals or possible lack of them. There was a great deal of a sly "You wait and see" attitude, as if they couldn't believe there wasn't a worm in the apple.

Al had only two or three casual glimpses of the girl to go on, but he thought the men were wrong. He'd been around. He knew the easy type. And he didn't think Jim's wife was one of them. She had all the equipment all right; but she didn't have the manner. She looked too satisfied, too untroubled—an air quite different from the restless, fundamentally dissatisfied manner of dames who were constantly on the make.

In some ways his conviction that Terese was virtuous made Jim's marriage the more incomprehensible. In Conway people never really expected to get the Best, in women or in anything else about life. There was something—Al couldn't quite put his finger on it—but there was something ... It was unsettling that one of their boys, without fuss or bother, and as if it were no more than he was entitled to, had reached out and brought home for himself a woman who was all anyone could dream of wanting—as if nothing were too good for him.

Somehow in Conway you just accepted the fact—without even thinking about it—that there were all kinds of things that were too good for you, things that only people like Mr. Faber and the almost mythical Conway family could have.

At the entrance to the gates Al met Jim. As they walked together down the asphalt road between the parking lots Al surreptitiously studied his fellow worker. Over his unruly sandy hair Jim wore a dun-colored felt beanie with a notched, turned-up brim. It rode forward jauntily over one temple. His eyes were a bright, good-humored blue, and there was a sprinkling of freckles over his straight nose. He was as tall as Al but not quite so athletically muscular through the shoulders. They both wore grease-stained khaki pants and matching shirts with the collars open and the sleeves rolled to the elbows above hairy forearms. Their feet kept time in heavy-soled laced shoes that covered their ankles.

There were no other pedestrians within yards of them either way, and suddenly Jim said in a low voice, "What do you make of this CIO talk, Al?"

"I ain't made up my mind yet. How do you size it up?"

"Well, to tell the truth, I ain't thought much about it." Jim grinned boyishly. "Had other things on my mind lately." Then he went on more seriously. "Of course my dad don't like it. Says we'd be giving up our independence to a bunch of pie-cards in Frisco and back East. George, though, he's all hot for it. Ma's made 'em quit talkin' about it at home, to keep peace in the family."

Al raised his eyes to the tiered windows of the gray cement building looming up ahead of them, the green crest of the hill showing in contrasting softness above it.

"I dunno. At first I didn't think much of it. Always better to let sleeping dogs lie. But—"

His voice faltered. There was something he felt he would like to have said, but, frustratingly, he knew he couldn't put it into words. Something about his pride in the mill, its bigness, its efficiency, the quality of its product. Something about wishing you felt more responsible for all that, more publicly responsible, that is. They all did feel responsible, of course; but somehow they didn't get any—any recognition, he guessed it was, for what they and their fathers had put into the mill. People just thought of the Conway Mill in terms of Conways, not in terms of the Jim McGowans and Al Bowens. And there was something—a sort of intuition that if they all belonged to one big organization that meant *all* of them, they might assert themselves, have more of a feeling, among themselves anyway, of what they meant to the mill.

All he could say, though, rather lamely, was, "But maybe if we went CIO, did away with the craft setup, we'd have more say. And then, you know, there's a lot of guys that by rights should be getting more money, but nobody's makin' any real effort to get it for 'em."

"Well, in case we ever had to strike, we'd get further all in one local," Jim said reluctantly. "Been a long time, though, since anything like that came up. Back in '35 when the Machinists got their contract was the last time such a thing ever happened."

"At that, us machinists ain't been gettin' the kind of contracts you hear about 'em gettin' around the Bay and even down in L.A. in some of the plants."

"Well, of course we got more advantages here—cheap rent and—uh—nicer surroundings, like the park and the clubhouse and our own school."

"Yeah, that's true."

They walked on into the mill thoughtfully.

CHAPTER 6

Mrs. Faber was away on one of her periodic shopping expeditions to the city, so Marguerite and her father had dinner alone in the dining room whose french windows looked out across a brick-floored terrace and an expanse of lawn terminated by an arborvitae hedge. It was a warm spring evening, and they took their fragile china cups out to the terrace to enjoy their coffee in the twilight.

Marguerite wore a simple turquoise linen frock and high-heeled white linen pumps over bare feet. She crouched on a round leather hassock and set her cup and saucer on a low, glass-topped table, clasping her hands over her knees. Mr. Faber leaned back in a comfortable chair and lit his cigar.

"I saw the most astonishing creature this morning," Marguerite said idly, "standing across from our driveway and giving us the once-over. I've been wondering who she was. Does anyone on Office Row have out-of-town guests?"

"Not that I know of. What did she look like?"

"Like something off a magazine cover. Black hair that she had sense enough to leave alone. Heavy enough that it belled out at the ends of its own weight. Big dark eyes, and a figure like an *Esquire* calendar. I was really startled. I wonder where she came from."

"Maybe it was Jim McGowan's wife. I understand the tongues have been wagging ever since he brought her down. Seems she's much more beautiful than the housewives on the East Side feel one of their number has any right to be."

"Do you suppose that's who it was? I don't wonder, then, if they're all in a tizzy. She is much lovelier than you'd expect a mill hand's wife to be. You see, she has chic, as well as beauty." Marguerite took a sip of her coffee thoughtfully. "A sort of inborn chic, not a cultivated one. A woman can tell, even in one glance as I had of her. She's one of those women who doesn't have to be taught about hair styles and make-up and the right lines and colors in clothes for herself. Some women have a sort of instinct that way. Even in a house dress, they sense what is right for themselves. And she has it."

"How long did you say you looked at this paragon?"

Marguerite laughed. "Just while I passed her in the car. But I'm very observant."

"You must be."

They sat in silence, listening to the sleepy twittering of birds, the croaking of a bullfrog in the fishpond north of the house. Miles Faber sighed.

"Tired, Daddy?"

"A little."

"Working too hard?"

"No. No more than usual." He smiled at her affectionately. "My observant daughter. Fact is, I'm a little worried."

"Trouble at the mill?"

"Not yet. But it's brewing. And it's my job to stop it before it boils over, and for once I feel a little inadequate. Guess I'm getting old."

"What is it? Or can't you tell me?"

"If I do, it's confidential. You're not to discuss it even with your mother."

"O.K."

"There's agitation again for bringing the CIO into the mill. Seems to crop up every so often. Like burr clover in the lawn."

The girl shook her head commiseratingly. "Who starts it?"

"Paid organizers, of course, from the CIO. They get around talking to a few picked men, get the talk started, and the first thing you know they're passing out leaflets at the gates. It hasn't reached that stage yet. That's what it's up to me to prevent."

He rubbed his hand wearily over his eyes. "They aren't going to like it in the head office if it comes to an election, even if the CIO loses. It's up to me to keep things from getting stirred up to that extent." He uttered a wry chuckle. "It's supposed to be easy, isolated as we are in these idyllic surroundings." There was a bitterly ironic note in the superintendent's voice as he went on. "It almost makes me laugh sometimes. They think around here that I'm God. If they only knew. I'm under the gun worse than anybody. I'm supposed to see that production keeps up; I'm supposed to keep the workers happy; and on top of everything else I'm supposed to economize." His eyes narrowed angrily. "If those damn soreheads in the mill knew how I had to fight to get a new compressor or a new conveyor belt or even planks for the loading platform, instead of having them repaired and repaired till the whole damn place is ready to fall apart, they'd think twice before they started grouching for more wages. But no, *they* blame me if the machines break down, and the head office blames me if the men get discontented."

Marguerite reached over and patted his thigh. "Poor Daddy." She studied the hedge for a moment with thoughtful eyes. "Which ones are carrying the ball for the CIO?"

"Johnny Rodriguez is the main one, but he has help. Even George McGowan is campaigning for it. And we suspect one or two others. Old Owen Euman at the hotel, for one." He knocked the ashes off his cigar with a vicious tap of his forefinger. "But Johnny's the ringleader. I wish to God old Manuel Rodriguez had gone back to *Mejico* with the rest of that bunch the company brought in during the First World War; but no, he marries a Mexican girl from town and stays right here. Manuel isn't so bad, still just goes along in the yard gang minding his own business. But this son of his is another story. I've suspected for a long time Johnny was a radical. He's too smart for a Mex. Always has been. Got through high school with high grades. And he's got a way of looking at everything with those soft eyes as if he was just innocently interested when actually he isn't missing a thing. I had a hunch even then to tell Combs not to put him on when he applied for work after the war. But Combs is the best personnel manager we ever had, expert at sizing people up; and I don't like to interfere with my help. Believe in giving 'em authority and not interfering, and Combs apparently thought Johnny was O.K." He paused and frowned. "He's popular. The men all like him, even though the Rodriguezes have always been sort of kept apart by the rest of the people on the East Side, not brought into their social life. You remember, Marguerite, they had quite a stir over there when Johnny started coming to the Friday night dances at the clubhouse, big as you please. Nobody dared tell him Mexicans weren't welcome, and finally when he stuck it out they just gave up and took the attitude, 'Well, just one, I guess, won't matter.'"

"Yes, I remember. We went to the Christmas dance that year, and I noticed that he danced with all the girls. An attractive boy."

Her coffee was cold, and Marguerite pushed it aside on the table. She clasped her hands again around her knees and regarded the darkening hedge. A vagrant idea fluttered through her mind, and she almost smiled at it, laughing at herself. The thought of the boss's daughter luring the stalwart young workman from his purposes with her subtle wiles ... helping Daddy by corrupting the incipient labor leader ... At some time she must have read too many melodramatic romances.

After a moment she spoke questioningly. "Isn't there some way of influencing him? Toning him down?"

"We've tried that. At least Combs has. I told you Fred knows his business. He dropped a word in the right place and a couple of years ago he had Johnny promoted to a machine so he was taken into the Machinists local. That usually cools off their highfalutin ideas about their fellow workers, makes them aristocrats who can look down on the others who aren't eligible for membership in a craft union, but," he concluded sourly, "apparently it didn't work with Johnny." He scowled. "His ambitions probably run along the lines of being a bigshot union leader. Can't be anything else."

Marguerite had been visualizing Johnny Rodriguez. There was something dashing, slightly exotic about him, with his thick black hair, the soft, deceptive eyes her father had spoken of, the deep, natural tan of his skin. Despite the Americanization of his ancestors, he had an Indian look about him—the romanticized Indian look of the Noble Red Man, like Alessandro in *Ramona*—perhaps because he was taller than either his father or grandfather and carried himself straighter, as if consciously and intentionally. He wasn't really handsome, she mused, but he was attractive.

And that irrelevantly made her think of the beautiful girl who had stood and looked at her in so unabashed a manner. Marguerite narrowed her eyes. It would not have been nearly so surprising if it had been Johnny Rodriguez who had found and brought that woman to Conway. He had that sort of an air, as if nothing were too good for him, as if, no matter how incongruous it seemed, he just might walk out and pick the loveliest-looking girl he saw off life's display rack

She unclasped her hands and leaned one elbow on the glass table top, her cheek against her fist. She kept seeing the two together, incongruous, unsuitable in their juxtaposition, yet somehow not surprising.

CHAPTER 7

Mrs. McGowan gave her bridge party as planned in Terese's honor, inviting some of the younger women like Lorraine Bowen and Gloria Hanson, who were not members of the club.

Terese consulted Florence about what to wear, and as they looked over Terese's half of the wardrobe hanging in the bedroom closet, Florence had to suppress a spiteful impulse to recommend something flashy and unsuitable, like the one formal of black satin with red velvet roses appliquéd along the hem. But the family reputation was involved as well as Terese's future standing in town, so from the not very extensive choice provided Florence suggested a white waffle piqué with a demure high collar and extended shoulders which covered the upper arms like modified wings.

Terese gave a little throaty giggle. "I'm scared, to tell the truth, meeting all those strange ladies; and I can't play bridge hardly at all."

"Well, you'll have to learn," Florence said practically. "All the married ones play." She was torn for a moment between family pride and resentment of her sister-in-law's overshadowing beauty. She would have enjoyed seeing Terese make a fool of herself at the party, but at the same time she was an asset to the McGowans, gave the family class, and you wanted her to make a good impression.

"Get some cards," Florence ordered abruptly, "and I'll go over the bidding with you."

At the party Terese looked, her mother-in-law reflected to herself, like an angel. The guests all privately admitted as much to themselves, but with the additional sentiment that she was about as approachable as such a heavenly visitor would have been. She smiled at each one with what was actually an uncertain shyness but which gave the impression of poised reserve. Over the tables she did not participate in the banter and light gossip. In her inexperience at the game, she was concentrating mightily on the cards, determined not to disgrace herself, not to let them see she wasn't used to fancy bridge parties. When she answered a polite question dealing with anything but the game, her manner was abstracted, for her thoughts were tightly gripped upon honor counts and what it meant when one's partner said three clubs.

When the ladies were taking their leave after the coffee and the cake decorated with pink rosebuds and the pineapple ice cream made in Mrs. McGowan's refrigerator, the pretty girl who was about her age and who lived down around the corner from her on the street leading to the park, and whom Terese wished would become her friend, said formally, "You must come and see me sometime."

Terese smiled warmly and rejoined, "You come and see me, too."

"Well—uh—I've been meaning to. I will some of these days," Lorraine responded hurriedly, taken aback and somehow distrusting the sudden brightness of Terese's expression. After the rather stiff deportment the guest of honor had exhibited all afternoon, Lorraine wondered if this abrupt brightness were not "put on."

When Jim came home that night, in the safety of his presence Terese's pleasurable excitement broke out undisguised.

To his query of "Well, how was the party?" she clasped her hands like a child and exclaimed, "It was lovely! Your mother had flowers all *over*, and all the embroidered tablecloths for refreshments, and individual score cards. Here, I'll show you." She darted to the coffee table and held out the pink-ribboned pasteboard.

"But I didn't get everybody's names straight. I was so nervous trying to act right—so I wouldn't disgrace you," she chuckled. "And scared about my playing. Honestly, I'm terrible. I had one of the lowest scores. But everybody seemed very nice." Her face sobered. "I hope they liked me."

"How could they help it?" her husband teased affectionately.

"Well, I did want to make a good impression." She giggled with a quick change of mood. "Honest, I was so refined it hurt."

In the two-story white house facing the park Marge and Byron Vale were eating their dinner at the dining room table of the house which was a replica of the McGowans' except that it faced west instead of south. Their twin sons were now freshmen at the university, so the Vales were alone. Marge was telling her husband about the party.

"It wasn't," she said reflectively, "an unqualified success. That girl somehow just doesn't get over. And it's too bad. She has an air of being aloof, disinterested. And the way she plays bridge—my God! I could tell the girls were a little offended. They thought she just didn't care, considered cards rather boring. But"—they had finished eating, and Marge lighted a cigarette—"it wasn't that at all. She simply doesn't know the game very well. And the way she seemed sort of preoccupied and stiff—it was from being ill-at-ease, among strangers and all." She frowned. "I told Gloria and Emily Fraser that on the way home, but they'd have none of it. They're just determined that she's stuck-up."

"Once they get better acquainted they'll get over it," Byron observed.

"I think so. But I hate to see people so obtuse. It's odd the way people seem to react with distrust to that girl. It's more than the way you naturally reserve judgment of a stranger."

"She's too pretty," Byron Vale said dryly, "and too smart-looking—in the couturiers' sense of the word. If she had married into the Fabers or even someone on Office Row, they'd all gape at first, but take her for granted. But to have looks and style and poise and be not too obviously stupid seems like too much for the East Side, like defying fate."

"They're coming to the dance Friday night," Marge observed. She shrugged. "I guess they'll get used to her."

CHAPTER 8

The Friday night dances had been going on for years. They were the only really successful collective social activity that had survived in Conway. They began at eight and ended at eleven-thirty, and no one would have dreamed of being late. Miss Schweitzer played the piano, old Mr. Cantoni fiddled, and Orin Finley, who was a bachelor from the hotel, played the guitar. And Tom McGowan called the squares. The dances had begun as Old-fashioned dances, and this they had remained. The orchestra's repertoire was rather extensive: polkas, two-steps, schottisches, the *varsovienne*, and waltzes, always waltzes, about every third number. A convention had arisen that two-steps were always "whistle" dances. Every so many bars Orin blew a sharp blast on a whistle tied around his neck, and all the couples changed partners, making a wild scramble out of it, with no formal "progressive" character to the change.

When folk dancing had become a national rage, some of the couples who had joined the classes in the high school in town attempted to educate the Friday night Conway dancers into the variety of established patterns provided in the books. But somehow the dances at the clubhouse stubbornly refused to be formalized or to follow mimeographed patterns. When people did a schottische they just schottisched, taking the required number of running steps and the kicks, round and round the hall, and the same with the polka, relentlessly performing the basic steps, rejecting the elaborations imported from countries across the sea.

The couples who went to the classes discovered, too, that Tom McGowan's calling of squares was a little unorthodox, that he inclined more to the hoedown than to the established, complete patterns. And they found that the squares in the Conway clubhouse didn't look nice, the way they were supposed to. Everybody had a different "style," and it didn't lead to a unified effect. It seemed that the approved style for Western square dancing was a quick-stepping, smooth movement resembling a prance, but at the clubhouse some people galloped, some did buzz steps on the turns, some shuffled or even kept moving in place to a sort of jig, and some even *bounced*.

Byron Vale, as principal of the school, had had to take note of and instigate folk dancing for the children, in line with the trend; and he had watched with interest at the Friday night dances when the young Fosters and the Adamses attempted to pass on what they had learned at the night school instruction in town.

His eyes had held an ironically amused gleam as he surveyed the couples in their every-man-for-himself versions of the polka, their wheeling, unpatterned waltzes, the vigorous following of the square-dance calls, all in step but each participant giving a different interpretation to the step.

He had a conviction that this was more typically *American* folk dancing than any you could learn under formal instruction, that here in the clubhouse at Conway was one of the few real folk gatherings to be found in the country's increasingly mechanized, urbanized society. It made him think of the remark that the American people were like a lot of wild jackasses all pulling in different directions. Here where they came together purely for fun they resisted disciplined patterns. Even in the formalized square each man must move his body in the manner that best suited his own instincts about the dance, whether it ruined the general impression or not. The expression in Byron's eyes was withdrawn, ruminating. This characteristic of the American people could be either their downfall or their salvation. He was not sure which.

Looking back, it seemed to Byron Vale that this dance was the real beginning of the trouble—in so far as Terese was concerned. Although no dramatic scenes took place, it was a memorable night for most who attended, standing out among the other Friday nights.

The McGowans came in a family group, Tom and Gladys, Florence and George, and Terese and Jim. Terese wore a full, circular pink skirt and a pink eyelet peasant blouse, both trimmed with bands of narrow black velvet ribbon. The women had learned that she sewed, and this homely domestic hobby had softened her strangeness somewhat. But this costume, the product of her skill with the needle, neutralized their tendency to look with favor on a woman whose tastes were simple enough to run to dressmaking as a pastime. The frock had a flair, a simple originality that again set her apart as something exotic and out of reach.

Terese danced first with Jim and then with his brother George. She faltered and lost step in the unfamiliar dances, watching the others with laughing anxiety, but she caught on quickly, and before the evening was over had mastered most of the basic steps.

Jim conscientiously introduced her to people she hadn't met before, looking proud and awkward as he did so. The women who had attended the bridge party were not exactly rushing about bringing their husbands up to be introduced, but Gladys McGowan valiantly towed them forward from time to time with an "I want you to meet my daughter-in-law."

Al Bowen was the first man, after Jim and George, to ask Terese to dance, at which Jim politely reciprocated by asking Lorraine. While she and Jim whirled about in the waltz, Lorraine laughed and chattered gaily and studiously refrained from glancing about to follow the pink figure in her husband's arms.

Johnny Rodriguez came a little late, accompanied by three or four men from the hotel, among them Eddie, the cook, and Owen Euman, the older man in baggy pants who had seemed to doubt the suavity of Eddie's greeting to Terese the day she had passed the hotel.

The people were all a confused jumble in Terese's mind; she couldn't yet sort them out—who was married to whom, and who was a parent to whom, and who were brothers and sisters and who just boy friends and girl friends.

But when she came back to her place from waltzing with Al, she noticed that Florence had left the chair beside her mother and was down near the entrance talking vivaciously to a very dark young man in a figured rayon sport shirt and tan slacks. Then she heard Jim mutter sotto voce to his mother, "I see Flo made a beeline for Johnny the minute he showed up." And Mrs. McGowan frowned at him with a shushing expression.

Jim and Terese sat out the next dance, which was the *varsovienne* and which looked a little too complicated for her to try as yet. She saw Florence take the floor with the Johnny Jim had mentioned, and followed them with appreciative eyes as they glided through the graceful back-and-forth movements of the dance.

"I'll watch this time," she had told Jim, "and next time I'll try it."

"It's easy," he assured her. "Listen how the music goes." And he sang softly, so only she could hear, "'Put your little foot, put your little foot, put your little foot right there.' That goes on two times each way. And then"— he paused to wait for the music—"you change and it goes, 'Don't you see my new shoes, don't you see my new shoes?'"

Her eyes alight with laughter, she looked up at him. "Oh, that's cute!"

He smiled down at her indulgently. "Haven't you ever heard it before?"

Her hair swung softly against her cheeks as she shook her head. "No, never."

They smiled at each other, and he reached over and squeezed her hand gently; then each of them glanced about embarrassed, to see if anyone had noticed, before they met one another's eyes again with a tenderly conspiratorial air.

Terese looked back at the dancers and thought she was just about as happy as anybody ever got to be.

Johnny Rodriguez came back with Florence to where the McGowan family was sitting, but it was Mrs. McGowan who introduced him to Terese. Florence seemed to assume the two had already met.

When Johnny led Terese out on the floor for the next dance, almost everyone in the room watched them. Like Marguerite Faber, the people here, too, seemed to find them a surprisingly fitting pair. There was something illusively appropriate in their being together.

Making an even later entrance than had the group of men with Johnny, Lester Coleman appeared in the entrance doorway while Terese was dancing with Johnny. In his somewhat overlong plaid jacket and light gray slacks hanging loosely from pleats at the belt, Lester stood negligently smoking a cigarette, observing the room with a sophisticated air made possible by the way his eyebrows slanted in two straight lines toward the center of his high forehead under the receding brown hair.

Every town has one—the perennial bachelor, the "ladies' man"—and Les was Conway's. There was always talk about one married woman or another who was supposedly dallying with Lester Coleman, and Les did nothing to discourage the talk.

His father had worked in the mill but had died when Les was in high school, after which Les had supported his mother until she too passed away when he was in his middle twenties. Then Lester had gone on "baching" in the little house his family had always occupied. For some years now he had been in charge of one of the machines at the mill and a member of the union to which Al Bowen and Johnny Rodriguez also belonged.

Les was known as a snappy dresser, and he always drove an automobile of some distinctive but outdated make. His first had been a Stutz touring car, and there had been a Chrysler roadster with a rumble seat, and, briefly and painfully, an aged Cadillac whose previous owner had managed to do some obscure but irretrievable damage even to that magnificent engine. Currently he was driving a twelve-cylinder Packard of some antiquity but of undeniable "class," with its unmistakable radiator lines and its bright yellow body and its stained canvas convertible top.

Lester had so far seen Terese only from a distance, but he had heard plenty about her. Now he studied her narrowly as she danced with Johnny.

People noticed his careful consideration of the new woman, and a little tingling of excitement coursed through nerves in the room. This would be the real test for Terese McGowan—how Les Coleman made out with her. It was a test every reasonably comely woman in Conway had had to undergo at one time or another.

When the music ceased Johnny walked with Terese back to her chair and stood aside a little to talk with George McGowan. In a few moments Owen Euman sauntered up to join them. They spoke desultorily for a few minutes and gradually moved apart, their conversation seeming to become more cohesive.

Jim sat beside Terese and inquired, "How'd you get along with the three-step?"

"Not so bad. He"—she motioned with her head toward Johnny—"showed me, and I caught on pretty good." She lowered her voice. "He talks just like an American, but he's Mexican, isn't he?"

"Yeah, but he was born here in Conway."

"Well, he's nice. Nice and respectful, but not stiff or anything. Friendly, I mean."

"Oh, Johnny's a good guy."

Jim saw Lester Coleman sauntering toward the group made by Johnny and George and Owen, and he was about to add for Terese's benefit, "But there's one you don't want to trust too far," when Al Bowen accosted him on the other side. "The next one's a square. You and Terese want to get in?"

As Lester strolled up to the three men who were now talking quietly and intently in low voices, Owen Euman saw him and closed his mouth sharply on the middle of a word. His eyes moved meaningly from Johnny to George, and they both glanced aside toward Lester, who greeted them nonchalantly, "This a private conference or can anybody sit in?"

"Just chewin' the fat," George replied noncommittally.

Lester threw a meaning glance from one to another of them. "Guess we got plenty to chew about lately, huh?" His low laugh was conspiratorial yet somehow meaningless.

"Around this town there's always something to talk about," Johnny said pleasantly.

It was then, when Lester had made himself seem like a trusted member of the little group, that Mr. Faber and Marguerite appeared in the half of the double doorway that stood open.

One after another, but with considerable speed, people noticed who had come in. Everyone continued to laugh and talk as usual, but the Fabers' entrance acted like a sedative on the spirits of the crowd. And an unspoken "Why?" hummed through their thoughts.

Not that it was too unusual, having the superintendent drop in at one of the dances. He and Mrs. Faber made a practice of coming once every few months. And sometimes Marguerite had come with them, even bringing a friend with her, when she was at home for a weekend from college. Everyone knew, however, that the Fabers came (when they did) as a democratic gesture, a living proof of how in Conway they were all part of one thing—the life of the mill. It was an unconvincing gesture, however, since none of the families on Office Row participated in the dances, a participation which might have served as a bridge between the East Side and the Faber residence.

Tonight Mr. Faber's appearance produced an especial tingling of shock along their nerves, an unacknowledged guilt reaction. The union talk was now spreading even out among the women, and although some of the foremen, like Tom McGowan, and some of the machinists, like Bert Adams, and all of the handful of carpenters, like Greg Hanson, were trying to pooh-pooh it away, the majority of the unorganized employees were becoming increasingly interested and excited about "going CIO." Accompanying that excitement, however, was a vaguely defensive feeling in regard to Mr. Faber, who was, after all, a good guy.

And now when he demonstrated his being a good guy by coming to enjoy the dance with them, it made a person feel uncomfortable. It was the older men and their wives who made the first sociable moves toward the Fabers. They had, after all, known and worked for Miles Faber longer.

Mr. Faber and Marguerite watched the square dance with hearty smiles, and when the next number, a waltz, began, Lester Coleman sauntered up to Marguerite and asked her to dance.

People around the hall thought, "He would." Lester, they considered, was well supplied with gall. Usually only the older men asked Marguerite to dance. The younger ones, especially those who were unmarried, would have been afraid of being thought presumptuous.

Marguerite's eyes had sought out Terese the first thing, and as she danced now, holding herself well away in the circle of Lester's arm, she watched Terese dance with Jim, her face happily smiling, the wide pink skirt flaring on the turns so that her shapely bare legs showed to above the knees. Somehow the girl was less startling tonight, Marguerite mused, here in the crowd, dancing with her husband. She was still, of course, the most exquisite thing in the room; but the crowd, including men as it did, seemed to take her in so that she merged with the rest of the people. It was rather strange, Marguerite thought, this phenomenon of the girl seeming to become more just one of them when surrounded by her husband and relatives, dancing in the group—for she was even more beautiful now in that low-necked blouse and the clear pink cotton skirt than she had been in slacks and a sweater.

It had been Marguerite's idea to attend the dance. Her father had shaken his head tolerantly. "My dear, it won't do a bit of good. This thing has gone beyond a point where personal loyalty to me will carry much weight. To tell you the truth, I don't see how we've managed to fend off complete unionization of the mill this long." He had paused and then said sardonically, "You know, in some ways I'm getting a rather ironical satisfaction out of this development. The company has always preferred to deal with the AF of L rather than the CIO; and I told them at the head office at the time that it would be better to steer the men toward a general AF of L union covering all the employees than to let in just the Machinists and the Carpenters. But no, they knew best. It was better to let a few top men into the aristocracy of the craft unions. That would hold the others, since the Machinists and Carpenters would never retreat to a general union. And now"—he shrugged—"you see what's happening. And they'll blame me for not managing better," he concluded sourly.

"It won't be decisive, of course," Marguerite maintained stubbornly, "but with some of the older ones, you'll see; it'll have an effect, just one social evening spent among them, being one of the boys. They like you. They don't want to fight you. Meeting you face to face, socially, right at this time, it'll slow things down a little. It'll give some of them a disloyal, guilty feeling," she pointed out cogently.

"Well, it won't do any harm," he conceded. "And I suppose it's part of my job, keeping up friendly relations with the employees."

Marguerite rather wished that the first "friendly relation" that had been forced upon her had not been Lester Coleman. While she was not precisely conversant with the standing of each member of the East Side society, she had long known that Les was not one whose favor you would choose to curry if you wished to stand in good with the East Side people. They accepted him resignedly as one of their own, but he swung little weight among them.

None of Les's usual slyly presumptuous manner toward women was in evidence now. He was deferential, not to say fawning, toward Marguerite Faber. At the same time he simmered with self-satisfaction at the general impression he was sure he was making. The nonchalant way he had asked Marguerite to dance, his aplomb in guiding her about the floor, the *sangfroid* with which he conversed with her as they danced. Surely everyone was being impressed by how easily he mingled with the upper crust.

When he had delivered Marguerite to her father's side once more, he sauntered off after a few moments and, mentally distended with triumph, moved baldly toward his next social conquest.

He spoke genially to Tom McGowan, with the effect of slapping him on the back. "Hi there, Mac," and to Mrs. McGowan, "See the whole family's here tonight," and, "How's tricks, Flossie?" in a condescending, subtly intimate change of tone.

"'Lo, Les," the latter responded with an indifferent air of acceptance. At the moment Florence was the most eligible girl in Conway, and naturally Les had paid her some attention despite the dozen or so years' difference in their ages. Florence had, in fact, come to depend on his attention to some extent. As a last resort she could count lately on Les walking home with her from the dances, or taking her for a drive on a Saturday evening in his car, winding up with a beer or so at a roadside bar, excursions which Gladys McGowan viewed with some uneasiness.

With gay camaraderie Les addressed Jim, who was standing facing the women. "How's it going, Jim, old boy?"

"O.K.," was the laconic reply.

Jim knew quite well that Les had never formally met his wife, but he perversely refrained from making the expected gesture, even when Les smiled expectantly down at the girl watching them with a pleasantly vacant expression.

Les, however, was not one to be put off by the social derelictions of others.

"Well, what do you think of the social whirl in Conway, Mrs. McGowan?" he inquired blandly.

"It's very nice," Terese smiled.

Les let his eyes rove the room with the tolerant air of a sophisticated visitor. "We manage to have a good time. Eh, Jim?"

"Yeah."

The musicians let loose just then with the strains of a two-step, and Les smiled down at Terese. "How about it? Like to start this out with me? It's going to be one of them 'whistle' dances, so you won't have to put up with me long."

Terese was rising as he ended these remarks. It never occurred to her to refuse his invitation. And she found that in some ways she felt more at ease dancing with Lester than she had all evening. He was a type she recognized and knew how to handle. It was like slipping into a familiar habit, parrying his meaningless, thinly disguised verbal advances. These would-be wolves who tried to pick up a pretty girl like herself were an old story, reminiscent of the public dance halls she had visited with groups of girl friends in the city, of Playland at the beach, and the ice-skating rink, and the paths of Golden Gate Park on a Sunday afternoon. She neither worried nor cared, with Lester, about what kind of an impression she was making, for she sensed immediately that he didn't count.

That, however, was a mistake in judgment on her part, for Lester was to "count"—and climactically, almost disastrously—in her life.

Eyes followed Terese and her partner even more intently than they did Mr. Faber and Marguerite, who had begun the two-step together. And many of the eyes detected the relaxation in Terese's manner as she grinned at Lester, retorted lazily to whatever he was saying—her command of the situation in this first brush with their "man about town." And in some of the minds there arose vaguely a cynical "Probably two of a kind" estimation of Terese's attitude.

This judgment was rooted in a loosely formed conviction that a really innocent woman would have been flustered, made a little uncomfortable by Lester's brazenly flirtatious manner. Then and there some of the more perspicacious observers decided that Terese was probably "not all she should be."

George had asked Florence to dance and she accepted ungraciously. She had been sure when Lester came up to them that he would ask her, and it was a comedown to have to go out on the floor with your brother. Her eyes rested resentfully on Lester and Terese. It was true she was only keeping Les in reserve, so to speak, an insurance against too many empty evenings. Johnny Rodriguez was her real interest at the moment; but it was annoying to find yourself passed up for a married woman, your brother's wife at that.

At the blast of the whistle Terese loosened her hand from Lester's and glanced about expectantly. Al Bowen was moving toward her, away from his previous partner. She turned from Lester and held out her arms as Al caught her for the next stretch of two-stepping.

"I'm glad I got you this time," she said with an ingenuous smile. "Not knowing the dances very well, I feel safer when I'm with someone I've danced with at least once before and know they're somebody that doesn't let me stumble over their feet."

"Don't speak too soon," he retorted cheerfully. "There's always a first time. I can step on other people's toes as good as the next one."

They laughed and went on talking, and Al said, "We ought to get together some night pretty soon, you and Jim and Lorraine and me, play cards or have a few beers or something."

"I'd love to." She looked up into his eyes eagerly. "You know," she confided, "I've noticed your wife and thought I'd like to get better acquainted. She's more my age, and all, than some of the others."

Although the whistle blew just then, they stood with their hands clasped, their arms still lightly together as Al suggested earnestly, "I tell you what, I'll talk to Lorraine about maybe having you folks over to dinner next week—"

"I'd love that," Terese said with a glow on her face as they separated, and she turned absently to the hand on her arm, which turned out to be Johnny Rodriguez's.

CHAPTER 9

When Jim and Terese were at home that night undressing for bed, he spoke hesitantly. "I should have said something—about Les Coleman. You want to be careful how you act toward him. Don't seem too friendly. He doesn't have a very good reputation where married women are concerned."

Terese turned with one hand on the elastic top of her panties. Her eyes widened with surprise.

"That dope!" She let the elastic snap back against her skin, and a current of amusement enlivened her voice. "Jim, you're not *jealous*—of him!"

"Of course not," he denied gruffly. "But people talk. He's been mixed up with two or three married women in town, and you don't want people suspecting him of getting anywhere with you, and if you act too friendly toward him in public, people might get the idea there was something to it where you're concerned."

For a moment Terese's expression was undecided, as if she might make up her mind to be cross, but then she laughed. "As if I'd look twice at *him*. Why, his kind are a dime a dozen where I come from. How could anybody think I'd even give him a thought?"

"Well, you'd be surprised what people can think around here," he grunted. "Especially the women. That's all they've got to do. Sit around and think up ideas about each other."

"Oh, Jim, that's not fair. They're all as busy as can be."

"Yeah, doing what?"

"Why, keeping house and taking care of the kids."

"How much time does it take to keep a house this size? And seems to me Byron Vale's got most of their kids down at school from eight-thirty till three-thirty every day."

Terese hesitated and then finally pulled off the nylon panties which had been part of her trousseau and reached for the bottom half of her pajamas. She had been about to argue the point, but she remembered that already she had noticed here in Conway that the women who talked the most about how busy they were, how they just never got caught up with their work, were the very ones who spent the most hours having morning coffee in one another's kitchens and standing on the path talking when they met coming to and from the store. Talking. And there had to be subjects for the talk.

"You think," she said slowly, "they gossip a lot here?"

"Think?" He snorted as he swung his legs under the covers. "I know." He crossed his arms under his head and mused aloud. "I don't know why it is, in a little place like this where everybody knows everybody else, they should be so willing to think the worst of everybody else all the time. Suspicious of each other, it seems like."

"But why should they be suspicious of each other?"

"I don't know. And it's not just the women. You see it down at work too. Seems as if everybody's always looking for somebody else to try to get ahead of him, take advantage of him." He turned his eyes on her soberly. "It's a terrible thing, some ways you look at it, the way nobody really trusts anybody else."

Terese pushed out her lips mutinously and then relaxed them and began to button her pajama coat resolutely. "You exaggerate," she said briskly. "I think they're all nice and friendly. They have been to me, anyhow."

Down the street in the Bowens' front bedroom another couple were talking as they prepared to retire. Lorraine had been stiffly polite to her husband for the past hour and a half. Al was puzzledly aware of her haughty manner, but he had not connected its origin with the portion of the two-step he had danced with Terese, although it was from that time that the frost had set in.

As Al hung his sport jacket in the closet be glanced at his wife speculatively. "Didn't you have a good time tonight?"

She was standing at the vanity table stripping the rings from her fingers. "Oh, I had a lovely time," she replied affectedly, then she met his eyes inimically in the mirror. "I noticed you seemed to be enjoying yourself all right."

"Of course I enjoyed myself. Why shouldn't I?"

Lorraine was near to tears, and she turned away sharply to conceal the fact. "No reason. No reason at all," she said with patently specious airiness.

Al put his hands on his hips and demanded angrily, "What in the hell's eating you, anyway?"

"That's right. That's right! Swear at me. Go ahead, swear at me." Her lips trembled pathetically. "On top of everything else."

The man looked at her in honest amazement, his pugnacity fading as he tried to figure out what ailed his wife.

"What do you mean—everything else? Wha'd I do?"

"Oh, nothing. Nothing at all. Just made a spectacle of yourself over that woman. Just couldn't keep your eyes off her, talking a mile a minute when you danced with her, couldn't even bear to let her go till Johnny Rodriguez practically pulled her away from you. That's all. That's all you did. Lot you care how I feel, having everybody seeing my husband joining the stampede toward her."

Expressions indicating astonishment and anger jostled each other on the man's face, but as he regarded his wife, slowly they gave way to a look that was predominantly one of sympathetic concern.

"Look, honey," he said placatingly, "you got that dame all wrong. You know what we were talking about at the end of that dance? You. She was sayin' how she'd been wanting to get acquainted with you—"

"Huh!" Lorraine ejaculated scornfully, and, "Huh!" once more, attempting to make it a snort.

"Look," Al reiterated, "I know a little bit about women; and I'm telling you, even if I did have my eye on her the way you mean—which I don't— I wouldn't get to first base, me or anybody else. That's a fact, honey; a man can tell. She's not the type."

"I'm sure you're quite an authority on women," Lorraine declared sarcastically.

"Oh, the hell with it," he retorted with sudden petulance, and grabbed pajamas off the hook on the back of the closet door. Whereat Lorraine finally let go with the tears she had been holding back. She threw herself on the bed and burst into a tirade broken by sobs, and Al raised his voice exasperatedly as he jerked out of his clothes and into his pajamas.

They had forgotten the open bedroom window facing the Fraser home, and were unaware that Emily Fraser stood in her robe and slippers before the raised window of her own living room, straining to hear every word. As the voices sank to a mumble after the Bowen lights went out, and finally were silent altogether, Emily hurried across to her bedroom, where Bill Fraser was almost asleep, and poured forth an excited report on what she had been able to hear.

"It was about that woman all right—Jim McGowan's wife. I kept hearing

Lorraine yell 'Terese.' She's mad because Al took so much notice of her. Jealous." She enunciated the word with relish. "He did dance with her several times. I remember now. And you know Al. He was quite a devil with the girls before he got married. Well, I must say, I'm not surprised. He always was quite a flirt. And I guess there's something to it about this Terese if Lorraine's getting wise already. A woman can tell about her husband. And if she sees reason to call him about it already— Well, where there's smoke, you know—"

Bill Fraser grunted a few times in response and finally said vaguely, "Oh well, maybe Lorraine's just jealous. I don't think Al's really interested—"

"Humph, that's what you think. You wait and see—"

It was unfortunate that Mrs. Fraser heard only the loud portion of the scene which had transpired next door, for it did not end with Lorraine's hysterical collapse and Al's angrily defensive response. As quarrels do, it worked itself around to where it was eventually resolved in mutual apologies and sentimental endearments on both sides. As he calmed down Al had begun to see his wife's jealousy as rather touching, an affirmation of her intense concern with himself. It was even a little flattering that she should become so upset for fear his attention was wandering from herself. And under the influence of his reassurances and protestations of utter devotion to her own person, Lorraine's hurt feelings and suspicions melted into what was at first a soothing self-pity and then a general softening toward the offending husband, until finally she allowed herself to be blissfully convinced once more of his love.

This phase of the clash between them took place, however, in the quiet and darkness of the bed, in muted voices and in murmurs which did not carry from the window. So Mrs. Fraser—and those who would hear about the scene from her—could not know that in the making-up of the quarrel the two had come back from the distance apart to which it had hurled them to a greater closeness than before, that actually the open fight over Terese had woven and strengthened another strand of the emotional bonds that marriage was weaving between them.

But although Terese was the innocent spark which had set off the explosion that resulted in so emotionally satisfying a reconciliation, none of the resulting tenderness in Lorraine was to be wasted on Terese. Her jealousy of the beautiful newcomer had deeper roots than those centering in Al, and although Lorraine knew she'd have to be nice to Terese, for appearance's sake, she had no intention of liking her any better.

CHAPTER 10

Lester had walked home with Florence, and they stood at the front steps for a few minutes after the older McGowans entered the house, indulging in aimless remarks that terminated in a tentative date for a drive on Sunday afternoon.

Around the corner, Lester crossed the street diagonally, heading for his own home two blocks down. As he passed the brown-and-white house occupied by the Rodriguezes, he noticed a light in the kitchen at the rear. While he talked to Florence he had heard the rumble of male voices passing on the street and recognized one of them as Johnny's. No other single men who lived down this way had been at the dance, so now Lester wondered about the group who had passed. Even if he had turned around to look from where he stood with Florence, he might not have been able to recognize individual figures in the party, for the nearest street light hung from a pole in front of the hotel over half a block away, and the boughs of the oak trees shaded the unpaved sidewalk anyway.

Now, seeing the light in the Rodriguez kitchen, he grew suspicious, It must have been a bunch going home with Johnny—to talk. Curiosity joined the suspicions.

Stealthily Lester tiptoed up the driveway until he could see in the window between the tieback cretonne curtains. He took a step backward, closer to the lilac bush beside the driveway, where he merged with its shadow.

It was as he had thought. George McGowan and Owen Euman—and, surprisingly, Eddie McGillicuddy—sat around the square, oilcloth-covered table, and Johnny stood facing the window pouring coffee from a white-enameled percolator, one hand on the glass top to keep it from falling off into the cups. He was laughing and saying something, and the others were stirring sugar into their drinks, lighting cigarettes, speaking to one another.

Lester considered the cook's blunt profile. So Eddie was in with them. Eddie hadn't been at the dance. They must have met him near the hotel and invited him along.

Lester wished he could hear what they were saying, but he didn't dare move up directly under the closed window for fear a casual eye might fall upon him. The thought of the group gathering in Johnny's kitchen had suggested "plotting," but somehow they didn't look as if they were plotting. They just looked like a bunch of guys shooting the bull over coffee and smokes.

There was something wistful in Lester's expression as he watched the men in the white light of the kitchen. He felt left out and lonely. He did not admit it to himself, but he would have liked to be in there too with a coffee cup in one hand, a cigarette in the other, a long-winded anecdote on his tongue.

But his eyes hardened as they rested on Johnny Rodriguez, who had just shown his even white teeth in a grin. A traitor, that's what he was, a traitor to his own union. Talking up CIO while he paid dues to the Machinists local. Those others—Owen Euman, a sort of glorified janitor, that's all he was; and George McGowan on the loading crew; and Eddie, of course, who was nothing in so far as the mill went—you couldn't expect any more from such as them. But here was Johnny, on the gravy train, ready to sell his own union brothers out, make them dependent on the whims of the membership of a union that would take in everybody down to sweepers and common laborers in the yard.

As he turned away and crept back toward the street, a small, vindictive smile took shape on Lester's thin lips. They needn't get to feeling too smart. They might find out yet what was what here in Conway. They might be surprised, just a *little* surprised, if they knew how fully Mr. Combs was cognizant of what was going on, of who was pushing things, who taking the lead and who was consorting with CIO organizers. Lester suspected it wasn't so easy anymore to fire people and make it stick, especially if the people were members of the Machinists or Carpenters, disloyal to those bodies though they might be; but Lester had a rather childlike faith in the wisdom and cunning of the men who wore white collars, and he didn't doubt that if they were kept informed they could figure out some way so that you'd never have a lot of dopes causing trouble by voting on wages and conditions and—worst of all—detracting from the present prestige and extra privileges of the smart ones who had had sense enough to get organized a long time ago.

As Lester walked along home the sense of loneliness which had smitten him when he stared into the Rodriguez kitchen was blotted out in vague, dreamy thoughts. There would be no question of his chances when openings for advancement arose. Certainly soon a foreman's job, and who knew, maybe someday even more, if the company trusted you. As surely they must trust him. And then there would be *new* Packard convertibles, and dinners and drinks at the best hotels in town instead of in Main Street restaurants, and all his clothes tailor-made.

CHAPTER 11

Miles Faber wondered if perhaps he was old-fashioned. After all, he had been with the Conway Corporation for thirty years, and when he began with the company they hadn't had such things as Specialists in Labor-Management Relations.

He managed to smile back at the bright young man who had driven down from the head office and who was now closeted in the superintendent's office with him and Fred Combs.

The young man's name was Mr. Gorham, and he smiled often. Mr. Faber was, in fact, getting pretty tired of the sight of Mr. Gorham's teeth. And he realized, with sudden, surprised insight, that one of the things about Mr. Gorham that irritated him was Mr. Gorham's clothes. Both Miles and Fred Combs wore business suits of hard-finished worsted material and white shirts with stiffened collars. But Mr. Gorham's deep gray flannel suit was cut on "sport" lines with patch pockets on the coat and conservative pleats at the waist of the trousers, and he wore a pale gray nylon shirt with a soft collar, and gray suede shoes. Somehow Miles couldn't keep from stealing surreptitious glances at those shoes.

Conscientiously he brought his mind back to the truisms Mr. Gorham had been spouting for fifteen minutes.

"... the main danger of an organization covering all the employees is that it leaves them wide open for radical influences. It's true the CIO has been doing a fine job of rooting out the Communists from their ranks, but the more inclusive the union, the more likely you are to have a few troublemakers active in it."

He paused and started up again. "To go back to what I said earlier, perhaps the wisest thing would be to encourage the AF of L Laborers to draw in some of our men who would qualify."

"You know what the scale is in the Laborers union?" Mr. Faber inquired dryly.

"Yes. Yes, I realize it would be expensive, but"—the teeth again, Miles noticed irrelevantly—"it might be cheaper in the long run. For instance, even a week's shutdown in case of a strike would run into money, and when you have them all acting as a unit they're more likely to get reckless along those lines."

Miles decided that he had endured diplomacy and oblique talk long enough. Mr. Gorham had not made the trip down from San Francisco without specific instructions in mind, and Miles was tired of feinting around while the Expert worked psychology on him and Combs to get *them* to decide for themselves what to do.

"O.K.," he said bluntly, "what's the deal? What do you propose we do?"

Mr. Gorham's teeth came into evidence again, but it was obvious that he was displeased. He wanted Miles to utter the solution now that he, Gorham, had indicated it subtly.

It was Fred Combs who obliged. "Way I look at it, this is the slack time of year anyway. Long about September and October is when we're at peak production. Couldn't we have an—er—temporary layoff, for an indefinite period?"

Mr. Gorham looked thoughtful and then showed his teeth at Fred. "You know which ones to lay off?"

Fred nodded. "I know."

Miles opened the humidor on his desk and selected a cigar.

"It may run us into trouble. I understand there'd be—say six or seven men we wouldn't need for a while, and at least three are members either of the Machinists or the Carpenters. They could either take it to those locals or have the CIO bring in the NLRB."

Gorham shrugged. "When work slacks off we're not obligated to run full crews." He smiled. "And yet—I believe the others would get the idea from your choice of those whose services could be dispensed with."

"Oh, they'd get the idea all right," Mr. Faber said dryly.

"I'll admit," Mr. Gorham said judiciously, "the spring is a bad time. General employment figures always rise in spring and summer. The men aren't so worried about getting jobs at this time of year, but they always have to look forward to fall and winter, and I'm sure they realize the unemployment rolls at that time of year have been rising annually for some time now."

They batted it back and forth for a while longer, but Miles raised no serious opposition to the plan, although it went against his own judgment. He realized, however, that despite Gorham's manner of approaching the subject, there was actually no choice open to him and Fred. Gorham had not come down for this conference for nothing. His veiled message was in actuality an order emanating from echelons higher than himself.

Later in the day, when the Specialist in Labor-Management Relations had departed in his Buick coupé, Faber observed in a disgruntled tone to Fred Combs, "I look for trouble over this."

Fred replied equably, "Oh, I don't know. There's nothing open about it."

But Miles was thinking that Johnny Rodriguez, Owen Euman, George McGowan, Bill Fraser would head the list who got pink slips next Friday. It would be unmistakable to the men.

"I'm afraid," he said gloomily, "they won't take it lying down."

"What can they do?" Fred countered. "We're in the clear. Our production figures show a decline which could justify a layoff. They've got nothing to put their finger on. Anyway, it doesn't hurt to show 'em who's boss now and then."

Faber regarded his personnel manager vacantly for a moment before he turned away.

Sometimes he wondered who was boss. The men thought he was, the head office in San Francisco thought it was, and in the final analysis the heaviest stockholders probably thought they were.

Miles's office jutted out with corner windows from the main office so that he could see from his desk the vast windowed side of the mill proper, behind which men controlled engines, trundled dollies up and down ramps, fed raw material into machines, and sent the finished product along conveyor belts.

The disquieting feeling had been growing in Miles for some time that if it ever came right down to it, it might well be that out there were the real bosses. It was perhaps for that reason that he had no enthusiasm for situations that called for "showing" who was boss.

As in all such organizations, rumors had a way of seeping back and forth between the mill and the office, seemingly by osmosis. In the mill portion of the establishment there was no question but that there were regular sources of information for the managerial personnel. The human sources of these leaks were suspected but not definitely known. On the office side, however, there were no specific persons who could be nailed even in conjecture as conscious "informers" to the workmen. But the seepage existed. Decisions made in the private offices somehow became suspected in the mill before they were put into effect. It happened inadvertently for the most part and couldn't be traced back, as could the gossip from the workmen which reached the ears of Miles Faber or Fred Combs or Jack Morgan. It might be a private secretary who dropped an indiscreet remark, or the switchboard operator, or a filing clerk who put two and two together and said something to her sister who was married to a man whose brother worked in the yard at the mill. At any rate, somehow, rumors got started.

It might have been only that the men had some imagination and that they figured what the logical next move of the company would be. However it came about, within two days they were buzzing covertly among themselves about the possibility that the most outspoken supporters of CIO might be laid off, and within twenty-four hours more the names of the seven men who were to be the victims were being passed along as fact.

The rumors were startlingly correct.

On the second day after Mr. Gorham's trip down from the city, Johnny

Rodriguez and George McGowan and Owen Euman stopped at the store after work and stood beside the large red metal box at the front whose cold, watery depths contained bottles of soda pop. As they helped themselves and stood drinking cola beside the box, they talked in undertones.

"Of course," Johnny said, "they pick up things in the office the same way we do in the mill. It's the old grapevine stuff."

"Grapevine, hell," George growled. "How come they got it down so damn pat? The very guys that have taken on the responsibility for passing out membership cards. You know we've been careful. I haven't mentioned to my dad, for instance, who the guys are that have definitely promised to help set the ball rolling. And I warned Bill Fraser particular not to say anything to Greg Hanson—living next door to each other the way they do, and Greg being dead set against us."

"Well," Johnny said, "it's pretty generally known which ones of us are most outspoken in favor of a change."

"Inside the mill, yes," Owen put in. "But how did that information get to Combs and Morgan so quick—and so accurate?"

"That's the rub," George nodded gloomily.

Owen turned himself slowly and looked out of the front windows as a figure passed outside. It was Lester Coleman, bareheaded and still in his work clothes, a completely unglamorous figure in his shapeless gray jeans and oil-stained shirt.

"There's your answer," Owen grunted.

"The son of a bitch," George muttered.

The next time Johnny and Owen met the CIO organizer for an evening conference in a back room of the CIO offices in town, they told him of the rumored dismissals. The organizer was a lean, weathered man who looked as if he might have worked once with his hands but who was obviously now several points removed from physical labor.

He nodded sagely several times and responded to the story, "That's good. That's all right. The minute they lay you guys off we'll appeal immediately to the NLRB. And under the stress of this crisis you should be able to sign up enough more men so that we'll be in without a ripple." He paused and grinned cynically. "I guess the management out there figured the men would scare easy. Well, they're asking for a showdown. They'll get it."

Owen Euman sucked on his pipe and said seriously, "I can't figure Faber tryin' a stunt like this. He knows better. Way I figure, he had orders. The big shots in San Francisco, they figure paternalism has always worked in Conway. Our people are softened up. So they figure all they have to do is crack the whip when we get restless and we'll crawl back into line. But Faber knows better. It ain't," Euman went on philosophically, "just us.

It's characteristic of the American people. If you can keep 'em from hearin' the whip and knowin' for sure it's there, they'll go along real docile. But once let 'em hear it crack and they'll buck like hell."

CHAPTER 12

Terese knew that there was talk at the mill of changing unions—or something. She heard Jim and his father talking about it in the kitchen at the old folks' one evening when George was out somewhere, and heard Mrs. McGowan charge her husband, "Now if you're going to get in an argument, you can just go outdoors. I won't have any more of it in the house."

And Jim had mentioned it at home once or twice, but Terese was still too preoccupied with being a housewife to feel that it had much to do with her. This was man stuff, and not her concern.

She waited for a call from Lorraine, and on Tuesday morning it finally came. Terese was ironing in the kitchen when Lorraine knocked at the front door. She had safely turned off the iron, so, somewhat effusively, she bade the guest take a chair in the living room and sat down herself on the edge of the davenport with her hands clasped about her knees, watching the other expectantly.

Lorraine had decided she couldn't get out of it. If she didn't ask the Jim McGowans over for an evening, it would cause talk. After all, she had gone to the bridge party in Terese's honor; they were near the same age; their husbands were sort of friends. People would think she was afraid of Jim's beautiful wife if she ignored her completely. Lorraine heartily wished, though, that there were some good reason for keeping Terese on the outside of the "nice" bunch on the East Side.

But she did her duty, albeit a little stiffly, and invited Jim and Terese over to play canasta the next evening.

Terese was wearing a yellow sun-back dress with only straps over her shoulders, and even at ten in the morning she looked fresh as a daffodil. Lorraine noticed that, and it fretted her a little. Somehow, even when they wore clean, starched house dresses, most wives seemed to look slightly bedraggled until early afternoon. During the course of dishwashing and bedmaking and scrubbing out the bathroom washbowl, your lipstick faded and face powder mysteriously vanished and your hair separated and the starchiness departed from your skirt.

Lorraine did not stay long, but Terese went back to her ironing with new buoyancy, thinking already of what she would wear the next evening and dreaming ahead to the days to come, when the rigidity would relax between her and Lorraine, and Lorraine would come and sit in the kitchen while she went right on with the ironing and they talked over all kinds of intimate things, like how soon they wanted to have babies and how much they had paid for their washing machines and whether an automatic was really the best.

Terese felt that now she was really getting "in" in Conway, that pretty soon she wouldn't feel like a stranger anymore.

The things that happened that Tuesday were all little things, seemingly of no importance. Such as the way Terese forgot about watching the time, and only realized after the ironing was put away that it was a quarter to twelve and that she had meant to go to the store for a loaf of bread and a head of lettuce for lunch.

It was a pleasantly warm day, so she dashed out of the house without the bolero jacket to her dress. As she hurried down the street few people noticed her, but those who did were struck by how bare she looked with her back and shoulders exposed. Everybody had been wearing those dresses for several years, but most of the women put on the jacket when they left their own yards. And even if they didn't, other women seemed to be not quite so noticeably uncovered.

When Terese came out of the store with her purchases in a brown paper bag held in the crook of her arm, it was several minutes past twelve, and down the long driveway toward the mill dark figures were appearing outside the entrances.

Lester Coleman had slept later than he meant to that morning, and in order not to be late had driven his car to work. Usually anyone who took his car came back at noon with the springs sagging from extra passengers. But on this day no one had jumped into Lester's car as the crowd flowed out of the mill, even when he called out jovially as he turned into the parking space, "Anybody want a lift?"

A few had shaken their heads, courteous enough to respond at least. But most of the men within hearing of his invitation had acted as if they didn't hear.

He pushed the gears into position defiantly. All right. The hell with them. He wasn't so dumb. They were blaming him because the office knew what was what. Well, let 'em. That's all. Let 'em. Rodriguez and old Euman and George, naturally they were sore because he didn't happen to agree with them. But there was no reason for the other guys—guys that saw things the same way he did but were too chicken to do anything about it—no reason for them to act as if they didn't know whether they ought to speak to him or not. Chicken, that's what they were. Scared of getting in bad with Johnny and that bunch when all the time they were also scared of the trouble Johnny and them were stirring up.

As the Packard tore off down the drive Owen Euman stared after it morosely. "The bastard," he said out of the side of his mouth to Johnny Rodriguez, who walked beside him.

Johnny shrugged. "There's always one like him. Some ways you almost have to feel sorry for a guy like him."

"If we get the pink slips in our envelope Friday night, it ain't him you should feel sorry for."

Johnny slowly turned his head and looked back over his shoulder at the uneven lines of men behind them, some talking and laughing, others striding along alone and silent.

"Maybe it isn't so bad as it looks," he said consideringly. "This may backfire on 'em if they fire us guys that everybody considers the most militant. The men don't like it—even the fellows that don't want a change. It may be just what we need to cinch an election."

"Gonna do us a lot of good, ain't it," Owen growled, "if we ain't even workin' here anymore?"

"If the plant goes CIO," Johnny said confidently, "they can force 'em to take us back, even if they should let us out now. Anyway," he said in a heartier tone, slapping the older man's shoulder, "it's all just talk as far as we know. Nothing but a rumor. May not a bit of truth in it."

"All I've got to say," Owen muttered with a scowl, "he'd better never let me catch him alone in a dark alley some night. That's all I've got to say."

"I know how you feel, but that sort of stuff doesn't get you anywhere. There's too much at stake to let a little jerk like Les Coleman get us in trouble by giving him an excuse to run squawking to Faber that we beat him up."

"Yeah, I know. I was just talking," Owen mumbled.

Johnny's dark eyes rested briefly and rather anxiously on the older man's set face. Owen had a reputation among the men as being "radical" when he got riled up. By radical they meant something more like hotheaded, extreme, rather than the usual political sense of the word. Although Owen was that, too, Johnny realized. At least more so than the general run of the populace of Conway. But in a peaceable, gentle way. It was only when Owen was mad that he became radical in the way the men used the word. He had become milder with increasing years, but there had been a time when every so often you heard of Owen and some other fellow mixing it with their fists, even once right on the job. The old-timers all knew you had to handle Owen with kid gloves, not risk having him fly off the handle, and they did so as a matter of course, for they knew that at heart he was a good guy. "Salt of the earth," they would have told anyone who asked about Owen Euman.

It would have been quicker for Lester to turn right from the mill yard and go past the service station and the hotel on his way home, but he instinctively chose the route where the most people, especially women, would see him passing in his car with the top down; so he turned left to go past the store and along the streets facing the park.

Terese had just turned the corner after leaving the store, and as Lester saw her hurrying past the post office windows he pulled up and called, "Can I give you a lift?"

Grace Schweitzer, on her high stool inside, saw Terese step toward the car after a moment's startled hesitation, saw Lester lean forward to push the door open, and saw Terese smile companionably as she slipped into the seat.

"You're a lifesaver," she laughed. "Now maybe I'll get home in time to have a plate on the table, at least, before Jim gets there."

"Out stepping, eh, while the old man's working?"

"Oh no, nothing like that. Just careless about time. I had a caller this morning," she added importantly, "and"—with a complacent giggle—"you know how us girls are, get to talking and don't realize what time it is."

This was something of an exaggeration, but it was the way she liked to see herself—the young housewife so popular that she entertained friends even before lunch time.

"Wouldn't kid me, would you?" Lester smirked. "About it being a *girl* that took up your time."

Terese slid a sidelong look toward him, one of tolerant amusement tinged with disapproval. "What minds some people have."

"Girl as good-looking as you, a fellow can't help getting ideas."

"Well, you just keep those ideas locked up in your own little head where they belong." They were in front of her house now, and she smiled. "Thanks a million for the ride. Now I may get the coffee started before Jim gets here."

He was leaning back negligently with an elbow on the car door after having braked to a stop. "How about inviting me over for coffee sometime—when the old man's not home, of course."

Terese had hugged her paper bag closer and put one hand on the door handle preparatory to getting out. She turned her head and regarded him with eyes narrowing a little. "Listen, kid—relax," she said flatly. "I guess I've heard about all the approaches there are, and I'm not impressed, see? I just want to get along here and be friends with everybody, and that includes you. So let's just leave it at that, huh? I wouldn't want to have to get tough about it."

He reached over and patted her arm that was clasped around the groceries. "O.K., baby. I'll consider myself slapped down—for now."

"Honest," she said with a wondering shake of her head, "you're a case.

I don't see how you've kept from getting in trouble if you go around handing out that line right and left."

She pushed the door open and climbed out.

"I'll see you at the dance Friday," he called chummily as she moved away from the car, "if not before."

"O.K.," she said indifferently, and turned on the path to add, "And thanks again for the lift."

"The pleasure," he countered insinuatingly, "was all mine."

As she hurried up the path Terese smiled to herself, thinking, "What a drip. That awful clumsy line. I'll have to tell Jim. I guess Jim was right. He's a character to stay clear of."

As she turned sideways to push open the front door, her eyes fell on Lela Adams, who was stretched out in her bathing suit on the lawn next door, taking a sun bath. Lela's face was buried on her folded arms, so Terese did not speak to her; she only thought idly, "This must be her day off."

It was Lela's day off. She was a telephone operator at the exchange in town, and her husband Bert was a machinist at the mill, one of those who could see no advantage in losing his identity in a general labor union. Lela drove to work each day in a shabby but still sturdy Model A Ford coupé. Between her job and her housework, she had not had time to cultivate her new next-door neighbor's acquaintance.

She had been lying just far enough away so that she could not hear what the two were saying over the sound of the idling car engine, but she heard Lester's call that he would see Terese on Friday and her laconic "O.K."

When Lela related the incident later, her statement was that they talked "for a while" after the car stopped. And by the time several other people had repeated the tale, Terese and Lester had "parked in front of her house" and the implication was that they had conversed anywhere from ten to twenty minutes. Lela also made note of and reported the smile that had stayed on Terese's lips as she walked to the house afterward.

By the time Jim came in five minutes later, Terese was in a flurry of kitchen activity involving the separating of lettuce and the thickening of sauce for creamed tuna fish, and the first thing she had to tell him about was Lorraine's call and her invitation. This topic kept them busy most of the forty minutes Jim had at home, and Terese did not think again of the lift Lester had given her.

CHAPTER 13

Another little incident which was later blown up to unjustified proportions by repetition took place in one of the toilet rooms at the mill that afternoon. Al Bowen and another fellow named Sam, who lived at the hotel, were leaning against the washbasins having a cigarette when Lester came in. After completing the mission for which he had entered, Lester also prepared to smoke. Conversation between the other two had staggered and finally collapsed after Lester's appearance.

Now Sam, to save the situation from too indicative a silence, observed with a slightly baiting manner, "I hear you took the little Frenchy for a ride this noon."

Al glanced at Lester in surprise, then cast his eyes down toward the cigarette in his hand, turning it in his fingers, waiting for enlightenment, at the same time feeling annoyance at the term Sam had used to designate Terese. Behind Jim's back the men frequently spoke of his wife as "the little Frenchy," managing to put an illusively lewd connotation into the epithet.

At first Al hadn't thought much about it, only hoping nobody forgot sometime and used the phrase in front of Jim, for it would not only make him mad but would hurt his feelings, and Al had always liked Jim, younger though the latter was. And now, since his quarrel with Lorraine over the girl, Al had become uneasy at the attitude people seemed to be assuming toward her. There was something unhealthy about it, something that he felt intuitively was dangerous, not just to the girl but to the people who refused to accept her.

"Yup, I don't lose any time," Lester was replying with a smug grin. "Old Johnny-on-the-spot Coleman."

"Think you're gonna get anywhere?" Sam jibed.

"That'd be telling."

"You've got about as much chance with Terese McGowan," Al grunted, "as you have with Lana Turner."

"Oh, you think you've got the inside track, huh?" Lester retorted nastily.

Al set his eyes on Lester's face and held them there as he dropped his cigarette butt on the cement floor and stepped on it.

"I ought," he said coldly, his eyes still unwavering, "to punch you right in the teeth."

Lester looked as if he didn't know whether to be surprised or frightened. He seemed to decide surprise was the safest reaction.

"Ain't you got no sense of humor?" he croaked with what was supposed to be a laugh.

"'Tain't funny," Al said, and walked out.

Lester looked aggrievedly at Sam. "What d'you suppose is bitin' him? We were only kidding."

Sam was young and not overly bright. He pushed back his black sateen cap by the brim and said, "Jeez, I dunno. You think he is stuck on her?"

"Could be," Lester said in his most sophisticated manner. "Could be."

During the afternoon Sam found occasion to recount this little exchange to several other men, all of whom listened with encouraging interest, one might almost say with prurient interest; and naturally the more the tale was bandied about, the more dramatic it grew, until finally some people were telling how Sam had to step between them to keep Al from jumping Coleman then and there.

Walking down the long driveway after work, Al happened to fall into step with Jim McGowan. Both were tired, and they did not talk much. Ahead of them a group of four men walked abreast, with Lester Coleman on the extreme edge. It was obvious, if you watched the group, that Lester had attached himself to it uninvited. He almost trotted, keeping pace with the others, and his head was constantly turned toward the rest of the irregular line they made, as if he had to pay close attention and keep butting in in order to stay a part of the conversation.

Al's eyes were disapproving upon him, and after a moment he blurted out to Jim, "It's a funny thing how you can go along for years takin' somebody for granted, and then all at once everybody gets a bellyful at the same time." He nodded toward Lester. "Everybody's known Coleman was an ass-kisser from 'way back, and nobody thought much about it, but here lately all of a sudden everybody's had all they can take of him."

"Yeah, I guess he wouldn't win any popularity contests right now."

Al's vexation was rising with the contemplation of it, and he proceeded unthinkingly. "I almost took a poke at him in the can this afternoon. Shooting off his mouth about having given your wife a ride home from the store at noon. Tryin' to make something out of it—"

Al broke off abruptly, belatedly realizing that these were the kind of remarks which could "make trouble." His eyes had been broodingly on the figures ahead, and now he didn't look at Jim.

"You know how Coleman is," he went on brusquely, trying to tone down the implications of his remarks. "Woman says 'hello' to him on the street, and he thinks he's made a hit."

"Yeah, I know," Jim said quietly.

He had looked surprised when Al mentioned the ride, but now he only added equably, "He better keep his dirty tongue off my wife's name if he knows what's good for him."

As Terese and Jim sat at the dinner table later, Jim casually asked the question which, simple as it was, he had somehow not been able to phrase acceptably since he got home. "Did you get a ride this noon with Les Coleman?"

"Oh yeah, I meant to tell you, and it slipped my mind, I had to rush so about lunch. What a character!"

"I wish," Jim said restlessly, "you'd pay some attention when I talk to you. I told you the other night to steer clear of that guy."

"Oh, for heaven's sake, Jim. I rode around the block with the jerk. You sound as if I'd been dating him."

"Well, that's the way he's already made it sound, shooting off his loud mouth down on the job."

She regarded him incredulously, and then her eyes narrowed, sparkling dangerously between the lashes. "That's disgusting," she said distinctly, and stood up suddenly, pushing her chair away with the backs of her knees. "You're all disgusting," she concluded sharply.

Jim raised his eyes, startled by her quick change of mood. He knew Terese had a temper, the quick, shallow, and meaningless kind. One night when she had been trying to mend the placket of an old cotton skirt and for ten minutes it hadn't gone right, she had suddenly looked as she did now, and with an explosive "Hell!" and a quick ripping movement of her hands she had put the skirt out of commission for good; and he had heard her in the kitchen one evening exclaiming, "God damn it!" and had come out to find her flinging a whole panful of scorched Italian squash into the clean white sink. Each time, a moment after the explosive action had relieved her feelings, she had grinned sheepishly and then returned to normalcy with a "Well, that's that."

It was the same sort of thing now. "You all make me sick," she stormed. "This stinking little town. A woman can't speak to a man on the street, it seems like, without people thinking she's a chippy. Even your own husband."

"Listen, don't get on your high horse with me. *I* can't help how people look at things. I'm just telling you you gave Coleman a chance to brag about how chummy he's getting with you."

Terese stamped off into the living room, still expressing her displeasure in shrill tones, and Jim followed, arguing doggedly.

Lela Adams had been outside her own house, playing the garden hose on the roots of the shrubbery, about fifteen feet from the McGowans' open kitchen window. She kept her back turned and her eyes on the shrubs, but her ears fairly reached out toward the voices next door. It was disappointing when they receded toward the front of the house and words became indistinguishable. She moved along the little cement path toward the fuchsias under her own front porch, but the McGowan bedroom intervened now between herself and the living room next door.

Over the pattering of the water and the screaming of some children running past on the street and the yapping of a mongrel dog in the next yard, Lela hadn't been able to hear every word, but she had heard enough to know they were quarreling about Les Coleman.

All in all, they were such little things that happened that day touching Terese. Time would have diminished the momentary importance of the interpretations read into them. But there was to be no time. Instead the several little events of that day were to be bloated and distorted through the lens of the one big event of the night.

CHAPTER 14

As the Friday night dances were a tradition in Conway, so Tuesday night was traditionally Stag Night at the clubhouse. A long, narrow room lay next the dance floor, connected with it by square archways over which sliding doors could close to shut off the main hall. This smaller room was the "game" room. It contained a pool table and scattered card tables surrounded by old-fashioned, round-backed wooden chairs. A single wood-paneled door opened from it into the alley behind the hotel.

The company's original intention in providing the clubhouse had been to have it available as a center for daily use by the community's residents. But it had worked out, for some reason now forgotten, that the men gathered there only on Tuesday evenings to play poker or cribbage or pinochle, to enjoy a case of beer paid for out of a kitty, to play pool and generally chew the fat, free for one evening from feminine society. All the other evenings the game room stood mustily vacant, the cigar and cigarette and pipe smoke clinging to the air from week to week.

Jim had not wandered down to the clubhouse on Stag Night since his marriage, but he had planned to go for a while this night. While the flare-up between him and Terese was dying down, he had wondered if maybe now he shouldn't go. She might get sore again. But her annoyance with him had been as short-lived as it had been with the skirt and the squash. By the time she was ready to wash dishes she was humming to herself as she stood before the sink.

Terese was going over to spend the time with "the folks" while he was gone, and at eight o'clock they set out together, Jim walking around with her onto the next street and so down the block to the older McGowans' house. He went in with her and found that George had already gone and that his father, who was sunk into a chair in the front room behind the city paper, was not going at all.

The older man was in a disgruntled mood. Much as he disapproved of the men's restiveness in wanting the upheaval involved in wholesale reorganization of their unions, he had been dismayed by the rumors of the selective layoffs that were coming up. It was no way, he figured morosely, for the office to handle things. So now he was just plain mad at everybody, with no desire for social contact with anyone concerned.

"I ain't," he informed his son gloomily, "gonna go over there and listen to 'em argue all night. I want some peace and quiet for a change."

"O.K." Jim shrugged. "Don't need to jump all over me. I ain't took sides one way or the other. I'm willing to go along with what the rest of 'em want."

His father gave him a scornful glance, grunted "H'mph," and put the newspaper up in front of his face.

Mrs. McGowan sighed humorously, "You men. Always taking things so seriously."

Her husband lowered the paper and glowered at her. "You'll take it seriously all right if they go and get a CIO union and we get pulled out on strike every whipstitch, losin' two or three months' work a year."

"Well, I've learned not to cross bridges till I get to them," she retorted.

Mr. McGowan held the paper over his face again, and in a few minutes Jim went out.

His father had been wrong about the tenor of the gathering that night. It was as if, for Stag Night, the men had declared a truce. No mention was made either of rival unions or of layoff rumors. They concentrated on the dime-limit penny-ante game and the pool table and a pinochle game while Owen Euman and old man Cantoni, who owned Jim's house, silently played chess in the corner.

Al Bowen came in late, sometime after nine-thirty, and stayed only an hour or so. He explained to the bunch watching the current game of pool, "Damned if I didn't fall asleep on the davenport after dinner. Forgot it was Tuesday night. Lorraine asked me when I woke up, 'How come you aren't going to Stag Night?' She was all ready to go to bed and read, so I decided I'd run over for a few minutes. Felt rested up after my sleep."

"What's a matter," Eddie McGillicuddy inquired loudly, "won't she let you sleep nights? Christ, you been married almost a year, ain't you? Ought to be lettin' up on it now."

They all laughed, thinking once more that that Eddie sure was a card, and Al made a flippant response.

Johnny Rodriguez left the hall a little before ten, replying jokingly to the protesting voices, "I'm not as young as I used to be. Gotta get my rest."

George McGowan said to him in a wry undertone, "You may have plenty of time to rest pretty soon."

"Well, I want to be in good condition to stand the shock," Johnny grinned, and then, "Kidding aside, I've been up late two or three nights in a row, and I'm pooped."

In a few minutes the chess game concluded, and Owen Euman departed quietly by himself. Eddie McGillicuddy was next to go, also alone. Jim dropped out of the poker game about ten-fifteen, and he and George walked back to their folks' house together. Al Bowen took his leave alone soon after, and from then on the others straggled out in twos and threes, with the four remaining poker players holding out until midnight.

If anyone noticed that Lester Coleman had not showed up—late enough, as was his custom, so that his entrance was sure to be noticeable—nobody commented on it. Either no one missed him or they all figured he was ashamed to show his face just now.

It was a clear, starlit night, but dark beyond the feeble light hanging from the eaves at the corner of the clubhouse where the alley met the street. The blinds at the windows were all closely pulled. Once on the street, however, the center light over the intersection by the hotel gave sufficient illumination so that the night did not seem dark.

When the two McGowan boys came up the steps at their parents' home, through the window they could see the three women in the living room.

"Where were you," Jim asked his sister, running a finger under the hair at the nape of her neck and giving it a playful flip, "when we came over?"

She moved her head away from his teasing fingers and said, "I was over to Marge Vale's. She was showing me how to fix my eyes the new way." She lifted her face complacently. "Like it?"

Jim looked and laughed out loud. "You look like pictures I've seen of Theda Bara taken back in the twenties."

"It's the latest thing," she said in an aggrieved tone. "I've been tellin' Terese I'd show her how."

"Well, just never mind," Jim said, "I like to have my wives look human."

Florence pulled the mirror from the purse lying beside her on the davenport and with a pleased expression surveyed herself in it.

"Les liked it. Said it made me look exotic."

"So that's where lover-boy was tonight," George put in. "I wondered why he never showed up at the hall. But I guess even he doesn't have guts enough to come around right now."

"He was going there," Florence said indifferently, still studying the effect of her eye-shadowed, mascaraed, penciled organs of sight. "I just happened to meet Jo and Tina on the street after I left Vale's and we met Lester coming out of the park and he walked around the block past the store with us."

"Sounds like the long way round if he was going to the clubhouse."

"He wasn't in no hurry. He left us at the alley behind the service station and us girls walked on around here by ourselves." She squinted sideways at her eyes in the mirror and added indifferently, "He said he was going to drop in at the clubhouse. Anyway, he started up the alley between the station and the store."

"I guess he got cold feet," George observed.

"Would you boys like a cup of coffee?" Mrs. McGowan inquired maternally. "We just had a cup after Florence came in."

"Not me," Jim said firmly, "not after three bottles of beer. I'm sloshing now. I think we better get moving, honey," he said to Terese. "Seven o'clock comes awful early."

Terese yawned. "I'll say."

CHAPTER 15

It was, distressingly, children cutting through the alley on their way to school who discovered Lester's body. It lay next to the cement foundation of the hotel, in the corner made by wooden steps leading to the back entrance at the end of the building closest to the service station. The boarders at the hotel used these steps infrequently, usually only when going to the clubhouse or as a short cut to the store. When they left for work in the mornings it was through the double glass doors of the lobby, going out from their breakfast in the dining hall at the front of the building.

The children ran directly to Byron Vale at the school, bursting into the empty classroom where he sat at his desk. They were pale, their eyes dark with excitement, small features strained, bodies tense with the conflict between horror and the pleasurable stimulation of being the bearers of such cataclysmic news.

Byron went immediately to the spot, taking the two oldest boys of the group with him, ordering the others to remain on the school grounds.

Despite their dazed, eager importance, the boys lagged back as they neared the steps, gesturing nervously ahead to show Byron where to look. He moistened his lips and put his hand to his throat in an involuntary gesture as if to relieve pressure there.

On the right front of Lester's head, just missing the eye, there was a brownish dent several inches long and about three inches wide, it seemed, although Byron's mind recorded automatically the thought that it might look wider because of the damaged skin tissue with its dried blood. As Byron's eyes moved away, escaping the sight, he noticed the ends of pipe leaning against the railing of the steps, and he remembered that two plumbers had been working under the house here yesterday. The pipes were black with age—abandoned obviously, left here probably until the plumbers should return today to finish their repairs and clean up. One piece about three feet long had fallen at an angle, resting on the second step from the bottom, its end on the hard-packed earth near Lester's legs.

In an automatic response to an instinct for neatness, Byron's hand started out to raise the pipe into line with the others, and then he jerked his hand back frantically before it touched the rough cylinder. Abruptly, then, he felt himself come awake from the trauma of revulsion which had frozen his senses since his eyes fell on Lester's wound.

He turned his head and met the boys' wide, fascinated, uncertain eyes. He took a deep breath and said quietly, "Go in and see if you can find Eddie or somebody, and send him out here. Then you fellows go back to the playground." He gave them a pale, reassuring smile.

When Eddie came out in his apron, peering down over the steps, all he said was, "Jeez!" He kept saying it, letting a few seconds elapse between times.

"I didn't want to leave—it alone," Byron explained, his voice scratching a little. "Will you just—stay here while I phone the sheriff?"

Eddie looked at him dazedly. "Jeez, the sheriff?"

As Byron ran up the steps he heard Eddie mutter, "Jeez," again in an awed tone.

When he had telephoned the authorities in town, Byron stood still with his hand on the phone. It had occurred to him as the natural thing that he must let the mill, in the person of Miles Faber, know what had happened. He glanced at his wrist watch. It was a little past eight-thirty. He would take a chance that Faber was at the office early.

His call was put through immediately, and he heard the superintendent's calm voice. Byron explained briefly and announced that the sheriff and coroner would soon be out.

There was silence for two or three seconds, and then Faber's voice: "When did it happen?"

"He's in his good clothes, so it couldn't have been this morning."

"You didn't say how. Was it a shot, a knife—"

"No, it looks like a blow on the head. I—I think it crushed the skull."

"Well, thank you. For calling me. It's a terrible thing."

"I thought you should know."

"Yes. Yes, that's right."

Byron hung up and went down the short, gloomy corridor to the back steps. Eddie stood in the sun, beyond the cool, damp oblong of shade from the building. His eyes lifted in relief as the principal appeared.

When he had descended the steps Byron's eyes fell on the pipes, and he halted suddenly, speaking sharply. "Did you pick up that pipe?"

Eddie looked down blankly. "Maybe. Yeah, I guess I did. It was crooked."

"You shouldn't have touched it." As Eddie looked at him with surprise, Byron added, "I know. I know, under stress a person does little things automatically, like straightening things that're out of place. But that length of pipe may have been the weapon. There're fingerprints to consider."

Eddie licked his lips and glanced at the pipe uneasily, then said defensively, "It's too rough. It wouldn't take prints."

Byron felt in the side pocket of his jacket and brought out cigarettes. "Smoke?" he asked.

Eddie reached forward gratefully to take one, and Byron seated himself on the steps.

"We'll have to wait till Sheriff Schofield gets here."

"Yeah." Eddie pulled deeply on the cigarette and looked down the alley past the clubhouse and the end of the hotel, beginning to get hold of himself. After a moment he spoke half to himself. "It's a funny thing. I knew somep'n'd happen. Felt it in my bones. I told a bunch of the guys right in there in the lobby"—he stabbed his cigarette toward the building—"told 'em there'd be trouble. I had a—whadda-you-call-it—premonition, first time I ever saw her."

Byron raised his head, frowning. "Her? What do you mean?"

"That woman of Jim McGowan's," he returned patiently, as if the other should have known.

"My God, man, how do you connect her with this? Let me tell you no woman did *that*. It had to be a man and a strong one."

"Sure, but you wait an' see, she's mixed up in it. She's bad medicine; I said so right from the start. The kind that makes trouble. Don't it add up? She comes in, and bang, we got a murder. I ask you," he demanded cogently, "we ever have a murder before she came here?"

Byron regarded him with an appalled expression and then he said earnestly, "Listen, Eddie, this is serious business. Somebody'll probably get sent up for it. And you wouldn't want it to be an innocent man. You want to be careful what you say to Schofield and his men. It would be a terrible thing to cast suspicion on the wrong person just on account of loose talk. And God, man, you know what's been going on around here lately. Les was about as popular as a skunk at a Sunday school picnic. Any of us go shooting off our mouths too much and half the town may be suspected."

Eddie's rather flat face ridged itself into a frown indicating difficult concentration. "Guess you're right, at that. But," he added assertively, "I got a feeling, that's all. Call it a hunch if you want to. That woman, she's out of place here. Too rich for our blood, if you get what I mean. And somep'n' like that, it leads to trouble every time. Like I said, did we ever have a murder before?"

Byron frowned and looked away toward the frosted window of the rest room at the end of the clubhouse, thinking discouraged thoughts about this almost superstitious distrust of the strange, the desirable, the beautiful—as if it must somehow be dangerous.

CHAPTER 16

When he had replaced the telephone Miles Faber sat with his eyes fixed on the triangle of leather which held down the upper right-hand corner of the blotter on his desk. He seemed to be studying the wavy gold line marked into the black leather as a decorative border.

One thing he knew he must do, now. But he would have to get in touch with the head office first, to explain. Mr. Gorham. Since the order had come from him.

His hand moved toward the button that would summon Hilda, his secretary. Then his fingers drew back. This was Wednesday. Friday was payday. The notices would go out then. He might not get a reply in time.

He moved to lift the phone, but again he paused, remembering switchboard operators on both ends. This was not something to be overheard.

He glanced at the leather-bound date clock on his desk and stood up abruptly. In the outer office he spoke briefly to Hilda, who was organizing her desk for the day.

"Will you call my wife; tell her I had to leave suddenly for San Francisco and will be back on the ten o'clock train. I haven't time to call myself. I'll just make it now."

"But, Mr. Faber," the girl protested, her hand going to a stack of papers at the side of her desk, "these—"

"You'll have to postpone everything. Anybody else who calls, tell them I was called away. If it's important, make appointments for tomorrow."

He jammed his hat on and hurried off without speaking to anyone else. In town he parked his car in the graveled station lot just as the fast train for the city whistled at the highway crossing.

Before noon he was in Gorham's office on Montgomery Street, and for once Mr. Gorham's manner betrayed a feeling of inadequacy to the situation in which he found himself. Miles Faber's intransigent attitude was mainly responsible for Mr. Gorham's loss of competent control of himself and of the other man, and hence of the entire situation. He was reduced to calling in E. J., a second vice-president, who promised to see them in his office at two o'clock. Gorham invited Faber to lunch with him, and by mutual agreement they did not discuss the matter until they sat around E. J.'s desk.

When the whole story had been repeated to E. J. with Mr. Gorham's sentiments added, the vice-president increased his judicial expression, regarded the edge of his desk carefully, shifted his gaze to the window, and finally smiled at Miles Faber in a fatherly manner.

"Couldn't it be that the man's death has no connection with his—er—status at the mill? After all, he must have had an—er—private life." He smiled and made a gesture with his head toward Gorham. "I'm rather inclined to believe with Harry that there's no reason to change our—er—strategy because of this unfortunate occurrence. As a matter of fact, may not this excitement tend to take the men's minds off this union difficulty, be another factor in—er—dissipating trends toward their taking action? With police about and suspicion—er—rampant in the village, and the dismissals on top of it, it seems to me it will all act like a dash of cold water on the—er—restlessness that seems to have developed."

Faber stared at the vice-president almost with incredulity. When he spoke, at first it seemed to be with some difficulty in controlling his voice. "You don't seem to realize—I know Conway. I know the mill, the people there. I've known for a long time that many of the workmen suspected Coleman of being a talebearer, if not an outright paid spy for the company, which of course we know he wasn't. It wasn't necessary. He was a natural-born toady, always thinking to advance himself by servility to us in the office and by keeping Combs informed every time a man took an extra five minutes in the can. Coleman thought nobody knew the role he played, but a lot of them did. The only thing was, they didn't think he was important. There was seldom any information he could pass on that they thought mattered. But it had obviously leaked out that we knew just who to fire in this case—as a threat. Let's admit it; that's what these particular layoffs are. And somebody got in a fight with Coleman over it—knowing he supplied the right names; and some one of this radical bunch killed him. I'm as sure of it as if I'd been there. All right, we go ahead with the layoffs. That proves it to everybody, that Coleman was killed because he put the finger on these men—"

"In that case," E. J. put in soothingly, "won't it turn the—shall we say the decenter—elements in Conway against these men? Won't they be actually a little relieved to have them out of the mill? After all, we have a fairly high type of people there. They won't condone murder. And the whole thing may shock them into a quieter attitude, may make them more willing to continue as they have been doing when they see the violent results of this dispute over rival labor organizations."

Faber took a long breath and then he said bluntly, "No. Your whole analysis is wrong. I may not be versed in psychology"—he directed a somewhat bitter glance at Gorham—"I don't know all the reasons why people act the way they do. But I know the mill and I know Conway. This won't scare the men, calm them down as you think it will. Layoffs, yes; that scares them; but connect a murder with those layoffs, and no matter which side the men are on, it's going to excite them. The drama in this particular situation may—probably will—drive the majority of them closer together, make them close ranks—not *against* the crowd from which Coleman's murder came—but *for* them, to protect them. I'm not making predictions. I don't know just what will happen. But I know; I can feel it; the effect will be bad on relations at the mill. This is no time to be showing the iron fist inside the velvet glove. It's no time for bringing things to a head. Our only hope of an eventual peaceful solution to this union crisis is for us to lie low now, pull in our horns until they get over this excitement about Coleman. We should keep out of it now. There's no use throwing a match into an explosive situation by firing men, any or all of whom may be suspected by the police, and who may turn out to have the majority of the men's sympathy on that count.

"Coleman wasn't popular. Even the side he allied himself with in the present squabble considered him a dubious asset. They all look askance at the police. That's nothing peculiar to Conway. People have a tendency to close ranks against the police. It's a sort of blindly self-protective instinct among working people. And now if it looks as if the management was working with the law and is out to 'get' whoever killed Coleman, it's going to create bad feeling against the office. No matter which side the men were on before, they'll resent our publicly picking out the men who had the most reason to hate Coleman. It might even throw some of them that are still on the fence over onto the CIO men's side, arouse sympathy for them because they're being persecuted over the death of a man nobody liked."

Miles rose with an abrupt movement. "God damn it, *I'm* the one who has to keep the mill producing. You want me to have a wildcat strike on my hands—or at the least a tense, rebellious atmosphere to upset the men and tear down efficiency?"

"Don't you think, Faber," Mr. Gorham said with a touch of superciliousness, "you're a little overfearful?"

Faber looked at him for a second, then he raised his head and stared stonily out of the window. "I've been with the Conway Company for over thirty years. During that time I've never acted except in the best interests of the company. If you want to take steps to retire me, O.K. But if I'm still superintendent on Friday, the suspension notices don't go out. That's all I have to say."

"Well, of course," E. J. said, "if that's the way you feel, that's how it will have to be. The affair isn't important enough that any of us would *insist* upon interfering. You're in charge at the mill. We'll have to abide by your decision. And we appreciate your discussing it with us first."

As the train cleft the darkness that evening, bearing him back to Conway, Miles Faber leaned his elbow on the window sill and watched the lighted ranch houses flicking past after dark intervals. He was tired—even, he realized now, a little unsure of himself. He had been vehement and decided when he talked to the men in San Francisco; but was he, after all, overexcited, reading too much into the situation at home? Was he getting old, perhaps, and afraid—afraid of the people at home, so afraid of them that from subjective motives, unwillingness to face their resentment and disapproval, he dared not fire their leaders? Was it actually this, rather than objective reasons having to do with disruptive conditions on the job, that had motivated his actions today?

He took his elbow off the sill and leaned back on the seat. The hell of it was there actually was a peculiar, restless, explosive undercurrent in the village just now, a heightened tension that always accompanied labor's organizational changes.

CHAPTER 17

It was typical of Sheriff Schofield that—after registering the overt physical facts which could be observed in connection with Lester Coleman's demise—instead of immediately canvassing the victim's friends and neighbors in the village, he went first to the mill office for data on Lester's background. The sheriff's was an elected office, and Schofield had the political acumen that was a requisite to winning elections in the county. He did not intend to run the risk of committing a *faux pas* in conducting the investigation. The best way to avoid this was to see the head men first.

Schofield was not a particularly prepossessing man. Without being grossly overweight, he still managed to convey an impression of clumsy heaviness. His face was square, the features rather blurred, and the members of what criminal elements there were in the county considered the expression in his small blue eyes a "mean" one. The head of the county detective bureau, a Mr. Marcus, a medium-sized man with plain brown hair and a deceptively blank look on his face, accompanied the sheriff into the office building.

Finding Mr. Faber out, they were shunted into Jack Morgan's office, whose door read "Assistant Superintendent."

In the absence of Mr. Faber, Jack Morgan had little taste for handling this unexpected problem in "Public Relations." Even as the two men entered his small office he had a brilliant inspiration, and it was not long until he was suggesting helpfully, "I'll tell you, Sheriff, I think the man you really ought to see is our personnel manager, Mr. Combs. The men and their lives and—uh—et cetera are more in his line. He's very conscientious and knows all the workmen personally. I'm sure he could tell you more about Mr. Coleman's possible—uh—enemies than I could."

Morgan mentally gave a relieved sigh as the officers trekked out to call at Combs's door.

Combs was no happier to see them than Morgan had been, and he privately cursed Faber for taking off like this when they were faced with so delicate a situation. He, too, suspected that the motives for Coleman's murder sprang from the ill feeling generated during this union dispute, but he did not accept that answer as conclusively as the superintendent had done. His was the problem now, however, of indicating the way for the sheriff to follow. He had pondered briefly as to whether it might not put the fear of God into the men if this crime were openly acknowledged as a result of the labor trouble that was brewing, if this horrible result of interunion contention might not sober them and make them feel it was better to let sleeping dogs lie when murder came as a consequence of fighting over what union was to represent them.

But there was another even more serious angle to be considered, and that was the company's Good Name. After all, Fred considered, it wouldn't look nice in the newspapers, having the sources of a murder traced back to causes lying within the Conway Mill. The company always avoided that type of publicity. The village of Conway was, in fact, one of the bright stars in the company's reputation, the peaceful, pleasant, model Company Town.

Even during the preliminaries in the conversation between him and the officers, Fred's mind was busy coming to a decision. He knew more, perhaps, about the villagers and their relationships than anyone else in the office did. He considered it his duty to do so. For a moment he indulged in an irritated thought of his wife. He would be even better informed about the East Side's private life if only Eleanor weren't so uncooperative in respect to mingling with them socially. He had to find out everything secondhand through people like Coleman and through keeping his ears open to people like Grace Schweitzer at the post office and Angela Amatelli at the store.

Schofield was making an inquiry, couched in intentionally general terms, as to Lester's standing with his fellow workers on the job, and Combs pursed his lips judiciously, realizing that this was the territory over which he must pick his way delicately.

"Well, the man wasn't exactly popular. You see"—smiling deprecatingly—"Coleman was a bachelor, and he fancied himself as a Don Juan. And he was also something of a dude. And, you know, other men don't usually respond very well to that type. I wouldn't say he was disliked; just not especially popular. As a matter of fact, the men sort of made fun of him, considered him rather ridiculous. Poor fellow," he added as an afterthought.

"Been in mix-ups with women, then?"

"We-ell, yes and no. I never heard of anything serious. I don't think Coleman ever let himself get too involved. He was a sort of neurotic type, I should say; it pleased his vanity to have it *look* as if women couldn't resist him."

"Um," the sheriff rejoined. "Any particular woman he was mixed up with lately?"

Fred's thoughts squirmed uneasily. He didn't want to actually *involve* any particular person. Still, if the officers were not to be led astray, he had to give them something to go on. His fingernail picked at an ink spot on the blotter. "Well, lately he's been going around some with an unmarried girl, Florence McGowan. Her father's one of our foremen. But as far as I know, it's a very casual thing."

"Any married women been mentioned in connection with him lately?"

Like the sudden projection of a close-up in a movie, Terese McGowan appeared in Fred's thoughts, exotically beautiful (for Conway), as yet to him a somewhat unknown quantity and, he knew, still a sort of nine-days wonder on the East Side. The idea struck him with some force, and honestly so. My God, might it not be that there—somewhere around the beautiful stranger—lay the real answer to the crime, rather than in the union dispute? He had seen her himself several times—on the street, in the store. With that sleek black hair, those mysterious dark eyes, the calm, aloof expression, there was something of the *femme fatale* about her, the type who set dark forces to work in male breasts. And he had heard that Coleman had immediately pricked up his ears at sight of her. Any man would notice her, of course; so certainly to a neurotic type like Coleman she would have an irresistible allure. And her husband of less than two months, would he not be excessively uxorious toward this rare prize?

There had been a slight pause while these reflections shot through Combs's mind and the officers regarded him impassively.

"I don't know," Fred said slowly. "That is, I haven't heard anything definite—just vague references. But there is a new woman in town that no one seems to know much about—what sort she really is, you understand. She just doesn't seem to exactly fit in, if you know what I mean. And she's—she's—" He sought for words, and ended inadequately, "Well, she's beautiful. And come to think of it, I can't imagine Coleman not making a try, at least, to gain her—attention. In fact, now that I think of it, I've heard vaguely that she's caused several little domestic scenes in town. The wives naturally view her with suspicion. She's—well, she's different."

"I see."

As they stood beside his car after leaving the office building, the sheriff gave final instructions to his detective, Mr. Marcus. "I'll drive you back to the hotel to pick up Pete, and then I'll leave you two on it out here. You heard what this guy had to say. You and Pete nose around here in the neighborhood, see what else you can pick up, and come on in to the office later in the day and we'll see what we've got. Tonight, when the men are off work, you can come out again. By then we may have a pretty good line on things, might even know who to bring in."

Marcus, settling into the front seat beside his boss, said practically, "We'll scout around first, these two dames, the people that run the store, and some of these McGowans' neighbors and so on. Pete's probably been picking up stuff already; he'll have ideas where to start."

CHAPTER 18

The detective whom they called Pete said he had learned nothing while they were away.

"Anybody," he told Schofield aggrievedly, "that might have heard or seen anything is at work. They were havin' this doings in the hall, and all the women were home; so the men are the only ones that were near the scene last night, and they aren't available yet."

"Doc," Schofield observed, speaking of the county medical examiner who had come out with the ambulance, "says he's been dead all night, won't be able to place the time very close till after the autopsy. All we know is it must have happened after dark."

"Well," Marcus sighed with the air of one settling down to work, "we'll find out from this Eddie character where these McGowan women live and start on them. Girl friends," he interpolated for Pete's benefit. "Personally, I wouldn't be surprised if it turned out to be Eddie. He's an unbalanced type."

As Pete and Marcus started up the street after ascertaining the McGowan address from the cook, Pete announced gloomily, "It's one of them needle-in-a-haystack deals. I'd be willing to lay you even money we never even make an arrest. Too many people."

Pete, although he was an accurate and thorough investigator, was a natural pessimist. He took a gloomy view of humanity, believing any or all of it capable of anything from perjury to criminal arson or mass slaughter.

It was now approaching eleven o'clock, and practically every living soul in Conway had learned that Lester Coleman had been killed the night before. Details were garbled. Some believed he had been shot, the weapon being everything from a twenty-two rifle to a forty-five pistol. Some were under the impression that he had been stabbed; still others had gathered it was strangulation. That he was dead, however, was universally known.

One of the very few who had not heard the news was Terese McGowan. She had no telephone, and none of her neighbors had seen fit to run over and inform her of the tragedy. At the moment when the detectives mounted the front steps at the Tom McGowan residence Terese was sitting in a low chair before the screened northeast window in her living room, enjoying the cool breeze and basting ruffles onto the French bathing suit she was making to take sun baths in. As she stitched she listened to a daytime radio serial with an abstracted expression. One of the idle thoughts that had gone through her head was that maybe they shouldn't wait too long to have a baby, and if they did have one before too long she hoped it would be a girl. You could really let yourself go on making clothes for a girl. There was simply no scope for imagination in little boys' clothes anymore. From the time they first staggered to their feet it seemed as if all they wore were T shirts and jeans. While with a little girl ... Her mind wandered off into a world of eyelet embroidery and ruffled lawns and starched ginghams trimmed with rickrack.

Florence answered the doorbell at the McGowan house and looked taken aback at sight of the two strange men. She wore a rose-colored flowered seersucker housecoat and bright blue open-toed bedroom slippers. She hadn't got around to pin curls yet this morning, and her hair hung in limp strands along her temples. When she learned that the men were from the sheriff's office and wished to question her, she looked terrified.

"Sit down," she gasped. "I—I'll get my mother. She's back in the kitchen."

Mrs. McGowan appeared just then in the doorway to the hall which led to the kitchen, where she had left her next-door neighbor sitting at the table while she came forward to investigate. When Florence had breathlessly explained the two strangers Mrs. McGowan half turned, saying hurriedly, "I'll tell Mrs. Phipps we have company."

Marcus spoke up. "If your caller is a neighbor, ask her to wait with you in the kitchen while we talk with your daughter a few minutes, and then you can both come in and we can ask you both a few questions."

Mrs. McGowan eyed him suspiciously and then cast an anxious glance at the staring Florence.

"We prefer to talk to people alone when we're gathering information," Marcus explained calmly. "It's customary."

The flat "It's customary" seemed to paralyze Mrs. McGowan's mental processes, and she withdrew reluctantly.

Marcus nodded at Florence and said, "Sit down," which she did, while he and Pete did likewise.

"Mr. Coleman was a friend of yours, we understand?"

"Sort of."

"When did you see him last?"

"Last night."

"Tell us about it, will you? What were the circumstances?"

Haltingly, and in a voice that was almost inaudible at times, Florence repeated the story she had told her family the night before.

"And what time was it when you reached home?"

"I'm not sure. I know it was after nine-thirty. Maybe later. Dad had already gone to bed."

Marcus digressed a moment. "Where does your father sleep?"

"Upstairs."

The detective glanced about the living room, seeking stairs.

"The stairs go up at the end of that hall," the girl explained.

Pete rose idly and went to the doorway to the hall which ran back to an outside screened door. On the right he saw an opening ending in a step, and on the left and closer to the living room a door from which came a murmur of voices. That was probably the kitchen. He registered the fact incidentally that someone who had presumably taken those stairs up to bed needn't necessarily have stayed there. He could have departed unobserved.

"And your brothers," Marcus prompted, "how soon did they come in after you did?"

"Oh, I don't know. Half an hour, maybe. Mom and Terese and I were just sitting in here talking, after we had coffee in the kitchen."

"You were going steady with Mr. Coleman?"

Ever since she sat down Florence had been conscious of her untidy appearance and had kept futilely poking at her hair and clothing. Now she was startled into forgetfulness of her sartorial deficiencies.

"Oh, mercy no," she denied shrilly. "It was just casual. I've always known Les. I wouldn't say I *went* with him."

Florence's vanity had been brought into play, and for a few moments she forgot the dreadful significance of the detectives' visit, overlooked also the fact that they would not understand the significance in Conway of a girl's not having any boy friend but Lester Coleman. When Les had begun to show interest in her she had wanted to corral that interest, had resented his paying more attention to others like—well, like Terese—but at the same time she would have resented being linked with him in the public mind as "Les's girl friend." These characters now sitting in the living room were *men*, and automatically she sought to give them an impression of herself more fitting to her own conception of Florence McGowan.

"In fact," she added with a trace of archness, "there's one or two boys would differ with you on that point—my being a special friend of Les's."

Marcus saw his cue and resignedly played the necessary role. For a moment he became more Man than Detective. "Got another fellow on the string, eh?" he smirked, with an air of "Well, now, we'll get off business for a minute or two."

Florence knew, if she were *really* honest with herself, that she couldn't lay claim to much of a place in Johnny Rodriguez's thoughts; but he was the one she wished was her boy friend, and it was pleasant every time she found a chance to say his name out loud. And, after all, he had danced with her three times at the dance two weeks ago and had walked alone with her as far as the front walk after the dance, going on then to his own house. And a month ago he had taken her to the show in town and they had stopped at the drive-in afterward for a sandwich. Of course it had happened accidental-like. She had seen him in the store and walked home with him, telling him en route how she was just dying to see the new Bette Davis picture in town, and he had said he was thinking of going, would she like to go along.

"I wouldn't say 'on the string,'" she demurred coyly, "but I think Johnny would be surprised if he heard I was supposed to be Les Coleman's girl friend."

Marcus smiled with great friendliness. "Johnny?"

"Johnny Rodriguez. He's a machinist at the mill," she added casually, hoping to impress the men. Then she felt a stab of caution. "Not," she appended airily, "that I'm tied up with Johnny either. What I mean to say is, don't get the idea there was anything *between* Lester and me."

She leaned against the sofa back complacently. She guessed she'd handled that pretty good. Disassociated herself from Les, and hence from his murder, and given the impression that Johnny was interested in her while not definitely *saying* so in such a way that it would get back to him and make her look foolish.

"I guess," Marcus said innocently, "Coleman wasn't the type to tie himself down to a steady girl friend. I understand he was friendly with your sister-in-law too."

Florence's muscles stiffened noticeably for a moment, and her eyes became wary as she was thus rudely jerked out of the comfortable mood she had settled into.

"Terese?" she snapped.

Marcus smiled deprecatingly. "Oh, I didn't mean anything—serious. Just I understand Coleman went for a pretty face"—he smiled flatteringly at the girl—"as is obvious from his having gone around some with you."

"Gossip," Florence sniffed. "Les couldn't be polite to a good-looking woman without people trying to make something out of it."

Florence was irritated. It was all right for *her* to belittle the importance of her relations with Les, but it was another thing to have it implied that he had had his eye out for other women.

"My sister-in-law," she said loftily, "has an unfortunate manner—it doesn't mean anything," she interpolated hastily. "But she gives men the impression—" She fumbled, and wound up, "Well, you know."

"Must be trying for your brother, her husband," Marcus observed sympathetically.

Belatedly Florence saw the spot she had put herself—and Jim—into.

"Oh, Jim," she said, wide-eyed, "isn't the jealous type at all. He understands how it is. Men just will make passes at a girl as pretty as Terese. And Jim never thinks a thing about it. He knows it doesn't mean a thing. As a matter of fact," she rushed on effusively, "I don't think it ever occurred to him that Les tried to flirt with Terese. He's just not the type to notice such things."

The two men just looked at her noncommittally. They did not say so, but each felt that he too knew something about the probable mental processes of men lucky enough to have unusually beautiful wives.

In a few minutes they had Mrs. McGowan and Mrs. Phipps come in and obtained a repetition of Florence's story of the evening.

CHAPTER 19

As they walked down the street, bent on interviewing Terese, Pete grumbled again, "You wait an' see what I tell you. We'll never make an arrest. Too many people, too many angles. And no evidence. No material evidence. No footprints, no fingerprints, not enough blood so any of it probably got on the assailant, no witnesses, weapon available to anybody. This is the kind of case I don't like."

"Hell, it's narrowing down," Marcus said impatiently. "Any kind of a break and we'll nab him. Ten to one it's the husband. He and the brother meet our friend fancy-pants in the alley; friend husband tells him to lay off the passes at his wife. Coleman talks back, and friend husband picks up the pipe and lets him have it. And the brothers beat it home, maybe not even knowing the bastard's done for. It was dark; they might have figured he was just knocked out."

"O.K. So that's the story. Now prove it. That's all we gotta do—prove it."

"Ever hear of a confession?" Marcus retorted.

"This is just one angle," Pete persisted. "Wait'll we pick up a dozen more motives during the day. You'll see."

"God," Marcus sighed as they turned in at Terese's walk, "what a crapehanger!"

Terese regarded them questioningly as they came to the screened door, making no move to admit them. So Marcus chose a direct approach.

"Mrs. McGowan?"

She nodded.

"We're investigators for the sheriff's office. No doubt you've heard of the accident last night—"

As he paused, she shook her head dumbly.

"May we come in, then, and tell you about it? We're checking the activities of the residents in this neighborhood at the time."

Terese looked from one to the other doubtfully and opened the door.

The men took chairs, and she sat on the sofa with her knees together, her hands clasped on them, her eyes moving from one man to the other. "What happened?" she asked faintly.

"Some children on their way to school found Lester Coleman dead this morning," Marcus said with intentional ambiguity.

"Oh-h." It was a soft, shocked sigh. "Oh, that's too bad."

The big dark eyes were candid and ingenuous. Trained though they were to be objective in their reactions to personalities, both detectives were somewhat diverted from the purposes of their call in fascinated contemplation of the woman they had decided was the heart of their case, for she was not what they had expected.

She wore a plain white house dress with a square neck. Like Florence, she had not been groomed for visitors. The skirt of her frock was wrinkled, and Terese too wore house slippers over bare feet. Her hair had been combed but once, and that just after rising, and she wore no make-up; but Terese had none of the frowzy look her sister-in-law had worn. The men had somehow expected a sleek, masklike glamour. This woman had glamour all right, but not of the kind they had expected. She was confusing somehow. A woman was not supposed to look beautiful in a slightly soiled house dress, without lipstick and with sewing thrown carelessly across the chair from which she had risen.

As usual, Marcus did the talking. From Terese he got the same story of the last hours of the previous evening that he had had from Florence. And then he began to probe for the nature of her acquaintance with the deceased.

In answer to his question as to when she had first met Coleman, Terese lowered her eyes and studied the feet of an armchair. "I think it was last Friday at the dance. I may have seen him around before then. I think I did. I noticed his car, but I never actually met him before the dance."

"Ever been here to your house?"

She looked at Marcus suspiciously. "No."

"Weren't he and your husband old friends?"

"I suppose so. In a way," she said slowly. "They've both always lived here."

When he and Pete went out together it was always Marcus who did the talking, but today he noticed a different quality in Pete's silence. Except when the girl glanced his way—at which time Pete's eyes wandered elaborately—the silent detective kept his gaze fixed upon her so intently that finally the woman became uneasily aware of it, sending occasional furtive glances in his direction.

When the two men went down the walk half an hour later, Pete broke his silence.

"Well, that's that. We gotta get another theory."

"What d'you mean?"

"She didn't have nothing to do with it."

They were at the path which served as a sidewalk, and Marcus halted involuntarily. "How do you figure?" he snapped. He glanced back at the house and observed wryly, "If I ever saw a dame a man might be tempted to commit murder for, she's it. By God, she's got everything."

"She ain't the type," Pete stated flatly.

They started to walk on slowly back toward the hotel, and Marcus said irritably, "Nobody figures her as the murderer."

"She ain't the type that starts men fightin' over her," Pete elaborated stubbornly.

"Type, hell. What do you mean?"

Pete's surprising viewpoint gave Marcus an annoying discomfiture, for Pete was a man whose opinions they relied on at the office. He was unpolished, uneducated, had none of the frills coming to be accepted as necessary in police work; that is, formal knowledge of criminology and sociology, and technique in meeting the public. But Schofield used him on every "big" case that came up, for Pete had a knack for noticing things that escaped other people, and with startling frequency the things he noticed turned out to be key points in evidence.

"There's two things," the big man said ponderously. "She's satisfied, and she ain't dumb. Now you take these dames that play men off against each other; in the first place, you can spot it every time—they're dissatisfied, life ain't exciting enough, they wish things was different someway. And this dame, she thinks she's sitting pretty. She's got no motive to stir up trouble just for the hell of it. And then, like I said, she's no dumbbell. I don't say she's no Einstein—"

Marcus's mind flinched under the necessity of disentangling the double negative. The terms of communication used in the sheriff's office were not such as to bring joy to the heart of a professor of English, but even there Pete's use of the mother tongue sometimes caused pain. His colleagues endured stoically, however, knowing that often Pete's most perceptive mental processes were couched in terms that did the greatest violence to grammar. Marcus's mind made haste to catch up with what his partner was saying.

"—but she's smart enough to see there's no percentage in risking what she's got by flirting with this one and that one just to build herself up in her own mind. Far as that goes, a dame that good-looking don't have to be vain. She ain't ever worried about her looks. See what I mean?"

"Supposing all this is true," Marcus rejoined grumpily, "how's her husband going to know? He could still be jealous."

Pete stared down the street thoughtfully. "No, it's a funny thing about jealousy. Unless a person's cracked, they ain't usually jealous unless they got cause to be—maybe nothin' outright, but they can kind of feel the other party pullin' away, even if the other party don't actually do nothing. And a husband—unless, like I say, he's kind of off balance himself—he can feel whether he needs to be jealous or not. See what I mean? Now this guy McGowan, he knows his wife better'n other people do. He'd get a feeling about her. And I looked her over good. Unless her man's some wizened-up little dope that ain't very bright an' deep down inside himself knows he don't amount to much, he ain't goin' around worryin' right now about anybody takin' her away from him. A man can feel it when he ain't in any danger. And unless I'm way off the beam, that woman's husband is safe—for the time being, anyway."

They were nearing the hotel where they planned to eat lunch. Marcus sighed. "Quite a psychologist, aren't you?"

They paused at the corner before going on to the hotel steps.

"Hell, no," Pete denied emphatically. "I never had no use for all them fancy names for things. I just know human nature, that's all. In this game you gotta. An' God knows I've seen enough of human nature, an' most of the time it ain't a very pretty sight. I tell you"—he regarded his colleague solemnly—"sometimes people almost scare you, you know that? It ain't so much the big things they do. It's the little mean, petty things. I tell you,

I'd almost rather see 'em ram a real knife into somebody else than do the way they do, running around stickin' knives in each other in ways it don't show. At least it's honest an' you got somethin' you can get your hands on when they come right out in the open and shoot somebody."

"Well," Marcus broke out, making a move to walk on, "you may have doped out human nature so we're on the wrong track in this case, but *I'm* not convinced. I'm going to keep this woman angle in mind."

Pete stood still and gazed off across the street. "I been thinkin' about somethin' else off and on all morning."

Men were beginning to straggle up the street and mount the steps further down, casting curious eyes at the two on the corner. Pete turned his head and considered them briefly.

"You know," he said in a low voice, "they been having a union beef out here."

Marcus turned back to face the other, frowning. "No," he said, "I never heard anything about it."

"It ain't generally known, but they are. They're thinking of kickin' out the crafts an' goin' CIO."

"How do you know?"

"Oh, I picked it up around."

Marcus gave Pete a sharp glance. If Pete had "picked it up," it was probably true. Pete made no bones about his attitude toward politics. It was a racket, and he wasn't interested. He couldn't have told you who was chairman of the United Nations Security Council and was probably vague about who was the United States Secretary of State, but in anything pertaining to county affairs he was a political encyclopedia—although he would not have considered his knowledge "political." He usually knew more, however, about what was going on and who was currently on whose side than did Schofield. He "picked things up" in bars, at church suppers, at Chamber of Commerce luncheons, from waitresses at lunch counters, from taxi drivers, from his wife's housewife friends, from telephone operators he had taken the trouble to "happen" to know personally. And although he had probably not read three books in all his adult life, he read every local daily paper in the county minutely and laboriously.

It was because of all this that Pete had a steady job in the sheriff's office, regardless of who held the post after election. You couldn't trust Pete to conduct an official interview; you couldn't put him in charge of anything that required other men working under him; but you always kept him on tap.

So Marcus turned now to listen.

"I been thinking," Pete said. "Feeling always runs high, specially in a tight little outfit like the mill, when you got somethin' comin' up there's two sides to. Might be a good idea to find out which side this stiff was on."

"I'm surprised," Marcus said dryly, "you don't know."

"Well, to tell the truth, I think I do. I ain't heard definitely about this issue. But I've seen this character around. He used to go to public dances in town and like that. And I know his type—"

"Type again," Marcus breathed wearily.

Pete ignored the aside and went on phlegmatically, "He was the type: find out which side his boss is on, and that's his side. Like I said, I don't know all the dee-tails yet about this squabble, but you don't have to be a mind reader to figure the management would be for leavin' things the way they are; so that'd be Coleman's side. So we find out who's on the wrong side an' start concentratin'. Union stuff, guys get pretty riled up, you know."

Marcus looked down to where the last of the men were entering the hotel, and his expression was discouraged.

"We'll talk it over with Schofield," he said, and added bitterly, "You sure like to complicate things, I'll say that."

CHAPTER 20

News of Lester's death had seeped into the mill during the morning. The twenty-five men at the two long tables in the hotel were subdued as they ate lunch, speaking in hushed, shocked tones, acutely aware of the two detectives whom Eddie had prudently placed at a small table to the side.

The boy of seventeen who was Eddie's helper and the waiter at mealtimes looked unhappy when Pete jerked his head toward the longer tables and said, "No need to treat us special. We'd just as soon sit at one of the main tables."

"Eddie said," the boy stammered, "Eddie said to set places for you here. We already had the other tables ready."

As they sat down the detectives met one another's eyes comprehendingly. Eddie, knowingly or not, was isolating them.

Marcus spoke in an undertone over the meat loaf which was the *pièce de résistance* of their meal. "You got a line on the stag party from the cook?"

"Didn't get much. There was about thirty guys there. This Eddie left around ten. A fellow named Rodriguez and another by the name of Euman had left not long before he did. After that he don't know who left— he says. And there was one guy, name of Bowen, came in extra late—after nine-thirty. That's all I could find out."

"Wish we knew the approximate time of death," Marcus grumbled.

"He might've lived for a while afterwards. Them head injuries're tricky.

Not always instantaneous. Way I figure it, it happened sometime between nine-thirty and—at the most—eleven. Sometime after he left them girls down by the school and came on up the alley here. We gotta find out who left the joint between them times. Then we got it narrowed down. So far we know of Rodriguez, Euman, McGillicuddy, the McGowans—and, oh yeah, Bowen, the one that showed up after nine-thirty."

"We'll get all of them tonight, after work and during the dinner hour."

"Of course," Pete said dispassionately, "there was people that didn't go to the party. No reason somebody else couldn't of done it."

"That's a lovely thought," Marcus rejoined sourly. He looked across the piece of rather dry cake covered with white sauce which had been set before him, to the tables across the room, and stood up abruptly. He walked over to the first table, and all the heads turned toward him.

"You all know, I guess, that my partner and I are working on last night's accident. We need to find out who was at the clubhouse last evening. When you finish your lunch would those who were there please step into the lobby for a few minutes. We'd like to talk to you." He grinned genially. "If we make anybody late for work on account of it, we'll settle it with the boss."

Only seven men tarried in the lobby after the meal. One was Owen Euman, one the young man, Sam, who had joked with Lester about Terese in the washroom the day before. The other five had left the stag party in a pair and in a trio respectively, after the departure of the McGowans, and they vowed they had seen no one either outside or in the halls of the hotel when they came in, and had heard nothing unusual before or after retiring. Poor Sam had been alone when he crossed the alley in a diagonal line from the clubhouse door halfway along that building to the back steps of the hotel at its far end.

"But I never seen a thing," he asserted earnestly. "The whole place was deserted. And it was pretty dark. There's a light at the corner of the clubhouse on the street, and there was a light upstairs in Eddie's room over the steps; but honest to God, I never saw Les. Maybe I could of if I'd been looking for a man there, but I didn't."

Marcus let the others go before Owen Euman, who had taken out his pipe and smoked while the men talked.

"Now as I get it," Marcus said with a friendly air, "you left a few minutes after this Rodriguez did; and the others say he mentioned the time—ten o'clock. Was he out of sight when you came out?"

"I didn't see him."

"Did you look up and down the alley?"

"Nope. Wasn't no use to. It was dark down toward the store end anyway."

"Did you hear any footsteps?"

"Nope."

"After you came into the hotel, did you see anyone?"

Owen hesitated slightly. "Nope."

"You went directly to your room?"

"Yup."

"Didn't stop at the bathroom?"

"Oh—well, yeah; I did that."

"No one saw you in the hall?"

"Not as I know of."

Marcus smiled ruefully. "This must be a quiet hotel. Do they all go to bed with the chickens?"

"I went up the back stairs," Owen said. "May have been somebody here in the lobby. I didn't come in to look."

Startlingly, Pete's harsh voice broke out of its silence. "Which side you on in this union fracas out here? AF of L or CIO?"

Marcus saw the older man's jaw muscles tense as his teeth gripped harder on the pipestem. Slowly he turned his head in Pete's direction.

"What's that got to do with it?"

"There wasn't much love lost on Coleman around here, was there?"

Owen took the pipe from his mouth. He regarded the bowl. In the second while he sought for a safe reply, Pete went on, "Coleman favored leavin' things the way they were, didn't he?"

Owen raised his eyes, but Pete continued inexorably, "He was kind of an annoyin' type, I figure. Might make guys that didn't agree with him pretty sore sometimes."

Owen opened his lips, appraising Pete warily, but still the usually silent detective did not wait for a response. "Before the day's over we'll find out in general how people were lined up on this issue. I figure you for favorin' a different type of union out here. You don't belong to none now, do you?"

Slowly Owen shook his head. "No."

Pete had finished. He sat now, his usual phlegmatic, imagelike self. Marcus was still somewhat taken aback over Pete's undisciplined interruption. As he gathered his wits to resume control of the inquiry once more, Owen spoke to Pete, his voice heavy with restrained antagonism.

"People don't kill each other over differences of opinion on things like union policy."

Pete's face stirred in a sardonic smile. "Ever read the newspapers? They even use atom bombs on each other when they can't agree on policy."

When Owen had been dismissed to return to work, Marcus turned on his confrere. "What was the idea? Tipping your hand like that?"

"It was a shot in the dark," the other confessed smugly. "But we found out somethin', didn't we? This old guy's a shrewd customer. And now we know how he's got it figured. *He* isn't bein' taken in by a lot of crap about dames. He figures it's on account of the union dispute, just like I do. Seemed to me it was more than that. He acted like he *knows* that's it."

They talked again to Eddie, discovering that his room and that of his helper, Herbert, were in the rear of the hotel, over the steps where Lester's body had lain, and that the two corner rooms between Herbert's and the corner one by the street were vacant.

"Everybody," Eddie explained, "wants a room at the front or on the ends. Nobody wants the rear ones. That corner one out to the street belongs to a guy named Wilson, and he's in the hospital having appendicitis."

Herbert, it seemed, had attended a movie in town the evening before, riding in with friends, and hadn't got home until nearly midnight, coming into the hotel through the front entrance.

As the detectives set out from the hotel, Pete announced glumly, "Far as I'm concerned, we can quit right now. We ain't never gonna find out who done it, find out so we can pin it on 'em, anyway."

Marcus shook his head impatiently. "God, man, we just started. We've got two angles—the woman, and this labor trouble. Time we interview some more of these men tonight—in their homes where we can catch the wives too—we may have more dope than we can handle."

"O.K., you wait and see," Pete advised discouragingly.

CHAPTER 21

In the morning, when the news had passed from man to man through the mill, it had been mostly shock and excitement which predominated in their minds. There was no fear, and the curiosity as to what had really happened there in the alley was unlocalized. By afternoon, however, the "I wonder" latent in their reactions had crystallized into words here and there. Groups had discussed the murder on the walk to and from work, and wives had entered the discussions over lunch tables.

Many of the men, after the first bewilderment when their minds had accepted the fact that Lester Coleman had been killed, had thought right off the bat of his role in the expected layoffs. With horror these had silently reflected that one of the CIO sympathizers must have let the stool pigeon have it. But no one said it aloud. You knew and worked next to Johnny Rodriguez and George McGowan and Owen Euman and Bill Fraser and the others. You hesitated to name your suspicion to others who also knew and worked with them.

And then at noon your wife, who felt secure in saying whatever she thought in your presence, let loose her own and the neighbors' morbid conjectures—which included, of course, the union angle and what a rat Les Coleman had been. But almost universally the women's otherwise unoccupied minds had ranged gloatingly over other possibilities as well.

One wife on the north edge of the East Side phrased it succinctly: "I always knew someday some man would put a stop to his carryings-on. Look at the women he's had affairs with! Gloria Hanson, that Mrs. Treadwell that moved away last year, and there was talk once about him and Lela Adams. He couldn't expect to get away with it forever."

"But all them women, it's over and done with, far as I know. Only woman I know of him bein' mixed up with now is the young McGowan girl."

The wife had screwed up her face thoughtfully. "McGowan. I wonder. There's Jim's wife. I hadn't heard nothing about her and Lester. But they all say she looks fast. *I* can't tell. All I know is she's too good-looking for me to trust. But I wonder. He's been sort of going with Flo, so naturally he'd be thrown with this woman some." She eyed her husband avidly. "Do you suppose—"

"How would I know?"

"Well, you know what? It looks funny. That's what it does. This happening right after she comes here. We never had no murders before."

"She's only been here three—four weeks," the man protested doubtfully.

"That's long enough—for that kind."

Lorraine Bowen, more subtly and with more honest reluctance, was edging up to the same conjectures in her home. Al had expressed his own painful, unwilling entertainment of the idea that Lester's death might have been a result of his role of stool pigeon.

"But for God's sake," he wound up, "don't go saying that to anybody."

"Oh, it can't be, it can't be," Lorraine denied anxiously, remembering that Al had gone late to Stag Night, had walked down the alley alone, that Al sympathized with the bunch Lester had been out to get, that now Al might be lumped in with Johnny Rodriguez and that gang, and if suspicion fell on them—well!

"No, I don't believe it."

Her eyes stared vacantly at the stove's oven door, and then she said abruptly, "Listen now, I don't want you getting sore, think I'm just jealous or catty or something, but I want to tell you something that happened yesterday evening right after dinner when you were taking a nap. Emily and I were over in Gloria's yard sitting around in her lawn furniture having a coke together, because it was still so nice out, and Lela Adams was going down the street on the other side—it was her day off, and she came over and Gloria got her a coke, and we were just talking, and Lela told us Les Coleman drove up in front of the house yesterday with Terese and they sat there talking in his car as chummy as you please, and she heard him making a date with her when she got out of the car; and Lela said Terese was smiling as if she was pleased all the way in the house. And then just before Lela started up the street and saw us—she was on her way over to her sister's for a minute—she heard Jim and Terese having a terrible row and she heard Les's name even if she couldn't hear all of it. And she did hear Jim say, 'I told you to stay away from that bastard.' At least"—she paused doubtfully—"I think that's what she said he said."

Al's eyes rested, troubled, on his wife; and he too was remembering Lester in the washroom. And his own thoughtless remark to Jim. His throat felt dry as he spoke in an abstracted tone. "I just can't see Jim— he's—Jim's such a good-natured guy." He frowned angrily. "Hell!" he ejaculated. "There wasn't enough to it. If he'd caught her sleeping with the guy—maybe— Oh, hell no, Jim wouldn't kill a guy just for trying to date his wife."

"It might have been accidental," Lorraine ventured uneasily. "They might have got to fighting and he hit Les too hard."

"No," Al retorted violently. "I don't believe it." His eyes as they rested on his wife grew stern. "Listen, don't mention any of this to anybody."

Lorraine looked back worriedly. She had no more taste for causing Jim trouble than had Al. After all, she had almost been in love with Jim once.

"It isn't just me," she said anxiously. "There's Lela, and Emily, and Gloria, and Lela's sister, and Bert. God knows how many people she told. And," she said with sudden dismay, "she'll make it sound worse *now*."

As his wife spoke Al had thought of more names for the list. Sam, and all the men he had told about Lester's remarks in the washroom.

"I hope somebody doesn't blab all this to the cops," he said faintly. "If it was anybody but Terese they probably wouldn't, but with the way everybody seems to resent her—" He drew a deep breath.

"That's what's so awful," Lorraine said sharply. "Jim being on the spot, and it being all her fault." She gave a little gasp. "And my gosh, they're coming over here tonight!"

"So what?"

"My God, do you think I want her in the house now!"

Al's fingers disrupted the usual flawless alignment of his hair. "Oh Christ, we're running away with ourselves. I don't believe any of the McGowans had a thing to do with it. Les Coleman had more people disliking him than you could shake a stick at."

Lorraine was not paying attention. On second thought she was deciding it might be worth the excruciating ordeal of having the cause of a murder in her house. They might find out something, having Jim and Terese over.

CHAPTER 22

Jim walked back to work after lunch with his brother George, and they talked soberly of what they had learned from the womenfolk at home.

"You can see what they're doing," George said. "They're checking up on the people that left the clubhouse during the time they think he was killed. And of course they'd check on Flo, her being the last person to see him alive."

"How did they know that, though?" Jim said slowly. "That she did see him last night?"

"I suppose they heard she went out with him some, so they naturally inquired to see if she'd seen him last night."

"How'd they find out she ever went out with him?"

"Somebody told 'em, I suppose. Eddie, probably. His tongue's loose at both ends."

"Yeah, I suppose."

"They can't be too interested in you and me," George mused broodingly, "or they'd have made it a point to see us this noon."

"Why should they be?"

"For Christ sake, Jimmy, grow up. We must've left the clubhouse when he was out there, dead already or hurt bad. How do they know one of us didn't hit him?"

"Why would we?" Jim asked blankly.

"Why would anybody? Wasn't he plain asking for it? I wouldn't have been surprised any time to hear of him being beat up. It's just damn bad luck that whoever did do it finally happened to have a lead pipe handy and swung it too hard."

"Well," Jim said deprecatingly, "everybody knows you and me were never tough guys, goin' around getting in fights."

"Look, baby-face," George said impatiently, "even you know about the pink slip I'm slated to get in my pay envelope Friday. Think that was going to make me just love Mr. Coleman?"

"But the cops wouldn't know about that."

"Maybe not about *that*—yet. But if they don't know already, they soon will find out about this union fight, and they'll track it down fast, who was who and all that. People in this town aren't exactly noted for being closemouthed. Those detectives'll pick up plenty here and there. *Now* do you see why it looks bad for you and me, especially me? One thing in my favor is we were together. It's an alibi, even if it's a weak one. They'll figure, of course, you'd stand by and lie for me, being my brother, even if you saw me do it."

"Jeez, I never thought of it that way. When Terese told me about them coming to see her, I figured it was just routine, checking on who was at the clubhouse last night and when they left and all."

That afternoon Jim felt as if every man who passed his machine was covertly scrutinizing him and wondering about him and George, wondering if he had helped George by holding Lester while George slugged him. Jim felt very uncomfortable.

He would have been even more horrifyingly uncomfortable if he had known that most of the surreptitious glances sent his way were expressions of sympathetic wonder. The men could understand. The thought was slightly chilling, but there was no real condemnation of the boy. They could see how an ordinary run-of-the-mill fellow like Jim could be goaded into desperation by the thought of a prize like his Terese being sullied even in idle gossip through the actions of a louse like Lester Coleman. It would be bad enough if a man's wife were an ordinary nice-looking girl such as most of theirs were, but if you had been lucky enough to get a real beauty like Jim's wife, her defections from grace would be even harder to take than would those of an ordinary wife.

Most of the other married women in Conway who had been "mixed up" with Coleman had become so during periods when everybody knew the couple in question had been "having trouble" anyway, and since other marital factors had preceded and accompanied and followed the fling with Lester, he had seldom been more than a mere additional irritant to the husband. But when everything else was O.K., as it appeared to be with the Jim McGowans, when they were, in fact, still in the first rosy flush of young love, a person could see how it would drive a man wild to see a snake in the grass trying to weave its way into his Eden.

It had been around eight-thirty in the morning when Lester's body was discovered. By three-thirty in the afternoon the case was solved as far as the residents of Conway were concerned. Only one held out with vocal disagreement, and that was Angela Amatelli at the store; and she had to curb her tongue, be discreet in her disagreement, for, as Joe kept reminding her, in business you couldn't take sides, there were times when you had to keep your mouth shut.

Lorraine and Emily Fraser had walked down to the store together. It was the quiet time in the afternoon, and Joe was helping a truck driver unload cases of canned goods at the alley entrance to the store. Angela and her two customers stood and talked, having a cigarette together, keeping their voices low, as if by speaking in confidential tones they could subsequently deny having said anything they might later wish to disavow.

"I don't think," Lorraine said virtuously, studying her cigarette in the downward rays of light from the row of high windows over the shelves on the west wall, "that she really *meant* anything, fooling around with Les like that. That is, I suspect she was just amusing herself." She sighed lugubriously. "I sure feel sorry for Jim."

"I hope," Angela said tartly, "you aren't going around saying stuff like that to the cops."

"My God, no!" Lorraine cried. "I don't want to get Jim in trouble."

"It's too bad," Emily Fraser said primly, "he ever married her." She couldn't resist adding innocently, her mind on the fight at Bowens' that she had heard after last Friday's dance, "I don't think it was just Lester that that woman had made a play for."

Lorraine's eyes darted toward her neighbor, and something twisted keenly in her as she too remembered. The knife blade of discomfiture came forth in the sharpness of her next words. "I don't think there's much doubt about it now; she's no good. If Jim did do it, I don't blame *him*, but her."

Angela jammed her cigarette out in a metal tray engrained with ancient scorchings and coated with dead ashes. Resolutely she reminded herself of Joe's admonitions about arguing with customers.

"I wouldn't be too quick," she said shortly, "to lay it on Jim. There's other reasons people might have to hit Lester over the head." Her eyes raised slowly to regard the other women through her thick lashes, and defiantly she violated Joe's policy. "He wasn't too popular with some of the guys at work. There was trouble about other things—things that had nothing to do with women."

The eyes of both Lorraine and Emily were wary as they rested on Angela. They had not spoken of it to each other. Indeed it had not set itself up in words in their own minds. But their husbands were among the CIO adherents. Bill Fraser was indeed one of the Seven, and both were prominent among those currently hating Lester Coleman. And Al Bowen had been alone in the alley between nine-thirty and ten. Bill Fraser had been at home, but no one but Emily could testify to it.

Lorraine, too, smashed out her cigarette in the soiled tray, her eyes following the action. Her voice was toneless as she said, "I don't think it's very smart to go around digging up reasons—and talking about them— as to why people might have been sore at Les Coleman."

"Nobody seems to mind pinning it on the McGowan boys. If people are going to be careful about throwing suspicion around, seems to me they shouldn't pick out any one person and lay it all on them, when nobody actually knows anything," Angela retorted.

"Well, naturally," Lorraine said stiffly, "everything we've said is in confidence."

"What I said was confidential too," Angela reminded them, her lips closing in a quietly triumphant smile.

As Lorraine and Emily walked homeward in the shade of the trees, Emily mused, "It's sort of funny the way Angela sticks up for that woman. You'd think, Angela not being very attractive herself, she'd resent Terese instead of siding with her."

"Maybe," Lorraine said thoughtfully, "it's on account of their both being sort of—foreign. You know, Terese's folks being French, and Angela being Italian. Maybe it's sort of a bond."

"Maybe." Emily said no more for a moment, and then she broke out soberly, "She's probably right, though. About people talking too much. After all, nobody *knows*. For sure."

"No. We don't."

CHAPTER 23

The detectives, Pete and John Marcus, were back at Jim McGowan's house that evening at six-thirty. Terese was washing dishes, and Jim rose from the sofa, where he had been reading the paper, to admit the men. They talked to him alone for almost an hour, going over, step by step, his actions of the previous evening.

When Terese finished the dishes and came in, Marcus indicated bluntly that they wished to interview her husband alone, so she shut herself up in the bedroom and made herself busy there and in the adjoining bathroom preparing for the evening's engagement, which she hoped these men were not going to spoil by staying too long.

Little by little Marcus led the interview deeper and deeper into Lester's life, and Jim tried valiantly to be both cagey and truthful in his replies. He had expected grilling on relationships at work and on the state of Lester's relationship to George, but this man Marcus barely touched on that. From time to time Jim shot a curious glance at the other detective who just sat there, seeming to take no part in things, just regarding Jim impassively from time to time and letting his eyes rove around the room indifferently.

"What did you think of Coleman going out with your sister?" Marcus inquired finally.

"Why—nothing much. It wasn't serious. Florence just went out with him to be going somewhere."

"Didn't he have a rather unsavory reputation—about women?"

"Well, I guess so." Jim moved uneasily on the sofa. To tell the truth, he had been embarrassed over Flo going out with Les, had felt it wasn't doing her reputation too much good. He felt that he should explain, for Florence's sake. "But you see, he was a funny guy. I tell you honestly, I don't think he'd ever try to go—too far with a woman unless he was absolutely sure she wanted him to. He'd flirt with 'em, and make quite a show about it; but he didn't really have much self-confidence. As far as—well, actually taking advantage of a woman, there wasn't much danger of that unless she let him know for sure she wanted him to. You see what I mean? So I never thought but what Florence was *safe* enough with him as far as that went, because I knew she just used him—as a convenience, so to speak."

Jim looked earnestly from one man to the other, hoping they understood.

"You wouldn't have been worried, then, say, at having your wife left alone with him?"

Jim uttered a wry chuckle. "Well, he wasn't the sort of guy a man would want his wife alone with—on account of his reputation, even though you might know there was nothing to it. It was the way other people would interpret it." As he spoke Jim was remembering yesterday evening's tiff with Terese, and a first stirring of uneasiness began to flicker in him, so that he added offhandedly, with a too-casual grin, "Not that I ever had that trouble about Les."

"Your wife," Marcus said silkily, "is very beautiful. Surely this character had noticed that?"

Jim interpreted these remarks as an "exploring every avenue" trend; so although he had come on guard, he was not unduly alarmed. He felt, in fact, on firmer ground than he had been when this man Marcus probed for information about Lester's standing with the men at the mill.

"Everybody," he said calmly, "notices that my wife is pretty."

"I suppose he knew you and your wife pretty well?"

"No. My wife has only lived here a little over three weeks."

"But she had met Coleman?"

"Yes. She met him at the dance last Friday evening."

"Has she seen him to talk to since then?"

Jim leaned over and picked up a package of cigarettes from the coffee table. His eyes looked straight and cold into the detective's. "Why don't you ask her?" He looked down at the cigarette he was deliberately extracting from the package. "If my wife was seeing too much of Coleman, I wouldn't know it, would I?" He looked up again. "That's what you're getting at, isn't it? And I'll tell you right now I don't like the insinuation. You may be policemen, but I don't think you've got a right to come into a man's home and make insulting insinuations about his wife."

"You misinterpreted my question," Marcus replied suavely.

When the detectives were outside Marcus lifted an eyebrow at his colleague. "Well, what do you think now?"

"Same as I thought before. I don't care what Schofield says the head guys in the mill office said, or what you think, you're all way off the beam on this dame business."

"You saw how he stiffened up when I mentioned his wife and Coleman."

"Yeah, I saw. It surprised him, and it made him sore. You think he'd be surprised if he really killed the guy on account of her? Not by a damn sight. He'd be waitin' for that line of questioning. And he'd have been damn careful not to act mad."

"Maybe he was just being subtle."

"Subtle, hell. That guy ain't no storybook master criminal. He's just an ordinary working stiff, about as subtle as—as I am."

"Well—" Marcus gave a sigh which cast the subject aside and went on, "I guess Bowen's next on our list. God, I love these cases where everybody and their uncle are involved."

"We're gettin' acquainted around here all right," Pete said stolidly.

When Jim and Terese crossed the street diagonally on their way to the Bowens' house the detectives were coming down the steps. The McGowans could see them in the porch light Al had switched on. Marcus and Pete turned west toward the park, however, and they did not meet face to face.

"I see you had company too," Jim said sympathetically when he and Terese were inside.

Al grinned a little too heartily. "Yeah, I guess they're really making the rounds. Come on, sit down, make yourselves comfortable."

"It's terrible, isn't it?" Terese said with bright sociability, sinking into an Early American maple chair with cushions and flounces and taking in as many details as possible of her new friends' living room. "I wonder who in the world did it."

Lorraine sent her a glance that even Terese thought "peculiar."

"I don't think it was premeditated," Al said judiciously. He opened a polished-wood box full of cigarettes and passed it around ostentatiously. "Smoke, anybody? I think it must have been accidental—that he died, I mean."

"That's the way I figure," Jim agreed quickly. "He got in a fuss with somebody out there and in the argument the other guy just struck out. Mad."

"Yeah," Al said. "I can't believe anybody we know would do it deliberately."

Terese had, of course, made up her mind to make the most of this entree into Lorraine's friendship, so now she laughed lightly, intent on seeming amiable. "I hope that's how it was. I'd feel kind of scared if I thought I'd moved into a town where people made a practice of killing each other."

"I've lived here all my life," Lorraine said, "and nobody ever got killed before."

Lorraine's tone had been that of a hostess keeping conversation alive, but somehow no one seemed able to carry on from there. They sat with eyes studying a cigarette or the carpet or the arm of a chair.

Terese was slightly puzzled. She hadn't thought it would be—well—stiff, like this. She had so hoped the evening would warm them all toward each other.

"Does anybody," she asked in a rash effort to keep things moving, "does anybody have any ideas about who it was? Or"—she glanced about uneasily—"shouldn't I ask that? Jim says he can think of a dozen people it might have been."

Her husband smiled at her with indulgent reproof. "That's the trouble, honey, it could be a lot of people; but nobody wants to pin it down to suspecting any one of them, people you've known all your life. It's all right, with just us here—Al and Lorraine—but you shouldn't even say right out that I can think of a dozen."

"I suppose that's so."

"Yeah," Al said heartily. "That's right." He laughed with exaggerated good nature. "Far as that goes, Jim, some people probably suspect you or me. After all, we were in the alley last night too."

"You ain't kidding," Jim said ruefully. "I wish now George and I had stuck around another hour or so. We're in a worse spot than you, though—closer to the whole thing in a way, on account of Flo being the last one to admit seeing him—her and Jo and Tina, that is. It kind of makes the cops notice our family."

Al turned the stub of his cigarette in his fingers, regarding it vaguely. "Yeah, I can see that."

"I suppose," Jim said, "they asked you a lot of questions about how well you knew him and how you got along with him."

"Well—yeah." Al frowned and added abruptly, "They kept digging around about other people too, though, and what I knew about who was and wasn't friendly with Les. I say 'they,' but it was the smallest one, Marcus, that did all the talking." Al chuckled as if it were not important. "Asked about you, as a matter of fact."

Jim grinned. "Hope you didn't tell them anything incriminating."

Al grinned back. "I tried hard to think of something, but I couldn't dig up anything."

Terese had been listening with a polite smile that had slowly become mechanical. All at once she shuddered and put her hands over her face.

"This is terrible," she said huskily, "joking about it like this." She lowered her hands and looked apologetically from one to the other of the two men. "It just hit me all of a sudden—that poor guy—yesterday he was alive and walking around and trying to enjoy himself, and now—look where he is—"

She shivered. "I know, Jim says he was kind of a crumb—about George and those guys they're going to fire. Telling on them, I mean. But I don't know, all of a sudden now—I just felt so—sorry. After all, he was human."

Jim moved down on the sofa, closer to her, and reached out to touch her hand. "Yeah, it is tough. Nobody would have wanted *this* to happen to him. I guess it does sound kind of heartless, talking about it the way we have."

Lorraine was regarding Terese uncertainly.

Al took up where Jim's words left off. He spoke reflectively. "There's something about murder. You're so shocked at it, it being so unexpected in the first place, and then your mind gets all taken up with who might have done it; and it's sort of like you said"—his eyes lifted briefly toward Terese—"people forget the human side. You almost forget it's a human life you're talking about."

Lorraine frowned and drew the tips of her fingers across her eyebrows. "Let's not talk about it. It—it's beginning to depress me." She looked at them with a deliberately bright smile. "I thought we were going to play cards."

Going home later, Terese said wistfully, clasping her hands more tightly on Jim's arm, "It didn't turn out like I thought it would. Somehow I felt as if everybody was—strained all evening. I—I felt conscious some way of every word I said."

"Well," Jim replied soberly, "I think this thing about Lester has kind of put a damper on things in general. It's like we were saying when we first came; for all they know, it could have been me and George fought with Les and killed him. You know how George hated him on account of Les opposing the CIO in such an underhanded way. And then—Al and Lorraine know that as far as you and I know, Al might have done it. He did come late and alone and somewhere around the time Flo says Les went into the alley. So you see everybody can't help wondering, and as a result nobody feels comfortable."

"Maybe," she said slowly. "Maybe. But I had a feeling that Lorraine kept looking at me in a specially suspicious way. I—I just felt somehow that she didn't trust me. More so tonight. She never has seemed very *warm* toward me, but I figured that was because we were strangers. But I don't know, tonight"—Terese shook her head—"she kept giving me such funny looks, as if she expected to see more to me."

They were at their own door, and as he pushed it open Jim slipped his other arm around her waist with a reassuring squeeze. "She was worried, probably. About Al—him being a possible suspect, and the cops having been there."

"Um, I suppose so."

CHAPTER 24

Miles Faber's house was dark that night when he got home from the trip to the city. Marguerite was out, and his wife was already asleep in the other twin bed. He would have liked to know what had developed in regard to the murder, but resigned himself to waiting until morning.

His wife Millicent awakened when he did and had breakfast with him, but she had nothing to add to the information he already possessed.

As Dora, the colored woman who did their housework, passed from view into the kitchen, Millicent murmured with a humorous inflection, "Now if we employed some woman from the East Side we'd have a front seat at the drama. She'd bring back all kinds of morsels of gossip."

"Well," Miles reminded her with a smile, "it was your idea to get help from town, and colored at that, so that we'd be protected from having our private affairs carried back into Conway."

"It's so unfortunate," Millicent observed restlessly. "Utterly the wrong kind of publicity for Conway, especially if the whole thing should prove to have its origins in something at the mill."

Fred Combs and Jack Morgan were at the office when Faber arrived there, and they went immediately into a huddle in Miles's office, where he told them what he had accomplished the day before.

"I had a hard time making them see," Miles said wryly, "that this was no time to make arbitrary dismissals."

Morgan spoke thoughtfully. "You're perfectly right. Coming right now, it would get publicity. For one thing, it would point the sheriff's men straight into the mill. And somehow or other these CIO organizers would make capital of it, twist it around to make it look as if conditions here were responsible for the whole thing."

"On the other hand," Combs said thoughtfully, "it might throw the whole thing in the lap of the CIO men, make them look so bad—as murderers, you see—that it would turn the majority against them and squash this election business right now. These seven men being fired right after the murder might put the fear of God into the men for good."

"Might, might," Miles repeated irritably. "In the meantime we're all over the front pages of papers all over the state. Make it a mill issue and it's big news. Keep it a little private homicide among a bunch of small-town people and it'll never go much further than the *Courier* in town."

"Yeah, that's right," Fred Combs nodded. "To tell the truth, I handled it that way—by instinct, I guess—when I was talking to the sheriff. Hinted that Coleman was our local Don Juan and it was probably woman trouble.

But somehow I never thought about holding off on laying off these troublemakers. I guess I figured the police were safely off on Coleman's private life and we could proceed as usual."

"Well, I think Miles is right," Morgan put in sagely. "We have to protect the mill, and if we do something that creates a stink right at this time, the public's liable to connect the whole thing up, think of it as all one mess; and we don't want that."

Fred Combs had moved to the window and was looking toward the ranks of steel-framed windows in the mill. "To tell the truth, I wouldn't be surprised if this whole thing had nothing to do with the mill and this union deal." He turned his head toward the other two men. "You know what the talk is in the village? Started, as near as I can find out, the minute the news came out."

"No. What is it?" Miles snapped.

Morgan said, "You mean the McGowan woman?"

"That's right. They're saying Coleman was hanging around after her and Jim didn't like it. And it seems Jim and George were at Stag Night and left the place alone about the time Coleman should have showed up there."

Miles Faber leaned back in his chair and scowled at the desk edge. "Jesus, I don't like this."

"May be nothing to it," Combs shrugged, coming back toward the desk. "You ever seen the dame?" he asked Miles.

"I saw her at the dance last week."

"Well, you can see, then, how she might cause trouble. Jim would naturally be jealous as hell. You don't run across a woman like that every day in the week."

"I've seen her around," Morgan put in. "It's not surprising if she causes trouble. To put it bluntly, she's too damned good for a mill hand. A dame that looks like that and carries herself like that don't belong in a place like Conway. She belongs in a penthouse in San Francisco or beside a swimming pool in Palm Springs. Naturally it's going to make her man edgy, trying to ride herd on a valuable property like that."

"It's too bad she ever came here," Combs declared sententiously.

When his assistants had gone Miles rose and went to the window where Fred Combs had stood, his eyes on the corner of the mill.

He was disturbed out of all proportion to the situation. Obscurely he felt that there was something wrong in the prevailing attitude toward Terese McGowan, and he had a guilty feeling now of having contributed to that attitude in some way.

The *Courier* headlines on Wednesday had declared that "Mystery Surrounds Death in Conway." The city papers recorded the known facts in stories of two or three paragraphs on inside pages, but on Thursday they had nothing to say, although the *Courier* announced that "Sheriff's Office Makes Progress in Conway Killing."

The "progress," however, was not noticeable either to Schofield or the two detectives assigned to the case. They sat in the sheriff's private office late Thursday afternoon, talking it over.

"We've talked to people steady for two days," Marcus said dispiritedly, his hands in his pants pockets, his feet stretched out, his head against the back of the straight chair, "and we haven't been able to shake a story, haven't found a scrap of anything that would give us an excuse to bring anybody in for more intensive questioning."

The sheriff sat with his elbows on the desk, his hands loosely clasped a foot above the blotter. "I've been thinking," he said slowly, "we've checked on what was going on at the time and just before and after the killing, concentrating on the scene of the attack." He drew toward him a small map of the village that had been provided by the mill office. Pointing, he proceeded to recapitulate:

"The McGowan girl, Florence, comes out of the Vale house here at roughly nine-fifteen. She meets these other two girls coming down the street past Vales', out for a walk. They go on down to the corner northeast of the business block. By the center light hanging in the middle of the intersection there they see Lester Coleman coming out of the path at the southeast corner of the park. They cross over and engage him in conversation. Then they all, still just out for an evening stroll, walk up past the front of the clubhouse, past the post office and the store, and around the corner to the alley. They stand there a few minutes chewing the fat, and Coleman heads down the alley to the clubhouse at the other end. Probable time: somewhere between nine-thirty and ten o'clock. Too bad none of those damn girls had any sense of time and none of their folks paid any attention to what time it was when they came in. At any rate, the girls go on around the service station which has been closed since eight o'clock, on past the hotel, and to the McGowan house, where Florence leaves them. All right. You see anything hard to explain in all that?" He surveyed the two men accusingly.

"Sure." Pete had been leaning over in his chair looking at the little map. Now he put his finger on the corner of the park where the girls had encountered Lester. "What was he doing comin' out of the park there when he lives"—the finger shifted to a spot a block behind the red X which indicated the Vale home—"clear over here?"

"Exactly," Schofield said sternly.

"We did try to follow that up," Marcus said defensively, "but nobody seems to know where he had been. At least nobody admitted seeing him before the girls met him."

Pete's blunt finger came down on the northwest side of the park. "This whole block," he said, "is the office crowd." The finger tapped along the paper, beginning at the end toward the Faber residence. "Combs, personnel manager; he's first. Egan, office manager. Morgan, assistant superintendent—" Flatly he delivered the names and titles of the occupants of the remaining three residences. Then he wound up unemotionally, to the sheriff, "You talked to them guys yourself, in the office."

"I didn't," Schofield snapped, "give you orders to lay off 'em."

"We wasn't born yesterday," Pete stated equably. "The Conway Mill brings in a hunk of tax money to this county. So me and Marcus here should go messin' around making the head guys sore, hinting they may be killin' off their employees."

Schofield uttered a four-letter word behind clenched teeth. "Nobody said anything about them being involved in the killing. But if Coleman was over there on Office Row seeing somebody that night, we ought to find out who and why. And," he added sarcastically, "if you boys have got such delicate feelings that you hesitate to offend the upper crust out there, I'll take care of it myself. Tonight."

Marcus heaved himself to a more erect position in his chair. "Pete here," he said, "is hipped on the notion it happened on account of this union deal. Me, I'm still of the *cherchez la femme* school of thought."

Schofield sighed. "And me, I've got a nasty hunch this is going to be one of those unsolved babies. There's no question about it—one of those guys that was gallopin' up and down the alley between, say, nine thirty-five and ten-thirty conked the bastard. That gives us Bowen, Rodriguez, Euman, the cook McGillicuddy, and the McGowan brothers. They've all got reason to dislike Coleman. But from what you report, none of 'em showed signs of cracking. They're like the three monkeys—didn't see anything, didn't hear anything, and aren't talking if they did."

"That's about the size of it," Marcus muttered.

Pete laced his fingers together and placed them over his belly. "I think I could dope it out—in time," he said musingly. "Fact is, I got a hunch already. But knowin' and provin' is two different things."

"If we know, we can usually work on the guy till he gives something away," Schofield said with a hopeful glance at Pete.

"Not if it's the one I think it might be," Pete said pessimistically. "He ain't the type to give under pressure."

"All right, mastermind," Marcus prompted, "who do you suspect?"

"It ain't really a suspicion even, yet. Just a kind of hunch. So I'd rather not say. But I'm going to keep my eyes open."

"Co-operation in the law-enforcement department," Marcus observed blandly, "it's wonderful."

Schofield frowned at his subordinate and asserted hopelessly, "It's a wonder to me somebody hasn't fired you long ago, Pete."

"Can't," Pete returned sweetly. "I'm too valuable."

CHAPTER 25

It got around the village—the way things did, without anyone being able to say exactly how—that Sheriff Schofield and that man named Marcus had called at each house on Office Row Thursday night; and it didn't take people long to guess that they must have been trying to find out where Lester had been before he came out of the park Tuesday evening.

The sheriff, to use his own term for it, drew a blank. He had detected a too-bland, too-innocent expression on Fred Combs's face; but a half hour's artful, diplomatic questioning had not shaken Fred's disclaimers of having seen Lester Coleman on that evening. And no one else in the block had seen the man, either passing on the street or in his home. They all seemed distressed that the sheriff should even ask them about such a possibility.

Schofield stood with Marcus beside the car and looked resentfully at the leafy bulk of the park with its dim lights flickering inadequately at intervals along the paths.

"There's another possibility," he said grouchily. "He could have been meeting the woman in there. After all, her husband was at the stag party."

"But her husband, the brother George, and both the mother and father say she came to their house with Jim and never left all evening. The in-laws wouldn't lie to cover her rendezvous with Coleman, if that's what was going on."

"They would if it protected the boy, Jim, after Coleman was dead."

"Yeah, but it would create a nasty situation for Terese McGowan in the family. They'd have to be pretty good actors to conceal how they'd feel about her if she'd been up to something like that. And I couldn't detect any undercurrents of that nature."

"This," the sheriff said violently, "is a hell of a case." He slammed the door after him when he got into the car.

People on the East Side had already entertained just such conjectures as the sheriff and Marcus expressed while they gazed at the park. If Lester had been coming from the park when he met the girls, might he not have been coming from a rendezvous with Terese while Jim was at Stag Night?

Emily Fraser and Gloria Hanson had discussed it at length beside

Gloria's baby's playpen that morning. There had been a certain coolness between the Hansons and Frasers of late. Greg Hanson, who was one of the better-paid carpenters at the mill, was inalterably opposed to any change in the status quo there, while Bill Fraser, who didn't say much, had nonetheless already signed a membership card in the CIO and made no bones about saying so, although the others who had signed up were keeping it quiet. The heat engendered by the murder, however, had partially overcome the coolness between the women. Lester's death was something they could discuss exclusively and without reference to the vagaries of their husbands' behavior.

"The only thing is," Gloria said with painful concentration, "I can't see Gladys McGowan, or Tom either, deliberately lying to protect that woman if she was cheating on Jim."

"But don't you see, they'd *have* to, to protect Jim and George."

"Yeah, I guess you're right."

The men inside the mill approached five o'clock Friday, the hour when they would file past the paymaster's window at the rear of the office wing to pick up their checks, with an increasing tension which superseded their wonderment and uneasiness about the murder.

Word that the layoffs had been canceled had for once not trickled out into general knowledge. There had not been time.

The mill had probably never emptied so fast as it did that Friday afternoon. Everybody wanted to be in the line when Johnny Rodriguez and the six others got their checks, wanted to watch their faces when they opened the envelopes.

Johnny was the first of the seven to get his check. He walked on a few paces and slowly tore off the end of the envelope, aware of the watching men. He noted with a sense of irrelevancy that his hands were steady. Somehow he wouldn't have been surprised if they had been trembling. His mind threw up the cliché, "This is it." Now that the time had come, surprisingly he felt rather eager. He realized that his attitude was a welcoming one.

He pulled out the long green check and peered into the gaping envelope. He held it a little closer, looking more intently. His eyes lifted blankly to the men surreptitiously eying him as they passed. He moved ahead with slow steps, his hand crushing the envelope, dropping it on the graveled path although it was against the rules to scatter paper on the driveway. He folded the check once and inserted it into his shirt pocket.

Then he glanced back and saw Owen coming behind him. He waited. Owen held his own opened envelope in his hand. He raised his eyebrows at Johnny, and Johnny shook his head. Owen moved his compressed lips in a puzzled twist.

Unabashedly they stepped aside and waited for George McGowan. The three walked on together then, talking in low tones. At the main gates they waited until each of the four others who had also expected pink slips had come abreast of them. The first two stopped, spoke briefly and shrugged, then proceeded on toward the village. The third joined them and they waited for the last man, and then they all walked on together.

Johnny and George and Owen turned in the direction of the hotel, while the other men went toward the store.

"Eddie's keeping a couple of bottles of beer in the icebox for me," Owen said. "Come on up to my room and we'll polish 'em off."

George had said it before, but now he repeated it stubbornly. "I don't get it."

Johnny chuckled. "Kind of an anticlimax, isn't it? We get ourselves all primed for a fight, and there ain't no fight," he finished with deliberate, humorous misuse of grammar.

In Owen's room, shady and cool on the east side of the building, they sat on the bed and the armchair with their feet up on straight chairs and considered the situation.

"There's something funny about it," George reiterated.

"Faber's behind it," Owen said quietly. "You remember he took off for the city Wednesday the minute he heard about Coleman. Eddie says Byron Vale phoned him when they found the body. Faber got scared the minute he heard about Les. He figured some of us killed him over what he done, and Faber was afraid it'd all come out, and he didn't want that kind of publicity connected with the Conway Mill. So he simply wiped out the motive. Think they'll ever admit now they ever had any idea of laying us guys off? If there never was such a scheme, how are the cops going to tie Les up to it as a stool pigeon somebody felt like killing?"

"It's odd," Johnny said soberly, tilting the water glass they had borrowed from Eddie and pouring beer onto its side. "If it was one of us that bumped Les off, the company has protected us by keeping us out of the spotlight that a layoff would have put us in."

"Ironical, ain't it?" Euman muttered.

"Maybe," George said, "they only postponed it. Maybe we'll get it with our next check two weeks from now."

"No," Johnny said, "it had to be now to be effective. In two more weeks we'll have enough men signed up so that we'll mean something."

"They may," George murmured uneasily, "figure the men won't trust us now, that they'll be afraid to line up with us, on account of the murder. Faber may figure the folks here are decent, moral people—which they are—and won't want any part of a—a black-hand kind of bunch that goes around killing their opponents."

"The only thing is," Johnny responded with a preoccupied frown, "it isn't working out that way. People don't figure any of us did it—not for those reasons, anyhow." He raised his eyes somberly to George. "You know what I mean?"

George reared up out of his chair and stamped across the room. "Hell yes, I know what you mean. None of the rest of my folks—except maybe my dad—have caught on yet. But I've got ears and eyes and I've got a little imagination. I can—I can *feel* it," he said explosively. He faced the others belligerently. "They think Jim did it because he was jealous of his wife. And it's all a damn lie. Jim and I never saw the bastard; and even if we had, it never entered Jim's head to worry about"—his voice dropped scornfully—"Les Coleman. The people in this town have got Terese wrong. She's a good kid. They're just jealous because she's got class." He scowled angrily. "You know what's the matter with 'em—inferiority complex, that's what. They get suspicious when something swell comes in and becomes part of us, figure they don't deserve it and so there must be a catch in it somewhere." He let out his breath gustily. "I don't know what the hell will happen if Terese ever finds out what they're thinking. She's—she's—well, she's a simple sort of girl, but she's no milk-and-water baby either. She's got a temper, and something like this'll make her mad as hell. She probably won't stay here if she finds out what their nasty minds have been cooking up about her."

Johnny ran his hand through his thick hair. "It isn't that simple. Like we've been saying, the first thing would be to suspect some of us guys that are working for the union." He frowned with the concentration of his thoughts. "But nobody—even Faber, you see, and even the guys that want to leave things the way they are—wants to see this thing lead back to the mill. They want to keep it a—a private affair. It's a funny thing," he said parenthetically, "the way we all subconsciously feel about the mill. We want to protect it. We don't like to see any funny business like this mixed up with mill politics. So you see how it is, George, the way things just happened to break, they all automatically seize on this thing about your sister-in-law."

"All I got to say is, it makes it nice for my family."

"Yeah," Johnny said heavily, "it's lousy."

"It was a mistake," Owen said sadly. "It's too bad it ever happened."

"It must have been an accident," Johnny muttered. "Must have been."

Owen carried his pipe a few inches away from his lips and nodded slowly. "I think so. I think somebody met Les in the alley and he started to talk, the way he always did, trying to worm his way in with people. And one word led to another, and whoever it was met him, they kept getting madder and madder, and maybe they just happened to rest their hand on one of them pipes, and when Lester made some specially cocky, insinuatin' remark, the way he could, the other guy just sort of picked up the pipe and swung before he really knew what he was doing. And then"—Owen drew in his breath deeply—"well, then it was too late."

George was staring out of the window gloomily. Johnny sat bent forward at one end of the bed. Without lifting his head, he looked up at the older man who sat gazing with melancholy abstraction at a knob of the bureau drawer.

Johnny closed his eyes, and when he opened them he was looking down at the faded linoleum on the floor. He straightened up.

"Well," he said, "all we can do now is go ahead and get enough guys signed up so we can put in our claim for recognition." He closed his lips and they curved in a wry smile. "Looks like maybe it's all working out to our advantage after all. Things'll work out more peacefully anyhow, probably."

"Yeah," George grunted. "Works out just dandy for everybody but us McGowans."

CHAPTER 26

There was no Friday night dance that week. The funeral was to be Saturday morning, and the coroner's inquest had taken place Thursday afternoon. Somehow everyone had felt that it would be poor taste to insert a dance between the two.

Almost everyone in Conway attended the funeral. The McGowans went together in the old folks' car. Florence had dug up a cap-like black felt hat and brushed it off carefully. She looked almost chic in her plain black suit and a net blouse that was only slightly too ruffly where it showed between the lapels. Florence had not yet heard the prevailing rumors about her sister-in-law, and as she dressed she tried to get herself up to look remote and mysterious, with an expression befitting the girl friend of the deceased. She had come around to the point of view that this was after all a pretty desirable role.

The villagers sitting in hushed discomfort on the pews in the soothingly decorated funeral parlor sent sidelong glances toward them as the Fabers came single file down the carpeted aisle. The two ushers had been escorting other parties to seats when the Fabers entered the rounding outer lobby whose atmosphere was laved by the muted strains of a pipe organ played somewhere in the distance. Marguerite took the lead down the aisle, with her mother and father following, her eyes surveying the pews for suitable seats.

At the end of one row, away from the center aisle, she saw the McGowans, and in the same glance saw that the end seats in the pew behind them were vacant and that these seats would give her a good side view of Terese, who sat at the end of the row of McGowans next her husband. It was not until she had turned in at the vacant places that Marguerite noticed she would be sitting next to Johnny Rodriguez. He glanced up as she entered the row, and their eyes met. She smiled faintly in recognition, and he ducked his head in a self-conscious nod before again staring gravely ahead at the flowers banked around the casket up front.

Marguerite forgot for a moment that it had been Terese McGowan she wanted to watch, and from the corners of lowered eyes she took in the brown tweed covering Johnny's thighs, his hands lying loosely cupped in his lap. His mother sat beyond him. Marguerite could see her hands in black cotton gloves hanging onto a plastic purse that rested on a black rayon skirt with a tiny white leaf design in the material. Marguerite leaned forward casually as if frankly to survey the congregation. As she did so, however, her eyes retained the sharpest picture of the Rodriguezes: Johnny neat and combed in his brown tweed suit and wine-colored tie, his mother sitting with shoulders habitually rounded, wearing a black straw hat with a flat crown and a narrow brim that supported a circlet of small yellow daisies, her black hair mixed sharply with white and coiled on her neck, her face brown and lined and a little tired, Johnny's father, with a look of Indian impassivity on his round face, his body stolid and settled in a navy blue suit with a white shirt and a black tie.

As Marguerite settled back, Johnny turned his head slightly and let his eyes rest on her briefly.

Marguerite felt subdued, almost reproved, as she sat still after meeting his eyes this second time. Had she read concealed disapproval in that impassive, unrevealing look? Had he seemed to indicate by it that he thought she had come here as if to view a show of some kind and that he considered such a purpose to be in poor taste?

She was a little disturbed at her own intense awareness of the young man beside her. Deliberately she fastened her eyes on the gray casket covered by a blanket of roses donated by the employees of the mill, reminding herself of why she was here. One of her father's workmen was dead, so naturally they had to "pay their respects."

And someone had killed the man. It might even be this man sitting quietly beside her in the brown suit. Her eyes shifted then toward Terese, whose profile was obliquely visible from her own position. People were saying he had been killed in a fight over this woman. As Marguerite studied the square shoulders in navy blue silk, the curve of sleek dark hair, the clean jawline, the flawless skin and the perfect line of eyebrow and lashes, the portion of smooth white forehead visible beneath the demure turned-back brim of a little blue-and-white hat, a feeling of incredulity rose in her. For the first time she realized that there was something pure and sweet and appealing about the young stranger, that it was these qualities, in fact, which made her physical perfection so startling. Nothing, Marguerite realized with a sense of shock, could be more incongruous than to associate this beautiful creature with something so shoddy and cheap and—weak was the word—as Lester Coleman.

Why, then, had the townspeople done it, and done so with such rapidity? Could it be, Marguerite thought bewilderedly, an unconscious effort to sully her perfection, to cut her down to their level? Was it small-minded resentment of anything superior to themselves, a feeling that she "showed up" the rest of them?

Marguerite slewed her eyes around to Johnny's unmoving profile. She had a sudden urgent desire to know what he thought. Was he, too, ready to believe this of the girl? Did he, too, desire to hew her down to size, make her seem cheap and—and common? The strength of her desire to know surprised her.

She lowered her eyes to her gloved hands and clasped them nervously. For that matter, for all anyone knew, Johnny Rodriguez might himself be the murderer. Marguerite was horrified to realize that the thought did not horrify her, that it would make no difference in her reactions to the man if it were he who had struck the fatal blow. Actually it was manslaughter more than murder. There was no reason to believe that the blow had been intended to kill. And she could see how a creature like Coleman could inspire rage in a spirited person.

Marguerite tried to put her attention on the services. The minister who had been chosen to conduct them had wisely cut his own remarks to a minimum and relied principally on prayer and reading from the Scriptures, interspersed with hymns sung in duet by an unseen man and woman.

Marguerite soon failed to follow the sense of the words being uttered. Her mind flowed on privately beneath the majestic cadences of the King James version of the Scriptures.

They had talked about the murder at home, of course; and her father had told her and her mother of his first fears when he heard of the murder— that it had come about because of friction among the men at the mill.

"But I may have been wrong," he had said, frowning. "They say that on the East Side everybody thinks it's tied up with that woman. And the people over there usually know what's going on among themselves."

"What do *you* think?" Marguerite had queried bluntly.

And her father had passed his hand over his hair in an uncertain gesture. "I don't know. I really don't know." Suddenly he smiled wryly. "Naturally I'd *rather* think it was a domestic squabble. That removes it from the mill."

His face sobered, and he went on slowly, "I shouldn't wonder but that's the way everybody feels, aside from the personal motives of keeping the thing separate from this division into rival labor factions. It's something," he said meditatively, "that the head office in San Francisco doesn't quite understand, the way the people here feel about the mill. To the central office the mill is an impersonal thing that they can set down in debit and credit columns, a source of either profit or loss. But to me, and also to the workmen, I believe, it's more than just our source of income. This may sound sentimental," he interpolated self-consciously, "but they love it—the mill. In an unformulated, inarticulate sort of way, perhaps; but they have an emotional feeling toward it. The head office doesn't see that when the men fight over representation and more money or shorter hours they're not fighting the mill. They actually have a dim feeling that they're fighting the mill's enemies and that those enemies are anyone who opposes the operation of the mill to the greater benefit of the men who run it on the inside. And, strangely enough, they often see its enemies as us who control it from what they consider the outside." He broke off and went on matter-of-factly, "So you see it could be that we're all too ready to place the blame as far away from the mill as possible."

"Really, Miles," his wife said with a touch of impatience, "it seems to me you're making too big a thing out of it." She regarded him penetratingly over her teacup. "I don't remember your ever being so—so intense about the mill before, as if it were almost something with a soul."

Marguerite had looked down at her plate, feeling embarrassed for her mother. Mother was so insensitive sometimes.

"Maybe I'm just getting old," Miles had returned with an attempt at lightness, but his voice grew serious again as he added, "I seem to keep being reminded lately that I've given over thirty years of my life to the mill."

"What nonsense," Mrs. Faber laughed reprovingly. "You've given your life to making an excellent living for yourself and your family and making us happy. Don't, for heaven's sake, try to picture yourself as a martyr to the company."

"I don't," he said with some acerbity. "I didn't mean that at all."

In the quiet chapel room of the funeral home, where the light was softly artificial, with no harsh daylight allowed ingress at any point, where the air was fraught with the scent of carnations and roses, where the music was throbbing and melancholy, where the sonorous biblical phrases were at the same time soothing and disturbing to the senses, Marguerite's undisciplined reverie led her into thoughts about her own life even while she sat ostensibly giving heed to another's death.

If her father's life had been "given," as he said, to the mill, to what was her own life committed? To nothing, really—as yet, anyhow. They had all thought it wise that she spend this past year after she finished college in the simple pursuit of pleasure. And she had done so. Visits to her friends, in Santa Barbara, in Phoenix, house parties at lodges in the Sierras for skiing, weekends at Palm Springs for swimming and tennis. There was a tacit understanding that after this summer she must settle down, decide what she meant to do. Two main paths lay open for her. She could marry Kenneth Swayle, who was a brisk, rising young lawyer in town and whom she had "run around with" for years, or she could stall him even longer and take a job for a while. She had majored in art at the university and taken a few dull courses in "Education," so that she was entitled to teach it if she chose. She had only to indicate her willingness and a place as an art teacher would be found for her in the town schools.

Her breast under the fine gray wool of her tailored suit rose and fell with a breath slightly deeper than normal. It all seemed somehow uninspiring and rather pointless.

Her downcast eyes moved to regard Johnny's hands, which were now clasped in his lap. The leg nearest her moved in a restless gesture, the knee straightening and the foot moving forward slightly on the carpet. His hands unclasped and one of them pulled at the trouser leg, loosening it over his knee.

Marguerite glanced up sideways, and Johnny looked at her, aware that his restless movement had caught her eye. Involuntarily his lips moved in a faint smile, and Marguerite's stirred in response. It was as if they had spoken, admitting to each other that funerals were a trial.

Marguerite looked down again at her gloved fingers entwined in the handle of her purse. She wondered about Johnny. She supposed he never looked into the future with the same kind of restless indecision that she had just experienced. Was he, she wondered, content just to look forward to "giving himself to the mill" on his level, as her father had done on his? Or did he have ambitions such as her father had irritably speculated about, ambitions to rise in the labor movement, be a big shot someday like John L. Lewis or Harry Bridges? There was not much doubt that if the CIO came into the mill Johnny would be one of its officers. Certainly he deserved to be, working as hard as he had to bring it in.

At last the services were over. There was no invitation to view the body, and the gathering slowly filed out into the sunshine.

CHAPTER 27

Florence McGowan learned on Sunday afternoon what was being said about Terese and Jim and Lester. She and her girl friends Jo and Tina were taking a bored stroll around the village, wishing they had something to do, preferably something along the lines of dates with men.

Jo was a plumpish girl in her last year of high school, and Tina had been in Florence's class and was now working in the office of a real estate firm in town. The three of them had wound up sitting in a sunny spot on the park lawn.

They had been talking about the murder, and Tina addressed Flo cautiously. "You've heard what they're saying, haven't you?"

"What?" Flo prompted suspiciously.

"Well, I don't see why you shouldn't know. Not that *I* think there's anything to it," Tina protested virtuously. "But it's going around that your brother Jim was sore at Les because Les was making a play for his wife."

Florence stared at her friend vacantly, absorbing this statement. Then the blood rose in her face, staining her forehead.

"It's a lie!" she exclaimed hoarsely. "Les had just barely met her. Anyway"—her voice cracked with strain—"everybody knows he was running after me."

Tina looked down and picked at the grass. "Well, all I know is what they're saying," she mumbled.

Florence glowered toward the east. "This town," she breathed. "I never— well, I never. The very idea." Her eyes veered angrily toward the other girl, suddenly alert. "My God, then I suppose they think my brothers—"

Tina's eyes moved uneasily, refusing to meet Florence's. "All I know is what I heard—" She broke off. "For heaven's sake, don't go telling *I* said it. I just thought you ought to know."

Florence scrambled to her feet. "Who said it?"

"Why, I—I don't know. It's just—going around. You know how it is."

"Who told you?"

"Now, Flo," Jo said unhappily, "don't get all upset. It's just—talk. We don't know who started it."

Suddenly Florence attacked them with a muted shriek. "Fine friends you are; that's all I've got to say. Talking about my family behind my back. And you know," she added hysterically, "*I* was—was the woman in his life," she finished after a quick mental dive into memories of the literature she habitually read.

Furiously she turned and rushed away across the grass, disregarding the other girls' distressed calls of "Now, Flo— Gee whiz, we didn't mean to— Don't go and get sore at us—"

The McGowans' old-fashioned front porch faced the main road into town, and Tom and Gladys sat there now, idly marking the infrequent cars which passed on the way out of town, enduring the boredom of a vacant Sunday afternoon.

"Maybe," Mrs. McGowan said vaguely, "we should have gone for a ride— or something."

Her husband glanced up the street. "Here comes Florence. Looks like somebody set a firecracker off under her."

Gladys peered in the direction from which her daughter approached. "She does look mad. Now what, I wonder? Honestly, that kid. I wish she'd settle down, either get a steady job or get married. She's so restless."

Florence stamped up the steps and demanded accusingly, "Do you know what they're saying?"

Her parents regarded her blankly.

"They're saying Jim and George were mixed up in Lester's murder. On account of Terese. Because Jim was jealous!"

Mrs. McGowan's head moved swiftly to right and left, her eyes sweeping the vicinity. "For heaven's sake, don't yell," she said tautly. "You want all the neighbors to hear?"

"Who told you that?" Tom demanded.

"The girls, Tina and Jo. They said it's all over the village."

Her parents regarded the girl with pained, thoughtful eyes. It was the first time the thing had been put into words for them. But they were not so wrapped up in themselves as their daughter was in herself. They were more sensitive to currents in the air they lived in. So her announcement was not entirely a surprise; it was more like a confirmation of unformulated prior knowledge.

"I had a feeling," Mrs. McGowan said heavily, "that there was something in the air. I—I just sort of sensed it."

"Well, we knew, of course," Tom added lifelessly, "that Jim and George were suspects, being in the alley when they were, and them detectives taking so much time over their stories. But I never exactly connected Terese up with it." As he spoke, though, he realized that he should have thought of that angle, Coleman having the reputation he did. Abruptly and irrelevantly he flared up at his daughter. "I don't know what *you* had to go and get mixed up with him for. You knew what he was."

"That's right, blame me," Florence whimpered, and sank onto the top step.

"I just hope," Mrs. McGowan said anxiously out of her own

preoccupation, "that it blows over before Terese and Jim find out about it. Jim would be mad at the whole town if he found out. It might cause hard feelings that'd never be lived down. And Terese"—she bit her lip—"she'd never forgive people here. I'm afraid, if she finds out, she'll never *like* people here, never feel satisfied in Conway again."

Florence raised her head. "I'll bet," she said slowly, "she'd insist on moving away, on Jim getting a job somewhere else."

Tom stirred in his chair. "We'll just have to hope they never find out. Maybe they won't. After all, it ain't the kind of thing you walk up and tell people to their face."

"Well, *we'll* never let on," Mrs. McGowan said decidedly.

Florence suddenly pounded the porch floor with her fist. "It makes me so mad!"

Mrs. McGowan looked down at her daughter speculatively, sympathetically. Poor Florence. It was more than outraged family loyalty that was eating her. Without being specific about it in her own mind, Florence had seen herself as the Woman in the Case, the one people thought of when they pondered the mystery of Lester's death. And now Terese had robbed her of that role. Parenthetically Gladys McGowan mused that Florence read too many of those silly magazines. Lester hadn't really meant anything to Florence, and Mrs. McGowan knew, with the mother's insight whose accuracy the offspring seldom suspect, that it was Johnny Rodriguez Florence wanted. It was too bad. If she really had her heart set on him, Mrs. McGowan would have been resigned to accepting him as her son-in-law, much as she shrank from the thought of a Mexican marrying into their good old Scotch family. But Johnny was a strange boy. Didn't seem much interested in girls. And of course right now Tom was so down on him—on account of all this foolish union stuff.

If only—Gladys's heart contracted fearfully—Terese didn't find out the way people were talking about her! If she did, she would drag Jim away someplace, probably back to San Francisco. Of course that wasn't so *far*. But it was such a comfort having him just around the corner. And she was beginning to get quite fond of Terese. She was the type, being sort of aloof and seemingly indifferent the way she was, that it took time to get close to; and Gladys was only now beginning to get used to her.

CHAPTER 28

June had advanced unobtrusively upon the world, and on Monday morning Terese recognized it consciously for the first time. The warmth of the sun was a little stronger but still soft; the breeze was as gentle as spring but with the last trace of chill gone from it.

When she carried the clothes from the automatic washer out to the clotheslines she thought, "What a beautiful morning," and as she began to hang them up she started to hum, "'Oh, what a beau-ti-ful morn-ing, oh, what a beautiful day—'" Her voice rose as she shook out the damp linens and pinned them over the wire lines. She had evolved a precise routine for hanging out washing. The sheets and dish towels and everything else that needed ironing but not sprinkling went on one line; on the next went starched clothes and all the other things which must be dampened down; on another went bath towels and socks and knitted underwear that needed only to be folded and put away when they were dry. There was something pleasantly soothing in this routine. It would have disturbed her a little to see a pair of socks hung between the pillowcases and the lunch cloths.

"'I've got a beautiful feeling,'" she sang, clamping a clothespin on the white shirt Jim had worn to the funeral, then bending to bring up one of her cotton skirts from the basket, "'everything's coming my way—'"

As she straightened, shaking out the skirt, a head and shoulders suddenly rose from behind the unpainted wooden fence that shut off the yard to the west. They belonged to "old lady Hanson," as everyone called her to distinguish her from her daughter-in-law Gloria.

Mrs. Hanson's eyes were owlish behind horn-rimmed spectacles, and her gray hair had loosened to hang in wisps around her face. Terese realized that her neighbor must have been kneeling behind the fence, intent on some rite of gardening. Terese had learned by now what she had not known when she first came to Conway—that you were expected to speak to everyone you encountered, on the street or in front yards or at the places of business. In this case she would have spoken anyway, having from the first day of her arrival been on nodding terms with Mrs. Hanson.

"Good morning," she called brightly.

Mrs. Hanson said "Morning" gruffly and disappeared below the fence, thinking, "The brazen thing, *singing*, and poor Lester hardly cold in his grave."

The exchanged greeting had broken off Terese's song, and now she glanced speculatively around her own backyard, reminded of it by Mrs.

Hanson's activities beyond the fence. The back of the house and the garage at the side shut in the square of grass bisected by a dirt path out to the clotheslines across the back. There was a somewhat languid fuchsia plant under the kitchen window and two or three luxuriantly spreading geraniums with scarlet blossoms along the garage wall. The string lattice provided for last year's sweet peas still clung with a neglected air to the back fence. Terese supposed she ought to garden too. Everybody else seemed to. In fact, she had heard a great deal lately among the women about "the yard keeping me so busy." She didn't know anything about it, but she supposed she could buy some seeds and follow the directions on the package. In fact, she guessed she would. It would be something to do.

Terese had already begun to realize that leisure could become excessive. There was only so much housework one could find to do, and you couldn't afford to sew all the time. Already she had more clothes than she really needed. And it didn't quite satisfy a person sitting around at the folks' in your free time, talking to Jim's mother and Florence, and as yet she didn't feel like running in on any of the other women at any old time, even Lorraine. So it might be a good idea to do what the rest of them did—burden yourself with a yard to keep up.

By eleven o'clock her work was all finished. She combed her hair and put on some lipstick. She had been wanting all morning to go over and invite the Bowens to come to *her* house this week on Wednesday evening. But she had wondered: would it be rushing things? Boldly she decided, however, that she was being oversensitive. It wasn't like her to worry about how other people were going to take her. But somehow ever since before the party Gladys had given her she had begun to feel uncertain, unsure of herself socially. She had never noticed feeling that way before. It must be Conway that affected her like that. Now that she recognized the condition, Terese decided to do something about it, to start overcoming this peculiar sense of insecurity that seemed to attack her when she was among the villagers.

She went around to the Bowens' back door and knocked, noticing that Lorraine's washing was on the line too.

"Oh," Lorraine said when she opened the door, and then she smiled politely. "Come in."

"I see you got your washing out already too," Terese observed brightly.

"Yes." Lorraine nodded to a chair by the table. "Sit down. I was getting my vegetables ready for lunch. I'll just go ahead and finish them." She stood at the sink, half facing Terese, and picked up a carrot and a small knife.

"We're having leftovers for lunch," Terese volunteered, "so I don't have much to do to get it ready."

Lorraine seemed to find no immediate reply to this. She brought her knife up the side of the carrot.

Terese had imagined them talking casually for a while before she introduced the purpose of her call, but now she found nothing to do but come out with it.

"I was wondering," she said brightly, "if you folks would like to come over to our house Wednesday night for another game."

Lorraine turned on the faucet and held the carrot under the stream. "I'm sorry," she said with meaningless polite regret, "but Lela has asked us over to see television at their house Wednesday."

"Oh. Well, how about Tuesday or Thursday?"

"Well, Tuesday's Stag Night. They're going to go on with it, I guess, even after ..." She let her voice trail off in a hardly detectable pause. "And then with the dance Friday, I expect Al will want to stay home and rest Thursday, after being out Wednesday too, you know."

"Oh—yes. Yes, I suppose so. Well, maybe next week."

"You can get in touch with me the first of the week sometime," Lorraine said carelessly, "and we'll see."

As Terese walked back across the street, for her the day might have been gray November instead of emerald June.

While she set the table slowly and emptied the contents of small bowls into pans for reheating, she fought against the formless depression that suffused her. In a way she wanted to tell Jim, when he got home, about how she felt, but in another way she did not want to. If she spoke about her mood she would be likely to cry. And she didn't want that. Behind her sense of being rebuffed she could feel a need to think forming, and if she spoke it out first, she would not think as clearly.

As she washed the dishes and brought in and folded the clothes after lunch her mind worked soberly on Lorraine, trying to analyze the difference in attitude that had taken place. There was no use in kidding herself—Lorraine had never been eager to make friends with her. But when she had come over last Tuesday to invite them to her house Lorraine had at least been willing. The slight stiffness in both their attitudes that Tuesday morning had been due more to unfamiliarity with one another than to antagonism. And then on Wednesday night Lorraine had not been as Terese expected her to be. During the evening there had been no gradual breaking down into greater intimacy, into easier acceptance between them. From start to finish Lorraine had been no more than the gracious hostess, carefully polite in her hospitality. Terese had thought perhaps it was on account of the murder and both Jim and Al seeming then to be possible suspects. You could understand how the knowledge of something like that hanging over their heads might preoccupy a woman until it cramped her social instincts.

But now the murder was almost a dead issue. Jim had said everyone believed that if the police had found anything to go on they would already have made an arrest. The fact that they hadn't made it pretty certain that now they never would. So Lorraine couldn't still be frightened and withdrawn into herself over that.

What had happened to drive her back from the path of tentative acceptance she had seemed to be pursuing last week? Terese was baffled.

CHAPTER 29

Still in a blue mood, she set out for the store and the post office, walking around the corner and up the street on the opposite side from Bowens' and not glancing that way. At the corner above the store she met Marge Vale crossing the street. Marge had always been friendly, so Terese was not surprised when the older woman quickened her step and came up to walk beside her.

"Lovely day, isn't it?" Marge said brightly.

"Yes, I guess summer is here."

"Sometimes I think June is the nicest month of the year. Warm but not too hot yet," Marge went on brightly.

Terese turned her head and saw Marge's eyes combing her face with a quick, alert expression that became even brighter as she met Terese's eyes.

Marge kept up her bright, inconsequential chatter until they reached the post office, while Terese grew quieter with each step. Recognition of Marge's brightness had penetrated her own dispirited mood. She could not help wondering what ailed the woman. She seemed to be trying so hard. And Terese couldn't figure out what it was the schoolteacher's wife was trying for.

She could not know of conversations between Marge and Byron Vale, and of how Marge had said, "It may be true what they're saying. In fact," she had sighed, "I suppose it is. We all saw how Les went for her that first night she came to the dance, but I don't like to believe it. That's what's so awful, by—the glee with which everybody has jumped at this explanation."

And he had said, "You can see how they would. It's complicated, but not surprising. There had to be a culprit, of course; and it's always the thing that's strange, alien, that they don't quite understand yet, that people are willing to blame things on."

"You'd think," Marge had said, "that they suspected her of having wielded the pipe herself, the way they pin the blame on her. Nobody seems to remember or care that if the prevailing theory is true, it is Jim who is a murderer. Yet I haven't heard a word of censure of him."

"The human mind," Byron had said philosophically, "is a wonderful and awesome thing."

Marge had slapped her palm down on the table so hard that the dishes jumped. "Well, I don't care, I'm not going to turn on her. So maybe, just amusing herself, she led Lester on and Jim found out and got sore enough to fight with him, disastrously as it turns out. That doesn't make the poor girl a pariah as far as I'm concerned. I intend to treat her decent anyway."

Terese walked on from the post office alone, disturbed by the peculiar manner she had noticed in Mrs. Vale—a sort of curiosity, and a determined cheeriness that gave itself away.

In the store Angela was waiting on two women, adding up their bills. Always when a customer came in Angela would raise her head and nod or smile or call "Hello," to acknowledge the newcomer's presence.

Today she raised her head, saw that the customer was Terese, and called out with an effusive smile, "Oh, hello, Mrs. McGowan. Be with you in a minute." She bobbed her head encouragingly, and her smile broadened.

The other two customers turned their heads and openly stared at Terese. One of them nodded, and then they both looked back at Angela's busy fingers.

Terese halted by the candy counter, suddenly alert in every nerve. "What gives?" she thought sharply. "What goes on?"

As Angela packed the ladies' shopping bags for them she looked down toward Terese again and smiled reassuringly, bobbing her head a little. The other two women had quit talking since she came in, and now they walked out, carefully not looking at Terese and passing Marge Vale at the door.

Marge came up to the counter, and as Angela waited on Terese both of the older women kept up a running patter of light talk, addressing every other sentence to Terese.

Terese walked home in a state of preoccupation, convinced now that something was wrong. Those women—Angela and Mrs. Vale—their manner had been solicitous. Yet as if they didn't want her to know that's what it was. As if she were sick or something. Terese thought perplexedly that she didn't get it.

That evening while she and Jim were eating she said worriedly, "Jim, is something wrong in town—about me?"

He lifted his eyes in astonishment and gulped to swallow the mouthful of food her question had caught in his mouth. "What do you mean, wrong about you?"

"I don't know exactly. But all day today I've caught people looking at me so—funny. And I told you about how—how—cool Lorraine was. Ever since then I've had a feeling, as if everybody was staring at me as if I was a—a freak or something."

Jim chuckled. "You're imagining things."

"I am not," she denied with sudden sulkiness. "There's something in the air in this town. I can tell."

Jim sobered. "Maybe. But I tell you, honey, I don't think it's about you—the way you seem to feel. I think it's the aftereffects of—Les. It jarred people, something like that happening on our doorstep. And then everybody was half mad at everybody else over the union question. It probably just made a bad feeling generally."

He paused, his thoughts apparently deflected. "Incidentally, I signed up with the CIO today. George got me to."

"You think it'll be better?"

"I don't know. George says it will, and I guess he knows. Way I figure is, if we're going to have unions in the mill at all, we might as well all be covered."

He leaned back on the rear legs of his chair, his hands clasped behind his head. "You know, it's sort of interesting. If I'd stopped to think of it, I'd have figured that Les being killed, him being the kind of stool pigeon he was, it'd have made everybody scared to have anything to do with the guys that was in favor of the CIO, for fear some of 'em might have been responsible for doing Les in. But it's worked just the opposite. Guys are signing up right and left. It's almost as if they felt they had to back up Johnny and George and old Euman, show everybody that they don't believe the CIO guys had anything to do with it." Jim looked at his wife earnestly. "You see what I mean?"

"Yes, I guess so. You mean they're sort of trying to protect Johnny and them from people thinking one of them did it?"

Jim let his chair down and lowered his arms. "Of course I think the CIO was set to get a majority, although it would have scared some of the guys out of joining if George and them had got laid off."

This talk with Jim diverted Terese's thoughts somewhat from her bewilderment over the changed atmosphere she had sensed in the village.

She was busy the next day with ironing and preparing a bed in the backyard for planting the package of snapdragon seeds she had bought at the store. On Wednesday it occurred to her that she hadn't seen any of Jim's folks since the funeral on Saturday. Briefly this struck her as odd. Florence usually came around at least once a day, if only for half an hour or so. When she had washed the breakfast dishes and made the bed Terese walked around the corner. She knew the women would be in the kitchen, so she took the little cement walk around the house and, mounting the steps, opened the door and walked in with a light "Hi!" to her mother-in-law, who was piling dishes on the sink.

Gladys said, "Well, hello, stranger."

Florence was sitting at the kitchen table eating strawberries and corn flakes. She turned her head to say "'Lo" and looked back into her bowl.

Terese sat down at the table and addressed Florence casually. "Thought maybe you were working, you hadn't been over for so long."

"I've been busy," Florence returned without looking up.

Mrs. McGowan began to ask questions. What had Terese been doing? Did she have a big washing this week? And Terese responded casually, going on to tell about her bed of snapdragons.

"Only thing about snapdragons, you have to watch out for rust," Mrs. McGowan informed her seriously.

"They don't have much selection in seeds at the store," said Terese. "Next time I go to town I'll go to that nursery on the way home and see what I can pick up." She glanced at Florence, who did most of the driving of the McGowan car in the daytime. "You going in today or tomorrow?"

Florence set down her coffee cup and said distantly, "I really don't know. I haven't made my plans yet."

Terese looked at the girl blankly, her eyes following as Florence rose with dignity and left the room, the soiled hem of her chenille robe sweeping regally across the linoleum.

She turned to Mrs. McGowan and asked wonderingly, "What's the matter? Is Florence mad at me or something?"

Mrs. McGowan had shot an annoyed glance at her daughter, but now she said dismissingly, "Oh, don't pay any attention to her. She's just in one of her moods. Got herself mixed up with the heroine of the last Joan Crawford movie she saw."

Terese smiled acceptingly, although her eyes turned speculatively to the door through which Florence had gone.

After dinner that evening Terese and Jim went into the backyard to inspect the incipient garden.

"It's late to start them," Terese said, "but I think I'll plant sweet peas there where somebody had them before."

They strolled down the driveway and stood looking speculatively at the front of the house.

"There's not much you can do here," Jim observed. "We don't want to dig up any of the lawn, and the rosebush dresses up the front of the place."

"Well, I could plant verbena between the path and the street."

A car pulled up before the Adamses' house, and they saw a couple named Foster get out and go up the walk. Just then old lady Hanson walked past in a clean house dress, her hair curled and controlled by a net. Jim smiled and nodded at her, and she said, "Good evening," and proceeded on to the Adamses' front door.

Jim sat down on the steps and remarked, "It's a nice evening. Let's go for a walk after a while."

"O.K."

Terese turned her eyes toward the street and saw the Bowens and Frasers coming along the dirt path under the trees. As they came closer Al raised his hand in salutation and there was a restrained chorus of greetings as the two couples went by.

Jim glanced at the house next door, commenting in a low voice, "Must be having a party."

Terese's face was averted as she murmured, "Lorraine told me they were going to see television tonight."

Jim raised his eyes to the silvery crossbars of the receiver on the Adamses' roof. "That's right, they had a set put in last week. Wish they'd invite us over some night."

Terese mounted the steps, brushing past him. Idly Jim rose and followed her inside. She had halted beside the coffee table, and he saw her raise her hand and brush her knuckles across her cheek. His eyes tarried on her bowed head, and he took a step forward, peering around at her face until he saw the tears hanging in her lashes. He lifted his arm and laid it over her shoulders, inquiring with distress, "What's the matter?"

She turned and put her hands on his chest, pressing her face against his shoulder.

"They didn't ask us," she sobbed, the words muffled in his shirt.

"Why, honey—" Taken aback, he began to pat her shoulder comfortingly. "Why, that's nothing. Nothing to get all upset about."

"I can't help it," she cried, and the tears suddenly came in a gasping flood. "It's just—it's just—too much—all of a sudden." She caught her breath and clung to him. "It just—came over me—"

He drew her down on the sofa, holding her, murmuring disjointedly, at a loss.

"I know it," she sobbed. "I've felt it—for—for days. People here don't like me!"

"Why, honey, that's foolish. Of course they do. How could they help it? You're just imagining things. You know we never have been chummy with the Adamses, her being away working every day."

"I know," Terese gasped, her outburst beginning to subside a little, "I know I'm being childish, but all of a sudden I couldn't help it. I felt so— so bad. It just seemed as if everybody was—against me; and I did so want to—to be in with people here, to be part of a crowd, have our own crowd—

you know—to run around with and—and have fun. And I can tell—they don't want me."

Jim looked worriedly baffled as he sought for an explanation that would be acceptable to her.

"I guess," he said cautiously, "it is funny they didn't ask us over too, being right next door—"

Terese nodded with melancholy but triumphant affirmation.

"—but I'll bet I know why. Bert Adams and George have been arguing every time they saw each other lately about this damn union business, and Bert knows I sided with George. And I'll bet he did it on purpose—left us out because he's mad because I wouldn't go along with him."

Terese had straightened and wiped her face with a handkerchief she found in her apron pocket. Her eyes focused rebelliously, consideringly, on the glass tabletop and then she burst out decidedly, "No! No, that's not true. It seems to me lately everybody explains everything by laying it on the union beef—or the murder. And it's not true. Al Bowen's on yours and George's side, and so is Bill Fraser, and they're over there, aren't they? So you see this—disagreement over which union's going to be in doesn't go that deep. Socially, they overlook it. No, it's something else. It's—it's me," she finished despairingly.

"Poppycock!" Jim snorted. "How could it be you? I'll tell you, maybe it's the murder. I was a sort of halfway suspect. Maybe the Adamses are sort of leery of me. Maybe they think George and I might have been mixed up in it."

"Poppycock yourself!" Terese retorted. "Wasn't Al Bowen just as much a suspect as you guys? He was out there, too, about the time it happened."

Jim said nothing, feeling stymied. Terese frowned across the room and suddenly clenched her fist and struck her knee with it. "No, there's something funny. Something smells. I can just feel it. And it's about me. And"—her voice sank consideringly—"it's got worse since the murder. I can see that now." Her tone hardened. "And I'm going to find out what it is if it's the last thing I ever do."

CHAPTER 30

By morning Terese had decided to corner Florence and cross-examine the girl. She was sure that, whatever the trouble was, Florence knew about it. Her haughty manner over the corn flakes had been a dead giveaway.

But when she went over to the McGowans' after breakfast it was to learn that on the previous night Florence had gone to town with one of her girl friends to spend a few days and, incidentally, to look for a job while she was there. Terese said nothing to her mother-in-law about the knowledge that she had become *persona non grata* in Conway. Even if Mrs. McGowan knew of her growing unpopularity, Terese was sure that the woman would deny it.

In the afternoon when Terese went to the store Angela happened to be alone. Again she greeted Terese effusively, and this time Terese read correctly the impulse behind the woman's manner. Angela was trying to show that *she* was on her side. The realization was both reassuring and disarming.

Joe came in while Terese was doing her shopping, and became busy restocking shelves at the rear of the long room. As Terese put her hands around the brown paper bag full of groceries she spoke impulsively. "Could I ask you something—confidentially?"

"Sure," Angela returned soberly. "Look, we have a little back room, sort of an office. I've got an electric plate where I make tea every afternoon. Come on back with me and we'll have a cup now. Joe"—she raised her voice—"I'm going out back a minute. Look out for things, will you?" And to Terese, "Just leave your stuff there."

As Terese followed Angela's plump shoulders toward the door at the rear she saw Joe cast an uncertain glance after them.

The back room contained an old-fashioned roll-top desk, a dark green filing cabinet of some antiquity, two rocking chairs with sofa cushions in the seats, and a somewhat decrepit swivel chair with a decaying sponge-rubber cushion. Angela plugged in the electric plate standing on a shelf against the wall and drew a kettleful of water from the faucet over a washbasin set into the corner. As she put a tea bag in each of two cups which shared the shelf with the electric plate she chattered of how you had to have some place like this when you were at the store all day, with apologies for the room's dingy appearance.

When they were settled with their cups of tea and a plate of packaged cookies, Terese began hesitantly, "I suppose you'll think it's funny, my coming to you with this; but I've felt that you were friendly, and—that's what's the matter. I've just waked up to something that I suppose everybody else has known all along, and that is that I'm just about as popular around here as a nice bouquet of poison oak. And, damn it! I'd like to know why."

Angela's face was still as she looked at Terese. She hadn't expected this point-blank "why?" And now she had to decide how to handle it.

"I won't," she said slowly, "try to tell you it ain't so. I'm awful glad you came right out with it to me, though. I *am* friendly to you. Right from the first"—she smiled gently—"I thought you were a nice girl, and that you'd be a real addition, as they say, to the village. But it's no use beating around the bush. A lot of people were—suspicious—of you right from the start. They thought you—didn't belong some way."

"Why? What's wrong with me?"

"Nothing. That's just the point. You were too—pretty. You dressed so nice. And you had a sort of—sophisticated manner right at first. That is, you looked at people and didn't seem to see they were there. It's a way city people get; and everybody here was born and raised small-town."

"But I'm not like that! Not stuck-up, if that's what you're trying to say."

"Of course you aren't, but it took people a while to get used to you. People always kind of hold off a little with a stranger, till they get their number."

Terese eyed her shrewdly. "O.K., so they held off. But they were softening up, beginning to take me for granted. But now, just in the last week, something's happened. All of a sudden it isn't just that they're stiff and formal, like to a stranger. Now there's something else; I can feel it; people have turned actually against me."

Angela studied her guest with worried eyes and knew she couldn't tell her. Terese herself had said "in the last week," but obviously she didn't connect it up with the murder. Yet it was so obvious. How could she have missed it? And Angela knew that if for some reason the idea that people might think she was connected with Lester's death was so repellent to the girl that she couldn't think of it for herself, then Angela could not tell her.

Word by word, she felt her way along. "It's hard to say sometimes why people act the way they do. They go along perfectly decent for a while, and then bang! the best of friends aren't speaking, and it's over some silly little thing that doesn't amount to a hill of beans. It's that way about you, probably. Somebody got sore at you about something and spread it around and now your name is mud. But I've lived here a long time, dear; I know how they are. They'll forget all about it one of these days. You just go on and pretend you don't even notice anything, and you'll see, it'll all blow over."

Terese frowned, and sighed. "I don't get it. I just don't get it." She accepted the cigarette Angela offered her from a package and leaned forward absently to the match the other held. "The reason I asked you," she went on, "was that if I had done something, maybe you could tell me what it was. It's partly for Jim's sake. He isn't going to be happy if people don't like his wife, won't associate with her. The feeling I've got is that they think I'm *bad* somehow. And yet what have I done to give that impression? I just don't get it."

Angela leaned forward and touched her wrist. "I know you're not bad, and there's others do too. You just trust us that are your friends. It'll come out all right; you wait and see. One thing, some people have been jealous of you right from the start, because, like I said, you're so good-looking. And another thing, you're a simple person—I mean that for a compliment, dear—and people sometimes don't understand a person like that. They figure they must be hiding something, must be a 'deep one.'"

"My God," Terese said dryly, "what am I supposed to do, take a knife and disfigure my face, eat like a pig and gain fifty pounds so I won't have any figure?"

Angela laughed. "You just try to forget it. And don't get to feeling you haven't any friends. You have. You'll see."

In spite of herself, Terese went home feeling better. Maybe she had exaggerated things. Maybe she just didn't understand yet the way things were in a village.

Angela, however, felt more stirred up than ever. That evening when the men dropped in after work for cigarettes or a couple of cans of beer to take home, she looked them over speculatively; and it was Johnny Rodriguez that she decided to pounce on. She hurried down to the candy counter where he was selecting a bar, took his nickel, and said urgently, moving out from behind the counter, "I want to talk to you. Come over here out of the way."

With a surprised look he followed her to the corner by the front window where the shelves held odds and ends of stationery and notions which were not in demand at the evening rush hour. She faced him and went on in a low voice.

"You know, of course, how they're all talking about Jim McGowan's wife."

Johnny nodded guardedly.

"Well, she stopped and had a talk with me, and the poor kid's got wise that everybody's down on her, but she doesn't know why."

Angela took a step forward and angrily poked a forefinger into Johnny's chest.

"Now listen, I wasn't born yesterday. Nobody can tell me she had a damn thing to do with the murder, and I think it's terrible the way people are making her out to be next door to a whore. I don't like it, see?"

Johnny backed up a step. "O.K. But what have I got to do with it?"

"You and a lot more of the men around here have got plenty to do with it. Nobody's fooling me. Lester got killed in a fight over this union business. The whole town knew what was going on and the way he was acting. And it was somebody on your side did it. It had to be—"

"Now you look here—" Johnny broke in, his eyes narrowing.

"Don't you 'look here' me, Johnny Rodriguez," Angela snapped, her own eyes glittering angrily. "Maybe you're a bigshot labor leader now, but I can remember when you were just another little brat hanging around waiting for overripe bananas we couldn't sell. Many's the time I've had to shoo you and the McGowan boys and the rest of 'em out that door when you wouldn't get out from underfoot. So you needn't get on your high horse with me."

"All right, all right. So what am I supposed to do? Run around telling people not to be naughty to Jim McGowan's wife?"

Angela placed her hands on her hips. "That's just exactly what I mean." Her finger went out again to poke his chest. "You can't get away from it. One of you guys—somebody on your side, anyway—let Les Coleman have it. And now, by God, you're not men enough to stand up and take the blame. No, you're all right in there helping out the whispering campaign to lay it on Terese McGowan, keeping suspicion off yourselves."

Angela, despite her vehemence, had kept her voice down, but passing customers glanced curiously at the pair in the corner.

Johnny took out his cigarettes and lit one. "I think it's too bad, too, the way they've settled on Terese, but nobody can stop these things, Angela. They just come up and keep growing."

"This wouldn't have kept growing if it hadn't been that everybody's so anxious to lay the blame somewhere besides on your precious union and to keep it away from the mill. My God, are the union and the mill more important than an innocent woman that never did nothing to anybody?"

"Some people might say they are."

"Well, I ain't one of them."

"They'll forget this in time, Angela. Maybe the girl feels bad now, but it'll all come out in the wash."

"That isn't the point. It isn't fair for people to think bad things about her when it's all other people's fault. And you can't tell me some people don't know more than they're telling. You guys are sticking together, protecting whoever did it. And I wouldn't care if it wasn't that you may ruin this poor kid's life on account of it. You know the saying, 'Give a dog a bad name' ..."

"You're taking a hell of a lot for granted, Angela. I don't know any more about who did it than you do."

"No, but you've got influence among the men. Right now it's Johnny this and Johnny that. They figure you're the main one responsible if they get a better union setup at the mill. You could do something about counteracting this story about Terese, get the men to talk against it, say it's all eyewash her ever having anything to do with Les. And I haven't seen you or Owen or Bill Fraser or any of your particular friends doing anything but join right in."

Johnny's eyes followed the downward course of the ash that he shook off his cigarette. "Seems to me about all she'd need right now is for another single man to come out suddenly showing an interest and sticking up for her."

"You men!" Angela snorted, and turned to go back to the grocery counter.

On his way home Johnny walked past the post office and the clubhouse with eyes cast down, his thoughts a guilty tangle after their invasion by Angela's recriminations. There was no reason that he personally should feel responsible for Terese's distress. It was too bad if the girl was unhappy, but he had kept his mouth shut, added no fuel to the fires of suspicion with which the villagers had enveloped her. And you couldn't expect the man who *had* killed Lester to come out and say, "Listen, folks, you're all wrong; the McGowan dame had nothing to do with it."

For that matter, Johnny argued with himself, how did he know it hadn't been Jim and George? But he had to tell himself that if the McGowan boys had done it, it would have been in an altercation connected with Les's stool-pigeon activities.

He lifted his head and crossed the street with a more determined step. Damn Angela. The union and the protection of the men in it were more important than some silly woman's hurt feelings over being snubbed by her neighbors.

But then he remembered Terese in her pink dress at the dance, with her shining hair, her glowing dark eyes, the satisfying clean lines of her face and body, and the gentle look in Jim's eyes when they rested on her. And it struck him in an unpleasantly forcible way that Jim was one of his union brothers now and that therefore Terese belonged to them too, in a way. Her beauty, her grace, they belonged to Conway and were part of it; yet the village had done its best to besmirch her perfection, to make her seem ugly and imperfect. And he had tacitly become a party to that effort.

Angela, damn her, was right. They were loading their own guilt upon the beautiful stranger. Both sides in the row had been willing to do it. Despite their difference of opinion over the rival unions, they had shown their real sense of solidarity by agreeing on a culprit who should carry for them the responsibility for the violence they feared even after it was done. Even, Johnny realized with a slight sense of shock, even the office and Mr. Faber had closed ranks with the men to shut the guilt away from the mill and onto the beautiful woman who was still a stranger.

Johnny went up the path at home with an unhappy feeling that there was nothing he could do about it.

CHAPTER 31

At the hotel, men were standing or sitting about in the lobby and along the veranda, waiting for the evening meal at six. There were exchanged looks and muttered words and questioning glances among them, for when they had mounted the broad, shallow wooden steps after work they had been faced by the detective Pete, dressed in a tired brown suit with a brown felt hat pushed back a little on his head, leaning back on the rear legs of one of the porch chairs, his shoulders against the painted wall of the building. He nodded and spoke to anyone who met his eyes, but otherwise he just sat there, something like a placid brown Buddha.

When the buzzer sounded for dinner he went in and took a place at the table and ate a hearty meal, making no effort to draw anyone into conversation, speaking calmly when spoken to, asking to have something passed now and then.

The men who habitually sat in the lobby for a while after meals with cigars or pipes or cigarettes rather uneasily took their usual places there after dinner; and their eyes rested noncommittally on Pete when he too came in and took a chair and just sat.

Finally one of the men said, "You still—uh—working on the case?"

"Sort of," Pete replied.

The men looked at him. They had nothing to say. Soon, one by one, they wandered off, upstairs or out to the porch.

One of the men glanced at Owen Euman. "Feel like playing tonight?"

Owen looked over at Pete, then turned his head back slowly. "Yeah, I'll play you a game."

The other man went to a corner cupboard and brought out a chessboard and a box of men. They set up the board on a small table and began to play.

Pete rose and came to stand beside them. "Mind if I watch?"

Owen lifted his head. "No," he said stolidly. "No, go right ahead. Watch." So Pete drew up a straight chair and sat down.

Owen's opponent was nervous at first. His eyes kept sliding toward the spectator. But Owen never looked aside.

Men passing in and out eyed the group surreptitiously. In the rooms upstairs and on the porch they talked. "What's he expect to get out of it, hanging around out here? He expect to find out something?"

Life had settled down after the funeral, as if the physical burying of Lester's body had also buried the problem of his death. Everybody had been willing to let the whole event sink slowly into memory with the little incidents of new days gradually covering it up. This stolid physical reminder in a shapeless brown business suit was disturbing, and resentment formed around it like mold on a decaying vegetable. If he thought he was going to pick up something, he'd find out, that was all.

When the chess game was over Pete rose wearily from his straight chair. Owen had won, and Pete addressed him. "You played good, considering you had somebody watching every move."

Owen picked up his pipe deliberately. "Some people play best under pressure."

"Yeah, I've heard that. Well, I'll be shovin' off. See you 'round."

Pete's expression was thoughtful as he went out and got into his car. It had been his own suggestion, and Schofield had acquiesced, that he should stick around out in Conway when he had a little time to spare. Officially the case was pretty well dropped for lack of evidence. No one but Pete would have cared to keep worrying it around between his teeth. But Pete was a funny guy. If he wanted to keep trying in his ponderous way, no one cared as long as it didn't interfere with regular assignments.

The following evening he was there again at five o'clock. He came into the lobby and glanced idly at the city daily on the old "library" table in the center of the room. Eddie saw him and came to the archway leading to the dining room.

"Thought I'd have dinner with you again," Pete vouchsafed idly.

"You must like my cooking," Eddie observed sarcastically.

"Yeah. I do. No objection, have you? This is a public eating place, ain't it?"

"We got a license."

"I'll probably be dropping in pretty often."

Eddie moved a step into the room. "What are you up to?"

Pete's eyes were on the headlines of the paper as he answered carelessly, "Sooner or later somebody always talks, and I like to be around where I can hear when they do." He raised his eyes to Eddie's face.

"Nobody around here's going to talk. Nobody knows anything."

"No? What makes you so sure? You think it"—he jerked his head toward the rear of the building—"was suicide? If it wasn't, then somebody knows something. And if more than one person knows something, it's going to look bad for the second party that knew things he didn't tell us."

Eddie stared at him with a baffled expression before he turned, muttering, "I got a meal to get ready."

When Owen Euman passed through to the dining room on his way from his room upstairs, Pete fell into step beside him and took the chair next to his at the table.

"I guess you've lived here at the hotel quite a while," Pete ventured affably.

"Yeah."

"Twenty or twenty-five years, ain't it?"

"Yeah."

"Guess you and Eddie are both old-timers here?"

"Yeah."

"Somebody was tellin' me Eddie's been cook here for ten years."

"Yeah."

"Guess you and him've got to be pretty good friends in all that time."

Owen looked at Pete and said, "Pass the bread."

The men across the table and on either side of Pete and Owen had been listening closely while they pretended to be interested only in the food. Up and down the table every diner was conscious of Pete sitting beside Owen. Everyone knew how he had stayed and watched the chess game the night before.

The men who could see Owen from where they sat realized that now the older man was getting mad. Anger seemed to emanate tangibly from the spot where he sat. There was a tingling of excitement among them, an expectancy of drama. They knew, even if this dumb policeman didn't, that it wasn't safe to bait Owen Euman if you didn't want him bursting out at you in withering fury. They expected at the least to hear Owen flare out with a "Mind your own damn business." But he held his tongue, kept his eyes on the food in his plate, and chewed determinedly.

Rather disappointedly the men concluded that, well, Owen had been calming down as he got older, and anyhow—with a cop investigating a murder—a man didn't dare fly off the handle.

CHAPTER 32

On this Friday night Terese looked forward to the dance with misgiving rather than pleasure, for this time she knew she would not only feel, but be, unwanted. Angela, however, was right. She mustn't give in to it. She would have to brazen it out, act as if she didn't know.

She stood before the huge round mirror of the new vanity dresser in the bedroom and regarded herself gravely. She had put on the white piqué dress she had worn to the bridge party, but the sight of her own beauty did not bolster her self-confidence as it usually did. Looking at her reflection, she saw what Angela meant. The sleek black hair, the long, curved lashes, the classically regular features above the pure white of her frock, they made her a picture. And these people here, they read pride and arrogance into her physical perfection.

Fleetingly Terese thought of the Church and the seclusion of the confessional. Although her father was what he called a freethinker, her mother was somewhat erratically faithful and she had seen to it that Terese took the formal precautions of loyalty to the faith. She thought now, Have I been guilty of the sins of pride and arrogance? But she lifted her chin, denying guilt. No, she had done nothing. It was the others, who had rejected her without cause, who were guilty of wicked behavior. She would not humble herself before them, sore and unhappy though she felt, and sorry as she was for Jim's sake.

Across the park Marguerite Faber stood in the entrance hall saying good night to her parents, who were going into town for an evening of bridge.

"I hate to leave you all alone," Mrs. Faber said perfunctorily. "Somehow I understood you had a date with Kenneth tonight."

"Oh, I'll be all right. Have fun."

Mrs. Faber kissed her daughter lightly on the cheek and went out with her husband, whereat Marguerite turned and ran leaping up the stairs two at a time. She changed quickly into a sheer, full-skirted dress and sandals, threw a short coat over her shoulders, and ran back down the stairs.

It had worked out nicely. All the time she had intended to go to the dance this week, but she had known she must keep it from the folks. She never had gone alone, and her father did not approve of too frequent attendance. He said it would look almost like spying on the part of the Fabers if they showed up too often to watch and listen while the employees disported themselves.

Marguerite had deliberately not analyzed too closely her reasons for wanting to be there this time. She wanted to see if Terese McGowan came, and if so, how people acted toward her. She wanted to see, in fact, how they all acted after the death and the funeral. She wanted to study Johnny Rodriguez in relation to all these things. Rather shamefacedly she realized that her interest was that of a spectator at a show of some kind. Underlying all the rest, however, was simply a desire to be there; and it was this which she did not attempt to define too closely.

Although it was just across the park, she got into her car and drove around the block to park a few yards down from the entrance to the clubhouse. Partly she did so to make her arrival seem casual, as if she had just been passing by and stopped in. Partly her driving the car was due to uneasiness at being out alone in the darkness. One could not forget that a man had been killed in the evening darkness of Conway.

The hall was lighted by old-fashioned bulbs covered with homemade paper shades, survivors of a decorative scheme for some long forgotten "special occasion," and now the couples were whirling under the yellowish-white light to the strains of "After the Ball." Marguerite stood aside by the entrance doors and watched, smiling in response to scattered nods of greeting. She sensed vividly the stir of surprise evoked by her presence, and was secretly amused. She knew what they were thinking: the Fabers hadn't dropped in since the Christmas dance, and now here was Marguerite at the dances both preceding and following the murder. They would say to themselves: it looks funny.

She saw Terese dancing with Jim, and Marguerite's eyes softened as eyes will when contemplating an affecting work of art. It was a shame, she thought with sudden resentment, for people to talk so meanly about a creature so lovely. Marguerite had wondered, placed some credence in the gossip; but now her doubts suddenly vanished and in an instant she became violently partisan to the beautiful dark-haired girl dancing with a grave expression in the circle of her husband's arm.

These horrible people, she thought, are making her the scapegoat for something that happened as a result of their own sordid scramble for more money and power at the mill.

As she took inventory of the crowd Marguerite saw that Johnny was not there, and she could not deny her disappointment.

One of the foremen's wives came up to greet her with overemphasized affability, and as the crowd on the floor flowed out to the side lines when the music ceased, Marguerite moved into it, speaking to this one and that, pausing to exchange amenities here and there, but always covertly watching the McGowans, as everyone else was doing. They sat in a row, Gladys and Tom, Jim and Terese. George stood beside them for a few moments, then moved away in answer to a jocular remark addressed to him by someone in a group beyond them.

A middle-aged man—at his wife's instigation, Marguerite was sure—asked her for the next dance, but she noticed that no one approached Terese, that she and Jim sat alone while the older McGowans were on the floor.

At the end of the dance Marguerite saw Johnny Rodriguez and Owen Euman and Eddie McGillicuddy enter in a group. At almost the same time she saw Marge Vale skirt the floor and drop into the chair beside Terese, fanning her neck with a handkerchief and making some laughing remark. Marguerite was delivered by her partner to a spot near where Byron Vale stood, and she approached him gaily, exclaiming after a few moments, "I must go over and speak to Marge. I haven't seen her for ages." She linked her arm in Byron's. "Come with me."

He looked down at the girl quizzically and accompanied her conspicuously across the bare, polished floor. Marge saw them coming, and although she was hardly more intimate with Marguerite Faber than were the others in the room, she called out as they came near, "Hello, there. I'm awfully glad you came out again. You know Jim's wife, don't you?"

Marguerite smiled amiably. "No, I don't believe I do. But I saw you two weeks ago," she said to Terese, "so I feel as if I'd met you."

Terese smiled, but Marguerite could see that it came with difficulty. The girl's eyes were brilliant, but her face looked stiff, as if to smile were a muscular effort; and Marguerite guessed how it was. It was as plain as if she had been here to watch since the first of the dance. No one but Marge had come up to say hello; formal nods and abstracted smiles had been the only greetings accorded Terese, and Marguerite was positive that no one had invited the girl to dance except her husband, her father-in-law, and her brother-in-law.

Jim had risen politely, offering Marguerite his seat, and she accepted with pretended gratefulness. Seating herself beside Terese, she confided, "I must be out of condition; one dance and I'm ready to take the load off my feet."

While this exchange was going on Angela and Joe had entered the hall. They spoke to a few people, and Angela doubtfully observed the little group that had formed around Terese. She "knew her place" and would not ordinarily have intruded herself socially on one of the Fabers, but Angela had listened all day to remarks whose tenor was "I wonder if she'll have the crust to show herself at the dance, after what's happened." And Angela had come with the firm intention of "being nice" to Terese, prudently not mentioning that intention to Joe, who had such an obsession against "taking sides." So well primed had Angela been for this purpose that even Marguerite Faber could not deter her, and with earrings swinging and the loud print of her dancing skirt swaying from her plump hips, she swept diagonally and also conspicuously across the floor with a ringing "How are you, Gladys?" to the elder Mrs. McGowan, who had self-consciously seated herself beside Marguerite.

"Nice to see you out, Miss Faber. My, how nice you look, Terese. White is so becoming to you. I wish I could wear it. I look terrible in white. Hello, Marge, and Byron."

Having done her duty, she beamed happily at everyone.

Terese's hands were clasped tightly in her lap. Her eyes went almost furtively from one to another of the group that was tightening around her, and her knuckles showed whiter as she caught a glimpse of the fatuously pleased expression on Jim's face. She knew he was thinking that this should reassure her in respect to her fears for her social position in Conway.

But it only terrified her. She was shrewder than Jim about some things, and she knew that it was the others—the ones keeping coldly away beyond the circle of the Vales and Marguerite Faber and Angela—who really counted in Conway, counted as far as she and Jim were concerned, anyhow. They were the ones with whom she must live and play if she were to remain in Conway—the Lorraine Bowens, the Gloria Hansons, the Lela Adamses. And this partisanship of the ones who were almost "above" the men in the mill would only antagonize them more.

She was, however, moved by this display of friendship, and astonished at Marguerite Faber, for she had recognized the sincerity in the other's manner.

The music had begun again, but none of this little group danced. They seemed reluctant to break up the protective coating they had formed around Terese, and they stood bulging out into the dancing space, seemingly oblivious to the detour they made necessary.

Terese looked stonily off across the hall through the space between Byron and Angela, and her eyes fell on the trio of Johnny, Owen, and Eddie, all of whom happened to be looking her way. Her mouth tightened, and her eyes met Johnny Rodriguez's, and she felt a sudden rising of antagonism within her. For the moment that group represented to her all the ones who stood away, across the hall, watching her with suspicious, unfriendly eyes, the ones who meant to keep her out, to isolate her.

She lifted her chin and held Johnny's gaze defiantly, and he was the one who dropped his eyes. He turned his head and found that Owen was also looking thoughtfully toward the group across the hall.

"Quite a high-toned bunch gathering around the McGowans tonight," Johnny said dryly. "Too bad Flo is away. She'd be in her glory."

Owen nodded and uttered a hoarse chuckle. "I was just thinking," he said slowly, "that it's funny the way things seemed to have lined up over that girl. You might say she's got management and the professions and small business all lined up on her side, while the working class all seems to be agin her. Ironical, kind of."

"You and your radical way of looking at things," Eddie said disapprovingly.

Johnny frowned and cast a fleeting glance across the room. "Yeah. That is the setup. And it's"—he moved his shoulders uneasily—"it's not right. She's one of us. We should be the ones standing up for her instead of running her down."

"You guys're always goin' intellectual on me," Eddie complained.

"Kind of a paradox," Owen murmured.

"Well," Johnny said more vigorously, "I never did like the way things have been going, and I like it even less now. I feel like a heel myself, even though God knows I never said anything to help build up this story that's been going around. But I have to admit I never did anything to discredit it, either, and so I feel partly responsible. And incidentally, Owen, you can add another category to the ones that've lined up on her side. The law. That detective wouldn't still be snooping around the hotel if he thought Les was killed on account of Terese McGowan."

Both Eddie and Owen regarded Johnny warily.

"You tryin' to say," Owen said quietly, "you think we ought to line up on her side too?"

"Maybe I am. There is such a thing as justice, and from the office on down we've all conspired to let this girl take the rap as far as public opinion goes. You spoke of 'management' as if the Faber girl represented it, but I don't think that's quite accurate. Miles Faber and Fred Combs and Jack Morgan have been just as satisfied to have Les's death laid to Terese McGowan as us guys in the mill have. I think the Faber girl's making up to Terese the way she seems to be doing is a sort of breaking away. I'd be willing to bet dough her folks don't know she's here tonight."

"If you don't think that woman was mixed up in it," Eddie said harshly, "you must believe it was some of our guys."

"Maybe it was; maybe it wasn't. I don't know. But I've come to the conclusion it doesn't work to try to protect him if it was one of our guys. You see what happens. Doing that just makes life miserable for some innocent person, and indirectly makes us look as if we stood for that kind of violence."

"Cripes," Eddie snorted.

"It's a problem, all right," Owen said philosophically.

CHAPTER 33

Marguerite was beginning to feel that this massed front on behalf of Terese was becoming unwieldy, too static. It needed to break up, become more fluid; so she leaned closer and whispered, "I have to go to the little girls' room. Do you want to go with me? I feel so conspicuous, taking off alone toward it."

Terese was already rising as she spoke, relieved at the chance to move around. "Sure, I'll go."

As they skirted the dancers Marguerite said confidentially, "That dress is just darling. Do you mind if I ask where you got it?"

"I made it."

"You did! I guess I should have known, though. It has that little touch you just don't get in readymade clothes. I've often thought I'd like to try to make something sometime, so I could have it just the way I wanted it. If I get reckless someday and buy a piece of material, would you give me a few pointers on how to go about it?"

"I'd be glad to," Terese said.

Their appearance as they pushed open the door in the far corner of the room was that of two young women engaged in light but absorbing intimate conversation, and Marguerite was smugly aware of it. She hoped that she was helping to "show" these nasty-minded little people.

When they emerged from the little cubicle with noses freshly powdered and lips more deeply reddened, Marguerite had no intention of letting Terese get stuck again on a chair among her relatives; so when they neared the group of men at the entrance, in whose center stood Johnny, Owen and Eddie, with George making it a quartet, she linked her arm in Terese's and said gaily, "What's this, the stag line?" She was glad the brother-in-law was in the group. It made it more natural for Terese to tarry there for a moment, as she was being made to do by the arm linked in hers.

The music was just beginning in polka time, and George smiled back. "We were just waiting for some pretty girls to dance with." He held out his hand. "How about it, Terese?"

Terese went to him gratefully, and they stepped onto the floor.

Marguerite's expression sobered in momentary disappointment. It wasn't with the girl's brother-in-law again that she had hoped to set her moving. Absently her eyes lifted, and she found Johnny Rodriguez regarding her quizzically. With a faint chagrin she realized that he had read her motive and her present thought. Impulsively she grinned at him ruefully and murmured, "Well, I tried."

"Dance?" he said in a low, amused tone, and they went onto the floor.

"I'm surprised to see you back so soon," he observed casually. "You don't usually come to the dances so regular."

"No law against my coming whenever I like, is there?" she retorted.

"No." There were a few seconds of silence before he added, "You seem to be taking a sudden interest in the proletariat."

"I've been hearing that the 'proletariat,'" she rejoined tartly, "has been acting very peculiarly lately. About Terese McGowan, I mean. Turning on one of their own, you might say."

"And I have heard," he answered dryly, "that it was the representatives of capital that first gave the cue to look her way."

"I doubt that. That they were first, I mean. You people over here were pretty eager, it seems to me, to find a scapegoat, even though the office did co-operate in finding one for you."

"Why are you so interested?"

She uttered an ironic little laugh. "I suppose because right now I'm bored. Have more leisure than brains." She glanced up at him whimsically. "Give me twenty years, and I suppose I'll be a typical clubwoman, busy with 'good works' and butting into other people's lives to make up for the dullness of my own."

Johnny met her eyes uncertainly. This was something he had never expected, and didn't know how to handle now that it had happened—this sudden establishment of an easy, friendly accord between himself and the boss's daughter, this realization that they were hitting it off well together, that if she had been anyone but who she was, he would have wanted to see more of her.

She held his eyes for a moment and then looked away with an amused gleam in her own. There was another pause before she said, "Look, seriously, I'm distressed about Terese. She's very unhappy, and it isn't fair."

"I thought," Johnny said heavily, "maybe she wouldn't catch on, that it would blow over without her ever knowing what they were saying. She always seems to be so kind of living in a little world of her own."

"Nobody can fail to get it when people turn against them. That's one of the things that seems to hurt people the worst in life, being rejected by the people they have to live with."

Johnny's eyes sought out Terese, whirling with George in the polka.

"So you think she knows?"

"Of course she knows," Marguerite reiterated impatiently. "She doesn't have a hide like a rhinoceros."

The music ended then, so they could not pursue the subject to greater clarification, and Marguerite did not realize that Johnny had been left with the impression that Terese knew not only that people were talking but what they were saying about her.

They were at the far end of the hall, and as they moved back toward the entrance doors Marguerite said, "Ask her to dance, won't you? You have a lot of standing in the village. If they see you giving her a friendly hand, it might help to break down some of this feeling."

"Well—sure, I'll dance with her," he said uneasily. "Although, considering what they've got against her, it may do more harm than good."

"No. No, you have a good reputation in that respect."

"Thanks," he said dryly, and then his step faltered. "Oh-oh, look who's here."

Marguerite followed the direction of his eyes and saw nothing but another common-looking man in a brown suit.

"Who?" she said, puzzled.

"The detective working on the case. That one in a brown suit."

"Oh."

They had halted on the edge of the people standing in a loose group at the end of the room. Suddenly Johnny looked down at her with a sardonic smile. "You know," he said in a low tone, "I'm a suspect too. How do you know I haven't got good reason myself to want suspicion thrown on the McGowan brothers?"

She studied his face seriously. "I don't know. But somehow I don't think it was you."

Their eyes held gravely for a moment, and then they both looked away self-consciously and moved into the crowd. Johnny was disturbed. Nothing had happened. All he had done was dance once with the boss's daughter. But he had an eerie feeling that a great deal had happened, that changes had taken place, leaving him stirred and quickened in their aftermath.

It was not entirely a welcome feeling.

Owen Euman had taken a seat on one of the folding chairs against the wall. He seldom danced, but on Friday nights he always showed up for an hour or so to watch. Along with everyone else he had noticed the entrance of the detective Pete, and along with everyone else his emotional fibers had tightened with defensive antagonism at the man's presence. It was going a little too far, the bastard busting in on their social life, coming to hover like a big fat buzzard while people tried to enjoy themselves.

Owen's teeth clamped on his pipe as the detective lumbered over to deposit himself on the next chair.

"Evenin'," Pete said affably.

Owen's eyes blazed briefly toward the man and then looked straight ahead as he gave a grunt for response. After a second Owen muttered, "Surprised to see you here."

"Oh, I like to get around," Pete said blandly.

And then they sat there, neither moving, neither speaking. Pete alone looked relaxed, interested in the scene before him.

The next dance was a waltz, and with a sense of being obscurely compelled, Johnny crossed the room and smilingly asked Terese to dance. She accepted indifferently. Somehow by this time she felt rather numb, as if partially anesthetized by the avid, curious, and unsympathetic glances that she had been aware of ever since she came. The exaggerated friendliness of the few who had apparently for some reason decided to sponsor her only underlined the general air of hostility she could feel beyond them.

You can only stay hurt for so long before you begin to feel mean, and Terese had reached that stage when Johnny asked her to dance. After a few steps she glanced up at him and said with an edge in her tone, "How does it happen you aren't afraid you'll be contaminated by dancing with me?"

Her eyes flicked away and rested bitterly on Al Bowen, who was consciously not looking at her as he circled past with Emily Fraser.

"Everybody doesn't believe the talk that's been going around, and I'm one of them," he said awkwardly. "There's always a few people that gossip in a little place like this. You shouldn't pay too much attention to it."

Terese had stiffened, and then relaxed deliberately so that he wouldn't notice. At last, if she was clever enough, she would find out what it was. She could tell that this fellow thought she knew.

"How come you don't believe it?"

"Well, for one thing, I've known Les Coleman all my life, and I knew better than to believe anything he said, especially where women were concerned; and then maybe I'm a better judge of people than some. I just don't believe you're the kind of girl that would give her husband reason to be worried about a guy like Les, nor that Jim's the type to fly off the handle over unfounded jealousy."

Terese pulled away, the palm of one hand braced against his upper arm, the other dropping his hand.

"So that's it," she breathed, her face so white that her eyes were like coals, her lips a red scar against her sudden pallor.

She stood rigidly still, so that other couples had to swerve to avoid her and the startled Johnny. Her hands dropped, and her eyes blazed at the people around them who were beginning to stare. Suddenly she whirled and made straight for the entrance, brushing against dancers, not speaking, hardly seeing the human obstacles which fell back before her.

George and Marguerite had been close to the entrance doors, and Jim had been dancing with his mother a few feet away. All of them noticed the commotion at once, and both Jim and George dropped their partners' hands to move toward Terese, but she was out of the door before either reached her.

Jim had seen Johnny dazedly following Terese, looking shocked and worried. As he and George met at the doors, Jim said curtly, "Go after Terese and see what's the matter. I'll take care of Rodriguez."

He turned and faced Johnny with cold anger and suspicion, and jerked his head toward the doors. "Come outside."

Johnny fell into step a foot behind him and they went out, followed by Marguerite and Mrs. McGowan. Immediately everyone near the entrance began to flow toward it. Pete and Owen Euman had been seated close to the doors, and Owen was the first to go out behind the two women who had crowded after Jim and Johnny. When others reached the doorway they found Pete's solid brown figure in the center of it, facing them. The music had faltered and died, and all heads were craning toward the entrance.

"Everybody stay in here," Pete commanded in a normal tone of voice that had nonetheless assumed a note of authority. His eyes roved over them coldly, impassively; and the people fell back unevenly, reluctantly, as they remembered that this man was after all the Law, and remembered, too, the sinister event that had brought him among them.

It was Tom McGowan, who had been too far away to follow his family outside, who turned and signaled to the orchestra, commanding quietly, "O.K. Go on with the piece."

The orchestra had to make two starts before they hit the beat together. A few couples mechanically followed the music, but most of the dancers separated into buzzing groups against the walls.

Pete turned, pulled the doors closed behind him, and went unobtrusively out on the steps, below which, in the pool of brightness from the outside entrance light, the little circle stood talking in staccato tones. Neither Terese nor George was in sight.

CHAPTER 34

As soon as they reached the sidewalk Jim faced Johnny in the tense pose of a man prepared to fight.

"What did you do to my wife?" he demanded.

"Look, Jim," Johnny began placatingly, "it's not what you think. Give me a minute to explain—"

"It better be good," Jim snapped, setting his jaw.

"I don't know whether you know it, but people've been talking—about her; and I thought she knew. I was just trying to let her know that I was on you folks' side, that I didn't believe the gossip, but—it looks like she didn't know—what it was they're saying, and when I let it out—well"— he moved his hand in the direction Terese had presumably taken—"you saw how she took it. I swear, Jim, I wouldn't have said anything if I'd known she didn't know."

Jim had been glaring at the other fiercely, and now he tore his eyes away to glance seekingly around the worried group of listeners before he snapped, "What gossip?"

Now it was Johnny's turn to look helplessly to the others. It was Marguerite who took a step forward in response. She seemed to sense that if it must be said, it would come better from her, an outsider, a woman, the boss's daughter, one, in short, against whom Jim's anger could most harmlessly be expended. "It's partly my fault this happened," she said. "When I was dancing with Johnny, I was deploring the way some of the people have been acting, and I told him I knew Terese felt it; and I'm afraid I gave Johnny the impression she knew the reason—"

"What reason?" Jim barked again.

Marguerite swallowed, and plunged. "They—that is, some of them— think you killed Lester Coleman because you suspected him of fooling around with your wife."

In the utter silence which followed, the muffled sound of the music blended with the melancholy croaking of the frogs in the park fishpond.

Appropriately, it was upon his mother that Jim's eyes finally came to rest for confirmation or denial, and for reassurance.

She met his gaze miserably and put her hand on his arm. "It's true, Jimmy. They have been saying that, but"—her voice became stronger, argumentative—"it's just people who don't count. None of us here believe it. See, Johnny doesn't, or—or"—her eyes moved desperately around the circle—"or Owen. And the Vales and Angela Amatelli, and Miss Faber here. Nobody who really counts in the village believes it. It's just—just the—ignorant ones."

Jim had listened slackly, and now he turned away, and in turning it happened that he was facing in the direction of the mill, although it was hidden by the bulk of the business buildings between.

"Sure," he said harshly. "Sure. Nobody believes it. Nobody believes my wife is a tramp and I'm a murderer." He stared sightlessly at the clubhouse wall as if he could see through and beyond it to the mill. "Nobody but the guys I work with every day." He uttered a short, nasty laugh. "Nobody but my new union brothers that told me everything was going to be hunky-dory now, everybody being *together*—all for one, one for all."

He turned back and looked from Johnny to Owen. "You were the guys—solidarity, brotherhood, unity—" He looked as if he wanted to spit, but instead he uttered a short, obscene word and, brushing past them, strode off in the direction Terese had gone toward home.

Mrs. McGowan gave a little sob, and Johnny muttered, "Jesus. Oh, Jesus," his voice both angry and tormented.

Marguerite said pityingly, "The poor kids."

Owen stood staring after Jim's retreating figure, scowling deeply and saying nothing.

Mrs. McGowan drew in her breath and said listlessly, "Well, I'll go in and get Dad and go home."

Johnny turned and started to walk away, and Marguerite quickly followed him, falling into step. "I can't go back in there now either. My car's right here. Let me give you a lift home."

He looked at her vaguely, as if trying to place her.

"Please," she said. "Ride with me. I don't feel like being alone." Johnny frowned, looked at her and at the clubhouse where Pete was holding the door open for Mrs. McGowan.

"People," Johnny said gratingly, "would talk if I took to riding around with you."

She looked up at him humbly and then looked down at the toes of her sandals. "It's up to you," she said in a muffled voice.

The yellow light from the unshaded bulb glinted on her fair hair; her shoulders were rounded and somehow dejected as she stood with her head bowed.

"All right," Johnny said roughly, and grasped her arm above the elbow. "Come on. At the moment I don't give a damn."

Owen Euman, left alone, turned and plodded away slowly in the other direction, on the long way round to the hotel.

CHAPTER 35

Inside the hall Pete's deceptively slow eyes took in the avidly watching and listening people who witnessed the reappearance of Mrs. McGowan and himself.

He spoke to the woman in a normally pitched voice, as if they were just concluding a conversation and he was unaware of the expectant audience.

"I wouldn't worry too much, if I was you, about a bunch of ignorant gossips. I'm the one that's done the most work on this here case, and I guess I oughta know what I'm talkin' about. Us guys that are in the business, we approach these here things scientifically. We find out things other people don't know about; and for your peace of mind, Mrs. McGowan, I want to say right now we got inside information and we've known right from the start there wasn't nothin' to all this talk."

Mrs. McGowan had stood regarding him dumbly, and now she gave him a wavering smile. "Well, I'm sure glad to hear that."

As if he were still unaware that this was not just a private conversation, Pete said heartily, "Well, guess I'll be running along. You folks sure have nice dances out here. Think I'll have to bring my wife out sometime and take a whirl myself."

"Do that," Mrs. McGowan said weakly. "We're always glad to have people drop in."

As Pete went out she faced the hall defiantly, lifted her head, and made for her husband.

Pete stood on the step outside for a moment and scratched his head, lifting his hat with the movement. He'd probably get in trouble if the office heard about what he'd just said. Especially that "we" stuff. But hell, a man had to be a boy scout once in a while. Anyhow, if they were going to fire him for breaking the rules they'd have done it long ago. He stood in thought for a moment and decided that was all for tonight. Tomorrow he'd find time to come out again.

The dance broke up early. There was a tendency toward gathering in little clusters and talking in low voices after Tom and Gladys McGowan left.

Walking home arm in arm, Al and Lorraine Bowen were mostly silent.

"I wish," he said once, "all this about Jim and Terese had never come up."

"Well, at least we didn't have anything to do with it," Lorraine said virtuously, and she almost believed it. By tomorrow she would believe it wholly. "It was Lela Adams, really, that started it," she added.

Her opinions and her attitude had been readjusting themselves grudgingly ever since The Scene, as it was to become known in Conway. Bolstering her change of viewpoint was Marge Vale's attitude toward Terese. No matter what else anyone could say about Marge, she had always been smart. Marge was nobody's fool. And the way Marguerite Faber seemed to be taking up with Terese. Emily Fraser had whispered it around that she heard them talking, and Marguerite and that woman were going to get together and sew. Lorraine's eyes narrowed. Stranger things had happened. Suppose those two got chummy, with Terese even going to Faber's house with Marguerite. Terese's friends, too, might be drawn into closer contact with the big house.

With a falsely offhanded air Al said, "We were planning to go up to Hillsview Park tomorrow on a picnic and go swimming in the river. Why don't you run over in the morning and ask Jim and Terese if they'd like to go along? There's plenty of room in our car."

For a moment the old jealous resistance rose in Lorraine, but she could read Al's motives pretty well. He had always been uneasy about Terese, felt somehow guilty about the whole thing. Lorraine pondered quickly and intensively. If things were going to be different now, it would put a person in a good position, going out with the McGowans tomorrow. You would be able to let on pretty convincingly, "Well, we never had any part of all that dirty talk." She could even see why Al suggested that *she* be the one to go over and ask. It was the women Terese needed on her side.

So she said with artificial matter-of-factness, "O.K. I'll do that."

From the clubhouse to Johnny's house it was less than two blocks, down the street and around the corner. After the emotional tension of the past few minutes Johnny and Marguerite lapsed into prosaic, disjointed commonplaces in their talk. But when he stood outside the open car with his hand on the closed door Johnny hesitated, as if there were more that must be said. The headlights and the dim light from the dashboard enabled them to see each other fairly clearly, and they met one another's eyes questioningly.

It was Johnny who spoke, with a faint, inscrutable smile. "Are you coming to the dance again next week?"

"Do you think I should?" she countered.

"Well—it's a free country."

"So it is." She struck the steering wheel lightly with her palm. "However, it looks pretty silly driving a car just two blocks around the park to go to a dance. I did it tonight because somehow I was frightened. But I wouldn't do it every time, and I would still be frightened to walk home alone. Could I count on anyone seeing me home safely?"

He regarded her guardedly but not unsympathetically, and finally said, "I don't know. But—we'll see."

Marguerite laughed. "'We'll see.' That's what my mother always used to say—when she didn't really want me to do something I asked to do but was pretty sure she'd finally give in."

She pressed the car into gear and was away down the street.

Upstairs in her bedroom a little later, Marguerite moved across the cream-colored carpet and stood between the bright blue silk draperies which fell into soft pools on the floor, looking out of the window to the east across the dark treetops of the park, beyond which she could see an occasional light from the cottages on the East Side. She put her hands on the sill and pressed her forehead to the glass, looking out into the darkness.

Tonight she had felt for the first time like a part of this place, this village called Conway, this appendage to the mill. Before, Conway had been the place where she lived, but a place where she lived among strangers. But tonight she had taken part, been an integral factor in the little drama which had ruffled the lives over there beyond the trees. In the press of the moment the McGowans, Johnny, that odd old man they called Owen, had spoken and acted in her presence as if she were only another person from one of the East Side streets. Indeed, their actions had interpenetrated hers. They had reacted to the things she did and said, just as she had reacted to their behavior.

As she pulled the heavy shade down over the glass and turned back into the room, switching on the bedside light, her mind ran undisciplined on unrelated thoughts.

It was summer now. Before autumn she must make up her mind what to do. She thought of Byron Vale, reserved, opaque, going quietly about his job, a man all sides in Conway found it a little difficult to understand. And she thought of the school with its skeleton-like play equipment of slides and rings and swings lying still and dark now beyond the eucalyptus grove to the south.

Because she had felt vaguely at college that there must be some purpose incorporated in her studies beyond pure self-improvement she had acquired a teaching credential—a rather specialized one, in Arts; but she was a teacher. She could be a useful one in any school, with her ability to play the piano, her talents in dancing and sports, which she had taken up because she liked them. And certainly she could handle third-grade arithmetic and spelling.

She sat on the flounced vanity stool with one bare foot over her knee, the sandal in her hand. Byron Vale, as principal, did the hiring. If she asked him, he wouldn't dare turn her down. Neither would the school trustees dare withhold approval of Miles Faber's daughter.

As a teacher, taking care of their children all day, writing stern notes home about behavior problems, it would be a step down from being the Boss's Daughter. She would be an active part of their lives whether they liked it or not. And no one could say anything about one of the machinists in the mill going around with one of the teachers. That sort of thing did happen.

Marguerite heard her parents' car turn in the driveway south of the house, and she set her shoe down with a deliberate movement. Mother wouldn't like it. She would be frightfully disappointed. Mother had even looked with some apathy on her taking a job at the high school in town. What Mother really hoped was that she would become engaged to Kenneth Swayle.

As for her dad— Marguerite slowly unbuckled the other sandal. Once she would have thought he too would be disappointed. But now she wasn't sure. As he got older there were times when her father seemed confused. He said unpredictable things.

She took a quick, deep breath and stood up. But it didn't matter. It was her life, and at last she knew what she wanted to do with it. She would never have believed, only a few weeks ago, that what she would want to do would be to stay right here in Conway, being useful, mingling with the people on the East Side, becoming probably more and more like them as time went on.

It was taking her a long time to get ready for bed tonight. Again she found herself standing still, her fingers slow on the fastening at her waist, seeing Johnny Rodriguez's face softened in the dimness of the night, his lips smiling a little, his eyes gently teasing as he murmured, "We'll see." She felt short of breath, a sort of outward pressure all over inside of her.

It was ridiculous, and unsuitable. She must not think about this too much. As Johnny had said, "We'll see." But it still took her a long time to finish getting ready for bed.

CHAPTER 36

Jim had almost run the distance to his home, and he was somehow relieved to see light glowing through the draperies of the living room.

When he threw open the door George was standing there, evidently interrupted in restless wandering about the small room. Terese sat on the sofa behind the coffee table, her shoulders hunched forward, a cigarette between her fingers. Jim could tell by her eyes that she had cried, but now she only sat looking at him with a sullen expression.

Jim crossed the room and sat beside her, putting both arms around her and pressing his face against her hair for a moment.

"Well, what happened?" George said jerkily.

"I found out what this is all about," Jim said with a firmness he did not feel. Sickened as he was himself, he knew he must try to play the whole thing down for Terese's sake.

"I thought," he said gently to the girl, "that Johnny had got fresh or something, that it was him upset you. That's why I didn't come right after you. I wasn't going to let him get away with—with bothering you."

"It wasn't Johnny," she said heavily.

"No, that's what I found out. Me and Johnny and Mom and Marguerite Faber had a little talk outside, and I got to the bottom of it." He looked up at his brother. "People—some of them—have been saying *I* killed Les because I was jealous of him and Terese."

"I know," George said.

"You'd already heard it? Why didn't you say something?"

"What was the good? It would just make you mad and hurt Terese's feelings. This isn't the kind of thing, you know, that you can clear up by denying it. Naturally people would expect you and me to deny it."

"How could they?" Terese cried hopelessly. "How could they? Why, I don't think I ever saw the man to speak to more than twice."

She rose and flung herself away from the sofa. "What gets me is that they assumed right off, without giving it a second thought, that I'm the kind that would encourage that louse, that I would cheat on my husband." She faced first one, then the other of the men. "It shows, don't you see, the kind of impression they have of me. They think I'm cheap and—and bad. Otherwise such a thing wouldn't have occurred to them. Maybe it's terrible and selfish and—and small of me, but that's what gets me worse than their thinking Jim is a murderer—that they could blame this on me. Because anyone can understand and—and overlook it, a man accidentally killing another in a fight over a woman. But that they should think I'm the kind of a woman that gets her man into that kind of a thing with a cheap wolf like that Coleman person!"

Jim stood up and came to her, putting his arm around her comfortingly, but George spoke first. "Well, of course, people here don't know you, Terese. This wouldn't have occurred to them if they'd had time to get acquainted with you, if you weren't a stranger."

Angrily she jerked herself away from Jim and flared out at George, "They know me well enough to know better. I've been here over a month. They could have known me better if they'd wanted to. But they didn't want to. I can see that now. They're mean, petty, evil-minded, hateful people; and I hate them all. I hate Conway. I'll never live here again. I can't get far enough away to suit me!"

"Now, honey," Jim murmured soothingly, "they're not all so bad—"

"Don't tell me, don't try to tell me they're not cruel and mean and—and hateful. Look at them. Somebody killed that poor stupid devil. Somebody knows for sure it's all lies about you and me. And he's keeping his mouth shut, letting us take all the talk and suspicions. And you can't tell me there aren't others that know who did it. And they're all standing together, talking as hard as they can against us. And that's what you call nice people! Well, not to me they aren't. They stink, that's what they do, they stink!"

She collapsed in a chair, crying hysterically. The men looked at each other helplessly, and Jim looked meaningly at the door. George mumbled that maybe he'd better go, and went out with a worried backward glance.

Jim crouched beside the chair and tried to comfort the weeping woman. She put her hand behind his neck and pressed her head against his. After a moment she said brokenly, "I'm terrible, I guess, just going on about myself, what they think about me. But it's you, too, I feel bad about. Them thinking you killed a man. That hurts me just as bad, that they could think such things about you."

Jim eased himself onto his knees in a more comfortable position and stroked her hair, talking gently, insisting that "It's not everybody," mentioning the names over again—Angela, the Vales, Johnny, why, even Marguerite Faber—saying that none of the really nice people in town had taken any stock in that talk.

"I don't care," she kept insisting bleakly. "I can't live among people who would think such awful things about me."

And then there was a knock on the door. Both raised their heads in startled surprise.

Jim heaved himself to his feet, tucking in his shirt, which had pulled up from the trousers in the stress of the last hour's developments. Terese rubbed her fingers over her cheeks to wipe away the tears and straightened her legs to sit upright in the chair, and Jim went to open the door.

CHAPTER 37

Owen Euman was standing on the porch. "Can I come in a minute?" he ventured awkwardly. "I know it's pretty late, but—"

"Why, sure, come in."

Owen took off his hat and bobbed his head at Terese.

"Sit down." Jim indicated an armchair, and Owen lowered himself into it.

There was a moment of strained, expectant silence. Owen turned his hat in his hand. It was his "good" hat, a tan snap-brim felt that he wore to town and on Sundays and to the dances. He let it come to rest in his lap and said gruffly, "I had you folks on my mind. I hope you don't mind an old duffer like me buttin' in like this."

"It's all right," Terese said dully.

Jim stood beside her chair as if waiting.

"It's kind of hard to know how to begin. I was outside tonight, you remember, when you and Johnny had words, Jim. I guess you folks are taking it pretty hard."

"If I have anything to say about it," Terese said with a flash of spirit, "we're leaving this town. I certainly don't want to live where I'm suspected of murder and Lord knows what else."

Owen ran his forefinger down the crease in the crown of his hat. "What you said, Jim, about the guys you work with and the union, it's stuck in my mind. I never looked at it just that way, that by protecting the guy that did it we might be layin' another one of the"—he cleared his throat self-consciously—"brothers open to trouble like what you two are feelin' now. And I can't get it out of my head that that's wrong."

He looked from one to the other of them rather sadly. "Maybe I ought to explain about myself. I don't have no family, no ties that way; all I've got is the men I work with that I feel—bound to. Time past, I used to read a lot; and I remember something I read once—a quotation from Abraham Lincoln. Wouldn't mean much to you kids, I guess; but being situated like I am, it hit home with me. It was to the effect that the strongest ties outside family ones are them that hold the working people of all nations together. Well, not havin' no family, I guess I feel those ties more'n some would—not on an international scale, the way the quotation goes, but leastways here in the mill. I feel a—loyalty, specially toward you fellows in our new union, and I can't take it very good, feelin' I'm being *dis*loyal to them."

Jim had moved unobtrusively to sink onto a footstool. Both he and Terese watched the older man wonderingly.

"And I been feeling tonight maybe I'm not doing the right thing, covering up for the man that struck Coleman down. Maybe I'm doing too much damage to a fellow worker's life. Specially since I never did hold with terrorism, individual violence."

"You know," Terese breathed, "who did it?"

Owen looked down at his hat, fingering the brim, as if he still hesitated to commit himself, but he said at last, "Yes, I know. Up to now, when I see what a bad effect it's havin' on your lives, I hadn't thought anything about keeping still, because it was in some ways an accident. Not premeditated, I mean, although I will admit the man felt murderous toward Lester when he picked up that pipe and let swing. But some ways Les brought it on himself—couldn't let well enough alone, had to stop this man and put on a front of friendliness when everybody knew he was doin' all he could to stick a knife in our back, pointing us out so we'd be fired. But he was a perverse kind of fellow—had to stop you and talk, couldn't resist rubbing it in, all the time pretending he was innocent as a newborn babe of any bad intentions, actually lettin' on he might be considering joining up with us." Owen shook his head sadly. "Kind of a fool, he was, in the last analysis. But like I said, the man never intended killing him, just lost his temper and picked up the first handy thing."

He seemed to have momentarily forgotten his audience. "I've had to fight my temper all my life," he muttered almost inaudibly.

Terese was wide-eyed. She leaned forward, her hands in two fists in her lap. "It was you," she breathed.

"I wouldn't go so far as to say that," Owen said dispassionately. "I'm just putting it to you. How important it is to you folks to be cleared. And not only you but the other guys they'll suspect if they get doubtful that it *was* you. What's been on my conscience since down at the dance tonight is— have I got a right to keep still and leave other people under suspicion so that their lives get messed up over it? Specially since a good lawyer might show it was maybe just manslaughter, not murder."

Terese shivered suddenly. "I don't think it would stand up in court— manslaughter."

"I haven't worried," Owen said unemotionally, "about anybody being hauled into court. There's no evidence to bring anybody in on. All they can hope for now is a confession. I didn't feel my silence was going to send anybody else to prison. But while I been walking around tonight I realized there's another court that's pretty effective. They call it Public Opinion, but what it amounts to is the good will, the respect of the people you have to live and work with. Some ways it's as bad as prison to be deprived of that. I could see that about you folks when I seen how the little lady here reacted tonight when she heard how things stand."

Terese stood up with a violent motion and ran her hands through her hair on either side of her head above the temples. She stared down at Owen and exclaimed, "Be quiet a minute, both of you!"

She moved jerkily across the room, clasping her arms in front of her, each hand holding the opposite elbow. She cast a despairing glance at each of the two men, and they waited, their eyes upon her. In front of the bedroom door she turned and stood still, her arms falling to her sides.

"No," she said to Owen, "don't do it. It isn't worth it. Your life against our reputation." She took a deep breath. "After all, life is long. I guess I kind of forgot that. All I could see was my own hurt feelings right now, being shut out from the company of a few silly people that really don't matter to me in the long run." Her eyes rested thoughtfully on Jim. "They tried to tell me, George and Jim, that it wasn't everybody; but I was too upset to pay attention. There's Jim's folks—they believe in us—and Johnny and the Vales, and Angela. I know how her husband is—leans over backward to keep from taking sides—yet Angela made a public show of her friendliness toward me tonight, risking making her husband mad and offending half her customers. And that Faber girl. I can see now. She felt sorry for me, on account of what they've been saying. She was trying to show me she didn't believe it. And now"—she let her eyes rest on Owen—"you."

For the first time in hours Terese smiled, and it was a gentle, uninhibited smile, the expression of a mature woman, adding a new beauty to the purely external perfection of line and coloring inherent in her physical make-up. "It's like the boys said—all the people that count are on our side, have faith in us. And I guess we're not the first or the last people to be misunderstood by—by the public."

Her face sobered and she raised her clasped hands to her lips, the thumbnails against her teeth. "And it's not as if they really cared about Lester, poor devil. Nobody minds because he's gone. I guess they've mainly been so anxious to pin down the blame in order to keep suspicion off you other fellows that you said were suspected. Partly they were actually trying to protect the good name of the union bunch that you're so concerned about, Mr. Euman. Maybe we can't blame them so much."

She sank into her chair again with a weary sigh. "It isn't even as if they really cared if Jim and I *had* been responsible. They just needed somebody to blame it on."

Owen let out his breath slowly, and nodded.

Jim had sat silent, looking down, his expression growing more thoughtful as the others talked. Occasionally he glanced up briefly, his eyes resting on one face, then on the other. Now he spoke slowly. "About all that, I think Terese is right; and I wouldn't want anybody putting his own head in a noose just on our account. But there's more to it than that. Whether it was accident or whether it wasn't, a man got killed; and that's against the law. Any way you look at it, it seems to me like it ain't right to lie and cover up about it. The way I've always figured, if a person lets themselves do something that ain't right, they should be willing to stand up and take the consequences. And it ain't right in the first place, hittin' anybody with a lead pipe, whether they die from it or whether they don't."

As he finished, Jim met their eyes with defiant steadiness.

Owen's face was expressionless, but he dropped his eyes.

"It's easy to say what's right and wrong—theoretically," he said in a dead tone. "But what would you do if it was your life?"

Terese's dark eyes, turning from one man to the other, had begun to smolder. She rose to her feet as if under compulsion.

"You sound like a preacher, Jim." Her shoulders rose and fell in a shrug. "Sure, you're right. Just like what it says in the Bible about how people *ought* to live is right. But who ever carries it all out? Nobody. In this world you've got to be practical."

Her eyes dropped speculatively on Owen. "And who," she demanded flatly, "is going to be any better off if Mr. Euman goes and spills what he knows to the cops?"

She sat down again in the armchair, leaning back in a fairly relaxed position. "Besides," she concluded, "he's showed he's *willing* to do the right thing. So in a way he's already—atoned for it." She had been regarding Owen most of the time as she spoke, and now she turned challengingly to Jim. "He's got it off his conscience by confessing to us, hasn't he?"

Both men studied the girl with rather nonplused expressions. "I didn't exactly—confess," Owen demurred.

"Well," she said dismissingly, "you were willing to put things straight for our sakes and at your expense. That's good enough for me. And if it isn't good enough for the law—well, that's just too bad."

Jim's mouth opened, and closed again. He turned to Owen with a sardonic smile that was a stranger to his usually open, uncomplicated countenance. "I've always heard it's no use to argue with a woman."

Terese suddenly sat up straight, and her face seemed to have more color in it.

"You know something? All of a sudden I'm hungry. How about it, Mr. Euman, would you like a cup of coffee with us? There's enough pie left over from dinner for each of us to have a piece."

He turned his hat in his hands and said, ducking his head shyly, "Why, I don't care if I do, thank you."

Terese rose with an air of animation. "It'll only take a minute."

CHAPTER 38

It was early afternoon the next day when Pete found time to drop in at the hotel again. He had been sent into the country to investigate a continuing disappearance of expensive tools at a large ranch in the foothills, and it was only a few miles out of the way to stop in Conway.

It was quiet about the hotel. Men had either gone into town already or were napping or reading in their rooms, resting up for an evening there. A few stood around on the sidewalk outside the store and in front of the barbershop around the corner.

Pete was surprised to see only Owen Euman sitting in one of the circular-backed wooden chairs on the hotel veranda. As he came up the steps Owen regarded him with what might have been a quizzical gleam in his gray eyes.

"Everybody deserted you?" Pete inquired affably, taking the chair next to him.

"Oh, they're around," Owen replied laconically. "It's always quiet Saturday afternoon."

Coming from Owen, this amounted almost to loquacity, and Pete sat digesting the fact in silence.

"Still expectin' to solve the case?" Owen ventured after a moment.

"You think I ain't going to?" Pete countered.

"I wouldn't bet no big amounts on it," Owen answered dryly.

Pete studied the other man's profile with the curved black pipe stem protruding from it. The subject of his scrutiny was relaxed, calm. The tension that Pete had known was there before had loosened. Pete looked out to the oaks lining the road, and pondered. That concealed tension, that hidden resistance, had been what he had to work with. Now, if he were to go on, he must find another angle.

"Guess I'm kind of a funny guy," he remarked chattily. "I don't like to see anybody get away with murder. Sometimes people get a funny idea that if they didn't *mean* to do it, then they ain't really responsible." He shook his head deprecatingly. "But me, like I said, I'm funny that way. Don't believe in violence. 'Cause whether you call it that or not, any time a man raises his hand against another man in anger he's got murder in his heart. And me, I don't believe in it."

Owen held his pipe in his hand, and his eyes, too, were on the trees. "I don't believe in it either," he said heavily.

After a while Pete stood up. He looked down, and Owen lifted his head, meeting the detective's gaze. Their eyes held for an instant, and then Pete said, "Well, I'll be seein' ya."

"How much longer d'you think they're gonna let you keep on wasting the taxpayers' money running back and forth out here?"

"Next big case that breaks, I s'pose I'll be kept pretty busy. But I won't be so far away. Any time you come into town you'll prob'ly see me around. I keep in circulation. And I'll be out, now and again."

"You'll be wastin' your time," Owen said softly.

"Maybe not." Pete's small eyes made a swift survey of the older man's face, and with a thrust of intuition he added tersely, "Any time more'n one person knows something it ain't no secret any more. Sooner or later somebody says something. So I'll just go along keepin' my ears open." He turned toward the steps. "Well, like I said, I'll be seein' ya."

As if not of his volition, Owen's eyes rested on the detective's back with the ridge under the collar where the jacket did not quite lie smooth above the heavy shoulders. Beyond the brown jacket he seemed to see, as he had never done in actuality on account of the darkness, the motionless body that slowly grew cold and stiff upon the hard ground. There could be no hatred, no anger now against the pitiful object that had been a human being grown despicable because its poor little hopes and longings had taken the wrong paths in their quest for satisfaction.

Pete did not look back as his car headed toward town, but if he had, he would have seen Owen sitting hunched forward with his elbows on his knees, a hand on either side of his head, his pipe lying in the seat of the chair next to him.

THE END

THE MISSING HEIRESS

HEIRESS

BERNICE CAREY

CHAPTER 1

A report that some seventeen-year-old girl has been missing for twenty-four hours does not ordinarily throw a whole state's police apparatus into uproarious activity directed toward locating the errant lass. From long and boring experience the guardians of the law know that all too often in a few days she will be discovered at some hotel where she has no business to be, in the company of some man, young or old, who will then find himself in more trouble than he cares to be in—or that at worst some innocent bystander will come upon her body at the foot of a cliff or in a roadside ditch, at which time it will be tragically beyond help.

But when the girl is Virginia Wilkins Forester and will upon her twenty-first birthday fall heir to property worth roughly three million dollars, and when she has not been seen for twenty-four hours, during the latter half of which her family has without result had inquiries made among all her friends and acquaintances, the police are likely to move with a little more than their accustomed celerity. For the disappearance of the granddaughter of Henry Wilkins, the California oil magnate, will be News.

It was on a Saturday morning that Virginia vanished from the country estate established before his death by her grandfather in the rolling foothills that lap against the steep slopes of the Coast Range mountains south of the San Francisco peninsula.

Virginia was enrolled at a boarding school near Palo Alto and had been at home as usual for the weekend. Her mother, the former Jane Wilkins, was dead, and that weekend her father, Douglas Forester, had been in San Francisco, where he kept an apartment in a luxurious hotel most of whose windows provided ample views of the bay and one or the other of the bridges.

Henry Wilkins had also sired a son, who had in turn provided him with a grandson—named Henry in the old man's honor. Young Henry, now an orphan and also an heir to some three million dollars' worth of stocks and securities left him by old Henry, was now twenty and a student at Stanford. Technically Henry made his home with his uncle and cousin; and if Douglas thought of it at all, he had assumed that the boy would be with Virginia at Rolling Hills. But Henry had chosen to remain at his fraternity house instead of driving home on Friday evening. Even if he had been aware of this fact, Douglas would not have interrupted his own schedule to keep his daughter company over Saturday and Sunday. Mr. and Mrs. Arnold, the caretaker and housekeeper, were always there in charge of a hired man and a pair of housemaids who, Douglas sometimes noticed, were not continuous. Once in a while Mrs. Arnold complained that it was hard to keep steady help, being five miles from town the way they were.

When Mrs. Arnold telephoned Douglas at ten that evening to announce that at ten in the morning his daughter had left the grounds in the Ford convertible set aside for her use and had not yet returned, and that she, Mrs. Arnold, had telephoned everyone who might have seen the girl and that no one had, Douglas ran his fingers irritatedly through his hair, told the housekeeper not to worry and to let him know when Virginia did come in. For a moment after he had replaced the phone Douglas intended to let it go at that. But then he thought of accidents, kidnaping, and general skullduggery and suffered a twinge of concern. Since Douglas never did anything for himself that he could get other people to do, he telephoned his attorney, who was in his own apartment playing bridge with guests and who was not delighted by the interruption. But Mr. Trumbull was well paid to cater to Mr. Forester's needs, so he only sighed inaudibly and told his client not to worry.

When by the following morning a routine police check of accident records had supplied nothing but negative information, Mr. Trumbull immediately put a firm of private detectives to work, and when by midafternoon these operatives had found nothing but the girl's automobile parked on a side road just off a main highway near the estate, the police were notified in earnest, and the hunt was on.

The head of Virginia's school reluctantly admitted that the girl was— er—difficult, and hinted that she might easily have vanished of her own free will, possibly out of sheer meanness. Virginia, it seemed, had had a hostile personality, was inclined to sulk periodically, and was at times— well, a bad influence on the other girls. It was pretty obvious that exorbitant tuition fees were all that induced the school to keep the young heiress's name on its rolls.

Douglas at first and with guileless incredulity insisted that his relationship with his daughter was of the sweetest. But the detective from the Missing Persons Bureau finally elicited the information that Virginia had resented—just a little—her father's impending marriage to a charming San Francisco widow who expected to become mistress of the country estate and "be a mother to" Virginia.

Young Henry, when questioned, had been completely blank about what might have happened to his cousin. That he could have had no direct hand in her disappearance was clear from the fact that he had been constantly in the company of one or more of his fraternity brothers all weekend.

Checking revealed that none of Virginia's personal belongings had been taken with her except for the clothing she had on, an alligator handbag, a diamond-studded wrist watch, and a string of real pearls which she wore regularly. Mrs. Arnold *thought* the girl had worn a gray flannel skirt, a pale blue sweater and a gray suede jacket, and flat black slippers with one strap; but Virginia had so many sport clothes both at home and in her closet at school, of which no one had ever taken an exact inventory, that it was difficult to be sure of what she had had on.

There was an equal vagueness on the part of all concerned as to how much money the girl might have carried in the alligator bag. Since she received a hundred dollars a month in cash for spending money, and since it was early in the month, she still might have been carrying most of it.

By Sunday evening the facts of the case and a description of the missing girl were in the possession of every police body in California and its neighboring states, to say nothing of the rest of the United States; for the ubiquity of airborne vehicles made it possible that Virginia Wilkins Forester could have been spirited away to any corner of the country or even into Canada or Mexico.

By Monday the news broke in the newspapers, and all the way from San Diego to Portland the usual quota of blond young women who were five feet four and weighed around a hundred and fifteen pounds began to be hauled in for identification by overzealous public-spirited citizens. Hotels, rooming houses, motor courts were alerted to watch for the missing heiress,

CHAPTER 2

The Shady Dell trailer park lay alongside the main coast highway between San Francisco and Los Angeles and some twenty miles from the Forester estate, outside the city limits of the former agricultural center but now increasingly industrial city of San Jose.

When an occasional cynic inquired of Mr. or Mrs. Bean as to why they had chosen to call their establishment "Shady Dell," they would point with an air of reproving surprise to the melancholy eucalyptus which stood aloof at the southeast corner of the lot and to the frowzy pepper tree which overhung the northwest corner, covering the bare earth beneath it with a litter of its own leaves, dried berries, and match-thin twigs.

The Beans had read of the missing heiress, heard about her over the radio, and even had a telephone call from the sheriff's office requesting that they check their weekend record of admissions to the park with the possibility in mind that Virginia Wilkins Forester might have lurked in some transient automobile or trailer. The police were being that thorough.

On that Monday morning Mrs. Bean was making a desultory check of her account books anyhow, and she dutifully reviewed the weekend admissions. There were the elderly couple who were touring the West in a Chevrolet club coupé pulling a little twelve-foot job which was all right for just the two of them but which didn't even have its own shower. They had pulled out on schedule Sunday morning, waving a cheerful good-by as they passed her window which looked out on the entrance driveway.

Then there were the two young men, construction workers they said they were, on their way over to the San Joaquin to a new bridge job, who had come in Sunday and got off before sunrise that very morning. They could have had a woman secreted in the trailer, but she doubted it. They'd had the space directly across from the MacLarens; and if there'd been any funny business Josie MacLaren would have managed to see or hear something and have wasted no time in hot-footing it down to report to the manager.

Sometimes Mrs. Bean grew a little tired of Josie MacLaren's role of self-appointed arbiter of the manners and morals of Shady Dell; but the MacLarens were practically a meal ticket, having been there for six months.

Josie had even entertained speculations about the young couple in space Five, two places down from her own Number Three. It was a little funny, of course, the way they pulled in on a Sunday morning two weeks ago and then the same afternoon the wife left again, to go to Los Angeles to see her mother, who had been suddenly taken sick.

Josie had tried to make something of it, especially of the fact that she hardly saw the girl that Sunday, that she never came out of the trailer at all until she drove off in the car with her husband in the afternoon. When, however, you had been in the landlord business, one way or another, as long as the Beans had, nothing people did surprised you. And the girl, Mrs. Morgan, had got back again this last Saturday. Her husband had driven in to pick her up at the bus station and brought her out before he went to work at twelve o'clock at the service station west of town.

Josie hadn't seen more than the car drive in and go out again with just the young man, Mr. Morgan, in it. In fact, she hadn't laid eyes on the wife until yesterday morning, Sunday; and she had reported aggrievedly to Mrs. Bean the way it was funny, that woman shutting herself up in her trailer with the venetian blinds down all day Saturday.

Mrs. Bean had retorted rather tartly that after riding all night in the bus from Los Angeles the poor kid was probably sleeping.

It was less than half an hour since Mrs. Bean had got rid of Josie MacLaren. Mr. Bean had run into town on business, and Josie had dropped in while Mrs. Bean was drinking a cup of coffee at the plastic-topped table by the south kitchen window, so she had felt constrained to offer the caller a cup too.

The Beans' home was also the office of Shady Dell Trailer Park, with the desk in the living room of the three-room white frame house that stood beside the arch over the entrance to the lot. The flat-topped desk beside the glass door opening on to a cement stoop from which steps led down to the driveway detracted somewhat from the homey character of the living room with its wine-colored mohair sofa and matching chair, its tapestry occasional chair, its console radio, its dark green broadloom rug, its venetian blinds, and its lamps with cream-colored silk shades; but the kitchen was roomy and conventional with red and yellow cotton drapes; and the bedroom with its hooked throw rugs, its chenille spread, and flowing dotted-swiss curtains might have been in a regular house set on a regular lawn on a regular street.

Mrs. Bean had begun to surmise that Mrs. MacLaren's dropping in so often was not due so much to interest in the hostess as to the attraction of the house itself. She suspected that Josie liked the feeling of being in an honest-to-God, immovable house instead of in a structure that was ready to roll at the first throb of a gasoline engine.

Since the Morgans were their newest steady guests, Josie MacLaren's mind had been occupied with them that morning.

"She has red hair; did you know that?"

"No, I didn't," Mrs. Bean replied, draining her coffee cup with head tilted back. She wiped her lips with a paper napkin. "I only saw her through the window the day they signed in, and she had a kerchief tied under her chin then."

"Well, she has. I was going by yesterday when she was outside kissing him good-by when he left for work at noon. I doubt"—she stressed the word—"if it's natural, judging from the rest of her."

"What's the matter with the rest of her?"

"Make-up, an awful lot of it. One of them big, dark red mouths like Joan Crawford used to wear, and I couldn't swear to it—I was too far away—but false eyelashes, I'm pretty sure. And falsies, or I miss my guess. She had on a black slipover sweater."

Mrs. Bean had crossed to the cupboard for a packet of matches, and with her back turned she muttered, "What color underpants d'she have on?"

"What's that?"

"Nothing. I was just mumbling to myself."

"Well, anyhow, the impression I got was that she's kind of cheap. Common, if you get what I mean. He's got kind of a *slicker* look himself. You know, his hair, even though it's curly and short, has that shiny-black, greasy look, and I thought his eyes were pretty close-set, and kind of a *loose* mouth; you know, too red and sort of soft for a man."

"I thought he was pretty good-looking myself."

"That's it, a little *too* good-looking, especially in them white service-station suits, makes his hair and eyes look darker than ever. And he wears that overseas-looking cap to sort of on one side." Mrs. MacLaren sighed. "Well, I hope they're all right. Don't cause any trouble. Her running off the first day and not showing up again for two solid weeks."

"If I let myself worry about the guests' private lives, I'd never get any sleep. As long as they behave themselves and don't make too much racket or get drunk and lay on the road so I stumble over 'em, I don't care what they do."

"Oh now, Mrs. Bean, you know you don't mean that. Just yesterday Mrs. Camarilla and I were saying that's one reason we've both stayed on here so long at Shady Dell. Such a nice class of people. No fights and wild parties and all like that. Believe me, both her and me have traveled around and seen a lot, both of our husbands being in work that keeps us on the move, so to speak, and believe me, you can run into some awful funny people living in trailer courts. Some awful funny people."

"You can say that again," Mrs. Bean agreed placidly—and cryptically.

Now Mrs. Bean glanced at her account book and noted that the Camarillas were, as usual, paid up a week in advance. She had expected to lose them in September or early October when the cannery season was irrevocably over for the year. Mrs. Camarilla had informed her that the previous winter they had traveled to Arizona for the winter deal in lettuce; but although Mr. Camarilla was not employed in the cannery anymore, he had seemed to find a few days' work here and there, and it looked now as if they might stay on and draw his unemployment insurance during the rainy season. Being just the two of them and living rather quietly, the Camarillas could probably afford to do that.

Well, it was nice for Josie MacLaren, having Mrs. Camarilla around, although the MacLarens would probably move on first. Putting it bluntly, Mr. MacLaren was a peddler, and he had worked the area surrounding San Jose for almost three months. Josie spoke of him as being a Salesman employed by The Company, but Mrs. Bean was pretty sure he bought his patent egg beaters, can openers, and combination potato peelers and apple slicers outright from the manufacturer and was thenceforth on his own to sink or swim with them.

Her eyes on the ledger, Mrs. Bean made a quick mental survey of her domain, and with a last cursory thought of the missing heiress dismissed her as a possible unsuspected tenant. Joan Skaggs in Number One just across the way was the only person near the right age, and the Skaggses had been here a month already. The mister ran a bulldozer for the state highway department and was working on a job east of town. His daughter

Joan was sixteen and could be called blond if you stretched the term to include washed-out light brown hair, but Mrs. Bean had seen her wait for the high school bus out front every weekday morning since the Skaggses arrived, so Joan could hardly be an heiress in disguise.

Mrs. Bean glanced out of the window and saw Mrs. Skaggs shaking a dust mop from the steps of her trailer. Mrs. Bean was glad Number One had been vacant when the Skaggses came, so their house could be parked in front in full view from the road. It gave class to the whole place, a long silver-colored job with flowered drapes and glass shelves across the windows with those little pottery skunks and Bambis and squirrels set on them so everybody could see. Of course when they were ready to roll Mrs. Skaggs took the animals down. And they kept things so neat on their lot, no automobile tools and empty bottles and cardboard grocery cartons thrown around. And the lovely new Buick sedan looked so nice pulled up under the awning beside the house. Usually Mrs. Skaggs drove him to work so she could have the car for shopping and things during the day. Mrs. Bean gazed absently at the rounded corners of the Skaggs trailer and mused enviously that there must be good money in running a bulldozer.

As she sat thus, musing, Mr. Montgomery Grandon pulled past the window in his convertible with the top up. She glanced down at her records, reminded that the Grandons were a week behind again with their rent. And there was no excuse for it, her working steady as a carhop in that drive-in, and him on steady at the card club downtown, dealing for those poker games. Monty didn't gamble himself, his wife Billie had assured Mrs. Bean virtuously; he just played for the house. At any rate, they had money, and with no kids or anything they ought to keep paid up.

On the whole, though, things were in pretty good shape. They kept Seven and Eight, which were directly behind the house and office, open for transient trade. So now only Number Two, between the Skaggses and MacLarens, was actually vacant, and that only since yesterday, when it had been a relief to get rid of that family with four kids. Now the only small child left was the Ingleborgs' Ronny in Number Six, which was conveniently right next to the small playground at the end of the park with its sand pile, swing, and teeter-totter.

Mrs. Bean raised her head, roused by the close and rather loud sound of a motor, and when she glanced out her practiced eye informed her that a Plymouth coupé eleven years old had nosed in and parked before her door. Automatically she noticed the license plate and saw that it was a Kansas one. A weather-beaten trailer almost as old as the car seemed by its superior size and weight to have pushed the automobile into the driveway. It was an old-fashioned model, insufficiently streamlined, almost square, painted dark green below and brown above, the windows covered by plain tan shades.

Mrs. Bean "placed" the whole equipage accurately. These were not pleasure travelers. They would be scouting around for work, practically any kind of work, and they would be more or less permanent, depending on how lucky they were in their quest. They wouldn't add much tone to the place, but there was nothing to do but take them in, in vacant Number Two.

As the man got out of the car on the side away from her she went to the door, fitting her business smile over her features, an uncommunicative but receptive expression that had developed of itself over the course of time.

As they spoke of rates and regulations and the facilities available at Shady Dell, Mrs. Bean noted that the man was young, in his twenties, that he was tall—what she would call gawky—and thin, with the bone structure showing through the flesh of his face. His wife remained seated in the car and through the open window watched and listened listlessly.

From a cursory glance or two Mrs. Bean learned that she was younger than the man, probably still in her teens. Her innocuous little face was framed by a characterless haircut that was neither long nor short, curling irregularly at the ends, which were turned back in shorter lengths along her temples and above her forehead.

The man came in to the desk with Mrs. Bean, and while she wrote the receipt he offered with a stilted little laugh, "We're gonna be glad to settle down for a spell. Been on the road about three weeks. Stayed around L.A. for a while, but my wife didn't like it so much there. Too big. That is, it's too far from one place to another."

"What line of work're you in?" Mrs. Bean inquired with dispassionate civility.

"Well, I was farming in Kansas. Thought I'd look into the possibilities around here. Course," he added with an apologetic half laugh, "I realize it's a different type of farming out here."

Mrs. Bean regarded him curiously. "Well, there's a lot of orchards around this country. The Santa Clara Valley, you know. Famous for prunes. But you'd probably need experience with trees. Don't 'spect you have many orchards in Kansas. But further south, toward Morgan Hill and Gilroy, there's quite a lot of truck farming, cauliflower and such."

As she followed him to the door, Mrs. Bean added kindly, "If you should get on steady at some ranch, it's lucky you havin' a trailer. You could pull right in, family and all."

She came down to the car door and acknowledged the man's introduction to his wife. "Glad to know you, Mrs. Parsons." Pointing, she went on, "Pull in right over there. Guess you know about connecting up to the lights and water and so on." Leaning forward, she pointed ahead down the drive to her left. "Case you don't have your own toilet and shower, there's the washhouse. There's a washing machine and tubs, twenty-five cents an hour, lines in the back. Any questions or anything you don't understand about gettin' hooked up, my husband'll be back in 'bout half an hour and give you a hand. He just ran into town."

"Thanks. I think we'll make out all right."

When she came back inside Mrs. Bean's eye fell on the morning paper which lay on the padded seat of the occasional chair beside the desk. She halted and picked it up, staring at the photograph on the front page captioned, "Have you seen this girl?"

Sleek, silky, and apparently natural blond hair, parted on the side and drawn back smoothly off the face, fell in a long bob not quite to the girl's shoulders, the ends just curving in a seemingly natural wave which softened the coiffure's severe sweeping lines. Her hair was the only distinctive feature about the pictured "missing" heiress. Otherwise it was just a soft young face with an average-sized nose and a conventional mouth. Even the eyes had no peculiarities as to shape or setting. All you could tell was that they were probably light-colored.

Mrs. Bean laid the paper on her desk and then slowly lifted it again. That complete lack of distinction. It was what she had noted about the Mrs. Parsons who had just driven in. Mrs. Bean frowned faintly at the picture. Give Mrs. Parsons the same hairdo and a little more lipstick and set a camera to lighting her face just so, and the result might be rather similar. Of course Mrs. Parsons had looked older. No, not older, Mrs. Bean realized suddenly, just—tired. She had put the dullness of the girl's expression down to travel fatigue.

With a slightly impatient breath Mrs. Bean dropped the paper. As far as that went, take ten pounds off Joan Skaggs, bleach her hair and let it grow a couple of inches, and you could get a photograph that wouldn't look too much different from this one. When you stopped to think of it, it was rather odd the way pretty young girls looked so much alike, their faces smooth, unformed by habitual expressions.

Looking across the desk through the window, Mrs. Bean saw the Morgans passing on foot toward the highway. She inclined her head and observed that they turned right beside the pavement. She decided they must be going down to eat at the restaurant and bar up the road.

Momentarily Mrs. Bean sympathized with Josie MacLaren's disapproval of the new tenant. Glamour at cut-rate prices was what she looked like. Her hair, cut short and curled a trifle too much, could be natural. Some people did have hair the color of fresh rust. In the brief glimpse she'd had Mrs. Bean suspected Mrs. Morgan used eye shadow—probably green— in the daytime. She didn't agree with Josie, however, that the girl wore falsies. Because that somewhat excessive fullness through the chest only made her look too thick in the body for the length of her legs. And Mrs. Bean doubted that a girl who obviously paid so much attention to her appearance would deliberately distort her figure.

What most annoyed Mrs. Bean was the mat-like texture of the girl's skin, from pancake make-up, and the lavish magenta mouth. She found herself thinking. "If she was *my* daughter—" with vague reflections about washing of faces. And then she brought herself up short, realizing she had thought of Mrs. Morgan as if the woman were a little girl messing around with a grown-up's cosmetics. Why had she thought of the girl like that, associating her with extreme youth? She must be at least twenty. She looked it, anyway.

Mrs. Bean glanced at the folded paper which was lying now with the photograph hidden and only half the headline proclaiming, "Sub-deb Missing." It was that girl, of course, and the sheriff's office phoning them to be on the lookout. You had young women on your mind. And since Joan Skaggs and this Marjorie Morgan—her husband had spoken of her as Marge—and this new Mrs. Parsons, whatever her first name was, were the only women on the lot who might conceivably be seventeen years old, you looked them over as the authorities had asked you to do. But there was no chance of her and Ira, of course, being able to collect the ten-thousand-dollar reward the paper said was being offered for "information as to the whereabouts of Virginia Wilkins Forester."

It was too bad, too. They could use ten thousand bucks. Pay off the rest of what they owed on the property, for one thing.

CHAPTER 3

When she left the Bean residence Josie MacLaren passed up her own house and walked on down the crushed-rock driveway to call on her friend, Mrs. Camarilla, in Station Number Ten at the far end of the south side of the park, opposite the playground.

It seemed lifelessly quiet in the park that morning. The car was gone from beside the egg-shaped aluminum job in Number Four, next to her own house. Number Four was always quiet. Two young fellows lived there. Plasterers, they were, working on a new store building downtown. They had resided at Shady Dell for over a month now, but they seemed only to come home a little before four o'clock to take showers in the washroom and dress up and be off. For some bar, Josie supposed. They were always filling up the garbage can with crushed beer cans.

No one was in the washroom, although she noted that Mrs. Ingleborg had a washing on the lines.

Mr. Grandon was outside wiping off the hood of his car with a rag. He wore a light maroon sport shirt and gray pants with a discernible self-check and a sharp crease.

Mrs. MacLaren paused. "Nice morning after the rain yesterday, ain't it?"

"Yeah." Monty Grandon ran the polishing cloth along the body of his car.

"How's Mrs. Grandon this morning?"

"O.K."

"I notice she started on the evening shift yesterday."

"Yeah."

"I guess you folks like that better, you starting the middle of the afternoon the way you do. Get to see more of each other."

"Yeah."

A little discouraged, Josie glanced aside and saw that Peggy Ingleborg was outside her house saying something to her son Ronald, who was pedaling back and forth across the end of the drive on a red tricycle. So she turned away to approach Peggy.

Billie Grandon opened the door and stood there in a cream-colored fuzzy robe whose hem was discolored to an uneven brown from contact with the floor. She pulled the robe tighter across her abdomen, holding it on one side.

"You had company, huh?" she observed teasingly, holding her voice throatily low. Her uncombed hair was tossed in a sensuous dark cloud about her head.

"Nosy old bag," Monty growled.

"You know what I think?" Billie said, leaning pensively against the doorframe. "I think she's lonesome. She's the kind of a dame needs neighbors. You know, steady ones. I can just see her in some little old hick town in a house with a yard where everybody sits on the front porch evenings and yells across to the people next door."

Billie's soft dark eyes roved over the domed roofs of the trailers across the way to the green puff of the pepper tree's foliage up front. "Sometimes I don't know but that's what I'd like. I sure have moved around a lot, auto courts, roomin' houses, apartments—"

Monty had finished his loving ministrations to the dark red car, and he came to stand at the foot of the steps, smiling up at the girl.

"Nah, honey, you don't want to live in no one-horse burg. We got bigger plans, remember? A classy suite in some ritzy hotel, and us with our own little high-class joint, nothin' like this damn two-bit Four Leaf Clover Club where a fifty-dollar pot's big stuff. One of these days we'll hit somethin' lucky, get a stake and hit the big town. I'll make the right connections one of these days. You'll see. May have to work for somebody else for a while like I'm doin' now, but sooner or later we'll be up in the big time with the real high-class trade, and I'll be runnin' the joint, not just dealin', and you'll be swishin' around playin' hostess in two-hundred-dollar evenin' dresses."

Billie looked down at him and smiled, skeptically but with gentleness in her dark eyes. "Keep dreaming, big boy," she said softly. "It don't cost nothin'."

Meanwhile Mrs. MacLaren had called out brightly to Peggy Ingleborg, "Well, how are you this morning?"

Peggy turned her head with the brown hair held back off her face by a yellow ribbon tied in a bow. "I'm fine. How's yourself?"

"Just fine. Nice morning, ain't it?"

"Yeah. It was good to see the sun. I got my washing out first thing. Ronald! Come back this way. You've got to stay here at the end of the driveway. You want to get run over?"

"I hear Mr. Ingleborg got on steady up at Moffett Field."

"Yeah. Finally."

"All this defense work again, I guess there'll be plenty of jobs. Well, they say it's an ill wind—" Josie concluded with a humorous sigh.

Peggy put her hands in the pockets of her denim slacks and let a short laugh issue from her unrouged lips. "Kinda horrible when you stop to think of it. Bein' glad to see another war comin' up so you'll be sure of steady work."

"Well, it ain't *our* fault."

"No. No, of course not." Peggy drew in her breath deeply. "What burns me up is we might's well have stayed in the Project in Vallejo when Eric got laid off at the shipyards last year. He could get back on now, anyway. But no, he had to sink our bond money in this damn trailer so we wouldn't have to pay rent, and then start out lookin' for work someplace else."

"Well, it's a very nice trailer," Josie said soothingly, "bigger than most."

Peggy shot a glance at the long, silvery wall of her home and declared bitterly, "I hate it. Just try livin' in one sometime with a four-year-old kid. You'll see. Can't turn around without falling over somebody. Believe me, just as soon as we get a little ahead, we're going to sell this thing for a down payment on a house. I want to live like a human being again."

"I've been living in a trailer house for five years," Mrs. MacLaren said stiffly, "and I don't know as I'm any less a human being for it."

"It's different with you. You're used to it."

Rather abruptly Josie turned away. "Well, I was just going to run in and see Mrs. Camarilla."

Her feet crunched away across the gravel, and her head was held high and a little haughtily. For some reason she was nettled.

At the end window of the Camarilla house, between the cretonne draperies, she saw the pot of pink begonias standing inside on the window sill which was also a shelf over the built-in sofa that opened into a bed.

While she waited on the metal step for admission Mrs. MacLaren became aware of the pleasing, slightly medicinal smell of the eucalyptus tree which shaded the coach. She heard the engine of Monty Grandon's car and the scrape of tires as he turned toward the highway. And then Mrs. Camarilla was opening the door and saying fluidly in the low-pitched voice which seemed always intentionally held down, "Hello, dear. Come on in."

The interior of the Camarilla trailer had a settling effect on Mrs. MacLaren's nerves. That was one reason she liked to go there.

"I swear, Stella," she said now, "I don't know how you do it. I've never been in here when everything wasn't as neat as a pin."

"It's all I have to do," Stella Camarilla said simply, but with an undertone of complacency. "Sit down, dear."

Detouring around the coffee table, Mrs. MacLaren crossed in three steps to the sofa whose back rest consisted of the two bed pillows covered by cretonne slips to match the curtains. As she sat down one hand caressed the square black satin cushion worked with a gay design in gold and orange silk thread, one of a pair standing at the ends of the seat. Sensuously she rested her feet upon the hand-hooked rug which lay before the sofa and by the pressure of her feet moved it back and forth on the waxed linoleum. Her eyes appraised the chests of drawers with glass knobs which lined one side of the sitting room, facing the paneled doors which concealed the closets. In the center the drawers dropped in a square to form a little dressing table with a mirror running to the curve of the ceiling above. Lace doilies spattered the polished tops of the chests, each serving as a parking place for some piece of bric-a-brac. On one of them a table lamp with a pleated paper shade stood ready to throw light on the armchair which faced the sofa from the middle of the trailer. On either side of the sofa were wall-bracket lights with shades to match that of the lamp on the chest.

Down at the other end of the room a potted red geranium hung on a chain high over the sink, with sunlight shining in on it through the end window. The walls at that end of the room were completely cupboard-lined, with a break at waist height which extended upward three feet to leave room for stove, sink, and worktable tops, all spotlessly bare except for the electric mixer, a pottery cookie jar, a bowl of fruit, and a gay red teakettle on the stove. Behind the armchair which faced the sofa a folding table could come down from the inside of a cupboard door. Now, however, it had done its vanishing act, as it did every night, so that the chair and coffee table could be pushed into the kitchen area to make way for the bed unfolding from the daytime seat.

"You've done so much," Josie said enviously, thinking of her own house, which, no matter what she did, always looked like something people traveled in, not like a home where people lived. "You've made it like your own home."

"It *is* my home," Mrs. Camarilla replied. She seated herself in the flounced armchair with an air of elegance actually made necessary by the restrictions of the full-length "foundation garment" that molded her Junoesque figure. She reached forward to take a cigarette from a silver-plated box on the table. Delicately she inserted the cigarette into a black holder with a silver band around it and struck a flame from the table lighter, holding it gracefully to the cigarette. The large diamond of her engagement ring—which Mrs. MacLaren was not sure was real—showed noticeably with the movements of white hands garnished with deep red nail polish.

"I suppose," she said, as if in answer to a question implied in the caller's remarks, "it's because I've been happy in our little house. Happier," she added, as if to herself, her voice harder, flatter, as she half forgot the other woman, "than I've ever been in my life." Her eyes came back to Mrs. MacLaren, and her voice went down a note, smoothed itself out. "You see, Mr. Camarilla and I bought it when we were first married. It's where we've always lived together."

"Romantic, isn't it, kind of? Keeps your honeymoon right with you, a person could say."

Mrs. MacLaren gazed at her friend with unfeigned admiration. She felt privileged, being Stella Camarilla's best friend. At least she was her best friend here in the trailer park. Anyone could tell that Stella's black hair, puffed out youthfully around her face and neck, was dyed, and that she made up rather heavily—for her age—her face powder pretty white, her cheeks pink, her mouth a strong red, but she had the manner of a lady. You felt it right away. There was something about the floor-length housecoats with V necks that she always wore at home that increased the *grande dame* air.

"That's what I feel marriage should be," Stella said softly, "one long honeymoon."

"It's all right if you can do it," Josie returned rather cynically. "And of course you and Mr. Camarilla only been married three years. I bet life wasn't one long honeymoon with your first man, not from what you told me about Mr. LaSalle."

Stella sighed. "No. But you can't go by that. I was so young, and I told you how he treated me."

Mrs. MacLaren regarded her friend with sympathetic eyes. "I know. Some men, they're just naturally brutes. I will say Fred has always been awful good to me. Not very romantic, maybe, but dependable, I will say that. And speaking of men, what"—she jerked her head toward the wall facing the Grandon trailer—"d'you make of them two, the Grandons? I'd say he was quite a bit older than her, and I wouldn't be surprised if he didn't have kind of a mean disposition. He certainly ain't very friendly."

"We've never noticed any signs of them not getting along all right. They're quiet enough. Of course they're both away all evening."

"An unnatural kind of life, if you ask me."

"Yes, I hate shift work. Thank God Mr. Camarilla hasn't had any night shifts since we've been here."

"Where is he today?"

"This is his day to report for unemployment insurance. I didn't go in because he always has to wait in line so long. We may both run back into town this afternoon to pick up some things."

This prosaic turn of the conversation was not to Mrs. MacLaren's taste, so now she leaned forward a little and demanded, "You seen Mrs. Morgan yet?"

"No, I haven't. To tell the truth, I haven't been out of the house this morning."

"Well, I haven't seen her yet this morning either." Josie was impatient to have Stella meet the girl so they could exchange impressions. She had already treated her friend to a detailed analysis of Marge Morgan's observable physical endowments, and there wasn't a great deal more to talk about until one or the other of them made her acquaintance; and sometimes that was difficult. So often people who stopped in trailer parks weren't a bit neighborly. They seemed not to care whether they ever met anybody or not, probably because they knew how impermanent any intimacy would be.

"I still think," she went on argumentatively, "it's funny, her going off like that so sudden, when they just moved in, and now all of a sudden here she is back again."

"Maybe," Stella said with a faint smile, "her mother really was sick."

Josie pursed her lips, and her eyes took on a faraway look; and then she said triumphantly, "She just doesn't look like a woman who'd have a sick mother."

Stella chuckled with real amusement. "Josie, you kill me."

"You can laugh if you want to, but like I was just saying to Mrs. Bean, I only hope they aren't the kind to make trouble."

"Well, so far they've kept to themselves enough."

"Yes, but she wasn't here. Of course," Mrs. MacLaren added with a faintly wondering respect, "you're not much of a one to be concerned about other people. I've noticed that. People don't seem to bother you much."

"If other people leave me alone, I leave them alone."

Mrs. MacLaren thought admiringly once more that that was what she liked about Mrs. Camarilla, that aloof way about her, as if she was above vulgar curiosity; so ladylike it was.

When her caller rose to go Mrs. Camarilla stood on the steps, bidding her good-by cordially. "My, it is a nice day, isn't it?" she exclaimed. "A person ought to get out, a day like this."

Suiting action to her words, she descended the steps and walked to the corner of the house with Mrs. MacLaren.

"There they are now," Josie muttered conspiratorially, although the couple she meant were only just past the Bean residence up the driveway and could not have overheard normal conversational tones. Unceremoniously she took her leave with an "I'll see you later," and hurried away to be sure of coming face to face with the Morgans, which she did opposite the entrance to the washrooms.

Stella Camarilla stood with one hand resting lightly against the trailer wall, the other on her hip in a negligent but somehow theatrical attitude. She saw Josie halt and heard her accost the strangers brightly, "I guess you're the folks in Number Five."

Stella saw the young woman regard Josie blankly, but she could not hear the man's indistinct response. The girl nodded distantly, and the pair passed Mrs. MacLaren.

Josie walked on with her shoulders straight, her head held higher than usual.

"Mad as a wet hen," Stella thought amusedly but not unkindly.

Made curious by Josie's comments, Stella had taken as good a look as she could get of Mrs. Morgan from a distance of some forty feet, but she failed to see anything to cause such mistrust as Josie MacLaren had expressed. She realized, though, that it was a form of entertainment for Josie, thinking about other people. For herself, she could see nothing alarming in the girl's heavy make-up, nor even in her quick disappearance after taking up residence here. If you had a family, she supposed they were likely to make sudden demands on your time. Herself, she was just as glad that since her older sister's death some years ago she had no one but Tony. Her nieces she saw so infrequently that they didn't count.

She glanced at her small jeweled wrist watch and thought that he would be getting back pretty soon. She would go in and start lunch, she guessed.

As she turned she found that Ronald Ingleborg had approached her and was peering upward hopefully.

"Got any more cookies?" he demanded.

She smiled and touched his hair. "I'm sorry, honey. Not a one left. Maybe if I go to town this afternoon I'll get some more."

"O.K.," he said seriously, and without further dalliance started back to the tricycle abandoned beside the little playground.

Inside again, Stella turned on the radio built into the cupboard over the let-down table. A late-morning newscast was on, and she listened idly as she tuned it in more clearly. "—no further clues in the disappearance of socialite Virginia Forester. A reward of ten thousand dollars has been offered by her father, Douglas Forester, for information—" Stella's fingers, twisting experimentally on the knob, blurred the next words in a blast of noise, and when the station was clear again she heard only a fragment: "—beautiful blond heiress, missing since last Saturday morning—"

Thoughtfully she turned her head and looked out of the end window across the potted begonia. Saturday morning. Saturday. She had been walking back after emptying garbage in one of the large cans behind the washhouse, returning down the driveway instead of along the path behind the trailers. Incuriously she had noticed the Morgan car turning into its parking place across the way. Her only reflection had been, as she saw the kerchief-covered head of a woman in the front seat, that Mrs. Morgan must have got back. That had been some time between eleven and eleven-thirty.

With eyes still thoughtful she leaned over and mechanically picked up a cigarette from the open box on the coffee table. With equal abstraction she lighted it and inhaled.

Maybe Josie had something. Maybe something funny was going on. According to Josie, the girl had spent only a few hours here in the park on the Sunday two weeks before, and no one had had a good look at her.

Absently Stella touched her hair, delicately pushing at the ends. A blonde. And now Marjorie Morgan's hair was a bright henna. That would be easy; something a woman could do herself, even to the casual, curly feather cut the henna now glorified. A good rachel powder base, a lipstick brush to widen and extend the mouth, a good grade of mascara, and an eyebrow pencil discreetly used. And Josie's charge of falsies. Maybe Josie wasn't so dumb after all. In the brief glimpse she'd had of the girl today Stella had gained the impression of a rather pudgy figure. Squinting her eyes, Stella tried to visualize that figure with a less fulsome bust; and it seemed to her the result would be better proportioned, although still not much of a shape, one more on straight-up-and-down, boyish lines.

Ten thousand dollars.

But of course it couldn't be. That would be too much luck. But it was possible. But definitely possible. The boy was good-looking; and he was what he said, she was pretty sure, a service station attendant. So a spoiled brat with her own car to drive fell for him. Her family would raise hell, naturally. So she takes this way of running off with him, works it so her family can't get at her to break it up.

Possible, even probable.

Ten thousand dollars would be very nice. Tony worried so much. Especially when he was out of work, even though with just the two of them they could get by. But the car wouldn't last forever, and sooner or later she would run out of clothes. And there was always sickness to worry about. With ten thousand dollars they could invest part of it, have some security for the future. It would be nice to be able to do that for Tony.

She moved to the end of the trailer and put one knee on the seat, gazing out of the window meditatively.

The only thing was, if *she* could catch on, so could other people. Josie, for instance, already had the wind up. But not along those lines. Josie might never catch onto the real situation.

As she stared ruminatively out of the window Mrs. Bean passed, walking toward the end of the lot, rather stiff-legged, her hands in the pockets of the gray coat sweater she always wore over figured house dresses cut on a shirtmaker pattern, her gray hair as usual uncovered, combed straight back in a slight natural wave to end in mannish shingled ends that fit the curve of her head.

The Beans would be the natural ones to catch on if anything was not on the up-and-up, but this sight of Mrs. Bean was reassuring. Plain, practical, unimaginative, neither of the Beans paid much attention to their tenants as people. And if they had had suspicions, they would have acted already.

Swiftly Mrs. Camarilla's mind ran over the occupants of the other trailers. None of the others took any interest in one another. They lived shut up in their own affairs. So Josie was the only one she had to worry about beating her to it, and if Josie began to get wise she wouldn't have sense enough to keep it to herself. She'd come blatting it out to her friend Stella the first thing, thus giving her ample warning.

So she would take her time. Because suppose she rushed to the authorities right off and Marge Morgan really was just that: Marjorie Morgan. It would make Stella Camarilla look damn foolish and be pretty embarrassing all the way around.

As she stood with her hands on the window sill, one knee on the seat, their own club coupé drove past and turned into the parking space beside the trailer. Tony was home. With a pleased relaxation of her face she turned toward the door in welcome.

They embraced and kissed each other, and she took his hat and stowed it on the shelf in the long narrow closet.

"They didn't have nothin'," he said glumly, lowering himself into the armchair.

"Well, you got your unemployment check, didn't you?"

"Yeah. I got that all right. I dunno, maybe we should've gone south last month. This place is dead as hell this time of year."

"When your unemployment runs out," she said cheerfully, "we can take off for Arizona if you want, or Imperial or someplace. Why kill yourself working when you don't have to?"

She bent over and kissed his grizzled, curly hair and then smiled into his face, thinking again what a good-looking man he was, with his large straight nose and the square chin with a cleft in it. And to be so good, so gentle and unassuming along with it. Usually it ruined a man, being handsome, made him think everybody ought to dance attendance on him day and night, and as for sticking to one woman, being straight and on the level with her, well, it didn't happen once in a blue moon. She knew.

It was still a source of wonder to her, getting Tony. It was true, like it said in the song, "A good man is hard to find," and if sometimes she had to fight back the thought that Tony would have got farther in the world if he'd been just a little bit brighter, well, a person couldn't have everything, and as far as that went, she could think for both of them if it came to that.

"I'll warm up some soup," she said efficiently.

"I was thinking," he said, "how'd you like to go in town later on, and we could eat at Kress's or Newberry's 'fore they close, and go on to a show."

Stella would have preferred to find an excuse to meet Mrs. Morgan that afternoon, but she knew how it was; Tony got restless, not working, and the day the check came it made you want to spend a little, so she agreed readily. "O.K. We'll just have some soup now and get dressed after while and maybe window-shop a little and have an early dinner."

A definite plan had occurred to her even while she spoke. Instead of buying store cookies today with the Ingleborg kid in mind, she'd bake homemade ones in the morning and in the afternoon take some over to the Morgan dame, a nice, neighborly gesture to someone who'd just moved in.

Mr. Camarilla had brought that day's newspaper home with him, and after lunch Stella put on her reading glasses and carefully perused the front-page story about Virginia Forester. Tony had dozed off for a moment in the armchair, his head against the back, his lips slightly parted. She let the paper fall to her lap and slowly removed her glasses, which had a gold design running through the broad plastic frames.

Painstakingly she reconstructed the way it could have been. The boy had changed jobs two weeks ago, been transferred to San Jose from a peninsula station. He might have been living in a trailer right along, or he could have bought it before he moved. It would be easy enough for the girl to get away for a few hours that one day, since nobody had seemed to look after her much, if one judged by the fact that the day she disappeared nobody noticed she was gone until evening. So two weeks before she really took off, they could have established a new identity for her, whisking in and out with nobody getting a good look at "Mrs. Morgan," her face made up the way it was now and her still-blond hair covered by a head scarf.

So the boy picks her up on the road this past Saturday, whisks her back in again, and she spends the day cutting her hair and giving it a strong rinse and putting it up in pin curls.

If this reconstruction were true, it would be quick work for the police to verify it. The first thing, they could check on where Bill Morgan had lived previously and whether he had been married then, and on the address of the nonexistent mother.

Stella frowned. The police. She had nothing to fear from them. There was, in fact, no way in which they could connect the former Stella LaSalle with the present Mrs. Anthony Camarilla, who would certainly be front-page news if her disclosures led to apprehension of the missing heiress. Even if she was wrong and Marjorie Morgan was proved to be on the level, nothing would come of it as far as she was concerned.

But it was hard to overcome past habits and attitudes; and one of the most deeply engrained of these was the tendency to stay clear of dealings with the law. After the years she had put in outwitting the police without letting them catch on that she was doing it, and even being hauled in once or twice and being released for lack of evidence, a person didn't lightly run to them even for the sake of ten thousand dollars.

It was silly of her, of course. Nothing would happen except possible bad publicity, even if she was wrong. But silly or not, she decided to hold off awhile until she was sure.

For another thing, she thought with an indulgent glance at the napping man, Tony would be mortified to death if she stirred up a stink like that here in Shady Dell and it turned out there was nothing to it. And if, by any long, wild chance, the glare of publicity should reflect back into her past life, there were things that Tony didn't know and which she wouldn't want revealed. Newspaper reporters would undoubtedly interview her, and with newspapermen you couldn't be sure. Some of them moved around almost as bad as fruit tramps. Two or three times she had figured unimportantly in the news, and it would be just her luck to run up against some reporter with a long and photographic memory.

For ten thousand dollars, though, she would gladly take what was, after all, such a minor risk. Not for herself, but for Tony. It would mean so much to him, a lump of cash like that. For herself, she was content as they were: snug, self-contained, and, above all, quiet and at peace here.

But she must be sure so that everything would go quickly and smoothly and not stir up a stink of bad feeling such as being wrong would do, forcing her and Tony to pick up and pull out in embarrassed disgrace. It was strange how as she got older people's good opinion meant so much to her, even the good opinion of people like the Beans and Josie MacLaren, whom they would probably never see again after they left Shady Dell.

CHAPTER 4

The next morning the Camarillas slept late after their evening with the double feature, and after breakfast Tony wandered away outside, and since he did not come back in a few minutes Stella decided with satisfaction that he had found Mr. Bean around somewhere to talk to. When her housework was finished she set about making cookies. Mrs. Skaggs, she remembered Josie telling her, had offered to take the latter shopping with her today, so she did not expect to be interrupted by Josie.

While Stella mixed cookie batter, next door the Grandons were dawdling over coffee and cigarettes, still in their dressing gowns. This was Billie's day off, and they were discussing plans for the day in a lethargy not yet dispelled by the breakfast coffee.

"I wish," Billie was saying in a disgruntled tone, "you could get the same day off I do. We never get to go no place or do nothing."

"You can't always work it," he said irritably. "And we been lucky about it up to now."

"I'll drive you down and keep the car and pick you up after work," she said irrelevantly. "I'll do a little shopping before the stores close, and then I guess I'll eat out somewhere and see a show. Hope there's somep'n good on."

"I'm gettin' off at twelve. We can stop somewhere for a drink."

"O.K. At least it'll give me an excuse to dress up. In the meantime," she sighed, casting a glance over the tumbled bed and the cluttered sink and stove, "I'll clean this joint up and do the washing."

"I'll put the bed up," he offered magnanimously.

"Thanks, that's big of you."

"What'sa matter with you this morning? Sound'sif you got up on the wrong side of the bed."

"What d'you mean, the wrong side? There's only one side *to* get out of in this cracker box."

"Whose idea was it," he inquired coldly, "getting a trailer so's we could save the rent and get a stake ahead?"

"O.K., O.K. Forget it."

It was one o'clock by the time Billie, dressed in slacks and a boyish plaid shirt, walked over to the laundry room carrying their washing wrapped in a sheet, leaving Monty stretched out on the built-in seat smoking and reading a *True Crime Detective* magazine. When she walked into the cement-floored main room of the little building she came face to face with Marjorie Morgan, who was standing in the middle of the floor, apparently looking the place over.

"'Lo," Billie said carelessly, and went to drop her bundle on the old kitchen table beside the squatty automatic washer.

"Hullo," the red-haired girl responded, and stepped back a little uncertainly.

"You're the folks in Number Five, ain't you?" Billie observed amiably, untying the knotted sheet.

"Uh-huh."

"I'm Billie Grandon, across the way, Number Nine."

"Oh. I'm Mrs. Morgan."

"Yeah, we met your husband. At least Monty—that's my husband—and him've talked to each other outside. You been away, huh?"

"Yes. My mother was sick."

"Tough." Billie was expertly sorting clothes, stuffing white things into the round opening of the machine. "What was the matter?"

"Pneumonia."

"She all right now?"

"Yes, she got over it."

There was silence for a moment while Billie measured out soap and dumped it into the top of the machine. As she glanced at the other girl curiously, Mrs. Morgan asked, "Mind if I watch?"

"No. Not at all. Didn't you ever use one of these?"

"No."

"Had the old-fashioned kind, huh, with a wringer?"

"Yes."

"Well, there's nothin' to it, see? Close the door, turn it to whatever temperature you want the water, and that's it. Come back in half an hour and it's done. I always do out my stockin's an' undies an' stuff by hand in the stationary tubs while the white stuff's running. We don't have much, 'cause the restaurant has my uniforms done, and we send out Monty's shirts. He wears the colored kind that have to be dry-cleaned."

Marge Morgan withdrew her eyes from the clothes whirling past the circle of glass in the machine door, and let them rest on Billie. "I see."

Billie drew a package of cigarettes from her shirt pocket and shook some loose, holding them out. Her eyes were curious as she invited, "Smoke?"

The girl reached out and took a cigarette. When Billie had lighted it for her Mrs. Morgan asked consideringly, "You work?"

"Sure. What else can you do? I'd go nuts sittin' around all day."

The other nodded thoughtfully.

Billie leaned against the table, one arm across her body, its hand supporting the elbow of the other arm, which held the cigarette to her face. "What do you do?" she inquired sociably.

"Why, nothing, right now."

"I mean when you're working—or"—Billie paused and eyed her curiously—"haven't you ever worked?"

"Well, no. Not regularly."

"I see." Billie tapped the ashes off her cigarette onto the floor. "I suppose you got married as soon as you were out of school."

"Yes, that's it."

"So did I. But I been workin' ever since. Not," she added defensively, "that I *have* to, y'understand. Monty makes good money. But you get ahead faster, both workin'. We don't intend to be livin' in a trailer all our lives."

"That's a thought," Mrs. Morgan said, dispassionately surveying the other.

Billie dropped her cigarette and stepped on it. "Well, I better rub out these things I have to do by hand."

The other girl also dropped her cigarette and stepped on it. "I'll run along now. I'm glad to have met you."

"Sure. We'll be seein' each other."

"Yes."

When Billie returned to her home she said to Monty, "I was talkin' to that Mrs. Morgan in the washroom. She's a character. Dopey, kind of. I don't think she's very bright. Just kept lookin' at me kind of blank and sayin' yes an' no."

"He seems like a good guy."

"Oh, I guess they're all right. She's not bad-looking. Gets herself up snappy, I'll say that. Every eyelash in place. And I mean in place. Store-bought. She's never worked, she told me. Prob'ly her folks were pretty well off."

"Maybe we should get together with 'em sometime. Have a few drinks or somep'n."

"Got your eye on her already, huh?" Billie observed tartly.

"There ya go. Christ, I ain't even had a good look at the dame an' you're startin' in already."

"Experience is a great teacher. So they tell me," she concluded acidly.

"O.K.," he said angrily. "So who is it's always cryin' about we don't have enough social life? We oughta know people, have friends like other people. So I suggest somep'n, what happens? Right off, your goddamn jealousy pops up."

"O.K. Can it. So if I'm jealous, whose fault is it, I'd like to know?"

"So all right. I step out on you once, an' all the rest of my life I gotta hear about it." He flung the magazine toward his feet and glared at her hopelessly. Then he ran a hand over his sleek, thinning dark hair. "What's the matter with us, baby? We didn't used to be always beefin'."

"I dunno."

"It's livin' this way, I guess. It ain't normal. No privacy. We get in each other's hair. We need a hunk of cash, that's what we need. Maybe I should quit horsin' around. Get into a few games on my own, pick up a stake."

"We had that all out," she reminded him sharply. "You're in the business, you keep your nose clean. You deal 'em, let the suckers play 'em."

"Yeah," he said, "but I'm no sucker. The cards'll behave for me."

"Sure, an' the first thing you know you'll get in a game with somebody that can handle 'em just a little bit better than you can, and then where are we? No, the guys that run the games don't gamble. Once you start that, you're through. You know as well as I do the only way to get set up for yourself is to play 'em straight an' close to your chest. And we're on the way. We got a thousand tied up in the trailer and we got over a thousand saved."

"Peanuts," he interpolated glumly. "In one decent game I could build it up to ten or twenty."

"Look," she said patiently, "you know how that stuff goes. Start depending on making it that way, and you'll never quit, and we'll never get a business of our own. It happens every time. You've seen 'em. Look at Charlie Flores and Nick Evans. I could name you a dozen more. They could of stuck to their knitting and been someplace today, but what are they? Bums, just bums."

With a smile he leaned forward and grasped her hand, pulling her down on the couch beside him.

"O.K., honey, you win. Guess you'll keep me honest in spite of myself."

"Maybe we oughta say I'll keep you *dis*honest," she said ruefully. "Isn't it you who always says the only guy that never loses is the man that owns the table?"

"O.K., baby, we'll go on playing for the sure thing—the table."

"That's my smart boy." She laughed as he pulled her closer and kissed her.

CHAPTER 5

When Marjorie Morgan left the washroom she stood for a moment outside, looking up and down the driveway with its silent, boxlike houses up off the ground on wheels, separated from one another by the vacant spaces where their automobiles stood at night. Down at the end a little boy stood with his face against the high woven-wire fence, staring at a tractor chugging down the length of a moist brown field. She glanced at her wrist before she remembered she wasn't wearing her watch.

Out of the second trailer from the front on her own side of the driveway she saw a figure emerge carrying something wrapped in a newspaper. The girl wore jeans, a cardigan sweater, and flat sandals. Idly Marge watched her come down the driveway. Their eyes met across the distance, then the stranger dropped her own and did not again look straight at Marge. She turned beside the washhouse, and Marge heard the clink of the garbage can's lid. As the girl returned empty-handed, she cast another glance at Marge, again looked away self-consciously, and hurried up the driveway, holding her sweater closed over her chest.

At least that one didn't try to strike up an acquaintance, Marge mused wryly. Colorless little thing she was, no personality. And a pretty crummy-looking trailer she had. Marge glanced at her own abode. Not cute like hers and Bill's. Theirs was a regular little dollhouse. She supposed she ought to fix it up some with drapes besides the venetian blinds. Flowers would help, but—her eyes raked the bare surroundings—she didn't know where to get any. There were a few geraniums around the house in front and a flowering shrub beside its door, but she supposed they belonged to the landlord. And there was a climbing rosebush on the fence behind their coach, but it wasn't blooming now. You could always buy flowers, but she wasn't sure Bill would approve. He had harped so on how they had only so much money and had to economize. Economize. She smiled a little, repeating the word in her mind.

Slowly she crossed and entered the trailer, noting by the alarm clock that it was one-thirty. Brief calculation determined that this meant seven hours before Bill returned. She drew a deep breath, and then her eyes fell on the couch seat. A steel frame could be pulled out from under it, and the mattress unfolded upon that to make a double bed. A sensuous smile curved the widely reddened lips as she reflected that it was worth while waiting for the evening.

She picked up a copy of the magazine *Mademoiselle* and sat on the couch with her back against the cupboard at the end, her knees drawn up with the magazine open against them. Idly she scanned the advertisements and finally chose an article to read. When she finished it, she looked at the clock again. Five minutes to two. How slowly the time passed.

Her head turned alertly at the sound of steps on the gravel outside; then she sat up straight as she heard a knock at the door. Scrambling off the seat, Marge cast a quick, inspecting glance at herself in the mirror on the back of the closet door which had been left standing open. With one hand she pushed it closed and opened the outside door.

Stella Camarilla stood on the step in a flowered white jersey dress, holding a plate daintily covered by a napkin.

"I hope you'll pardon me for intruding," she said in her most mellifluous tones, smiling with dignified yet gracious restraint, "but I made cookies this morning, and I just thought, you being sort of a new neighbor, you might say—"

Insinuatingly she held the plate forward, and blankly Marge regarded it before her hand went out to accept the offering.

"I'm Mrs. Camarilla," Stella smiled, "in Number Ten."

"Uh, thank you. It's—it's very kind of you." Marge looked down at the embroidered napkin and said uncertainly, "You'll want your plate back. I'll put the cookies somewhere."

"Oh, no hurry. You can bring it back any time. I just thought you might be a little lonesome here all by yourself."

This character with the too black hair and the rayon jersey draped in folds over her bust where the white flesh came together in a crease just kept standing there with her air of pseudo-elegance, smiling with restrained expectancy, and Marge remembered the hours—six and a half of them now—that still had to go by. And besides, she found herself a little curious.

So she smiled rather stiffly and stepped aside. "Won't you come in?"

"Well, for just a moment." Daintily Stella stepped up in her high-heeled black sandals with the ankle straps. She had dressed carefully for this excursion.

"What a lovely, roomy place you have," she exclaimed politely.

Marge glanced about at the nine by five feet of floor space between the walls lined with the built-in necessities of living, and shot a suspicious glance at her caller. Then she motioned toward the seat under the end window, whose sides were provided by the walls of two chests of drawers. There were no loose armchairs in the Morgan establishment. As Stella seated herself elegantly and crossed her ankles, Marge lifted the napkin and said with real enthusiasm, "They look good."

"They go nice with a cup of tea in the afternoon," Stella observed blandly.

Marge shot her an oblique glance under sweeping lashes as she set the plate on the drainboard. "Would you care for some tea?" she responded, taking the hint.

"Why, that would be lovely—if it's not too much trouble."

"No, not at all." Rather awkwardly, conscious of the woman's observation, Marge turned on the electricity under the tea kettle; but as she got down cups and put tea in the cheap little pot, she began to enjoy herself, and while her back was turned she grinned rather impishly at the thought of herself in the role of hostess serving tea. The self-confidence which had temporarily deserted her returned. Shaking out a large paper napkin, she approached Stella and unhooked a panel from the wall, letting it down to be supported by a metal bracket so that it made a side table convenient to the caller's hand. Then with a flourish she spread the napkin on it and observed gaily, remembering to be careful of her language, "Ain't it a riot, the way everything pulls down and slides out and pushes in and shuts itself up in these here trailer houses?"

Stella so far forgot herself as to give the girl a sharp scrutiny, startled by the sudden nasal tones. But then she realized Mrs. Morgan had hardly said a dozen words up to now. She might have been mistaken in thinking there had been a different quality in the girl's voice before.

But she replied equably, "They sure do make 'em compact."

As Marge went back to the stove she glanced over her shoulder to inquire, "Lemon or cream?"

"Nothing, please. I take it straight."

Marge set the cookies and the teapot on the table and pulled up a straight chair. She emptied three spoonfuls of sugar into her cup and stirred while she looked over at Stella expectantly, as if wondering, "What now?"

Stella bestirred herself and began to talk about Shady Dell. The more, and the less inquisitively, *she* talked first, the more she might get out of the girl later.

"It isn't," she went on to say after a few introductory comments, "the very best type of trailer park. A little too bare. Some we've stayed in have grass and landscaping and everything. But it's small, and that's an advantage, less noise and cars pulling in and out—"

The girl sat listening, eating one cookie after another and washing them down with sips of tea. Stella glanced surreptitiously at the diminishing stack, and the girl noticed the glance.

"Jeepers," she said. "I guess I better leave a few for Bill. They're awfully good." She turned her head and glanced about seekingly. "Would you like a cigarette? Oh, there they are." She rose and fished a flattened package from under a cushion on the couch. Rummaging on a shelf among combs, boxes of hairpins, and hand lotion, she found a paper packet of matches.

Stella thrust her hand into a shallow pocket concealed at the seam of her dress and drew out her holder. Now, she thought, she could start getting down to business.

"You're a bride?" she said archly.

"Sort of." Marge regarded the older woman with a look of bland innocence from eyes made violet by the shadows of long lashes. "I suppose you've been married for years and years."

"Oh no, dear. Only three years."

"Second marriage, I suppose."

"Why, yes, as a matter of fact, it is. This is your first, I presume," she added with a slightly ominous additional sweetness.

"Naturally. Do I look old enough to have been married three or four times?"

Stella cast the ashes from her cigarette into the saucer of her teacup and murmured laughingly, "Of course I didn't mean that. As a matter of fact, I was just thinking how young you looked. How old are you, anyway—if you don't mind telling?"

"I don't if you don't," Marge retorted lazily, her eyes resting blandly on the other's face.

Stella's skin seemed even whiter than its coating of protective powder, and the edges of her lips seemed to become outlined more clearly. There was the barest of pauses before she purred, "Oh now, dear, you can see I'm past the age where I tell."

Marge drew up one foot and placed the heel on the edge of her chair, linking her hands around her knee, the cigarette between her fingers.

"I don't see why you should mind. These days glamorous grandmas seem to be all the rage. Every magazine you pick up, there's photographs of some movie star with a shoulder-length bob, wearing a sun suit and dandling a grandchild on her dimpled knees." She lifted her cigarette and took a puff. "Personally, I always figure those pictures must be touched up plenty. Judging from them, *I* could even be a grandma. You aren't by any chance, are you?"

Stella's face was a mask, but her fingers trembled on the cigarette holder. "I'm not that lucky," she said thickly.

"I'll bet," Marge said ingenuously, "you were a career woman. You have that sort of a sophisticated look."

"You flatter me," Stella said, the harshness close to the surface of her soft, sweet voice. She stood up suddenly. "But I must be running along. I had no idea I'd stayed so long."

Marge also rose. "Well, I'm sure glad you dropped in," she declared nasally. "And thanks a million for the cookies. Here, I'll give you your plate and napkin."

As Stella made her way to the door Marge slid the remaining cookies onto a plate from the shelves behind her and dusted Stella's plate off with her hand.

"They were awful good," she said politely.

"I'm glad you liked them. And thank you for the nice tea."

Stella stepped carefully down the bars of the metal steps, and swept off with her head held gracefully erect.

As she closed the door Marge's eyes gleamed triumphantly. "Guess that'll hold you," she thought to herself.

On the way to her own doorstep Stella got her vexation under control. Such rudeness. The little pipsqueak turning the tables and cross-examining *her*. Bold, brazen, no upbringing; that was for sure. No manners a-tall. Stella's step faltered a moment. Was that what you would expect from a gently reared young heiress from a swell private school, one who'd had all the advantages, such rude, common behavior to a guest? And her speech. Sometimes she sounded like a regular lady, and then again that coarse, inelegant way of talking slipped out. One of them was an act. But which one? Stella frowned to herself, hesitating at the foot of the steps. Still, they said those rich girls were regular hellcats, some of them, knew everything in the book by the time they were sixteen. That sly, bold manner this one had shown, deliberately needling an older woman who, on top of everything else, was her guest! Stella couldn't believe that breeding would so far forget itself. After all, she'd always heard that good manners became second nature to the upper crust. And that one—regular little tart, she was. It showed.

Of course, Virginia's grandfather, Henry Wilkins, had started out as a roustabout in the early-day oil fields in California and, according to legend, had died still a pretty rough, crude character, unpolished by the fortune he had acquired on the way up to being president of his own company. Maybe the coarseness had never quite been ground down, even now in the third-generation granddaughter. Her not being a lady might not mean anything.

Her thoughts shaken with uncertainty, Stella went on in to have a game of canasta with Tony as she had promised to do after her call.

Back in her own domicile, Marge cleaned up the tea-things and retired to the couch again with her magazine. In an hour she had exhausted all of its contents that interested her. She sighed as she looked at the clock once more. Just past three-thirty. Rummaging around, she found the package of cigarettes with one left in it. Listlessly she lighted it. Well, now she could walk down the highway to the cluster of buildings that served as a sort of business district: an open-front market, a service station, a restaurant and bar, where she could buy cigarettes, some fruit, a carton of milk, and slices of cold meat for sandwiches. Bill ate his dinner at a lunch counter across from the station. Again she calculated times. If she stretched it out she might make these activities last until five. So she supposed she'd better buy a pocket-sized novel off the rack in the market to keep her busy till eight-thirty. One thing you could say, it looked as if she was going to get plenty of reading done.

With deliberate leisureliness she arranged her hair and checked her makeup. The sun's rays were warm and slanting as she started down the driveway. Traffic roared out beyond on the highway, and the tractor still sputtered in the background, but here in the trailer court it was incredibly still. As she passed Number Two she glanced up and in the rear window saw the face of the pale blond girl. Their eyes met again, and instantly the face with the uncombed blond hair was pulled back out of sight as if by invisible strings.

"I'll bet," Marge conjectured, "she's bored too." She dismissed the thought that they might share and thus exorcize their boredom. She couldn't imagine having a thing in common with that frumpy little creature.

At the next parking space, Marge noted, there were at least signs of life. A bloated black sedan stood with its doors open toward the shining, streamlined trailer while two women lingered beside it with their arms full of packages, their veiled hats bobbing at each other animatedly. As Marge passed, Josie MacLaren pushed the rear door closed with her elbow and chirruped over her burden of brown paper bags, "I sure do appreciate your taking me along today."

Mrs. Skaggs pushed the front door closed with an efficient movement of her hip. "Not at all," she said briskly. "I was glad to have you. Any time."

"Well, I had a lovely time —"

Then they noticed Marge passing, her eyes taking them in.

Mrs. Skaggs nodded cordially. "How d'you do."

Marge nodded and murmured politely and passed out of their field of vision.

When she came out of the grocery and fruit stand, her own brown paper bag in her arms, she saw the cumbersome, bright yellow school bus stopping across the street. Three young people carrying books darted across the highway in front of her as traffic on both sides halted to let them pass. Marge was not far behind the trio as they walked along the packed earth beside the pavement, their voices shrill but the words indistinguishable over the incessant *swoosh* of passing vehicles.

Idly Marge surveyed them, her attention directed first toward the male member of the group, a tall boy with sandy crew-cut hair, a purple and white satin-finished jacket with knitted waist, neck and cuff bands hanging loosely on his narrow shoulders, pants the shade of army "pinks" rolled up to reveal blinding cerise-colored "fluorescent" socks above thick-soled blue suede shoes. A mere child, she dismissed the male disdainfully.

The girl on his right, toward the highway, was Japanese. She wore a pleated plaid skirt and a bright red jacket and had a little red bow in her short black hair that curled spreadingly on the ends. She seemed to giggle a lot and occasionally took little bouncing, skipping steps in her saddle oxfords and heavy white socks.

Marge surmised that she must live down the side road off the highway.

The back of the girl on the inside gave one hardly anything to notice or speculate about. A gray sweater above a straight skirt and ballet-type slippers. Her straight, light brown hair had a feather cut, and she didn't seem to be built very well.

With some surprise Marge saw this girl turn away from the others, looking over her shoulder with a smiling word to her companions, and walk under the arch of Shady Dell.

Without meaning to, Marge quickened her steps, and as she passed the end of the first trailer in the row, she looked in and saw the girl taking the two shallow steps in one bound and heard her call out, "Hi, Mom, got anything to eat?"

Marge was still looking back as the door slammed behind the girl. She walked slowly, and there was an unseeing expression in her eyes. She could still hear the flat, cheerful words, "Hi, Mom, got anything to eat?" with their note of assurance that meant the girl knew Mom would be there and that there would be something to eat.

The little boy from the trailer at the end stood at the corner of his house, stuffing cookies into his mouth.

"Hi," he said thickly.

"Hi, kid." She looked him over dispassionately and stood still to look around her. The space occupied by the Grandon car was empty, and although its car stood beside it the Camarilla place looked deserted. Neat shadows lay to the east of each structure. With a dry, brushing sound the trailing boughs of the eucalyptus moved slightly, pensively, silvery in the late afternoon sun. A radio squawked unintelligibly from the Ingleborg trailer. The tractor droned hoarsely at the far end of the field. And the sound of the highway traffic was like the steady, unnoticed pulsation of surf at the seashore. In an hour or so the sun would be gone. It wouldn't matter whether you were outdoors or in. But now the day was gently inviting. There should be something to keep a person out in it.

Marge turned her back slowly on her own residence and looked toward the arch. As she stood so, Joan Skaggs crossed the driveway, eating something that she held in one hand and with a step that was half skip, half run, mounted the steps of the Bean house and held her finger to the bell. Standing there, she continued to eat, facing down the driveway, of necessity seeing the other girl standing there watching her.

Marge turned away, and her eyes fell on the child who was carefully stowing two cookies in one pocket of his jeans. She whirled full around and went into the trailer.

CHAPTER 6

A little later at the Forester country home four people sat or roamed restlessly about the sunken living room, whose east windows looked out across the busy valley where long strips of highway and the untidy outlines of residential developments were softened by the broad squares of orchard foliage interspersed among them.

No one, however, was enjoying the view. The dark, polished floor broken by softly figured oriental rugs was the main object of contemplation by the room's occupants. In its effort to achieve an air of dignity and age the room had turned out rather dark, with its maroon-colored draperies, its occasional wall tapestries, its heavily framed landscapes done in greens and browns, its velvet-covered, vaguely antique, deep sofas and armchairs.

It was the cocktail hour, but even the lighted floor lamps and the fire blazing under the darkened old bricks of the mantel did not bring cheeriness to the long, ponderously elegant apartment.

Young Henry had driven down from Stanford after classes, and he sat on the raised hearth, facing the others, his knees apart, his pants legs pulled up so that his gay wool socks showed above rubber-soled brogues. A cigarette dangling from the hand hanging between his legs sent up a slim column of smoke which he watched with lusterless eyes.

From under her lashes Madeline Cummins watched her fiancé nervously. Her half-full cocktail glass stood neglected on the coffee table before her. For the sixth time in half an hour she ran her fingers over the smooth contours of her coiffure, as if to reassure herself that they were still intact. And then she smoothed the fine suede of her dark green suit skirt.

Mr. Trumbull, who had felt obliged to drop all other business and devote himself to the Forester case, leaned back in the down-filled cushions of a golden-brown chair and wearily took a swallow of his drink. If they'd just cut out the incessant talk. Everything had been said, every conjecture made, every possibility torn apart and put back together again. He felt as if he were going mad.

Douglas came pacing back from the broad steps terraced down from the entrance hall. He held his glass in both hands, turning it jerkily in his fingers.

"No," he said, as if pursuing an argument, although no one had spoken for a good thirty seconds, "I'm beginning to believe something has happened to her, that"—he surveyed them all solemnly—"she's met with foul play. How else can you explain it? She wouldn't *do* this to me—to us— put us through this hell, this agony."

Madeline thought to herself, "Oh, wouldn't she? Headstrong, opinionated little brat. Precocious, too." But she murmured soothingly, "Darling, you mustn't distress yourself. You know what I've contended right along. Amnesia."

Mr. Trumbull stared at the rug and tried not to hear. How long could they continue saying the same things over and over, each time with an air of having just thought of them? At first he had suspected kidnaping, but if it were that, they'd have had a communication by now. So there was nothing but the obvious: Virginia had been picked up, attacked, and killed. It happened all the time. But of course you couldn't tell them that. All you could do was wait for the body to be found.

"My own opinion is," Henry was announcing with youthful pompousness, "there's a man mixed up in it. She's just damn well run off with some punk."

"How could she?" his uncle snapped. "We've checked on every boy she knew."

"Well, she might have known one we didn't know."

"But Virginia didn't seem much interested in boys," Madeline demurred with a frown.

"She was interested all right," Henry retorted tersely. "She was a girl, wasn't she?"

"Don't keep saying 'was,'" Douglas barked.

"I'm just talking about the past," Henry explained aggrievedly. "And how do we know how she felt about men? We never saw her when she was out with her own crowd. And as far as that goes, she kept her affairs to herself, spent a lot of time by herself, too, come to think of it, dashing off to the club in her own car to play tennis or something. And she rode every day she was home, on Prince, or that little mare of hers."

"That was just on the trails here on our own place."

"The point I'm getting at is: did she ever advertise where she was going or where she'd been? As far as that goes," Henry concluded with a grunt that could have been ironical in intention, "did anybody ever ask her?"

"Mrs. Arnold," Douglas rejoined stiffly, "kept track of her pretty well. She's been with us ever since Virginia's mother died."

Madeline spoke up after having listened thoughtfully to the others. "If it is as Henry thinks, an elopement, I feel that perhaps the school should be blamed. They must have let the girls wander off the grounds during the week."

"Miss Fairweather says," Douglas protested, "they weren't allowed away from the school except one afternoon a week, when they could go to Redwood City or Palo Alto in the school station wagon with one of the teachers along. In town they were allowed to separate, but only in groups."

"If I know Gunny, she wouldn't stay part of a group any longer than she damn well felt like it," Henry interpolated.

"You could speak a little more respectfully of your cousin," Douglas remarked stiffly, "especially under the circumstances."

"I hope the boy's right," Mr. Trumbull finally put in. "Better a scandal than—" He broke off with a little cough.

In the kitchen Mrs. Arnold and one of the present pair of maids were discussing the same subject. Mrs. Arnold's eyes were the only ones in the house whose eyeballs were pink and the lids puffed from weeping.

"I can't help it," she was reiterating dejectedly, "I just can't help feeling responsible, partly, anyway. If I'd taken more interest, if I'd *insisted* on knowing where she was going whenever she left the house, if I'd made more of an effort and gained her confidence, tried more to take the place of her poor dear mother, this might not have happened. After all, who else was there to care for the poor little thing?"

"She had a father, didn't she?" the maid, Imogene, demanded.

"Oh well, but men—" Mrs. Arnold dismissed her employer drearily.

"I never noticed you were so crazy about her highness when she was here."

"I can't say," Mrs. Arnold replied, being difficultly honest, "that I did *like* her, but I didn't *dis*like her. She made it hard," she went on fretfully, "*to* like her. The way she acted like she didn't want you to get close to her. And she was always so impudent. And high-handed. Never called me Mrs. Arnold after she found out what my first name was. Always 'Esther, do this,' and 'Esther, do that!'" She shook her head sadly. "Yes, she was a trial, but she was just a child. I should have tried to make her love me. I think that was her trouble, not that nobody really loved *her*, but that she didn't have anybody to love. Her father, he hardly noticed her; and Henry, all he ever did was tease her, and, being older, never wanted to be bothered with her. So I should have put myself out more, been so nice to her she'd have had to love me at least," she sighed.

"Well, I wouldn't let myself brood over it if I was you, Mrs. Arnold. It ain't your fault she was a mess. And it's too bad if something's happened to her. But you can't get away from it, whatever the reasons for it were, she was a brat."

"The poor little brat," Mrs. Arnold murmured sadly.

"Poor little rich girl," Imogene snorted. "I thought that went out with the bustle. If she's still alive," she concluded briskly, "the ones I feel sorry for is the people that get mixed up with her."

Six o'clock was the dinner hour at Shady Dell, and the lights were warm behind the windows of the little movable houses lining the broad driveway.

The Skaggses sat on the benches around their narrow table with its woven mats under each pottery dinner service. A ruffled plastic apron covered the rayon dress Mrs. Skaggs had worn under her coat when she went to town. Mr. Skaggs looked shiny and slightly damp from his after-work bath. They were eating broiled steaks, and Mr. Skaggs had just observed, "Another two weeks, and I figure I'll be through here."

"Any idea where the next job will be?" his wife inquired.

"Over on the coast, I think. That rerouting on the Santa Cruz highway."

"That ought to be nice. Mountains."

Joan looked up and said flatly, "Just as I'm making a few friends. And here we go again!"

"You always say that, Joanie. Remember how you cried about leaving Stockton, and now all you can see is San Jose. You'll be just as crazy about the next school and the kids you meet. Won't want to leave Santa Cruz or wherever it is you'll have to go."

Joan was usually a docile child, but now she flared up, her cheeks pink. "Most girls my age have a steady boy friend. But look at me! I've never even had a date."

She looked down, her lips trembling, aware that she had revealed a desire that she was not willing for anyone to suspect.

"There's plenty of time for dates when you get a little older."

"You gotta remember," Mr. Skaggs said sternly, "I make good money. It's worth a little inconvenience to you."

"Money isn't everything," Joan muttered toward her plate.

"You just try getting along without it sometime," her mother reminded the girl curtly. "You're darn lucky, if you just knew it."

Next door, by the light of a weary center bulb, the Parsons were eating canned soup on the oilcloth-covered drop-leaf table. Delbert had been in to the county agricultural workers' placement office in the afternoon.

"Oh, I'll get somep'n all right," he said unenthusiastically. "There ain't much now. But I said I'd take anything, and they told me to come in every morning and they was sure they'd place me. I know what it'll be, though," he finished sourly. "Somep'n they don't usually get nobody but Filipinos or Mexicans to take."

"You gotta get somep'n," his wife, Darleen, said simply. "There just ain't practically no more money. Maybe I should look around for somep'n."

"Not," he said sternly, "in your condition."

"Well, I'm only three months along."

"That don't make no difference. A woman in your condition, she shouldn't be on her feet. I'm bound to get somep'n. They said so. Only thing is," he broke off with a frown, "there ain't no future in anything I'll get through the Farm Labor Office. But I'll keep my eyes open. Thing to do is get on steady at some big ranch where you got a chance to work up to foreman."

"We shoulda stayed where we was," Darleen said monotonously.

Delbert let his spoon fall into the soup with a splash. "You say that again, and I'll—I'll blow my top."

"O.K., O.K., keep your shirt on. But at least we had our folks back home. We wasn't all alone like this."

"Yeah, and a lotta good they done. There ain't one of our folks, yours or mine, that's got a pot to piss in theirselves. And I'll make good money, even the kinda jobs they'll send me on from the placement bureau. They may be kinda mucky an' backbreakin', but at least they pay somep'n in California."

"We'll never get no piece of land of our own out here; I can see that."

"I don't want no place of my own. In the long run you're farther ahead in a steady job for somebody else." At last Delbert smiled. "Quit worryin', honey, we'll make out."

"Oh, I ain't worried. Only—I'll be glad to get settled. And"—her light blue eyes went blank—"I miss the folks."

"We'll get acquainted, once we get set someplace."

"It ain't like your own folks," she repeated, still with that shaded look in her eyes.

Next door the MacLarens ate sliced bologna, delicatessen potato salad, and boiled carrots.

"I expect," Fred MacLaren was saying seriously, "we oughta think about movin' on. Today was the smallest day I've had around here. Guess I've just about exhausted the territory."

Josie cast him a quick, calculating glance from under her lashes and said with an artfully offhand manner, "I was talking to Mr. Ingleborg this morning. He got on up at Moffett Field; and I was just thinkin', all this defense work starting up again and so many young fellows bein' drafted, I bet you could get on someplace around here, at Westinghouse or someplace like that."

"You know," he said fretfully, "I ain't very strong and that war work wears me down. Did last time, you know that."

"Yes, but you lived through it all right, and last time we got enough ahead to pay for the car and this trailer. All I was thinking was, if you was to get on somewhere steady for a couple of years again, we could put something by again. You know we just get by on what you make now, hardly even that sometimes."

"But I like what I'm doin' now," he protested stubbornly. "I'm my own boss and set my own hours, and it's interestin' work, meetin' the public."

Josie set her teeth and suddenly broke out, "I ain't said much, 'cuz you're the one makes the money, so you're the one should decide how you're gonna do it, but you know this ain't no way for a woman to live, hand to mouth, and no regular home like a woman's entitled to. I've stood it a long time, Fred MacLaren, but I'm gettin' tired of it, just plain tired of it!"

He regarded her with surprise and resentment before mustering a faintly whining response. "I do the best I can. 'Tain't my fault I can't sell more."

"If you want to sell, all right, sell. But you could see first that your wife's properly provided for, especially when you got a chance like now, with another war comin' up and practically handing it to you on a platter."

"Well," he said hesitantly, "I suppose if it would be only temporary—"

"Besides," Josie declared clinchingly, "it's your patriotic duty."

"Oh, I don't know about that—"

"But you will put in your application around?"

"Well, I can do that, I guess."

Josie sat back and resumed her dinner, her mind made up. Once she got him into a regular job, she'd keep her eyes open, find *some* kind of a real house. They could sell the trailer to make the down payment, and then the monthly payments would take care of the rest. Fred would have to stay on a steady job. After all, she'd kept still—well, reasonably still—and put up with this crazy kind of life for a good long time now just so Fred would be happy doing what he wanted. It was about time she had something her way for a change.

Down at the end trailer of that row little Ronald Ingleborg sat on a high stool and made depressions in his mashed potatoes with the back of his spoon. Canned peas and bits of what had once been a hamburger patty made an uneven ring around the mound of potatoes.

"Stop that, and eat your dinner," his father commanded.

"I ain't hungry."

"He's been eating cookies all afternoon; that's what's the matter," Peggy volunteered resignedly.

"Miz 'Rilla gave 'em to me," Ronald announced placidly.

"She means well," Peggy said, "but I wish she wouldn't give him so many at a time."

"How is the duchess? Haven't seen her around for several days."

"Oh, she's around." Peggy giggled. "Only I'd say she looks more like a madam than a duchess."

"What's a madam?" Ronald inquired interestedly.

"Oh-oh. Little pitchers. It's another way of saying 'Mrs.,'" Peggy explained to the boy, and to her husband, "Now why did he pick up that word instead of 'duchess'?"

"What's duchess?" Ronald interrupted co-operatively.

"Another way of saying 'lady,'" Eric informed him curtly, and to his wife, "We've gotta start watching what we say. We forget how big a certain party's getting to be."

"I'd like to have just one hour a day," Peggy retorted, "when I wouldn't have to be in the same room with him and could act and talk like a human being."

"Well, his bed's curtained off from ours."

"Oh, lovely."

"O.K., O.K., in a couple of weeks or so we can start looking for a house. But I'm warning you, the prices they're asking are out of this world. How we'll ever keep up payments on a house and get something to put in it besides, *I* don't know."

"I'd just as soon have secondhand furniture," Peggy assured him eagerly.

"Think you get that for nothing?"

"Ronny's big enough now; I could put him in nursery school and get a job myself to pay for furniture."

"Find a nursery school first. The guys at work tell me they all got waiting lists a mile long."

"Well, he'll be in kindergarten next fall."

"Yeah, that's so."

Peggy leaned around the corner of the table and hugged Eric's shoulders. "I'm so glad," she cried, "that you're willing to at least consider getting a house. It's different for you; you're away all day. But you have no idea how tired I am of living this way—" She broke off to lean the other way and exclaim, "Ronny, watch that milk! Either drink it or leave it alone!"

"Well, I'll admit it's crowded," Eric conceded grudgingly.

"It's not only that; it's the people and everything. You never meet any nice people."

"What's wrong with the people?"

"Oh, nothing *wrong* with 'em, I guess; but it's all so temporary. If you did meet a couple you liked, next week they'd be gone, like as not, and you'll never see them again. And you can't entertain anybody or be entertained. Anyway, who is there here you'd want to associate with?"

"Oh, I dunno—" He broke off, and caught Ronald's saucer of prunes just as the contents were about to cascade over the edge of the table. "For Christ's sake, kid, be careful."

"Eric, you mustn't swear in front of him!"

Ronald gazed seriously at the prunes and repeated tentatively, "Chris'."

"You see?"

CHAPTER 7

The next day at one o'clock Marge Morgan ran up the small venetian blind at the end of her trailer and looked out moodily, facing another seemingly unending afternoon. Across the way Billie Grandon sat on her own steps, her feet extended to touch the ground, her full circular skirt pulled up to expose bare thighs to the sun riding at its highest in the unmarred blue of the southern sky.

Marge regarded Billie thoughtfully for a moment and then, catching up a cardigan sweater and draping it over her shoulders, she stepped outside purposefully and sauntered with a casual manner toward the other woman.

"Hi," Billie called cordially.

"Taking a sun bath?"

"Half a one. I had a good tan this summer, but it's practically gone."

"Mine too." Marge leaned against the front fender of the car with her hands in the pockets of her slacks.

"If a person wanted to," Billie informed her, "they could put on a bathing suit and take a blanket and lay in the sand pile in the playground and get a real sun bath. Ain't no kids playin' there much now, but"—her shoulders moved shrinkingly—"it's too chilly this time of year. For me, anyway."

"Aren't you working today?"

"I don't go on till three."

"Oh." There was a slight pause. "Is it very hard, your work?"

"All depends. When we're really busy, it's rough. Of course when you ain't busy, you get tired standin' around. So I don't know."

"There isn't much to it, is there?"

"What d'you mean, not much to it?" Billie countered curtly.

"Well, I mean all you have to do is write down what people want, go tell the cook, and bring it back to 'em."

Billie looked at her oddly. "Yeah, that's all there is to it," she said dryly. "Of course," she added, "there's the little matter of wrestling around heavy trays and gettin' the stuff set out so you don't spill hot coffee on the customers, and bringin' 'em more mustard and more ketchup an' more Worcestershire sauce an' more butter an' more cream an' more sugar and any other little item they can think up that's not included in the order. And actin' as if you was just tickled pink at their fresh remarks and corny jokes, and then gettin' a ten-cent tip—if you're lucky. Yeah, that's all there is to it."

"I mean," Marge continued, as if she had not detected the sarcasm, "anybody could do it, I suppose."

"Anybody, I guess, that can walk and can write and can add could learn how," Billie retorted ungraciously.

"What I mean is," Marge persisted, "I should think I could do it. I've come to the conclusion I'll have to do something. I'll lose my mind just sitting around over there all day."

Billie regarded her more sympathetically. "Oh. I see. Well, it's hard to get on any place when you're inexperienced."

"How do you get experience?"

Billie grinned. "That's the catch. It's what we all run into, starting out. But a person gets it someway."

"What about where you work? Do they need any more girls?"

"Not right now that I know of. But you never can tell. Right today somebody might not show up, and then there'd be an opening." Billie surveyed her neighbor speculatively. "Want I should put in a word with the boss?"

"Would you?"

"Well, I can do that much, and maybe you can run out and see him tomorrow. He might put you on the list. Course usually he gets new girls through the union; but if he takes you on, all you gotta do is join before you go to work. They have to take you in if you've got the job."

"Why do I have to join?"

"Why—why—you just have to, that's all. We've gotta be organized, or the first thing you know we'd be back workin' for just tips and cuttin' each other's throats to get 'em."

"Oh."

Billie regarded her wonderingly. "My God, honey, where you been all your life?"

With a startled movement Marge's eyes met Billie's. "Oh—Oh, I guess I was thinking about something else."

The door behind Billie opened, and Monty stood there in his plaid slacks and wine-colored shirt, his hair sleekly brushed, the narrow line of his mustache precise above his lips. Billie glanced up over her shoulder and then looked back inscrutably toward the girl.

"I guess you haven't met my husband," she said flatly, and in a general upward direction, "This is Mrs. Morgan, Monty."

"How do." He smiled. "I thought I'd come out and see what you girls was gassin' about so fast and furious."

Marge smiled composedly and cast a glance at Billie, who was studying her hands impersonally. "I guess I was pumping your wife," she confessed.

"Mrs. Morgan," Billie explained tonelessly, "is thinking of gettin' a job."

"That's nice. If you girls got on the same shift you could ride back and forth together," he said helpfully, inadvertently revealing that he had eavesdropped on their conversation.

"That'd be dandy," Billie muttered, eyes still on her hands.

Marge sent a puzzled glance from one to the other, and then measured the man with a coolly analytical expression. She smiled and dropped her eyes.

"I'd better be running along." Girlishly she appealed to Billie, "You will speak to your boss about me, won't you?" As a final touch that came as an inspiration and which she thought rather artistic, she added wistfully, "We could sure use the money."

Billie lifted her eyes to the suddenly ingenuous face above her, and her own expression softened. "Sure, kid, I'll do what I can."

Monty looked down at the top of his wife's head, and when Marge was out of earshot said carelessly in a low tone, "I guess you were right. She's pretty dumb."

Reassured by his disparaging tone, Billie murmured, "Oh well, she's awful young, just a kid really. Beautiful but dumb," she chuckled.

"Oh, I wouldn't say beautiful," Monty returned lightly, but his eyes rested with something of interest upon the trailer into which Marge had disappeared.

Without glancing up, Billie held her hand up over her shoulder. "Got a cigarette?"

As he pulled a package from his shirt pocket and placed a cigarette and a paper of matches in her fingers Stella Camarilla came sauntering, as if casually, along the driveway from her house. She wore black satin mules with Cuban heels and a black seersucker housecoat enlivened by a design of large purple morning-glories.

"Out enjoying the sun?" she asked.

"Yeah. Nice day, isn't it?"

Monty edged down the steps past his wife and leaned against the car. "Person hates to go to work, a day like this."

"Yes, a person does," Stella purred cozily. "I just felt sorry for Tony having to leave this morning."

"Oh, is Mr. Camarilla working today?"

"Yes, they called Bean's yesterday afternoon on the telephone. A few days at the cannery where he worked this summer. Some stuff to be boxed for a special shipment."

"Well, that's nice."

"Yes, he gets so restless not doing anything."

"I guess anybody does," Billie said equably. Lowering her voice, she nodded toward the trailer across the way. "She was just talkin' to me about chances for getting on where I am. But"—Billie shrugged—"she's got no experience."

"Is that so?" Stella said thoughtfully. "Wants to go to work, h'm?"

Billie shook her head in humorous despair. "Is she ever a babe in the woods! Wanted to know why she had to join the union. I can't figure her out. Sometimes she talks real intelligent and then again, honest to God, she acts as if she didn't know from nothin'."

Monty aimed his cigarette at the driveway, where it fell with the end still glowing. "There is something kind of funny about that dame," he said absently. "Something that doesn't quite ring true, if you get what mean."

"Oh, I think," Stella said quickly and soothingly, "she's just young and—and inexperienced, like your wife said."

Monty slowly moved his lower jaw back and forth sideways, unconscious of the movement. "Yeah, but I think that's what's kind of off the beam. Like Billie said, she don't seem to know from nothin', and yet there's something about her makes you think she knows the score." He snapped his fingers and then pointed his finger at the women. "I know who she makes me think of? I've seen 'em in high-class joints playin' the wheel or tryin' their luck at blackjack. Them society dames, they got a way of seemin' sure of themselves, as if all they had to do was keep a-going and everybody'd just naturally move out of their way. Well, this dame's got that same kind of look in her eye. Kind of—oblivious," he concluded triumphantly.

"Oh brother," Billie taunted, "have you got an imagination! She don't look oblivious to me. She just looks blank, as if half the time she didn't get you."

"I dropped in to see her yesterday," Stella said creamily, "and"—she glanced at Monty archly—"I'm afraid I can't agree with you, Mr. Grandon. She seems like a nice enough girl, but I wouldn't say she had any— background. A little common, I'm afraid," she finished with well-bred regretfulness.

"You said it," Billie agreed.

Monty shrugged. "Well, I won't argue with you women. I gotta admit you usually see through each other." He yawned. "Think I'll walk down to the market and get a paper."

When Monty returned no one was out of doors at Shady Dell, and he walked slowly down the driveway, reading the folded newspaper as he came. Inside, he lounged in the easy chair, half aware of the spatter of the shower where Billie was bathing in the cubicle at the other end of the trailer.

As she emerged and went about dressing for the day, he let the paper fall to his lap.

"I wonder why our friend"—he inclined his head toward the Camarilla house—"made a point of bustling out to see what we'd been talking about to Marge Morgan."

Billie ceased the contortions contingent upon wriggling into her girdle and regarded him with surprise.

"Why, she stops to say hello every once in a while."

Monty slowly lighted a cigarette. "Seemed to me it was Mrs. Morgan, not us, she was interested in."

"You're imagining things."

"Maybe. But she was awful quick to contradict my idea that Marge had a high-toned air about her sometimes."

"I don't see that myself."

Monty smoked in long, spaced drags, not replying. After a while he glanced down at the paper and observed idly, "I see they haven't found that Forester girl yet."

"I wonder what happened to her." Billie, in her slip and stockinged feet, was busy with her face before the mirror. "You know," she confessed with a sheepish giggle, "I actually caught myself looking over the customers yesterday, keeping an eye out for suspicious-looking blondes. But naturally, if she was kidnaped, by now they'd have her miles away from this part of the country."

"Wouldn't be bad, getting a line on where she is. That ten thousand bucks reward would be all we'd need."

"Boy, wouldn't it!"

Monty leaned to one side and pulled yesterday's paper off the uneven stack on a low shelf against the wall. He spread it out and studied the photograph. His cigarette was down to half an inch, and he held it gingerly between thumb and forefinger, squinting through the smoke. Then he flattened the butt in an ash tray on the arm of his chair. Curving his fingers around the pictured face, he shut out the hair, leaving only the features to bear his scrutiny.

"No telling where she is," he muttered.

"The police'll pick her up one of these days," Billie said cynically, "and nobody'll get the reward."

"A lot of people would like to have it," Monty said musingly. His eyes strayed to the oblong of windows through which he could see the matching oblong in the Camarilla coach.

"What you planning to do today?" Billie interrupted his reflections.

"Hang around downtown, I guess, after I drop you off at work."

"You oughta see the show I went to yesterday—at the California."

"Maybe I will. I'll come out to the restaurant to eat."

"And for Christ's sake," Billie said petulantly, "see if you can't get Tuesday off next week so we can go somewheres together, over to Santa Cruz or somep'n. This is no way to live."

"I'll see if I can get O'Hara to change with me."

When Stella had made her adieus gracefully and retreated to her own place, she stood irresolutely in the middle of the floor. The lack of information about Virginia Forester was still front-page news, and Monty Grandon had gone to buy a paper. He might never make the connection between his own observations regarding Marge Morgan and the news stories about Virginia Forester, but you couldn't count on it. If she wanted that ten thousand dollars she had better get moving.

The trouble was, the more she dilly-dallied with indecision, the more unsure of herself she became. Would the girl want to come out in the open, for instance, as a waitress in a drive-in restaurant if she were the heiress in disguise? Would her "husband" allow it, even if she herself were indiscreet enough to want to try it?

Stella struck her fist into the palm of her other hand, annoyed with herself for her own indecisiveness.

The smart thing to do was to take a chance. And if Marge wasn't the Forester girl, so what? Perhaps the other tenants wouldn't even know it was she who had turned the girl in—if it turned out she wasn't the heiress. If they suspected anybody, it would be Josie, with her curiosity and her addiction to gossip.

She was being extremely silly, worrying over what people would think, just because she had enjoyed so much the prestige she held here in this dumpy little trailer park, a prestige built up partly through Josie's admiring partiality toward her. She would dress and go out to the pay phone at the bar down the road this very afternoon.

Stella's fingers were on the zipper of her gown when there was a knock at the door and she saw Josie's face peering through the gap between the little drapes over the door's window.

"Hello, can I come in?" Josie called.

Although Mrs. MacLaren stayed for an hour and a half, Stella made no effort to hurry her. She wanted to arouse no suspicions that she had something up her sleeve. The Parsons had supplanted the Morgans in Josie's interest for the moment, and she went on enthusiastically about "the poor little thing's" being "so homesick she can hardly stand it" and about her own suspicions that the girl was "in the family way."

"She's got that kind of a drawn look they get. You know. And no pep."

"Maybe she's just anemic," Stella ventured idly.

"No, I can tell. Just like I can tell, I don't care what anybody says, there's something funny about that Mrs. Morgan."

"Funny?"

"She—" Josie paused and visibly indulged in thought. "She—wanders around—kind of lost like—after he goes to work. I've seen her."

"Well, she doesn't have much to do."

"I don't know why, but she gives me a feeling she's a bad one, something sly and deceitful about her."

Stella did not desire argument over "that Mrs. Morgan," so she agreed indifferently, "You may be right. Maybe," she added facetiously, "she's a gun moll hiding out after her latest crime."

Josie's eyes widened. "Do you think so?"

Stella was taken aback. She uttered an artificial laugh. "I was only joking, dear."

But Josie eyed her with interest. "Have you talked to her?"

"Well, I took her some cookies yesterday."

"Oh. Was she—How did she act? Friendly?"

A flash of impatience suddenly broke through Stella's suavity, and she said rather sharply, "Really, Josie, sometimes I think you're too suspicious-minded. After all, what do we care *what* Marjorie Morgan is?"

Josie pulled her head back stiffly so that her spine was very straight. "It isn't," she said primly, "necessarily suspicious to take an interest in other people."

"No, of course not," Stella rejoined, quickly mollifying. "Oh, I meant to ask you. Did you buy anything interesting when you went to town yesterday with Mrs. Skaggs?"

"Groceries, that's all, if you call them interesting. I kept wishing I had some money. I saw a lot of things I *could* have bought. But," she sighed, "there's never anything left anymore after you buy groceries—"

"Isn't it the truth," Stella agreed, and led her guest gently along on the high cost of living until Marge Morgan was left safely behind.

But when Josie trudged off home again her own thoughts reverted to Stella's strange reaction to the subject of Marge Morgan. It was as if Stella had some secret reason for not wanting to talk about the girl, as if she were hiding something. Josie had seen Stella go to the Morgan trailer yesterday and had watched at her own window to see how long she stayed. It had been a good half hour. She frowned to herself. Maybe Stella *had* found out something she didn't want to tell.

It was after three when Josie departed, and by the time Stella had herself suitably accoutered for a trip to the store it was past three-thirty. She was buttoning her fitted black coat around her when again there was a knock at the door. But this time she could see no face at the window. Opening the door, she found Ronald Ingleborg gazing up angelically.

"Got 'ny more cookies?"

She smiled. "Well, maybe one or two."

She turned toward the cupboard and, uninvited, Ronald clambered on into the room.

As she handed him the last two cookies from the jar, he said, "Thank you," and carefully, "madam."

Stella smiled. "Well, aren't you the polite little fellow."

"That's what my mamma says you look like," he explained cheerfully, "a madam." Seeing the strange look on his benefactor's face and interpreting it as noncomprehension, he elucidated further, "That's the same as miss-uz."

From outside came a piercing call "Ron-nee-ee!"

He scampered to the doorway and shouted, "Here, Mommy. Here." He turned his head and smiled. "G'by."

Stella took slow steps and stood in the doorway. Peggy Ingleborg, at the edge of the playground, called over, "I was just wondering where he was. I get worried when I can't see him."

Stella merely stared at her with hare black eyes and pulled the door closed. Her chest heaved deeply, once, as she faced back into the room.

Mechanically she picked a cigarette from the box on the coffee table. She would have to calm down before she went out. The nerve, saying such a thing, and before a child at that! And it wasn't as if she ever had—

"The dirty, sanctimonious little bitch," she muttered sibilantly through her teeth.

All she'd ever been was a landlady. Like Mrs. Bean. And if she rented only to single ladies and if they sometime! had—guests, was that her business? And so what if her rents were pretty high for that part of town, and if she sometimes took telephone messages to deliver to her tenants? Not a dime had she ever collected except in rent; and a nice, quiet, respectable house—er—place it was, too. And it wasn't her fault that the company that owned the property had finally refused to lease it to her again.

Anyhow, that was a long time ago now, and a more respectable, refined, better-behaved married lady than Mrs. Anthony Camarilla a person'd have to go a long way to find.

She crushed her cigarette out viciously and, straightening, caught her own eyes in the mirror. Intently she scrutinized her reflection, looking for something she could not find. Toward the last there was something pathetically questioning in her eyes. She touched up her hair, used make-up; but who didn't? She looked rather young for her age, maybe, but "Really," she thought, "there's nothing hard about my expression." She smiled experimentally. Rather a sweet expression, really. "And my clothes—quiet, refined, neat; this fitted black broadcloth coat with only one gold sunburst lapel pin; and a nice print dress." Her eyes were puzzled. Even the black wedgie sandals she had put on to walk in. Smart, yes; but not *loud*.

She shook her head and picked up a shiny black handbag with a gold clasp and went out the door, casting one resentful glance at the Ingleborg trailer.

She was slightly taken aback to see Marge Morgan leaning against the end wall of her own house, smoking a cigarette. But she went on, nodding a bit haughtily, with a "How do you do."

"Hi," Marge responded. "How are you today?"

Stella realized that she must act normal—just in case the alarm she was about to turn in proved to be a false one.

"Did your husband like the cookies?" she inquired.

"He was crazy about them."

"I'll have to give you the recipe. You cook, of course, don't you?" she added blandly.

The girl's eyes steadied upon her uncertainly a moment before she replied flippantly, "Not very well, I'm afraid."

"Never needed to, I suppose," Stella observed innocently but with eyes intent to catch the effect of her words.

Just then the car for Number Four pulled into the parking space next to them, and the two young men who were brothers and plasterers, according to Josie, climbed out of the machine still in their stiff white overalls and white, visored caps. They looked the women over carefully as they drove in but neglected to proffer any form of greeting.

"My, I didn't realize it was so late," Stella said briskly, "the Donelli boys home already. Of course, they get off at three-thirty. Well, I must be running along."

"Going shopping?" Marge asked idly.

"Just—an errand," Stella replied with a cryptic little smile and a last unreadable glance at the girl.

As Marge watched the older woman's progress along the driveway, she frowned slightly. "She acts," she thought to herself, "as if she was up to something." Could it be? But no—

Before Stella had come out of doors a low, heavy pea-green car had pulled in beside the Beans' residence towing a streamlined trailer painted the same color. The driver disappeared into the office, and as Stella approached the automobile her eyes rested idly upon the woman in the front seat, who was rather plumply and smugly middle-aged and who wore a tan beret over short russet-blond hair. Stella was too genteel to stare curiously, and anyhow she had a good deal on her mind; but as she came abreast of the machine she glanced again at its occupant, and their eyes met across the six feet of space. Stella's feet faltered slightly as if momentarily tripped by recognition, but she averted her eyes and took another step. Then her head turned and she looked back with startled eyes.

The other woman had leaned forward involuntarily. And then through the open window Stella heard her utter in a muted but incredulous exclamation, "Stella LaSalle!"

Stella turned full around. "Babe. My God"—her eyes traveled swiftly over the latest-model Oldsmobile sedan, the obviously luxurious trailer attached to it—"Babe Jackson. Well!" She let out her breath audibly. "Looks as if you'd done all right for yourself."

The woman lifted a hand covered by a stitched pigskin glove and murmured, "Not 'Babe,' Stella, please—"

A man in a tweed suit came out of the office door, and "Babe" looked nervously over her shoulder. The man was tall and heavy-set, and he also wore a beret and was drawing on his own pair of pigskin gloves. He was assuring Mrs. Bean in a hearty voice, "Number Eight. That's right. Oh, I'm sure everything will be fine. Fine!"

Stella stepped back, and the woman in the car faced stiffly ahead. The man came around the front of the car with a casual glance at Stella.

As the trailer moved past her, Stella glanced up to see Mrs. Bean standing on the steps with her arms folded, looking after the new arrivals with a proprietary air. Noticing Mrs. Camarilla, she observed with lifted eyebrows, "Some class, huh?"

Stella moved toward the steps, magnetized by curiosity. "They're going to stay here?"

"Just for the night. They're on a tour." She grinned. "That's what he said. Headed for Mexico."

"Where are they from?"

"Washington. Everett, I think he put down on the register."

"What does he do?"

"Well, after all, I couldn't get their whole life history in five minutes. Some big frog in a little puddle, I expect. You can tell they've got what it takes." Meaningly she rubbed the fingertips of one hand together. And then she sighed. "Must be nice, just traveling around all winter, seein' the sights. I've always said, even if I had money, if I was going to travel, I'd go by trailer. For one thing, you're not always packin' and unpackin' suitcases."

Stella murmured appropriately, but her eyes were on the manipulations involved in disconnecting automobile and trailer which were taking place down the way.

"You going someplace?" Mrs. Bean inquired.

Stella's eyes darted across the court and noted that Marge had disappeared. "I was," she said, and glanced at her watch, "but, dear me, I've wasted so much time I guess I won't bother. It's almost four-thirty already, and Mr. Camarilla'll be home before five. I guess I'll put it off till tomorrow."

This expressed decision was a surprise to her ears, but she realized as she started back down the driveway that she just wasn't up to the excitement and suspense she would undergo after that telephone call. Since she had waited this long, she could wait now until tomorrow, the first thing in the morning.

To tell the truth, this encounter with Babe Jackson had shaken her profoundly and for reasons she could not quite put her finger on. As she came up to Number Eight, she looked boldly down the opening between the car and the trailer. The door of the latter stood open, and the man was not in sight, but the woman stood beside the car, reaching inside for something on the front seat. She saw Stella and regarded her coldly, almost balefully; and suddenly Stella's eyes began to glitter in reaction to the distaste she detected in the other's gaze.

Deliberately she took a step closer and said in a low, taunting voice, "Fancy meeting you here. We must get together, talk over old times."

With a fearful glance at the house windows, the woman edged forward a step and muttered, retaining her supercilious manner with difficulty, "I can't think of anything we'd have to talk about."

"Oh no?" Stella's eyes roved over the automobile and hesitated unintentionally on the license plate whereat the other woman stiffened.

Stella's disposition had been curdling ever since the incident with the Ingleborg kid, and the only motive for her next words was an impulse to hurt or annoy anyone who came in handy; and Babe's uneasiness and dismay were a temptation.

"If you're too good to talk to me, maybe there are other people I could talk to—" She left the sentence dangling meaningly.

The stranger surveyed her distastefully but with trepidation. "You haven't changed a bit, have you?"

"Looks as if you have, considerably. I wonder what the folks in Everett, Washington, and even—him"—she nodded at the trailer house—"I wonder what they'd say if word got around about the old days in L.A."

"What good would it do you, raking all that up?"

Still motivated only by a vaguely malicious impulse, Stella cooed, "Maybe it would do me some good *not* to claim acquaintance with you— in front of—him. The least we could do is talk it over."

The other woman's lips tightened. "O.K., when can we get together? I suppose I can slip out."

Stella successfully concealed the fact that she was taken aback by this businesslike reaction to her mischievous needling. "My husband'll be home pretty soon now, but he leaves about seven-thirty in the morning. You won't be pulling out that early. Drop in sometime after seven-thirty."

"And if I don't?" the other said shrewdly, as if having reconsidered upon hearing the word "husband."

Stella's eyes went maliciously to the Washington license plate. "Well, I know where you live. Mrs. Bean just told me."

The other's face tightened, but just then her husband, capless and jacket-less now, leaned out of the trailer doorway.

"Oh, there you are, punkin," he stated in his carrying voice. "Wondered what happened to you."

The woman turned and smiled indulgently. "This lady just noticed we had an out-of-state license and stopped to speak of it."

She turned her back rather rudely and walked toward the man, so that Stella could only nod pleasantly in his direction and proceed on her way.

In extreme preoccupation she entered her house and sat down and lighted a cigarette. In some ways it was a wonder she had recognized Babe at all. Twenty pounds heavier anyway, and her hair, which had been platinum, now that light, natural-looking brownette, and practically no make-up, just a rose-colored lipstick. And her clothes. That straight-cut, completely unadorned suit, and low-heeled oxfords. And a silver costume necklace the only jewelry. Stella shook her head dazedly.

Of course she had good reason to remember Babe Jackson. One of her mistakes, and one that had cost her plenty. The mistake had been taking Babe in as a tenant. She wasn't the right type for an establishment like Stella's. Low-class she had been, but Stella hadn't realized it until Babe had her so tangled up with the law that only the expensive services of a fast-talking lawyer had saved Stella's own neck. Not holding her liquor, for one thing, and no sense of discretion about whom she entertained. Stella had, in fact, lost two of her best tenants after the trouble over Babe. Pamela, for instance, the aristocratic blonde with the English accent—who Stella knew for a fact had been born in Bisbee, Arizona. Stella could still hear Pamela's, "Re'lly, dear, if one is going to be embarrassed by persons of that class—" Pamela had moved out bag and baggage, and Stella never did get the same rent again for Pamela's suite.

Yes, her softheartedness in taking Babe in had cost her hard cash and almost thrown her into the clutches of the organized racket by the publicity the affair had generated. She never would have believed that Babe would turn out like this. Mrs. Bean had said, "Little frog in a big puddle." Small-town big shots, you could tell. He was probably somebody important in the Chamber of Commerce. They probably even went to church. One thing was sure, Babe had not caught him as the Babe Jackson Stella had known. She had been younger then and she must have got wise to herself, decided to calm down and play for bigger stakes. How and where she had hooked this Babbitt, Stella couldn't imagine, but hook him she had; and you could bet he didn't know many details about his wife's previous career.

That was why she had been frightened and nervous when Stella seemed bent on renewing the acquaintance. That Stella had no more desire than she to reveal the past to anyone had not seemed to occur to Babe.

The possibility of quick, easy money in connection with the Virginia Forester case seemed to have prepared the ground in Stella's mind for thoughts that would not have occurred to her a week before.

She had felt safe, relaxed, pleased with life as Mrs. Anthony Camarilla. They hadn't had much money, but they hadn't needed a great deal. Her own money had bought the trailer, and Tony's car had been just paid for when they got married. For the past three years she had been happy to live in the present, delighted with her marriage, with the lack of responsibility involved in living in a trailer. But that ten-thousand-dollar reward had reminded her of the future and of what a nest egg could mean, had made her remember with a shock that they weren't, after all, so young anymore.

And now Babe Jackson came along and instantly suspected blackmail. Stella smiled wryly. Showed what kind of a mind she had underneath the matronly, middle-class masquerade.

So then—maybe—why not? Certainly she had no love for Babe. Certainly the little tart had set her back financially and caused no end of inconvenience and even danger to herself, not to mention the other girls. Why not collect a little on the moral debt, at least, that Babe owed her?

Five hundred or a thousand. Stella frowned uncertainly. She had no way of knowing just how rich they were. Well, a thousand. Anybody could raise that. And it would serve Babe right. Stella punched her cigarette out viciously. Yes, she'd do it. She felt like getting even with someone. For what, she wasn't quite sure.

That Babe would show up in the morning, making some excuse to get away from her man, Stella had no doubt. She smiled reminiscently now, remembering. For Babe was afraid of her. She had forgotten that. Even before the last escapade when Babe had brought the police down on their heads, Stella had had occasion to get tough with the girl, her and her friends getting drunk and loud and attracting attention from the neighbors. Stella had always been a big girl, and strong; and one night when Babe had stood on the front steps, naked under a sleazy negligee, screaming after one of her guests who was wobbling into a taxi at the curb, Stella had felt constrained to haul her into the entrance hall and to slap her around a little when Babe became obstreperous over Stella's "interference." Always afterward Babe had had a healthy respect for her physically superior landlady. Stella had known then that she ought to send her packing, but Babe had cried and pleaded and promised, and like a fool she'd let her stay.

So all right, now that Babe was in the chips she could just make her former benefactress a little present. It was no more than fair.

She'd make up some story to tell Tony about where it came from. He always believed anything she told him, bless him.

Stella passed her hand over her forehead, and her facial muscles relaxed.

CHAPTER 8

When Stella went on after speaking to Marge, the latter contemplated the green automobile and trailer parked at the Bean doorstep, noticed Mrs. Camarilla hesitate as she passed the car and turn back. And then she watched the new tenants pulling into their allotted space.

In a moment Marge turned and went inside; but after the brightness of the daylight the trailer seemed dark and gloomy despite the blinds having been drawn clear to the top on all the little rectangular windows. She stood before the end window, surveying the scene beyond with a blind expression. Soon she faced back into the room. She picked up a comb and ran it through her hair, holding her head down before the mirror for a closer inspection of the parting on top.

Still holding the comb, she looked all around her at the strictly utilitarian walls and thought longingly of Billie Grandon. If only Billie would get her a job. For this was unbearable. She'd had no idea. The nights, yes, they were swell. But the days! Truly she had had no idea. You couldn't, it seemed, live on love, which she might have known if she had stopped to think of it. But a job, wearing one of those cute caps with a visor and a tight satin blouse and bell-bottomed slacks, that would be an experience at any rate. And experience was, after all, what she craved.

Restlessly she opened the door and stepped out again. She had no destination in mind. All she knew was that she must move or go nuts.

The young men in Number Four were pulling out again, dressed now—what she could see of them—in open-collared sport shirts and tweed jackets. She walked behind their car, and as it pulled away from her she saw that the woman in Number Three was standing beside her trailer talking to the mousy creature from Number Two.

As Marge approached, Josie called out cordially, "Oh, Mrs. Morgan, are you in a hurry?"

Josie was not one to let a previous snubbing stand in her way, especially since she had a frustrating feeling that other people were getting ahead of her in regard to Mrs. Morgan, what with her standing around talking to the Grandons and even entertaining Stella Camarilla in her house.

Curiously Marge paused. "No, I'm in no special hurry."

"Well, I wanted you to meet Mrs. Parsons. I'm Mrs. MacLaren," she interpolated beamingly. "I just felt you girls ought to get acquainted, both being brides, so to speak. You are a bride, aren't you, Mrs. Morgan?"

Marge eyed her with a sort of insolent yet speculative attention. "Well, in a way," she admitted.

Mrs. Parsons spoke up then in a small, high voice. "I've been married six months." She looked from one to the other of them with a meek assertiveness that was as surprising as if a rabbit had suddenly turned around and argued with its pursuers.

"You don't say," Marge remarked dryly.

"I'll bet you're a newer bride than she is then," Josie chirped archly, her eyes alert.

Again there was something insolent in Marge's measuring contemplation of the older woman.

When she said nothing Josie went on with nervous brightness, "You girls being both home alone all day, I thought you ought to know each other, help keep each other from being lonesome."

"How sweet of you," Marge murmured.

While they stood together Joan Skaggs had come out and was now approaching them on her way to the laundry room, progressing with a sort of sideways skip. She had changed after school to rolled-up jeans and a loose pull-over sweater that hung like a sack from her shoulders. Over her arm was something long, floating, and colorful, and she waved it gaily at the trio.

"Hello, Joanie," Mrs. MacLaren called. "What are you looking so happy about?"

Joan detoured toward them with the little half-skipping step. "Hi. I'm going over and wash my formal."

"My, my! Going to a party?"

"Um-h'm." The girl included the other two in her smile. "Friday night. In the gym." She held the dress up in front of her. "It's just my old cotton from last summer."

"Gee, it's purty," Mrs. Parsons said softly.

"Well, it fits me nice," Joan acknowledged smugly.

Marge reached out and touched the pink-and-white material. "Kind of a voile, isn't it?"

"Tissue gingham, the clerk where we bought it said."

Marge held the skirt out and nodded judiciously. "Not bad lines."

"Somebody goin' to take you?" Josie queried coyly.

Joan had crumpled the frock over her arm again, and she giggled, her eyes brightening. "Yup."

"A boy friend, h'm?"

"Oh, not exactly. Just a kid I know." Her hands wound themselves up in the dress as she added in a spuriously casual tone, "He rides on the bus. Lives in the auto court down the road."

"The one with the crew haircut and the purple and white jacket and the suede shoes?" Marge asked.

"Yeah, how'd you know?"

"I saw you getting off the bus yesterday. He looked sharp enough," she added seriously.

"He's a good kid," Joan said with an offhandedness that did not conceal her satisfaction over the date. "Well, I gotta get this thing in shape," she broke off briskly, shaking the dress, and trotted off toward the washroom.

"I'm so glad," Josie said in an undertone, "the poor kid's got a date. Moving around the way they do, she never really has a chance to get in with a crowd."

While Josie beamed approvingly after the girl both Marge and Darleen Parsons also gazed after her with quiet faces; and Josie, glancing from one to the other, thought that each pair of eyes was a little wistful.

Across the way the new man in Number Eight stood in front of his car in his shirt sleeves, smoking a cigar and looking about him like an explorer surveying new territory. He was bald except for a fringe above his ears, and his waist bulged on both sides of his belt.

"That's some outfit over there, isn't it?" Josie observed in a low voice. "Kind of flashy, though, all that green."

"They must be well off," Mrs. Parsons murmured enviously.

"I wouldn't be surprised."

The man met their eyes, smiled, and nodded cordially.

"We were just admiring your outfit," Josie called, taking a step toward him. The man also moved forward, as if pleased at having an excuse to speak. "We like it," he acknowledged modestly, raising his voice to be heard across the driveway. "Got everything real comfortable."

Marge was half inclined to move on, but she remembered she didn't have anywhere in particular to go, so she lagged behind Josie as the latter and the man exchanged conversational sallies, each time moving closer together.

"You're from the state of Washington, I notice."

"Yeah. Everett. Awful nice town. Ever been there?"

"No, we never have got that far north. I'm Mrs. MacLaren, and"—she turned hospitably—"this is Mrs. Parsons; she's in Number Two, and Mrs. Morgan from Number Five."

"How do," he responded with an inclusive smile. "Wilson's my name. You all stayin' here permanently?"

"More or less," Josie returned. "Guess you folks don't stay in one place long at a time."

"No, we're just seein' the country. Like the birds," he laughed, "headin' south for the winter."

"Carryin' your own nest right with you," Josie countered gaily, and they laughed together cozily. "I'll bet you've got it swell inside, judging from the way it looks outside."

"Well, it's comfortable," he repeated modestly, and then, "You folks like to see the inside?"

"Why, we'd love to," Josie exclaimed, "wouldn't we, girls?"

Mrs. Parsons smiled shyly and nodded, and Marge shrugged acceptingly, not caring one way or the other, merely making a mental note that it would be a painless way to kill time.

Mr. Wilson led the way importantly, opening the door and poking his head in to call, "Wanda, here's some folks'd like to see the house. O.K. if we come right in?"

As a voice from inside rejoined, "Of course, honey, bring them on in," he turned his head with an explanatory chuckle. "You know how it is. Might walk in and find my wife in her unmentionables."

They laughed politely and followed him into a surprisingly spacious room fitted with silver-colored kitchen equipment at one end and leather covered seats at the other.

Mrs. Wilson, dressed now in a pale blue woolly housecoat zipped up the front, graciously acknowledged the introductions to her husband's new friends and stood aside smilingly as he pointed out the features of what he described as "our traveling hotel suite."

Mrs. Parsons put her hand on the softly grained wood paneling. "A person wouldn't mind," she said softly, "living in a trailer if it was like this."

"My," Josie said enthusiastically, moving her foot back and forth experimentally, "real broadloom carpeting all over. Why, even Mrs. Camarilla only has linoleum, and she has her place fixed up the homiest of any I've seen." Her gaze traveled over the room inspectingly. "I don't think yours is quite as big as the Skaggses', but their place seems more crowded on account of there being three of 'em, I suppose."

At that, the Wilson trailer seemed slightly over-occupied with five of them in it, the ceiling just clearing the host's smooth-topped head. Marge was preparing to back unobtrusively out of the open doorway when Josie cried ingenuously, "What a comfortable-looking chair! Is it leather or that new plastic material? Mind if I try it?"

Marge watched in mild astonishment as Josie lowered herself into the dark red chair, exclaiming, "My, it is comfortable."

"That's Mr. Wilson's chair," his wife volunteered gaily. "I hardly ever get to sit in it."

Expansively Mr. Wilson gestured to the two girls poised uncertainly near the door. "Why don't we all sit down? You're in no hurry, are you?"

Marge and Mrs. Parsons looked at one another irresolutely.

"Well, I—" Mrs. Parsons stammered. "I—my husband will be back pretty soon—" Her eyes fell longingly on the deeply padded leather seat along the wall. "But—just for a minute." She darted rather furtively to the corner and leaned back on the cushions, her fingers moving caressingly over the soft leather. Marge followed and sat in the other corner, her eyes going curiously from one to another of her companions.

"Would you folks like a Coke?" Mr. Wilson suggested heartily. "There's plenty in the refrigerator."

"Well, if it's no trouble—" Josie acquiesced.

Darleen Parsons bobbed her head meekly in answer to the man's inquiring look, and Marge nodded absently. Her eyes kept coming back to Josie, as if fascinated.

Mr. Wilson offered cigarettes, which Josie and Darleen refused; and as he bustled about importantly while his wife procured bottles from the refrigerator, Mr. Wilson opened a drawer of the cabinet next to which Marge was sitting, searching for extra ash trays. Just as he pulled it open Josie spoke to him, wanting to know what line of business he was in, and he looked over his shoulder to explain, "Lumber. I own a little chain of lumberyards in Washington. Hard to get away when you're in business, but I have a good man now, my manager—"

Marge glanced idly into the open drawer and blinked as her eye fell on a squarish black object which was unquestionably some sort of gun. She lifted her eyes to the man's face, but he had found the ash tray he sought and was still speaking to Josie as he closed the drawer, apparently unconcerned over what it had revealed. "Well," Marge thought to herself, "I suppose people traveling feel they have to be armed."

She accepted a glass from the tray Mrs. Wilson offered, and listened indifferently to the talk. They were back on the general subject of trailers again, and Josie was babbling, "My friend, Mrs. Camarilla—she's down in Number Ten—a lovely woman—is the only one I've ever known that really honestly likes living in a trailer. Mrs. Skaggs, for instance, doesn't *mind*; but Mrs. Camarilla really likes it. It's too bad you won't be here longer. We have a really nice class of people, and you'd love Mrs. Camarilla. Everybody does—" She paused, her eyes having fallen on Marge, and she seemed to recollect something. "You've met her, haven't you, Mrs. Morgan?"

"Yes. She—called on me."

"Didn't you think she was a lovely person?" Josie eyed her sharply.

Marge had been bored for several minutes, and now she felt a certain malicious mischievousness, a desire to prick this garrulous little creature's happy composure. "She's all right, I guess. A little on the inquisitive side, maybe, but that seems to be a pretty common trait around here."

Everybody looked at Marge, and she thought, "Damn me, why do I always have to open my big mouth?"

Mrs. Wilson spoke first, and Marge caught an almost comradely glint in the woman's eyes as they rested fleetingly upon her. "That must be," Mrs. Wilson said suavely, "the rather imposing person with the dyed hair who stopped to speak to the manager as we came in."

Josie seemed at a loss for a moment, and Marge hid the grin which curved her lips by placing them over the rim of her glass and taking a sip of her drink.

It was plain Marge Morgan had not taken to Mrs. Camarilla. Inquisitive. But nobody could be less nosy than Stella. Josie was quite disgruntled as she came to the conclusion that something had taken place between those two and that it was something neither intended to tell her.

When to the accompaniment of Josie's protestations of gratitude for their hospitality the guests finally backed out of the Wilsons' trailer, Josie exclaimed, "Oh, my goodness, there's our car. Fred's home already, and not a thing started for supper!"

With her skirt flying out behind her, she trotted away as if Fred would be in mortal danger of starving if his supper did not appear at the same instant he did.

Marge raised her eyebrows at Darleen Parsons. "What a character!"

Darleen smiled timidly. "She's really nice though. Neighborly." She glanced at Marge sidelong. "My husband won't be home till after six tonight. I got lots of time. Would you—would you like to come in and sit awhile?"

Marge regarded the other curiously but uncertainly. Then she turned her head to glance about her. The sun was gone, but the air was only moderately cool.

"I'll tell you," she responded on an impulse that surprised even herself, "why don't we go for a little walk? I noticed there's a side road a little ways down the highway. We could walk down there and back."

"That would be nice. A person does get to feeling cooped up, but you hate to start out all by yourself and walk. It looks funny."

"Does it? I never thought of it. But I guess you're right. I used to walk a lot—by myself; but now that you mention it, I haven't felt like starting out alone here along the highway."

"It's good exercise, too. They say walking's good for you when you're like I am now."

They had turned past the Beans' house and begun to trudge down the roadside. Since Marge's suggestion that they walk together a new liveliness had come into Darleen's face, as if she had expected rejection and was disproportionately elated to find acceptance instead.

"I haven't told anyone else here," she offered shyly, "but I'm expecting."

Marge's eyes fell to the girl's flat abdomen. "A baby?" she blurted out incredulously.

"Uh-huh. Of course I don't show yet. I'm only three months along."

"Aren't you kind of—young?"

"I'm eighteen."

"Gosh," Marge said with an abstracted air. "*I* could even get that way. Of course I knew I could, but you actually being that way makes it seem—well, more possible." She regarded the girl curiously. "Aren't you scared?"

"Oh, some. But not much. It has to happen sometime."

"Yes."

They turned down the blacktop road that led between fields of turned earth.

"But," Marge continued as if to herself, "a person doesn't expect it to happen—yet."

"Well, if you get married," Darleen said practically, "you have to expect it."

"I just never—" Marge broke off and walked along with her hands in her pockets.

"Don't tell people, will you?" Darleen adjured her, and smiled. "I dunno why; it just slipped out."

"No, I won't mention it."

"I guess," Darleen confided, "not having no folks or no girl friends here, I just felt like I had to tell somebody, and you being more my age and all— Don't you," she interrupted herself abruptly, "get kind of lonesome?"

"Well, I guess I do. That is, there's nothing to do all day when your husband's away."

"My husband sure had a lucky break this morning. He came around by to tell me before he went out and reported for work. They got him a job driving tractor. Boy, it was more'n I ever dared hope for! They pay good for drivin' tractor."

"That's good."

It was much darker when they turned back under the Shady Dell arch.

"I sure enjoyed talkin' to you," Darleen said ingenuously. "I guess I nearly talked an arm off you. I don't know why, either. Usually I'm sort of quiet."

Marge smiled, rather patronizingly, "You were lonesome. That's what you said. Remember?"

"Yeah. Well—" She giggled. "Next time I'll let you talk. I guess it's partly because the only company I've had was Mrs. MacLaren, and she doesn't let the other fellow talk. Has she been to call on you?"

"No, but"—Marge inclined her head down the driveway—"*she* has. The one at the end. Mrs. Camarilla."

"Mrs. MacLaren just idolizes her. Thinks she's awful high-toned. You oughta feel honored that she came to see you."

"Well, I didn't." Marge frowned, looking down the driveway. "She gave me a feeling—as if—as if she was the sort of person you want to look out for. I don't trust her. I could tell, all she came to see me for was to look me over, see what she could find out—" Marge halted suddenly and looked at Darleen opaquely. "Well," she said brusquely, "I have to run along."

Uncertainly Darleen said, "Good-by," and stood gazing at Marge's retreating back. Then she called with a deferential note in her voice, "And thanks."

Marge turned her head. "Thanks?"

"For—for going for a walk with me," the other elaborated with shy confusion.

Involuntarily Marge smiled. She waved her hand and walked on. Dull, she thought, but nice. Something sort of—appealing about the awkward little thing.

She opened a can of beans and made toast and tea. She had a small feeling of triumph as she looked at the alarm clock after she had finished her meal. Six-thirty. She had managed very well in filling the late-afternoon hours; and now if she took her time about putting away the dishes and changing to her dressing gown, there wouldn't be so very much more time to get through before Bill came home. She sat vacant-eyed, smoking a cigarette, a pleasant expression on her face as she thought of Bill.

It was strange how it was the little things you remembered when he was away. Not the flesh-dissolving moments of climax, nor the mounting insatiability which preceded them; but little pleasant sensations, like the feel of the material of his white shirt sliding over his smooth skin under the pressure of her fingers, the rough irritation of his beard in the morning as his chin burrowed into the hollow made by her collarbone at the base of her neck.

A firm knocking on the metal door to her right brought Marge out of her reverie. Her fingers went to her lips as she realized that she had not refreshed her make-up since she went outside after four o'clock, and that in the last fifteen minutes she had eaten most of it off. She couldn't, however, leave whoever it was standing outside while she titivated. She hesitated a moment, then with a resigned shrug went to open the door. She blinked at the sight of Monty Grandon smiling up at her.

"Hope I didn't interrupt you," he said debonairly.

"No. I just finished eating." Then she demanded bluntly, "You want something?"

He grinned. "I hope you won't take me wrong, but I'm just killing time, waitin' till it's time to go after my wife when she gets off work. This is my day off. And I saw your light and remembered you were probably at loose ends, too, Bill not getting home till around eight-thirty, so-o"—he smiled in a humorously ingratiating way—"I thought maybe we could help each other kill time."

"Oh." Marge's tone was impersonal. "You did, h'm?"

"Don't get me wrong now. I just thought maybe you'd like to go down to the bar down the road and have a drink or two before Bill comes home. You know, the joint down by the market."

"Yeah, I know."

"Well, how's about it?"

"Thanks," she said formally, "I think not. I don't drink."

"O.K. You can have a Coke."

"I'm not thirsty."

He shrugged and grinned again. "Well, O.K. Just thought I'd ask. No hard feelings?" he prompted with a lift of his eyebrows.

"No hard feelings."

Thoughtfully Marge turned and went to the window at the end of the room, peering out through the slats at Monty's retreating figure. Her eye was distracted by the lights of the Camarilla trailer; and at the end window she saw Stella Camarilla's head against the interior lights. Stella's eyes, too, were intent upon the man who now passed out of her line of vision around the side of his own residence.

Her own blinds concealed Marge, but Stella's head was framed between the draperies, with the potted plant hanging above her like a bell. Since the light was behind the woman, Marge could not discern the expression on her face, but she saw Stella's head pivot to face the Morgan trailer, then turn again in the direction of the Grandons' next door. It was as if she cogitated, considered, tried to read the meaning of Monty's trip across the driveway.

A light came on in the Grandon coach, and in a moment Monty's head and shoulders appeared at his window. He stood for a moment staring directly at the window where Marge stood. Then he pulled the curtain down in front of him. At the same moment Stella withdrew from sight.

Marge sank down on the seat at the end of the room, frowning toward the floor, suffused with uneasiness. They had seemed to her, in that moment when each stood at his own window, each pair of eyes upon the wooden curtain behind which she cowered, like two rival birds of prey, with herself the prospective victim.

When the sun went down that day, tenuous clouds stretched in ragged banners across the sky, and by the time darkness came there were no stars.

During the night the rain began, waking the occupants of Shady Dell by its increasing tattoo on the metal roofs, arousing some to pull down open windows or to set pans under leaky ceilings.

The two in the Morgan trailer stirred, muttered sleepily of "raining," and cuddled closer in the warmth and coziness of bare flesh against bare flesh, and slept again to the lulling drumming of the rain.

By daylight the showers had thickened to a downpour, and while men ducked into automobiles and with a roar of engines backed out on the wet gravel and headed for the glistening highway, the wind howled between the coaches, the rain beat against their walls, and the sodden, pendent branches of the eucalyptus tree whipped against each other with a sound like crackling paper.

Once the workers' cars had pulled out against the rain—Mr. Ingleborg's, Mr. Camarilla's, the Donelli boys', Mr. Skaggs's—who would report in but who was not sure he would work, on account of the rain—there was an absence of life in the park. The trailers sat huddled like wet chicks in a barnyard, wetly enduring the storm, with only a yellow light here and there in a window to show they were alive. Several lower branches of the eucalyptus tree behind the Camarilla trailer broke loose with a sharp, cracking sound, to dangle by a heavy shred of bark or to fall heavily to the ground.

By nine o'clock the brief violence of the storm had subsided to a steady, undramatic rain, and in the trailers even the late sleepers were getting dressed or drinking coffee or listening to radios.

Mrs. Skaggs had done her housework and was settled down with her portable sewing machine, running up a pair of pajamas for her husband.

The MacLarens were facing each other dully over the table, wondering what to do with themselves all day, since he could not go out canvassing in the rain.

Delbert Parsons was bemoaning the fact that he could have been working if it weren't for the weather.

The Morgans were making inefficient but good-humored efforts to straighten up their house. Peggy Ingleborg was dressing Ronald, whom she had taken back to bed with her after Eric left. It was quiet and there were no lights at the Camarilla place; and the Grandons were lying wide awake but lazy, trying to make up their minds to get up. The Wilsons, suitably garbed in raincoats and rain hats, were hitching up the trailer and getting into their car, waving to Mrs. Bean, who peered out of the kitchen window and lifted her hand in a farewell salute.

By eleven o'clock the rain had stopped, and by noon patches of brilliant blue sky were showing between clouds turning creamy at the edges.

Since his day was ruined now, anyway, Mr. and Mrs. MacLaren drove downtown to go to an early matinee at the movies.

After their late breakfast Marge Morgan suggested to Bill that she might drive him to work, take the car, and spend the afternoon prowling the shops downtown, picking him up after work.

He hesitated before replying. "Better not—not just yet. Maybe next week we can start going out more."

She sighed deeply. "O.K. But I'm beginning to feel like the Count of Monte Cristo or somebody."

"You could listen to the radio," he suggested hopefully.

"Did you ever listen to the afternoon programs?" she inquired mordantly. "I suppose," she added bitterly, "I could take up tatting."

"Cheer up, honey; it won't always be like this."

"I should hope not."

When Bill had gone to work Marge busied herself for a while with a great stir of domestic activity, inexpertly sweeping and pushing the lint and dust over the threshold with the broom and then brushing it off the steps to the ground. In the cupboard where she had found the broom she also found an old undershirt of Bill's which she decided was a dust rag, and she went around assiduously wiping off all the flat surfaces. Then she bathed herself again meticulously and arranged her face and her hair. Yet it was still only two o'clock.

Resignedly she picked up the weekly magazine Bill had brought home the night before and, starting at the front, read every story in it, including the third installment of a serial whose first two parts she had not read and the final two of which she did not expect to see.

By then it was four o'clock and her eyes ached. Listlessly she put on a jacket and went outside to stroll aimlessly toward the highway. The trailer park steamed in the bright afternoon sun, and the leaves of the pepper tree and the eucalyptus glistened in their new cleanliness. Except for the occasional vocal exuberances of Ronald Ingleborg, who pattered about in little red rubber boots, it was an unusually quiet afternoon at Shady Dell.

At the arch Marge met Joan Skaggs, who had just parted from her two companions, the Japanese girl and the tall boy with the crew haircut.

"Hi," Joan greeted her as if Marge were an old acquaintance.

"Hi, yourself. How's everything with you?"

"Not so bad." Joan lifted her arm, over which hung a red raincoat, and brandished a pair of red rubber boots which she held together by the tops. "Mom made me wear the works this morning, and is it ever a nuisance draggin' 'em home."

"Well, it rained pretty hard."

"I'll say."

As Joan made as if to move along, Marge spoke up almost desperately, unwilling to relinquish even this slight social contact. "Did you get your dress all ready?"

"Uh-huh, it's all fixed. And Mom's gonna let me wear her string of pearls—imitation, of course—but they look neat with the square neck."

"The dance is in the gym?"

"Uh-huh. And he's gonna get to use his dad's car." Joan gave a happy little bounce on the balls of her feet. "I got gold sandals to wear too."

"What kind of a wrap are you going to wear?"

"Oh, just my short white coat." Joan eyed her interlocutor with sudden perceptiveness. "Like to come in," she invited impulsively, "if you haven't anything else to do? I'll show you the whole outfit."

"O.K. I don't have anything special to do."

As Joan pushed open the door she explained, "I brought Mrs. Morgan home with me, Mom, to show her what I'm going to wear tomorrow night."

Mrs. Skaggs looked up from the sewing in her hands and smiled pleasantly, the rays of the afternoon sun making an aureole around her as they slanted through the clear glass of the window. "I've just finished lengthening your slip to wear with the formal," she said, shaking out the length of white. "I put on a flounce and lace at the bottom of that, see?"

Joan had dumped her rain gear on a chair. "Gee, that looks neat."

She extricated the party dress from the crowded wardrobe closet and displayed the round-toed gold sandals while Marge murmured appreciatively.

"I'm hungry," Joan announced precipitately. "What's there to eat, Mom?"

Mrs. Skaggs raised her eyebrows at the guest. "I was wondering when she'd get around to that. They're usually the first words she says when she gets home." Then to the girl, "There's grape juice in the refrigerator and some cookies in the breadbox." And to Marge, "Can't you sit down for a while? Joan, put your things away so Mrs. Morgan can have that chair. How about you, wouldn't you like a glass of grape juice and some cookies?"

"Well," Marge demurred, "I didn't mean to intrude—"

"Oh, nonsense. We're glad to have you drop in. Joan, pour us all a glass. Use the tray."

Joan sprawled on the studio couch at the end of the room with her glass in one hand, a cookie in the other, and complained, "There's nothin' to do tonight."

"Don't you have any homework?" her mother asked.

"Did it all in study hall. Gosh, I wish we lived in town where there was other kids to run around with."

"It's probably just as well you don't," the woman declared primly.

"There *isn't* much to do here," Marge volunteered with a diffidence she herself could not quite understand. There was something about the two Skaggses that robbed her of all brashness and made her anxious only to make a good impression. "I get pretty bored myself."

"D'you play canasta?" Joan queried abruptly.

"Some. Not very well. Some of the girls at school played." Quickly she added, "Some of the girls I knew at school."

"Would you like to play a game?"

"I'd love to."

"O.K. I'll get the cards. Wanta play, Mom?"

"No, you kids go ahead. I'll have to start dinner pretty soon."

When Mrs. Skaggs arose to begin moving about the kitchen end of the coach, her eyes rested occasionally on the two at the other end, hearing the girlish exclamations, "Oh darn, you would. I was just waiting for that six. So *you* had them all the time." The occasional crows of triumph, the wails of disappointment, the little giggles which were as likely to come from Mrs. Morgan as from Joan. Mrs. Skaggs's eyes were faintly reflective as she went about her work.

Automatically she had lumped the two together as "you girls"; yet the stranger was a married woman, like herself; and she looked older than Joan, probably nineteen, anyway; yet now, with her back turned, one leg stuck out with the loafer-clad foot hooked over the bracket which supported the folding table on which they played, she seemed no older than Joan.

Mrs. Skaggs felt a stirring of compassion. One of those unfortunate cases of a mere kid up and getting married before she was fairly out of bobby socks, her carefree girlhood wasted. She looked like the wild type that *would* get married too young. With a slight concern Mrs. Skaggs glanced at her daughter's head bent over the cards. Maybe Mrs. Morgan would be a bad influence on Joan; maybe she oughtn't to encourage the association. She'd hate terribly to have Joan rush off and get married young. But then, they'd be moving on soon. There wasn't much likelihood of the two getting too chummy. It wouldn't do any harm to be nice to the girl. She did seem to be lonesome.

So when Marge took her leave, Mrs. Skaggs was cordial in her invitation to "drop in again sometime."

Joan had been the first to return to the park that afternoon, and while Marge was in the Skaggs trailer the Donelli boys had swept past with tires singing on the wet gravel; then the MacLarens' car crept conservatively back to its place, and Marge had no more than reached her home when Mr. Skaggs came, and then Eric Ingleborg. And, last, Mr. Camarilla.

He descended from his car rather stiffly and mounted the coach steps, pushing the door open in front of him. It remained ajar after he had stepped inside. Several minutes passed. Mr. Camarilla did not know whether it was three or five or even six or seven minutes before he came out again, leaving the door still open behind him. On the damp ground he stood for a moment looking about wildly. Then he ran with stumbling steps and occasional hoarse, inarticulate sounds to the Bean residence up front.

Mrs. Bean was in the kitchen slicing potatoes for a scalloped dish when she heard the pounding on the back door and a thickened calling of her name.

A distraught, haggard face met her eyes as she opened the door, and for a moment her mind refused to comprehend the breathless, desperate words, "My wife, my wife—Stella—she's shot—dead—"

Mrs. Bean gaped at him for an instant, and then she grasped his arm, pulling him inside and pushing the door shut behind him, calling toward the front of the house, "Ira! Ira, come here! Quick!" And to the man, still with her hand on his arm, guiding him to a chair, "Now, take it easy, Mr. Camarilla. I don't understand."

The man sobbed and then cried hysterically, "She's dead, I tell you! In the forehead. I found her like that—" Suddenly he dropped his head into his hands and shuddered. "Oh my God, oh my God—"

Mr. Bean hurried in, the evening paper still in his hand. "What's the matter? What's up?"

"It's Mrs. Camarilla. Something's happened." Mrs. Bean looked at the man in the chair and moistened her lips. Her tone was muted with horrified incredulity as she added, "He says she's been shot—that she's"— Mrs. Bean swallowed hard—"dead."

"Good God!"

Mr. Camarilla sobbed into his hands. "I don't know what to do."

Mr. Bean drew in his breath as if to steady himself, and looked hard at the man. Then he turned to his wife and commanded tersely, "You call the police. I'll go back with him and see—" His voice faltered uncertainly before he repeated flatly, "And see." His eyes flicked toward the dusk beyond the window. "You stay here. Don't say anything or let the rest of 'em know anything's wrong until after the officers get here." He touched Camarilla's shoulder. "Come on now. I'll go back with you."

Dazedly the man rose and led the way out. He jabbered incoherent phrases as they walked back to Number Ten.

Mr. Bean clenched his teeth before he stepped into the over-heated space where the electric heater had apparently been running for hours, for even with the door open it was hot inside.

The bed was open, and Stella lay on her back, her knees over the foot, her feet in satin mules resting on the floor. Her arms were thrown out, and a wraparound robe had fallen open across her torso to reveal a rayon satin nightgown. There was a round black hole between her eyebrows. Small rivulets of blood had coursed down the sides of her face to dry in black streaks on the white skin.

Mr. Bean put one hand against his throat and then stood with his hands hanging limply at his sides. Mr. Camarilla had sat on the edge of the bed, holding Stella's left hand with a warming movement, his other hand on her shoulder. Suddenly he bent and laid his forehead on her body and wept with no effort at control.

Mr. Bean looked this way and that, swallowed, and blinked his eyes. He put out his hand and touched the other man's heaving shoulder and mumbled indistinctly, and then looked around again at the room. It seemed hard to get his breath. And then he noticed the red coils of the heater in the wall and purposefully crossed and flicked the switch off.

CHAPTER 9

To Mr. Bean it seemed hours before the police car rolled up, with an ambulance pulling in behind it.

The little procession drew people from the other trailers as if it were equipped with suction which reached in and pulled them out as it passed. Bareheaded and coatless, they flowed down the driveway in the vehicles' wake, with Josie MacLaren well in the lead. Mrs. Bean stayed on her own doorstep, peering anxiously toward the scene through the darkness which was mitigated by the outdoor light poles behind each coach.

Eric Ingleborg, seeing the official cars through the window, crossed the driveway to inquire about what was wrong while Peggy hesitated in front of their door, waiting.

Marge Morgan peeped through the venetian blinds and remained staring at the ambulance and the unmistakable black sedan with its red spotlights. She frowned and watched, but she did not go out.

None of the questions which peppered the drivers who stood beside the machines was answered, and no one was allowed past the barricade the vehicles formed in front of the Camarilla quarters. Some of the occupants of the park had seen Mr. Camarilla drive in at five-thirty, however, and they soon agreed among themselves that something must have happened to Stella.

They did not wait long before one of the men who had arrived in the head car came out to address them curtly, requesting that they return to their homes to wait there until they could be interviewed.

Mr. Skaggs demanded belligerently, "What's going on here? We got a right to know why we're bein' ordered around like this."

"There's been an accident. Now if you'll please disperse so we can get on with our business, we'll have to take up that much less of your time." The officer turned and in a lower tone addressed the colleague who had remained beside the car. "Go up to the entrance and don't let anyone leave till we've talked to 'em."

"How about people comin' in?"

"The woman that runs the place is still up there. If she says they live here, O.K. But nobody else comes in."

When the neighbors had reluctantly withdrawn to their own domiciles, Captain Granger of the sheriff's detective force walked up the driveway with Mr. Bean and Mr. Camarilla while the sedan swerved about and came back to stop before the office, where another detective descended and accompanied the captain into the house with the two men. Meanwhile still a third automobile drove back to Number Ten, and the technicians went ahead with their work of photographing, dusting for fingerprints, and finally removing the body in the waiting ambulance.

With terse, businesslike questions Captain Granger elicited the statement from Tony Camarilla that Stella had been alive and normal, in so far as he knew, when he left the park at a little past seven-thirty to be at work at eight. Assuming for the moment that Mr. Camarilla's story was true, Captain Granger estimated that the fatal shot must have been fired during the early-morning hours. The breakfast dishes had been neatly stacked but unwashed in the small sink, and the fact that Stella was still in night clothes and that the bed was unmade bolstered this theory. The medical examiner had gruffly refused a statement as to approximate time of death until after an autopsy could be performed.

"Did you see or speak to anyone outside on your way out?" Granger inquired.

"No. It was raining. Nobody was around."

"How about the other cars? Anybody else left the place before you did?"

Tony shook his head confusedly. "I—I don' know. I think Mr. Ingleborg, he was gone. I think his car was gone."

The detectives interviewed Mr. Camarilla in the Bean kitchen, and Captain Granger went into the parlor-office to speak to the Beans while his companion kept the bereaved man company.

"How about these people?" Granger went straight to the point. "They get along all right? Any marital trouble?"

"They seemed to be," Mrs. Bean said flatly, "as happy a couple as any we've ever had here."

"Any bad feeling between them and any of the other tenants?"

"Not that we know of."

"Could it have been burglary?" Mr. Bean suggested.

"Doesn't look like it. There was a wrist watch and a diamond ring laying in plain sight on the shelf, and the woman's handbag hadn't been disturbed. Twenty dollars still in the billfold."

Mr. Bean said, "Um," and subsided moodily.

"Maybe," Mrs. Bean said hopefully, "a—a fiend. Sex stuff?"

The captain shook his head. "No signs of her being worked over any. Just the shot."

Granger pulled out a small notebook. "Let me get a line on the other people here. Who were the Camarillas chummy with?"

"Well, I guess the missus was friendlier with Josie MacLaren, in Number Three, than with anybody else. But they were on just ordinary friendly terms with everybody else."

"Let's take up first the people closest to their parking place. Give me their names, occupation, how long they've been here, and so forth."

Slowly, thoughtfully, Mrs. Bean told what she knew of the Grandons, the Ingleborgs. "And then I guess the Morgans are next closest to them. But they barely knew the Camarillas. Been here less than three weeks. And Mrs. Morgan, in fact, hasn't actually been around except since last Saturday."

"How's that?"

"Well, they rented the space"—she consulted her register book—"two weeks ago last Sunday, but Mrs. Morgan went away again the same day to visit her mother and didn't come back till last Saturday, so she couldn't have known Stella more than two or three days. He works in a service station the other side of town."

"Young couple?"

"Yes."

"O.K. Let's go on. How about your other tenants?"

Mrs. Bean outlined the facts she had on hand about the others in the order of their locations in the park and wound up with Number Eight, the Wilsons.

"But they wouldn't count. They just stayed overnight."

"What time did they leave today?"

"About nine," Mr. Bean broke in finally. "We didn't even see them to speak to this morning. They paid in advance."

"You have their home address? And the license number? May have to find out what they saw or heard. Meanwhile, now, I'll have to see these other people. Another thing, I don't want anybody moving out till we get this thing settled. If somebody absolutely has to, be sure we're notified first."

The two detectives started with the houses nearest the Camarilla trailer. Since the Grandons were at work, they talked first to the Ingleborgs; who had nothing helpful to contribute. Eric had pulled out before Mr. Camarilla and had been too sleepy and tired even to remember whether or not there had been lights in the end trailer, and Peggy had turned out their own lights and gone back to bed, taking Ronny with her after Eric departed, not getting up again until about nine o'clock.

Tiny, pale rims of light made rectangular markings around the closed venetian blinds of the coach in Space Number Five, and when the door opened to the officers' knock, the room inside was only slightly less dim than the out-of-doors with its high yard lights.

"Investigators from the sheriff's office," Granger announced, and stepped inside, forcing the girl to back up in order to avoid collision.

Granger hid his disapproval of the girl's appearance by his usual impassive expression. His trained eye had immediately catalogued the false eyelashes, the too highly arched brows, the standardized shape of the painted-on lips, the somewhat extreme fluffiness of the hair, which now looked merely brown in the light from two shaded wall lamps.

"We want to ask a few questions. May we sit down?"

"Why—I guess so."

Marge backed up to the far end of the room and sank onto the seat Stella had occupied during her call. Granger took the straight chair, and the other detective sat on the long seat against the wall. The captain pulled his notebook from his coat pocket and the pencil from his breast pocket. He glanced about the room imperturbably, then swiveled on the chair and, reaching back, pushed one of the buttons beside the door.

"Mind if we have some light?"

Two long bars in the ceiling whitened, trembled uncertainly, and then suddenly irradiated the room with a milky pallor.

Calmly, then, Granger regarded the young woman whose features had become still and set.

Efficiently Granger asked his questions, which Marge answered in a flat, nasal voice roughened by ungrammatical constructions. She knew little about Stella Camarilla, had talked to her perhaps twice, had never seen her before coming to Shady Dell. She and Bill had slept until nine or so, had heard nothing unusual that morning above the dinning of the rain.

The eyes of both men came back to her repeatedly with the impersonal scrutiny of trained policemen, revealing nothing, seemingly seeking nothing.

The county of Santa Clara was large, active, varied, wealthy, and often violent. It needed and could afford topnotch law-enforcement personnel. Marge knew that these were not hick cops. Mercifully she did not know that police who are well trained for their jobs have been taught to look at faces, not as the layman does, absorbing a general impression; but piece by piece, sorting and assembling each feature and group of features, noting the shape of the forehead, the bone structure about the eyes, the curve of a nose bridge and of nostrils, the line of jaw and cut of chin, even the shape and size of teeth.

Both men were silent as they walked away from the trailer. Granger's mind was groping for something. He couldn't quite place it, but there was something that girl's face should have told him. He was sure of it.

He halted out on the driveway and slowly pulled cigarettes from his pocket, mechanically offering one to Jerry, who watched him keenly.

"I wonder," he said, and held a match to his cigarette, "if there was some connection"—he jerked his head toward the Camarilla house—"between those two in the past. Let's see, this girl came here about two weeks ago—but she wouldn't have seen the Camarilla woman until this past Saturday. Mrs. Bean said the Morgan woman was just in and out and then away and didn't get back till last Saturday—"

His voice died, and he stared at the unlighted laundry room across the way. "Last Saturday," Granger muttered, and Jerry turned his head, startled, and glanced back at the Morgan trailer, then quickly at his superior.

"Well," Granger said with sudden briskness, "we better get on with our work."

"Just a minute," Jerry said softly. "I'm in on this. We split the ten thousand."

The captain sent him a sidelong look and grinned. "Why, sure, Jerry. I was just going to make sure, have her identified before I said anything. No use going off half-cocked."

"I just don't want there to be no mistakes. We both tumbled to it at the same time, so we both collect on the reward. Far as I can see, there ain't much doubt. Bring the eyebrows down where they belong, rip off them eyelashes, wash her mouth and take the falsies outa her sweater, and it's the Forester girl, red hair or no red hair."

Granger drew on his cigarette and gazed at the Camarilla trailer. "I wouldn't be surprised if this didn't wash the whole thing up. That Camarilla dame looked like she'd been around, knew a few angles in her day. If we tumbled to it, maybe she did too. Could be this Forester kid bumped her off to keep her from squealing—"

"Which," Jerry interpolated dryly, "was the one sure way to get herself picked up."

"Well, she's just a kid, only seventeen. She probably didn't figure this far ahead, or thought nobody but another dame like the Camarilla woman would see through the make-up."

"If she did do it," Jerry said soberly, "it may not be so easy pinning it on her. The Wilkins money. They'll throw everything they've got into it. The best legal talent—"

"Well, there's a gun somewhere. Looked like a .32 hole. Of course they've had all day to get rid of it—"

They had been standing in the middle of the driveway, speaking in muted tones. Granger turned now to look back at the Morgan trailer.

"We'd better take her in," he said flatly. "When we get back to the office we'll call Forester and have somebody pick up Morgan at the service station. Meanwhile we'll see what we can get out of the girl before Douglas Forester descends with his lawyers."

The girl inside the Morgan coach had been watching the dark figures of the two officers around the edge of the blind. Her tension had eased somewhat as they left the trailer, but as they turned back she withdrew from the window. When she opened the door she regarded the men antagonistically.

"You'll have to come along with us for further questioning."

Her hand tightened over the edge of the door. "You can't!" she said defiantly.

"Yes, we can," Granger countered quietly. "Put on your coat and come along now."

"I—I don't have to. You have to have a—a warrant or something."

"Now let's not have any trouble."

"But I haven't done anything!"

"Maybe not. But we have some more questions to ask you."

Uncertainly the girl stepped back, her hand falling from the door.

"Get a move on," Granger commanded curtly.

Reluctantly she picked up the cheap gabardine topcoat which lay on the padded seat and, with a mistrustful glance at the detective's face, sidled out in front of him. This was more than she could handle. If only Bill had been at home!

Granger knew that his time alone with the girl was limited. They wouldn't dare hold off on notifying her father, who would immediately wall her in with legal counsel. So as soon as she was seated in the back seat of the car between him and Jerry, he began, "All right, Miss Forester, let's have it. When did you first realize Mrs. Camarilla knew who you were?"

The girl's mouth opened, and she stared at the dim outlines of his face as mesmerized her.

"I didn't—I don't—I don't know what you mean," she choked.

"Look, let's not go through a whole rigmarole now. Your father will be notified as soon as we get to the office. This fancy getup won't fool him any more than it did us. And even if it does, we have your fingerprints from articles in your room at home, and they can't lie. So let's skip all the denials."

She took a deep breath and relaxed against the seat. Her shoulders lifted in a little shrug.

"Now that we've got that out of the way," Granger proceeded, "let's get back to my question. When did you find out Mrs. Camarilla knew?"

"I didn't know she did know. Did she?"

"Look, Miss Forester, can't we quit sparring?"

"Not 'Miss Forester,'" the girl snapped. "I'm Mrs. Morgan. Regardless of what my name used to be, it's Morgan now."

"I don't see how that could be. You're under age."

"Maybe so. But let's get this straight once and for all. It may not have been technically legal, but Bill and I went through the works, see? License, blood test, and a marriage certificate—suitable for framing. Maybe I gave a false name and maybe I lied about my age, but we're just as married as anybody else."

Granger surveyed her curiously, looking sideways to where she now sat ramrod-straight between him and his colleague. "Just as a matter of curiosity," he asked, "how did you work all that without getting caught?"

She eyed him suspiciously and then said a little wearily, "I don't suppose it matters, now that you've got me where you want me. I've known Bill for months. We got acquainted at the station where he worked when I stopped there for gas. We started seeing each other on the quiet. I knew my family'd raise hell if I tried to go around with him openly. A month ago we decided to get married. We got the license and stuff in Redwood City—I sneaked out of school to do it—and a few days later we were married there by a justice. I made up the way I am now and wore a hat to cover up my hair. It was blond then."

"Smart customer, this boy friend of yours," Jerry put in dryly. "All this mumbo-jumbo puts him in a better bargaining position when the whole thing comes out—"

"Shut up, Jerry," Granger ejaculated roughly.

Virginia turned her eyes on Jerry slowly and said, "You son of a bitch."

"That's enough of that," Granger expostulated, adding, "If you weren't who you are, you wouldn't get away with that kind of talk to an officer."

"Keep it in mind," the girl said coldly. "I was ready to forget my family, and their money along with them; but now that you've raked them up again for me, just don't forget who I am. I'm not some little floozy that you can push around."

"Did you bring the gun with you from home, or was it your—husband's?"

Virginia met his eyes, her own startled and interested. "She was shot?"

"It won't do any good to lie about this. We can check back, you know, on guns purchased by any member of your family or by Mr. Morgan."

Virginia shrugged. "Go ahead, check. I didn't even know the woman was dead till I saw them putting her in the ambulance. And then I only assumed it because she was all covered up."

The two detectives met one another's eyes over her head, and Granger shook his head slightly with rueful despair, while Jerry tightened and twisted his lips and moved his own head sympathetically.

By this time they had pulled into the courtyard in the rear of the courthouse, and the two men got out and hustled the girl into the building. Jerry guided her down a hallway and into a bare-looking but commodious office while Granger stopped at a desk in the anteroom. The sheriff himself was out, so Granger made the call to the Forester estate some fifteen miles away.

"Phil and Ernie are bringing the husband in now," he explained to the man in the outer office before collecting a stenographer and heading for the room that contained Virginia.

"Jeez," the stenographer muttered, "the Forester dame, eh? What's she like?"

"Pain in the ass," Granger replied tartly. "Makes you want to turn her over your knee and warm her britches. Personally, I don't see why they *wanted* to find her."

Virginia regarded the men ungraciously as they entered. She answered their questions warily and in monosyllables for the most part, but with a certain interest in the officers' tactics. Once she left a question of Granger's unanswered to pose one of her own, looking curiously from one to the other of the men. "Is this what they call the third degree?"

"It is not," Granger snapped.

"Because if it is I'll tell Father and Mr. Trumbull when they come, and if you're doing anything illegal you'll catch it. Mr. Trumbull knows everybody who is anybody in state politics."

Granger's inscrutable gray eyes for once wore a rather baffled expression as they rested on the garishly made-up girl. Turning slightly, he muttered to the stenographer, "See what I mean?" and the latter glanced up and grinned. But by the time the Forest limousine drew up at the side entrance, driven by Mr. Arnold, Granger had by hard work elicited from the girl a nearly complete account of every time she had seen Stella Camarilla and of what they had said to each other. He was still convinced that she had shot the woman to protect her own identity, but he realized that all the evidence was yet to be collected. The kid was too precocious, knew too well how to take care of herself.

It was no use trying to hold her. Douglas Forester's legal talent would demand that she be charged immediately if she were to be held, and Granger realized they had nothing as yet to put before a magistrate that the said legal talent could not blast to bits.

As he paused to cogitate the girl demanded, "Where's my husband? Did you send somebody after him?"

"We're questioning him," Granger said calmly.

"I want to see him."

"That'll be up to your folks when they come."

Virginia eyed him narrowly, and just then footsteps and voices were heard in the corridor, and Granger went to open the door.

With his first step across the threshold Douglas Forester came to a stop, his eyes fastened on the girl who had risen to face him, her shoulders squared, head erect.

"Good God," he exclaimed weakly. "Virginia. What have you done to yourself?"

"Disguise," she returned flippantly.

For another instant they eyed one another across the brightly lit room, and then Douglas uttered a sigh of relief and stepped forward. He put his arms around the girl and kissed her cheek. She let her hands rest on his biceps and submitted to the embrace.

"Thank heaven you're safe." He drew back and scrutinized her anxiously. "You *are* all right, aren't you?"

"As far as I know, I am."

"Virginia," he said faintly, and repeated, "Virginia. How could you?"

She lowered her eyes and said nothing.

Mr. Trumbull stepped forward and took her hand, cradling it in both of his. "It's wonderful to see you again, my dear."

"Hello, Trumbie," she responded with an impish upward look through the elaborate lashes.

Douglas turned to the silently observant officers. "We can take her home with us, I presume? Mr. Trumbull will attend to any official matters."

Captain Granger nodded.

"Just a minute," Virginia intervened. "What about Bill?" She turned to her father. "I don't know whether they told you, but I'm married now."

"You're—you're—what?"

"Married. I have been for almost a month. That's where I've been this week, with my husband. That's one reason I left. I knew you'd raise a fuss if I told you about Bill."

Douglas Forester's physiognomy was on the pale and aquiline side, by no stretch of imagination a choleric one; but now he suddenly looked apoplectic. His eyes flashed angrily at the policemen who surrounded them.

"Why wasn't I told about this?"

"We didn't have time," Granger replied phlegmatically. As an afterthought he added, "He's outside now, in another room."

"And," Virginia interpolated, "I'm not going anywhere without him."

"You're a minor," Douglas exploded, "and you'll go wherever I say."

"If Bill goes with us, I'll go home with you and talk things over. Otherwise I won't budge."

The eyes of the sheriff's men had all been fixed on the girl. Now, all at the same time, they shifted interestedly to her father. His face still had a red and swollen look.

Mr. Trumbull interjected mildly, "Now, Virginia, there's no use in taking that attitude—"

She looked at him and said rudely, "Shut up."

The men of the sheriff's crew again moved their eyes, fascinated, from one to another of the trio.

"Virginia!" Douglas's voice had become shrill. "You come along with us this instant!"

"Is Bill coming too?"

"No!"

She sat down. "Then I'm not going."

"I'm afraid you must," Mr. Trumbull observed coldly. "You wouldn't want us to use force, would you?"

She took a firm grip on either side of the chair seat. "If you try to force me I'll kick and scream and"—she paused—"and scratch and—and bite," she concluded, as if the last were a sudden inspiration.

The men all gazed at her.

"And how," she went on defiantly, "are you going to keep me after you get me? I can run away again, you know. Even if you hire a bodyguard, he'll have to turn his back sometimes, and the first time he does I'll conk him over the head with something."

Douglas and Trumbull stared at her aghast, then met one another's eyes with frustrated expressions.

Captain Granger put in almost diffidently to Trumbull, "We have a psychiatric department. Should I—" He hesitated, embarrassed. "We could call Dr. Davidson in."

"No," Douglas snapped.

Mr. Trumbull moistened his lips. "I think perhaps—" He glanced distastefully at their absorbed audience. "Perhaps if we retired to your house, Douglas, and talked this over quietly with the young man present—"

Douglas regarded his attorney uncertainly, and the latter's eyes darted unobtrusively toward the officers and met Douglas's again meaningly. He gave a little cough. "There were already some gentlemen of the press in the anteroom."

Douglas drew a deep breath. "All right."

Mr. Trumbull addressed Captain Granger. "Have you finished with this—er—Bill?"

"Our men have been getting his statement. I'll check to see if he can be released. On account of this other matter that I mentioned on the phone, we want them both available for further questioning if necessary."

At the reference to "the other matter" Douglas and Trumbull both cast despairing glances at Virginia.

"Is there any way we could get away without attracting further attention?" Trumbull inquired.

"Well, we'll do the best we can. George, go see if they've finished with Morgan. If they have, let us know and we'll escort you folks and him to the car at the same time. I'm afraid, though, you'll have to run the gantlet. The newspaper boys'll be out in force by now. Couldn't keep it quiet, something like locating Miss Forester."

In a few moments the deputy returned to say that Bill would be brought to meet them at the entrance, and with Douglas and Mr. Trumbull on either side of Virginia, the sheriff's men flanking them fore and aft, they made a dash for it. It was as Mr. Trumbull had expected. The limousine was surrounded by waiting photographers and reporters.

Virginia held back against the pressing arms of her escorts until she saw amidst the flare of the cameramen's flash bulbs the white trousers and hat of Bill's uniform diving into the tonneau of the car whose engine Mr. Arnold had ready. Then with a rush she also made for the open door. Douglas crowded in behind her and rudely shoved his way between the two young people in the back seat. The front door slammed on Mr. Trumbull, who had jumped in beside the chauffeur, and the long black car lunged forward, narrowly missing an assiduous photographer with flash bulb upraised and camera aimed.

Bill leaned forward, ignoring the man between them, and demanded of Virginia in a low voice, "Are you all right?"

"Right as rain," she replied cheerfully, and reached across her father to pat Bill's arm reassuringly.

"For Christ's sake, what happened?" he demanded.

"Didn't they tell you? Mrs. Camarilla was shot sometime today; and the big fellow, the one that's in charge, when he came to ask me what I knew about it, somehow or other recognized me. I'll never know how."

"So that's it," Bill said weakly.

"And," Virginia added brightly, "I think they think I did it."

Both men released startled exclamations.

"Good God Almighty," Douglas said on a despairing rising and falling cadence.

"Oh," Virginia said belatedly, "I forgot. This is my father, Bill, and, Father, this is my husband."

Douglas ignored the introduction and groaned, "If this is true, what you said about being suspected, it's even worse than I thought."

"It can't be, Virginia," Bill asserted with determined rejection. "If they suspected you, they wouldn't have let you go."

"Oh, they suspect me all right," she said complacently. "But I think Father's social position scared 'em, and Mr. Trumbull worried them too. They probably need more evidence before they really get tough."

Douglas straightened tautly and looked at his daughter. "Virginia!" His voice was muted with horror. "You didn't, did you? Kill the woman?"

"Father! How could I? I didn't have a gun. And besides, I hardly knew her."

"How can you think she'd do such a thing?" Bill snapped angrily.

"After everything else she's done," Douglas retorted irritably, "I wouldn't put anything past her."

"I—I know, sir," Bill said uneasily. "I—you probably won't believe me, but I'm sorry. That we had to do it this way. It—it just seemed—Well, there didn't seem to be any other way. I guess I should have been firmer, but Virginia—well—" He paused helplessly. "Well, you know Virginia."

"We will discuss this," Douglas said coldly, "with Mr. Trumbull when we get to the house."

"If you're thinking," Virginia said belligerently, "of annulment, you'd better think again, because I won't have it. Besides, suppose I'm pregnant. You wouldn't want an illegitimate grandchild, would you?"

"Virginia! Have you no modesty?"

"No."

"Virginia," Bill chided, "you know perfectly well you aren't—"

"How do you know—"

"Virginia!" Douglas roared. Then he leaned back, closing his eyes exhaustedly. He was not a roaring type, and this being out of character was wearing on him.

For the rest of the way they rode in silence except when Virginia said in a relieved tone, "Well, at least now I can let my hair grow back and throw away that lipstick." She reached down inside her sweater to tug at something and came up with a wide cone of sponge rubber. "And I can get rid of these things. You have no idea how hot they are to wear—"

"Virginia," her father repeated in an exacerbated tone, but his voice had lost some of its spirit.

When they reached the house Madeline and Henry awaited them in the hall of the entrance where the car pulled up. Madeline had remained at Rolling Hills to give comfort and moral support to her fiancé. She had telephoned Henry that his cousin had been found, whereat the boy had felt it his duty to drive down from the campus to lend an air of family solidarity to the homecoming.

Without the falsies and with the heavy lipstick rubbed off Virginia looked a little more like herself, so Madeline's eyes widened only slightly and her cries of greeting were not too colored by startled amazement. She grasped the girl's hands and kissed her unresponsive mouth; and Henry said, "Hi, stranger. You sure had us going around in circles," and put his hand on Virginia's shoulder and brushed her cheek with his lips.

Both he and Madeline had covertly and wonderingly taken note of the dark-haired young man in rumpled white pants and a windbreaker jacket who had accompanied the group into the hall.

Henry and Madeline had no more than executed their welcoming gestures when Mrs. Arnold appeared in the doorway of the corridor that led back to the kitchen. She hesitated uncertainly, but as Virginia's eyes fell upon her and the girl nonchalantly lifted a hand with a "Hi, Esther," she seemed deliberately to surrender to impulse and came billowing forward in a little rush, crying, "Virginia, Virginia, you're really home! Safe!" She hugged the girl convulsively and pressed her face against Virginia's hair. Then she pulled her head back, and her face quivered. "We were so worried. So worried." She clutched the prodigal again and gulped, and tears began to trickle down her cheeks. "You poor baby. Are you all right?" She held the girl off and gazed at her with brimming, anxious eyes.

Virginia nodded dumbly, at a loss for the first time since being reclaimed to her correct status. Then Mrs. Arnold grasped her shoulders and, with tears spilling from her eyes and her lips trembling, shook Virginia vigorously. "You ought to be spanked, scaring everybody like this. For all we knew, you could have been dead, or something else terrible. Don't you ever do anything like that again. D'you hear me?"

Virginia lowered her chin, and the effort with which she controlled the quivering of her own lips was evident. She moved her head in some kind of response to Mrs. Arnold's adjuration.

The latter had quit shaking her, and with a last little helpless pat on the girl's shoulders, still ignoring the others, she turned and rushed off toward the back of the house, overcome. Surreptitiously Virginia rubbed the back of her fist across her cheek.

The family had watched the scene in startled silence, and Bill had looked down at his hands as they pulled at his folded cap.

Douglas cleared his throat. "Virginia, go into the living room with Madeline and Henry. Mr. Trumbull and I will see Mr. Morgan in the study."

Virginia lifted her head and blinked her damp eyelashes. "Oh no, you don't. Any talks you have with Bill I'll sit in on."

Madeline and Henry exchanged puzzled glances.

"Virginia, won't you please be reasonable?" Douglas sighed.

"No. I'm a grown-up married woman and I'm going to be treated as such."

Madeline gasped, and Henry's mouth fell open, and both looked from Virginia to the embarrassed young man in the background.

"Oh—you must pardon me," Virginia suddenly addressed the astonished pair, "I haven't introduced you." Graciously she presented Bill first to Madeline, then to Henry. Madeline stammered unintelligibly, and Henry asserted, "Well, I'll be damned," frankly staring at Bill.

Douglas broke in, "Mr. Morgan, if you'll come this way—and, Virginia, go with Madeline and Henry."

Virginia met his eyes with cool dignity, and now her voice was level, no longer defiant, no longer argumentative.

"I'm sorry, Father. I meant what I said. I'm a married woman, and I intend to be treated as such. Come on, Bill, we'll both go to the study."

As she headed for a door down the hall, Mr. Trumbull met Douglas's eyes and shrugged slightly. The three men followed the girl into a room furnished with bookshelves, a desk, and leather-covered armchairs. Virginia had already switched on a floor lamp when they entered.

In the hall Henry and Madeline met one another's eyes blankly, and he repeated, "Well, I will be damned."

CHAPTER 10

Virginia leaned against the edge of the flat-topped desk with her hands in her pockets. "Now," she said, "let's get this over with, once and for all—"

"If you don't mind," Mr. Trumbull interrupted, "I'll take over now. Since, to avoid still another scene, we have allowed you to be present, Virginia, we shall permit you to remain, but you will please not interrupt. Sit down, Mr. Morgan."

"Thanks, I'd rather stand." Bill tucked his cap under his arm and pulled a package of cigarettes from the breast pocket of his jacket.

Virginia's eyes had narrowed, gleaming dangerously, but she said nothing.

"I wish to remind both of you," Mr. Trumbull said curtly, "that this so-called marriage is illegal and that you, Mr. Morgan, are technically guilty of contributing to the delinquency of a minor."

Bill dropped his match in an ash tray. "I can swear that I believed Virginia was over eighteen, which is the legal age for marriage in this state."

"All the newspapers reported her true age in last Monday's papers."

"Maybe I don't read newspapers."

"Let's quit fencing," Douglas broke in irascibly. "You know that we can make it hot for you if we choose. And we will if necessary, but I'd rather avoid further scandal. The best thing as I see it, Morgan, is for you to have a quiet talk alone with Mr. Trumbull, and he'll see what can be worked out."

"You're forgetting, Father," Virginia's voice intruded silkily, "in less than four years I'll be worth three million dollars. Bill would be a fool not to hang onto me instead of selling out now for a few thousand."

"That might be better than spending the next four years in the pen," Trumbull snapped.

"I don't know that you've got anything on him that would put him in jail. After all, we conformed to all the rules that society and religion demand, even if it wasn't quite legal."

Bill's voice broke in harshly: "Let's get this straight: I'm not making any deals. And I didn't marry Virginia for her money. I knew what we were doing was risky, but I thought we might get away with it, and I figured she'd be a hell of a lot better off married to me than she would be running wild the way she was. She needed to be settled down and have somebody to look after her, somebody that cared what happened to her and that she cared about. We weren't going to stay in the trailer forever. When things died down a little we were going to get an apartment so we could live decent. Maybe she'd have got a part-time job or something to keep her from getting restless. And I'd never have run off like this with her if I'd thought there was half a chance you'd consent to our even going steady or being engaged. And another thing—and you can make anything you want out of it—I never had any intention of keeping her from getting her money when she came of age. She's entitled to it, and when she's twenty-one you couldn't interfere with her life."

"Of all the brazen—" Mr. Trumbull breathed.

Douglas glared at the young man. "Do you realize that this child is only seventeen years old?"

"Seventeen years and three months and two weeks," Virginia corrected. "And I've been thinking of something else while I've been sitting here." She nodded at two photographs in oval frames on the wall. One was of a woman in a pompadour coiffure and a tucked shirtwaist with a high, boned collar and leg-of-mutton sleeves, the other of a man wearing a celluloid collar and a walrus mustache, his hair parted on the side to rise in a patently artificial wave. "Those pictures were taken much later, of course, but Grandma Wilkins was married one week after her sixteenth birthday. They eloped too. I've heard the story often. And if it weren't for Grandma Wilkins I wouldn't even be here."

"Times have changed since then," Douglas snapped.

"Maybe times have, but people haven't. At least not that much."

"This is all beside the point," Trumbull intervened irritatedly. "I think if both Mr. Forester and Virginia would leave us alone, Mr. Morgan and I could talk this over."

Virginia straightened purposefully from where she half sat against the desk. "I've had enough of all this. Now I'll do the talking—"

"May I remind you—" Mr. Trumbull began threateningly.

"I said it before, and I'm saying it again: you shut up. I'm young, yes, but I'm no baby. I'll admit most girls my age are drooling infants. And why not? They're babied and taken care of and looked after. But nobody ever babied or took care of me. It's true I've had money and a place to live provided for me, but otherwise I've been on my own, practically ever since my mother died, and I've learned to look out for myself. And I can afford to be independent because"—she bowed ironically toward the photographs—"thanks to Grandma and Grandpa, I know that when I'm twenty-one I won't have to ask anybody for anything. So—"

She took a deep breath. "Let's quit playing games and get down to business. I hold the whip hand, and you know it—"

Douglas looked at Trumbull with dismay. "She's insane."

Trumbull passed his hand wearily over his forehead. "You'd better get her off to her room. We'll never get anywhere allowing this kind of thing."

Virginia had taken a step or two away from the group. As she paced back again, her hands in her pockets, eyes on the broadloom carpet, she seemed to be ignoring her elders. Now she looked up at them candidly. "Even if it weren't for this murder, you would still be smart to give me my way, because you'd have a hard time controlling me. No school will want me after this, no matter what you pay them; and we'll be news from now on, much more than we were before; and if I don't get my way, I can bring on more unpleasant publicity any time I want to."

She surveyed each of them seriously. "You don't any of you quite believe it, but I'm telling you, it's true. That detective captain, Granger, honestly believes I killed Mrs. Camarilla. He thinks I'm wild. I guess I do look rather tough in this make-up. Apparently nobody else in the trailer park had any reason to kill her, and he thinks I did it because she recognized me—"

"Preposterous!" This was Trumbull.

"I know, but you must believe me. That's the bee he has in his bonnet. Don't you see? He figures there's a connection between my being there and her getting killed. Two unusual things happening at the same time. Therefore"—she threw out her hands—"they must be connected!"

"But, my dear child," Douglas protested, "they wouldn't dare. The granddaughter of Henry Wilkins!"

"Don't kid yourself. They'd love it. The police and the newspapers and the public." She regarded him tolerantly. "Really, Father, you're so naïve sometimes. They hate us, all of them. Envy, I suppose," she digressed with a judicious air. "The fact that our money protects us from the police most of the time makes them that much more bloodthirsty when they catch us where it won't protect us."

"Where does she get such ideas?" Douglas exclaimed helplessly.

"Anyway, you must see what I mean. I know. They really put me through the wringer while you were on the way in, kept wanting to know what I did with the gun. They're going to watch every move we make, always with that murder in mind. And don't you see, if we get to raising hell amongst ourselves, annulling marriages and me carrying on, it'll strengthen the motive I was supposed to have, that I was afraid to be found. On the other hand, if everything is peaches and cream and you give out to the reporters that it was all just young love and a romantic elopement, and if Bill and I settle down with your blessing, Father, why, where's their motive? Certainly I wouldn't shoot somebody to shut them up if I could come home to love and kisses whenever I chose."

"It seems to me," Trumbull said dryly, "this is a two-edged sword you're brandishing. After all, it is you who might be tried for murder if they can build up a circumstantial case. Therefore, for your own protection, it is up to you to be a good girl and do as you're told."

"No. It's Father and Madeline who would suffer from a long, messy session on the front pages. You see, *I* don't mind the unpleasant publicity; and as far as I'm concerned, prison is prison, no matter how you dress it up. If I'm going to be condemned by you to four years of restraint until I'm twenty-one, it's all the same to me whether it's here or in a house of correction. They'd never sentence me to execution. I'm too young," she finished, ironically demure.

"I think it's time I said something," Bill declared abruptly. "Maybe they think Virginia shot Mrs. Camarilla. But I doubt if they'll ever get enough evidence to arrest her. The way I look at it, though, knowing Virginia, you guys are going to have your hands full with her if you try to break us up. And like she says, she is old for her age. And anyway, she's seventeen. A lot of girls do get married that young. I know you don't approve of me. I don't have nothing except a job, and my family don't amount to anything. My folks live back in South Dakota," he explained parenthetically, adding defensively, "They're just as good as anybody else, even if they aren't well off. But whether you approve of me or not, that's neither here nor there. Virginia's satisfied"—his lips curved slightly in a smile as he met her eyes briefly—"and that's what's important. And all I can say, Mr. Forester, is I'll do my best to see that she's happy. If you want character references, you can ask the company I work for and the folks in my home town back east. I may not be the brightest guy in the world, but I've never got into any serious trouble, and—and"—he twisted his cap awkwardly—"I think a lot of Virginia and we seem to get along good."

He lifted his head and regarded Douglas bravely. "Maybe I'm wrong, but it seems to me that's as good as any father can ask for his daughter, three million dollars or no three million dollars."

Douglas looked nonplused and turned helplessly toward the attorney.

Trumbull dropped his eyes to the desk with a disgruntled frown and muttered after a moment, "Perhaps we'd better sleep on it. Take the matter up again in the morning. Personally, I don't feel we're getting anywhere."

Virginia spoke up. "Bill stays here tonight."

"He may occupy the remaining guest room," her father conceded icily.

"That's O.K." Bill spoke quickly to forestall a mutinous protest from Virginia. He smiled at her reassuringly.

So with sudden compliance she moved with the others out of the study. In the hall she announced without preamble, "I'm tired and I'm going to bed. Excuse me, please."

Turning her back on the men, she jogged up the stairs. In an exasperated tone her father called, "Good night, Virginia."

She turned with her hand on the banister. "Oh." And then, indifferently, "Good night. Night, Bill."

Inside her own room she glanced about with seeing eyes. It seemed as if her absence had been longer than six days, and it seemed much longer than that since she had really looked at the plain lines of the modern furniture and the turquoise and ivory color scheme enlivened with touches of bright coral.

She took a tub bath and put on a short night coat of heavy white silk and a warm white robe with a full skirt, and soft padded slippers. She sighed as she stepped across the yielding carpet. It was too bad that Bill could not be with her. She was so clean and sweet-smelling, and the room was so big and quiet and private. But she had interpreted his look in the study. It meant that if they wanted to win in the long run he thought it best now to go along, to accept cheerfully this first concession, that he be allowed to stay in the house, even on their terms.

Outside Virginia's door Mrs. Arnold hesitated for a moment with the tray in her hands. Her greeting of the girl downstairs had been unpremeditated. Without thinking she had followed her natural inclinations. But this gesture was deliberate, the result of thought, of remembering her feeling of responsibility for Virginia's disappearance, her sense of having been remiss toward the girl in the past, and of her resolve to be different if Virginia was ever found.

So she knocked on the door.

"Come in."

Steadying the tray against her body, Mrs. Arnold pushed the door open.

"I thought," she said heartily, "you might be hungry, so I brought you a little something. It's bad for you right at bedtime, but I guess this is a sort of special occasion, and a little celebration is in order."

Mrs. Arnold set the tray on a table beside the chaise longue.

"Angel-food cake!" Virginia exclaimed, and, lifting the lid of a tall china pot, "And hot chocolate."

"I knew how crazy you were about angel food," Mrs. Arnold said, forcing herself to sound bright and easy, "and as soon as I heard your father had gone to bring you home, I said to myself, 'Well, this is one time when we ought to have something special on hand,' so I whipped this cake up in a hurry."

"Why, Mrs. Arnold." Virginia looked down at the smooth linen napkin, the marshmallow waiting in the china cup. Her voice faltered. "Why, that was nice of you—"

"The way I figured," the woman blurted out, "it's *time* someone was nice to you. Do you want to sit in bed?" she suggested briskly. "I'll fix the tray over your legs and pour the chocolate."

"No, I'll sit here," Virginia said, perching on the edge of the chaise. "I'll have to brush my teeth again anyway."

As Mrs. Arnold poured chocolate into the cup, Virginia lifted her eyes to the woman's face. Somehow she felt disarmed, and as a result constrained to make some reciprocal gesture to this completely unexpected pampering.

"Did they tell you," she asked, "that I'm married?"

The lid clattered as Mrs. Arnold set the jug down. "Wha-at!"

"Yes, that's one reason I ran away. I knew Father would raise hell about Bill if he even thought we were going together. Probably ship me off to some Eastern school or something. So we figured the only thing to do was to cut loose completely."

Mrs. Arnold was staring at her. "Then that's who—the young man that was in the hall—I—I never paid much attention—I thought maybe he was just the one that located you—Well, I never," she concluded in a deflated voice.

She moved backward and sat down heavily on the dressing table stool.

Virginia began to enjoy the effect she was producing. "They think they're going to break us up, but they'll find out different. Um, this cake is delicious."

"How—how did you meet him?" Mrs. Arnold inquired weakly.

"He was working in a service station in Palo Alto where I used to stop for gas last spring when I took the car up to school with me sometimes. We got to kidding back and forth. He sort of flirted with me. And one day I came in just as he was getting off work and he asked me to go have a soda with him. It was Friday, and I was on my way home. We did that every Friday for a while; and in June when school was out we made arrangements for him to pick me up around here, places I could walk to from the house. I never went back to the station after that. We didn't want anybody getting wise that we were dating."

"Why?"

Virginia's eyes were scornful. "Can you imagine Father letting me go out with a fellow that worked in a service station?"

"No, I guess not."

Virginia sent the woman an impish glance through her lashes, her own now. "Many's the night when you thought I was innocently asleep in bed up here, I was out at a drive-in movie, or just parked someplace. Once we even drove as far as Santa Cruz and danced at the public dance hall."

With concerned eyes Mrs. Arnold watched the girl chase the melting marshmallow around the cup with her spoon, gulping it down with childish gusto when she had captured the gooey morsel.

"Well, I—I hope he's all right," the housekeeper murmured faintly.

Virginia eyed her shrewdly. "I know. You think it's just—sex. And I guess maybe it was, to start with, and maybe it still is mostly. Although," she went on thoughtfully, "I don't know just where you draw the line between just wanting a guy and—and having a good opinion of him. Love, I mean. Seems to me it's all mixed up together." She studied the dregs of the chocolate swirling in her cup as she moved it meditatively. "Tonight, though, there was something—more, something different in the way I felt about him down there in the study. I—I was—proud of him, I guess, the way he handled things. Stood back and let me run the show, didn't try to shove me out and do it all himself, but then, just as I was beginning to feel I'd come to the end of my rope—although I don't think I showed it—he seemed to know it, and he stepped in and took over, didn't act a bit scared or anything. He was so calm and sort of sure of himself. It made me feel stronger. Maybe that's what they mean by love—aside from sex."

"Well—well, I'm sure I don't know," Mrs. Arnold murmured. "But I hope so. Now that you're into it, I do hope so."

When the housekeeper had gone and Virginia was lying in bed with the lights out, she thought rebelliously of Bill far off down the hall in the third and last guest room—Madeline and Mr. Trumbull would have already appropriated the two more desirable ones—and she resented their senseless separation. After all, he was her husband.

Lying with the covers pulled close around her neck, her knees drawn up, her hands curled at her chest, Virginia felt little and young and unprotected. It was the way, she realized with surprise, that she always used to feel when she relaxed and let go and was alone and could quit even unconscious pretending. Like a lonely, weak little girl. And she realized now that when she was with Bill this was not her inner image of herself. Living with him, she had actually felt like her conscious conception of Virginia Forester—sure of herself, worthwhile, not a little girl.

She sighed audibly in the darkened room. Well, this was part of being a big girl, to take your time, play it smart.

But she wished Bill was with her so she could talk to him, because there was no getting away from it, she was scared. She had talked big down there in the study, defied them; but she did not really feel defiant about this business of the murder. She had told the truth when she said the detective captain suspected her of the murder. He did. She knew it. He thought she was wild and irresponsible and perfectly capable of such a thing. And he thought she had a reason for it.

It would probably never go any farther than that, but still it was not pleasant.

All at once she remembered something she had forgotten, and she frowned. The gun in those people's trailer—the ones from Washington.

Probably lots of people had guns. Probably the Beans and those two fellows in the next space to hers and Bill's, and the Grandons. But this one gun she had seen with her own two eyes. Had anyone else seen her see it? Would it help if the police knew of that gun? Would their knowing help to diffuse their suspicions, divert their thoughts from her? Or would it clinch the case against her if they learned it had lain within reach of her hand?

She must not be afraid. Suspicion was one thing. Definitely accusing her of the crime was another. For almost the first time in her life she was consciously appreciative of her father's social position, of the bulwark of Grandpa Wilkins's fortune which made possible the retention of Trumbull and as many more like him as should ever become necessary.

She fell at last into a troubled sleep.

CHAPTER 11

With the discovery of "Mrs. Morgan's" identity, the sheriff's office went all out in the investigation of what would otherwise have been the unimportant murder of an unimportant woman; for the Virginia Forester story was front-page news all over the state, and its connection with the murder placed the latter under a spotlight it would not otherwise have merited.

While Captain Granger interviewed the Foresters at the courthouse two other detectives doggedly questioned the remaining tenants of Shady Dell. The results were discouraging at first. No one had noticed any activity around the end trailer on the right-hand side at any time during the morning, and everyone who knew her had been just crazy about Mrs. Camarilla. At least they all strove to give that impression now. The Camarillas had, so far as anyone at Shady Dell knew, no acquaintances or friends outside the limits of the trailer park. None of the tenants admitted to knowing of any hard feelings between Mrs. Camarilla and any other member of the little colony. Only Josie MacLaren, between protestations of horror and intermittent tears, gave any indication that Stella was not universally beloved.

Even murder had not dammed Josie's garrulity, and in the course of her conversation with the detectives she paused once with a dawning gleam in her eye.

"The only person," she said slowly, "that I ever heard say a word against her—and that wasn't really a criticism—was that Mrs. Morgan in Number Five. I do remember how she made several slighting remarks about Stella in my presence, and"—bristling—"you can bet your life I shut her up in a hurry."

"Just what was the nature of these remarks?"

Josie frowned with the effort of recollection. "Well, it was more just a vague *tone*. Like yesterday afternoon when we were in those Washington people's house, Mrs. Morgan spoke of Stella as a 'person' in a sort of slurring way. I think she called her 'inquisitive,' if I remember correctly. But," she added hastily, "I don't suppose it really meant anything."

"You spoke of being in 'those Washington people's house.' Who was there, and what were the circumstances?"

"Oh, it was just Mrs. Parsons and Mrs. Morgan and I. Mr. Wilson invited us to come in and see their trailer. It was such a nice one. We had a Coke with him and his wife and just visited with them for a while."

Every trailer was searched for firearms, but all that were brought to light were a rifle belonging to Mr. Bean and a shotgun of Mr. Skaggs's. With the help of the overhead lights behind each parking space and of powerful flashlights the officers searched the grounds thoroughly and still found no gun, .32 or otherwise.

Captain Granger decided not to wait until morning to question the Grandons, whose trailer stood side by side with that of the Camarillas; and men were sent to the drive-in restaurant to interview Billie and then on to the Four Leaf Clover Club to talk to Monty, who was called away from his table to answer their questions.

Mrs. Bean had said the Wilsons were heading south and had spoken of doing the Monterey peninsula next on their tour; so word was sent out immediately to the Monterey County sheriff's office to have all trailer courts contacted in order to locate the Wilsons, slim as the chance was that while they prepared to pull out that morning they might have seen or heard anything pertinent to the case.

The Wilson equipage was found without difficulty, nestled under the pines within a short distance of the rocky shore line at Pacific Grove, some seventy-five miles from Shady Dell in another similar though larger park, this one labeled Ocean Pines. Since the Monterey County officers had been comprehensively informed of the facts and instructed by telephone as to what information was desired from the Wilsons, the Monterey sheriff co-operatively took over part of the burden from his neighboring officers and sent two deputies to ask the necessary questions of the couple from Washington.

They arrived only just in time to intercept the Wilsons, who were prepared to set forth on the Seventeen Mile Drive as the next leg of their journey. Mrs. Wilson was trying the door of the house to be sure it was latched properly, and Mr. Wilson was drawing on his gloves preparatory to stepping in behind the wheel when the two men approached them from the direction of the little rustic office near the road.

"Mr. Wilson?" the spokesman accosted him.

"Yes."

"We're acting on behalf of the Santa Clara County sheriff's office. We'd like to talk to you for a few minutes."

Mr. Wilson's eyes seemed to bug out slightly. "Why—why, sure. What's the matter? Anything wrong?"

"There was some trouble at the place where you stayed night before last, and we're hoping you may have information that will help in straightening it out."

"Well—well, anything I can do, of course, I'll be glad to— Trouble? I don't understand. What's up?"

Mrs. Wilson had remained still, her hand on the door handle, her eyes intent on the strangers.

"Could we go inside and talk?"

"Yes. Yes, I guess so."

As the men passed the automobile Mrs. Wilson slowly sorted a key from the bunch in her hand and opened the door, proceeding into the house ahead of the others.

"This is my wife," Mr. Wilson explained.

With some constraint the group found chairs, eying one another warily. The older, more heavyset man spoke first while his companion sat back impassively, obviously playing the role of witness.

"We understand you people pulled out of the Beans' trailer park at roughly 9 A.M. yesterday morning."

"That's right."

"One thing we would like to know—did you see anyone at this camp"—he consulted a slip of paper in his hand—"Shady Dell, that you had met before?"

"No. Not a soul."

"You, Mrs. Wilson?"

She shook her head.

"Could you give me an account of your activities yesterday morning up until the time you left the place?"

"Activities? Why, we got up, and dressed, and had breakfast—" Mr. Wilson paused and glanced at his wife. "I don't know what else besides—"

Mrs. Wilson spoke up. "You could hardly call that 'activity.' It was just what we always do. Why, we weren't out of the house or out of each other's sight."

"Unless you count," Mr. Wilson said, "when you took the garbage out. Remember, I said I'd do it, and you said never mind, and you—"

"Oh, that—" She laughed lightly. "It was just a step, and I was back in half a minute. It was raining, you know. But what is it that's happened? What were we supposed to have done, or seen? That you want to know, I mean?"

The officer noticed that Mr. Wilson looked puzzled, but he had looked that way ever since they first spoke to him.

"The woman in the end parking space, a Mrs. Camarilla, was found dead yesterday afternoon—shot through the head."

Mrs. Wilson exclaimed and pressed her hand to her breast in a horrified gesture. "Oh, my!"

"Say, that's terrible." Mr. Wilson sat forward in his chair.

"Did either of you meet the lady while you were there?"

"Oh no."

Mr. Wilson pinched his lower lip. "Say, could that be the woman you were talking to, Wanda, when we first got parked, the one that walked down the driveway?"

"I wasn't *talking* to her, dear. Just some woman went by and I just glanced up and she said, 'How do you do,' and I nodded. I hardly noticed what she looked like. My goodness, I wonder if she was the one!"

"Tall, dark-haired woman," the officer volunteered helpfully.

"Now, it could have been. At least, I think that woman was dark, though I just barely glanced at her."

"Well," the officer said briskly, "the thing is, you folks were up and around, around the time she seems to have been killed, and we'd like to know if you heard the shot or saw anybody coming in or going out. You might have seen somebody from one of your windows."

Mr. Wilson wrinkled his brow and thought hard, and finally shook his head. "I don't think so. It was raining hard, and I don't remember even looking out—to look around, that is—until we got out to get in the car. And I'm positive I never heard a shot, but I don't know as we would have heard it. There was quite a wind early in the morning."

"I don't remember anything either," his wife volunteered.

"Another thing, then, do you folks carry a gun of any kind with you?" Mr. Wilson thrust his head forward, antagonistic for the first time. "Now, look here—"

"We have a search warrant," the officer said imperturbably. "All the houses on the lot there have been searched, and just as a matter of routine we'll have to search this one."

"Well, really," Mrs. Wilson protested.

"O.K.," her husband conceded ungraciously. "We do have a gun, and I've got a permit too. Traveling around like this and staying in lonely places sometimes, a person has to have one." With a disapproving glance at the men he rose and went to the drawer whose contents Virginia had seen.

He opened the drawer and moved his hand in it, then he peered inside and stirred more energetically.

His head turned and he looked at the others blankly. "By God," he said tonelessly, "it's gone."

"Why, Rupert," his wife spoke up efficiently, "I'm sure it's there. I saw it yesterday morning." She, too, fished around and pushed articles aside, and then exclaimed, "Why, wherever—"

Mr. Wilson looked at her fearfully, and back at the men. Then he sat down.

"What type of gun was it?" the officer inquired easily.

"Thirty-two automatic." Suddenly Mr. Wilson raised his head hopefully. "Say, wa-ait a minute. I just remembered something." He turned to his wife with an animated movement. "You remember day before yesterday those women that came in to see the house and we gave 'em a Coke?"

"Yes?" she prompted expectantly.

"Well, that flashy one—I forget her name—anyway, she had red hair; she was sitting right there on the seat beside the drawer when I opened it to get some extra ash trays, and I saw her look right down at the gun; she seemed kind of interested, come to think of it."

"I remember," his wife said eagerly. "Not that I noticed her when you opened the drawer, but she was sitting right there all the time; and when they all got up to go, everybody just standing around the way people do, you know, saying, 'Well, we must go,' and then still talking. Well, that girl stood there in front of the shelves. It was sort of crowded, everybody bunched up opposite the drawer, and as I recollect," Mrs. Wilson said slowly, enunciating each syllable thoughtfully, "everybody sort of had their backs to her—you know, facing the door. Anyway, she was sort of back of the rest of us—"

Mr. Wilson grasped at the lead. "She could've reached in and took it and hid it under her sweater, stuck under the waistband of her slacks."

"Of course," Mrs. Wilson demurred, "that sounds like an awfully bold thing to do, with all of us right there in front of her."

"She could have had her hands behind her back," Mr. Wilson persisted, "and, if she had a belt on under her sweater, hooked it into her belt somehow in the back."

The officers had been listening silently at with unwavering attention, and now Mrs. Wilson turned briskly to the drawers.

"No, I can't believe it," she declared. "We've just mislaid it." Busily she went to work opening drawers and stirring at their contents.

The older officer spoke authoritatively. "We'll have to search the place anyhow when we leave. So never mind that now. This bunch you had in here day before yesterday, tell me some more about that."

Speaking alternately and sometimes in unison, the Wilsons recounted the details of the call. "Was this Mrs. Camarilla mentioned while they were with you?"

Wide-eyed, Mrs. Wilson glanced at her husband. "Why, come to think of it, she was. Mrs. MacLaren spoke about how this woman liked living in a trailer, and—" Her eyes took on an abstracted glaze. "I'm just trying to remember," she explained to the men. "And yes, now I remember, that girl, the redheaded one, she made some kind of a catty remark about the woman. Uncalled for, I remember thinking at the time; and Mrs. MacLaren, she seemed to think a lot of the Camarilla person, she said something, I forget what, to the redheaded one, showing she didn't approve of what the girl said." Mrs. Wilson turned anxiously to her husband. "Wasn't that right, Rupert?"

"Well, I remember her name coming up and the girl saying something. It was kind of—well, making fun of this Camarilla woman, I think."

Irrelevantly the officer inquired, "Incidentally, what route did you folks follow coming down here?"

"Why, we took Seventeen out of San Jose, around through Los Gatos and Santa Cruz. I guess we kind of took the long way round, but we heard it was awful pretty through that way, and we hoped the rain would let up so we could see something. Then we went through Watsonville and Moss Landing to Monterey and walked around on the wharf, had an early dinner at a restaurant out there."

The deputy was silent for an instant, digesting this information. He was making careful mental notes to the effect that the "redheaded girl" who these people had not yet learned was Virginia Forester had seen and had access to the missing gun, but at the same time they had been awful quick with the information, and you couldn't disregard the fact that they could have disposed of the gun themselves—a .32-caliber—and the murdered woman had been killed by a bullet from a .32. He thought dejectedly of the miles of wooded ravines along the Los Gatos–Santa Cruz highway and of the deep waters of the bay around the wharf in Monterey. The route they had traveled had provided plenty of places for "losing" a small automatic.

CHAPTER 12

On the evening before, the officers had deliberately withheld from the occupants of Shady Dell the fact that the erstwhile Mrs. Morgan was actually the missing heiress. The morning newspapers and radio broadcasts were, consequently, a shattering revelation to Virginia's former neighbors. They kept saying to each other, "I just can't believe it," or,

"Imagine! She was right here all the time. And worth three million dollars." Only Josie MacLaren went around asserting in high, outraged tones, "I knew all the time there was something funny about her. I kept telling everybody so. But would anybody believe me! Oh no. No, everybody just thought I was crazy."

When he was sure the news would be well disseminated among the residents, Captain Granger again invaded the precincts of Shady Dell. He was a prosaic man who did not believe in wild coincidences, and when on the same day two such startling occurrences as the discovery of a missing heiress and the murder of a woman who apparently had no enemies took place within less than a hundred feet of each other, he tended to look for a connection between the two. If the theory that had come to him the night before had any basis in fact, now that her former neighbors knew who "Mrs. Morgan" really was, he might be able to gather some inkling as to whether Stella had indicated that she did know the girl's identity, and whether anyone had reason to believe that the girl knew she knew it. To the people who had seen and talked to both women in the past three days the actions of both might now appear in a different light.

Systematically Granger trudged from coach to coach, alone this time, questioning, prodding, prying. He noticed a philosophical but uncomfortable attitude in those he talked to, as if they understood but didn't like the necessity of being involved in an investigation of murder. As his questioning inevitably revealed his interest both in the murdered woman and in the heiress, and in their relationship to each other, there was an awakening comprehension, an awareness, a questioning on the part of the questioned. He had not meant to implant suspicions in their minds, but he realized that his strategy made it inevitable.

He had not personally seen the Grandons until now, and in the somewhat stuffy, early-morning atmosphere of their trailer, with a haze of cigarette smoke and the smell of coffee and scorched eggs in the air, he took them over their story once more.

When he had found out what they knew of Stella's friendship or lack of it with the other tenants, he inquired offhandedly, "Did she get acquainted with Mrs. Morgan, who, I guess you've heard, is really Virginia Forester?"

"Yes, they met each other."

"Do you happen to know the circumstances, just how it happened?"

"We-ell," Billie said thoughtfully, "I think Stella said she went to call on her, her being a stranger and alone all day and all."

"Did she discuss the girl with you folks?"

"Well, not really *discuss*. But, let's see—was it Wednesday, Monty, that Marge came over and asked me about getting on where I work? I think it was. And Mrs. Camarilla came up afterward—we were sitting outside in the sun, and we did talk about Marge Morgan—or should I call her Forester now? Anyway, we just made a few idle remarks."

"Would you say Mrs. Camarilla seemed particularly interested in her?"

Billie was answering the questions while Monty sat back in a silence that seemed almost taciturn.

"I don't think so," she said, "but," with a glance at her husband, "I remember afterward Monty said he thought she came out on purpose to find out what we were talking about with Marge."

"In talking to you, did she give any indication that she thought the girl might be other than what she was—that is, that she thought there was anything funny about her?"

Monty and Billie were gazing at the officer with absorbed expressions, their minds obviously working hard on the ideas suggested by the line of his interrogation.

Monty looked down at his hands and replied slowly, "I'd say just the opposite. I was the one, come to think of it, said something about this girl reminded me of society dames I'd seen in places I worked; and the way I recollect now, Mrs. Camarilla was awful quick to call me on it. She said she'd talked to Mrs. Morgan herself and she figured her as being as common as they come."

"Now about yesterday morning." Granger cast a significant glance at the east windows through which could be seen the drawn blinds next door. "You're not more than ten feet away here." He paused interrogatively.

"We should have heard something?" Billie ventured.

"Didn't you?"

The Grandons met one another's eyes uneasily, a fact the detective noted.

It was Monty who spoke. "We both work evenings, and we're used to sleeping in mornings with cars starting up all over the place, engines racing to warm up and backfires sometimes. I know I was restless yesterday morning. The rain makes a lot of noise on this roof, and the wind was a regular gale. Seems to me I heard a loud crack once or twice, but I noticed after we got up that some branches were broke off the tree at the end of the lot. One extra noise, more or less, like a gun going off, wouldn't do more than disturb our sleep a little."

"That's right," Billie seconded.

Privately discouraged, the captain let it go at that.

He went next to Mrs. MacLaren. He had saved her until last, since she had seemed to be on the most intimate terms with Stella Camarilla. Since the weather had cleared Mr. MacLaren was out on his rounds once more. As the detective stolidly proceeded from one house to another, Josie had watched from behind her net curtains, fuming with impatience and fearing that she might be overlooked. She welcomed him almost effusively, and Granger now found himself the party subject to interrogation. He made vague replies but for a time allowed the interview to proceed in that manner while he listened politely to Josie's disjointed outpourings.

"I knew," she chattered after a while, "right from the start that there was something out of the way about that girl. Mrs. Morgan, you know. Although I never dreamed— It was just woman's intuition, I guess. I just felt she wasn't what she seemed. More than once I said so to poor Stella, but she always just smiled it off, sort of teasing me about taking so much interest in other people—"

"You spoke of your suspicions to Mrs. Camarilla then—that there was something false about Mrs. Morgan?"

"Oh dear, yes. And I told Mrs. Bean too. Her being away two solid weeks like that after just stopping by for an hour or so, you might say, and him staying on. But would they listen to me? Oh no. And to think that if it hadn't been for this happening to poor dear Stella her and that young man might have gotten away with it indefinitely. Were they really married, do you know?"

"They went through the forms. Whether it was legal or not is something else again."

"Well, I said right from the start, she'll cause trouble. She's just the type."

"You think then that there was some connection between Mrs. Camarilla's death and Virginia Forester's presence here?"

Josie's ready tongue was silenced for once, and her jaw hung slack. Then she gulped. "Why—why, no. Why, no, I hadn't thought of that. Was there?" she countered with returning vigor.

"I don't know," Granger answered simply. "But we have to look into all the possibilities."

Josie retired into startled reflection, and Granger waited. At last she murmured, "Come to think of it, it was unusual for Stella to go see her—take her cookies even. Stella wasn't the social type—that way. She always seemed satisfied with just her and Tony, friendly if other people wanted to be, but she didn't seem to need to seek people out. Other people moved in here—like the Ingleborgs and the Grandons—after the Camarillas had been here long enough to be what you might call old residents, and I don't remember Stella ever going out of her way to make any of them feel at home. Such things—well, they just never seemed to occur to her."

"You talked to Mrs. Morgan several times, I understand. Did she ever indicate what she thought or felt about Mrs. Camarilla?"

Josie's eyes were considering as they rested upon him. "She didn't like her," she stated absently. "And that's funny, when you come to think of it. Everybody liked Stella. And you'd think, her being so thoughtful and taking cookies to her, that Mrs. Morgan would have felt kindly toward

Stella."

"Did she ever—Mrs. Morgan, that is—come right out and say she disliked Mrs. Camarilla?"

"No. Oh no. It was just something you could tell. She—well, it was just a slighting way she had of speaking of Stella." Josie's eyes glazed with recollection. "For instance," she went on, "the day—Wednesday, I believe it was—that Mr. Wilson asked us in to look at their house—"

She went on to recount the conversation the Wilsons had already reported to the officer in Pacific Grove. Josie's account came out a little differently, giving the impression that there had been more specific derogatory implications in Marge Morgan's references to Stella, but it dealt with the same now blurred exchange of remarks.

When Granger returned to his office he gathered together all the reports on the case, including a detailed telephone account of the interview with the Wilsons. Closing the door against interruption, he reviewed the material on the case.

One thing stared him in the face all the way through. Again and again, from every witness, the statement recurred, "Everybody liked Stella." And all the information they had garnered about the Camarillas presented an innocuous picture of a quiet middle-aged couple living a rather unconventional itinerant life, perhaps, but with the husband respected in the places where he had worked locally, the wife in good repute with her neighbors. Quiet people who paid their bills and lived simply and who found it convenient to follow seasonal work in a trailer.

Only Virginia Forester "spoke slightingly" of the woman, had revealed an antagonistic attitude toward her.

Although the Camarillas seemed to be out of debt and to have enough money laid by to carry them a month or two if necessary, they were poor people. Ten thousand dollars would look very big to the woman. Granger rested the lower part of his face in his hand and recalled Stella's body and the room it had lain in. Her hair had been obviously dyed, and although she had worn no make-up in death, the cabinets in the trailer had been well stocked with cosmetic aids. She, perhaps more than anyone else at Shady Dell, had been competent to see past a job of hair tinting, false eyelashes, and a painted-on mouth. *He* had seen past them, assisted, of course, by a varied selection of photographs studied under magnification; but a woman like Stella might have been able to see through them assisted only by the necessarily inadequate newspaper photograph. And the girl had not wanted to be found. She had had to run away to get the man she wanted, and she had feared her family would separate them somehow if they recaptured her. She had perhaps an overconfidence in her disguise, had been willing to take the risk of fooling police investigators as opposed to certain disclosure if Mrs. Camarilla's suspicions drew both the police and her family to the scene.

Granger put the fingers of both hands to his forehead and pressed them there. But it was all ephemeral, based on probabilities, on vague recollections of what would be meaningless conversations if repeated in a courtroom. His only chance had been to hang onto the girl and keep putting on the pressure until she broke. And that chance was gone now that she was safely barricaded behind her father's money. He had been too hasty. He could have pretended not to recognize her until later, until she had been held long enough as a material witness to get what they wanted out of her. His actions had been natural, however, almost instinctive. Where a family like the Wilkins-Foresters was involved, the police were careful to stay well within the law in their treatment of its members. And he, too, had wanted to clinch the reward.

The only concrete, definite thing they might have had to go on was the gun, and it had disappeared—for good, he suspected gloomily. The girl, if it was in her possession, would have had all day to dispose of it, to bury it, perhaps, in a vacant lot, or hide it deep in some garbage can—not the one at Shady Dell, but any other one in some alley. She wouldn't normally be carrying a gun, although the husband could have had one. It linked up, however, the Wilsons' firearm being gone and Virginia's having seen it. The whole thing was too coincidental. Her hands, it was true, had shown no traces of powder burns when they gave her the paraffin test after apprehending her, but this was not definitive. She could have worn gloves and disposed of them.

Granger continued to ponder. It was a mistake to concentrate too much on one theory, no matter how pat it seemed. These Wilsons now. They had been at the place less than eighteen hours, and during those hours a woman was shot by a .32 bullet. They had admittedly owned a .32 and now could not find it. They, too, had had ample opportunity to "lose" it on a day's drive over rugged mountains and along precipitous sea cliffs.

Now Granger ran his hand through his hair. But Christ, to trace back through both the Wilsons' lives, starting with Everett, Washington, and back through the Camarilla past, which would lead all over the Southwest, would be a staggering task and probably a wild-goose chase. Besides, it was too fantastic. A prosperous small-town businessman and his wife, and an impecunious day laborer and his wife. What connection could there be?

And then there were the Grandons. The storm and their sleep-drugged condition could have prevented their recognizing the sound of a gunshot. But their trailer was only ten feet from the Camarillas'. They had conversed with Virginia at some length on more than one occasion, and they admitted suspecting that Mrs. Camarilla was taking an undue interest in the new tenant. Suppose they, too, had guessed her identity and had killed Stella in order to get the reward before she could.

But no. He rejected that theory quickly. They'd had all day to turn Marge Morgan in, and they hadn't.

No, it always came back to Virginia Forester, and the fact of her possible—indeed, probable—motive, and the incontrovertible testimony that she had at least seen a .32 automatic the day before the murder and had had an opportunity to purloin it for future use.

And then there were always the personalities to be considered. And you couldn't get away from it. The girl was willful, reckless, undisciplined, used to getting what she wanted. And you couldn't deny she had courage—or maybe bravado was a better word for it—the cunning with which she had handled her disappearance showed that. Also, she seemed to have a complete disregard for other people. If he had ever seen a likely candidate for the execution of a quick, impulsive, and rash killing, she was it.

There was nothing to do but go out to the Forester place and talk to the girl again. He rose, picked his hat off the rack, and went to get Jerry to accompany him.

CHAPTER 13

When Virginia awoke that morning her little white clock read eight-thirty. She must have been more tired than she realized, for she had meant to get up early and seek Bill out to talk things over before the others appeared at their usual hour around nine o'clock. She decided against dressing, and stepped into a long navy blue silk housecoat that zipped up the front to a little round red collar at her throat. As she combed her hair she frowned at herself in the glass. The collar did not go too well with the new shade of her hair, and she hesitated over her face. The bright hair, too curly from the home permanent she had given it, demanded the darkened brows and lashes and a bigger, gayer mouth. Her own coloring and the pink lipstick she had formerly worn left her face inadequate to the hair.

She knocked quietly at Bill's door, and after a moment opened it to see that the bed had been occupied but was now empty. Her expression clouded and her lips tightened angrily. Had they managed to spirit him away already?

Lifting her long skirt in both hands, she ran down the stairs, prepared to do battle. At the entrance to the dining room on the south side of the house she halted, deflated by the sight of the three men somewhat stiffly consuming their breakfasts. Her stormy expression faded, and Virginia said calmly, "Good morning, everybody."

Bill grinned. "Good morning."

Her father said coldly, "Good morning."

Only Mr. Trumbull rose politely and pulled out a chair for her as he murmured an indistinct greeting.

Douglas pressed the buzzer beside his plate to summon a maid.

"Where's everybody else?" Virginia asked cheerfully, unfolding her napkin.

"Henry drove back to the university to make a ten o'clock class," Douglas vouchsafed, "and Madeline left word last night that she would ring for breakfast in her room. She didn't think she would feel up to coming down this morning. This whole thing has been very upsetting to her," he concluded with a disapproving look at his daughter.

"Tough," she responded laconically, and turned to Bill. "I just remembered. Today and tomorrow are your days off. Doesn't that work out lucky? It gives us two days to work out what we're going to do. After breakfast I'll put on some jeans and heavy shoes and show you around the place—" She broke off as the maid entered. "Oh, hello, Imogene. You still here?"

"It—it's nice to see you back," the girl murmured uneasily, with a sidelong glance at her employer.

Virginia giggled. "This makes me think of the story about the little boy who ran away from home after lunch and changed his mind and came back in time for dinner, and when he came in said, 'Well, I see you've still got the same old cat.'"

"Virginia!" her father exploded.

Virginia raised contrite eyes to Imogene's face. "Oh, I didn't mean to compare you to a cat."

Imogene had set the girl's orange juice before her and poured her coffee. She uttered an uncomfortable note of sound intended to resemble laughter, and stammered, "That's all right," and escaped.

"Mr. Trumbull," Douglas announced, "has to return to the city this afternoon. We'll have to get things settled before he leaves."

"You aren't going until after lunch?"

"Probably not," the lawyer returned.

"Well, you'll have to wait until I get dressed, anyhow, before we go at it again. I feel so untidy," she said calmly, "in just a housecoat. Although personally I still don't see what there is to discuss. Oh, by the way, have you had the morning papers?"

"We have."

"Is it in all of them?"

"It is."

"And the murder?"

"Yes."

"I'll take them up to my room and read them before I dress. I'll bet they really knocked themselves out on this. Finding me and a murder besides—"

In the distance they heard the front door chimes. Douglas fixed his eyes accusingly on the girl. "That," he said, "is probably more—as it has been euphemistically phrased, I believe—gentlemen of the press. The telephone and the doorbell have been ringing steadily since before eight o'clock this morning. Mrs. Arnold has been delegated to answer the telephone, and Mr. Arnold has alternated between the front door and the back of the house, turning away reporters and photographers. At this moment he is out posting the grounds with 'No Trespassing' signs."

"Whoo! What it is to be famous! I suppose they want interviews with me."

"They will receive none. Mr. Trumbull and I prepared a statement for the newspapers last evening. It has been given to the wire services. And that," Douglas concluded ominously, "is all."

"O.K. by me—for the present," Virginia agreed. She winked at Bill across the table, and he shook his head warningly, but with a slight smile.

Purposely Virginia dawdled over her breakfast, but her father and Mr. Trumbull smoked cigarettes and sat on doggedly over fresh cups of coffee. Finally Douglas consulted his watch and said, "It's nine-thirty. Will you be dressed, Virginia, to meet Mr. Trumbull and me in the study by ten-thirty?"

"Make it eleven-thirty," she said airily. "I want to read the papers first. Besides, I'd like to talk to my husband alone for a few minutes before I go up to dress."

"I don't think that will be necessary," Douglas stated.

Virginia's face began to darken with a scowl, but Bill spoke up in an equable tone. "That's all right. We'll have plenty of time to talk—afterward."

Virginia relaxed. Bill had been so subdued during breakfast that she had begun to fear he was being affected by his position as an unwelcome guest, but this was almost a threat, as if he had come right out and said, "We'll go along with you. We'll accede to your wishes while we're guests here. We'll talk with you again. But it won't do any good."

Douglas and Mr. Trumbull had already done a good deal of talking between themselves, with the attorney summing up the situation for his client. "There are two courses open to you. You can accept the situation, recognize the marriage, and come to some kind of agreement with the two of them as to how they're going to live and where, and perhaps even get her to go on and finish her education, at least until she has the equivalent of a high school diploma. In that case you are under no legal obligation to assist her financially. It would be up to you whether you wished to give her an allowance. There is no way, of course, to use her inheritance as a threat. It comes to her without strings at the age of twenty-one."

Douglas's frowns and muttered phrases as his adviser outlined this course were answer enough.

"The alternative is to obtain an annulment of the marriage immediately. This can be done with very little trouble—legal trouble, that is. Evidently, however, this course would entail a great deal of trouble with Virginia herself. You would have to provide her with utterly reliable chaperones. I use the plural, because I fear it would be necessary to keep her under almost constant surveillance in order to avoid further—unpleasantness—"

"What about a school? Some other one, of course. I suppose the Misses Fairweather wouldn't let her on the place again—after this."

"It's possible. An Eastern school, perhaps, one in an isolated locality. But even the best of them are inadequate as—as—well, prisons—" He chuckled self-consciously to show he meant it as a joke.

Then Mr. Trumbull raised his eyebrows meaningly. "There is just a chance that she might be subject to—er—economic pressure. A few days of the kind of life she's just had may have taught her a lesson. In some ways it is unfortunate that she was apprehended so soon. If they realized that if they persist in this defiance they will have to live on the young man's income, it might put a different face on things—for him, at least."

"All right," Douglas said abruptly. "We'll try that." He groaned. "God, Trumbull, this is a terrible ordeal. To be defied by one's own child, and to feel"—he paused and confessed shamefacedly—"so helpless about it. It's—it's humiliating."

Mr. Trumbull had turned to one of the broad windows, where he stood with his back turned to Douglas, gazing out at the slope north of the house, at whose base the autumn gold of maple leaves made a softly warm border to the drab greens of the underbrush flowing back up the hillside.

"And that, my dear fellow," he thought but did not say aloud, "has probably been a large part of your child's unconscious motivation all along—the desire to humiliate you."

It was nearer twenty minutes to twelve than eleven-thirty when Virginia joined the men waiting for her in the study. The getting seated, the wary exchange of amenities as an overture to the business at hand were hardly concluded when there was a knock at the door and Imogene announced that a Captain Granger from the sheriff's office wished to speak to Miss Virginia.

"Show him in here," Douglas instructed her wearily.

"There's two of them," she added in a flustered manner.

"All right, all right, bring them in."

Douglas went to the door and greeted the two officers stiffly. Granger looked about at the assembled group and said stolidly, "We'd prefer to speak to Miss Forester alone."

"As her father I feel I have a right to be present at any interviews with my daughter."

"And I guess," Bill spoke up diffidently, "as her husband I'd better be here too."

"We're attempting," Granger insisted doggedly, "to get to the bottom of this murder. Miss Forester was around the place for several days. She may have information we need. I believe she could concentrate better and give us more assistance if there weren't so many people around." He looked directly at Trumbull. "If necessary, we could issue a warrant to have her brought into our office for further questioning."

Trumbull spoke dryly to the girl's silent but increasingly truculent defenders. "The officers will have no objection to my being present as Virginia's legal counsel. I think it best, Douglas, that you and Mr. Morgan wait in the living room."

Virginia had stood silent, her eyes moving from one of the men to another. As her father and Bill walked reluctantly out of the room she sat down in a straight-backed chair and folded her hands in her lap.

"I feel," she said, "like a dummy in a store window. People just push me around. Nobody dreams of asking me what I want."

Trumbull motioned the men to seats, and himself sat down behind the desk.

"Well, what do you want now?" Virginia demanded impertinently.

"We understand that on Wednesday—that's the day before yesterday—you went into the house trailer belonging to some people named Wilson, along with two other women with whom you had been talking in the driveway."

"Yes."

"Would you tell us what happened during this call on the Wilsons?"

"Happened? Why, nothing. We just—went in, and looked around, and pretty soon we came out again. I personally didn't care much about going in the first place. I just trailed along with the others."

"I mean, what was said, what you all talked about, how long you were there, and so forth."

Virginia glanced at Mr. Trumbull uneasily, and he nodded guardedly.

"Well, we all stood and looked around to see how it was furnished, and Mrs. MacLaren sat down—uninvited, incidentally, and then Mr. Wilson asked us all to sit down—"

"Just where did you all sit?" Granger interrupted.

Virginia contemplated the floor across the room while she brought the scene back in memory. She told him where they had sat. "And then Mr. Wilson served Cokes to everybody."

"Yes? Anything else?"

"Well, we drank the Cokes and we got up to go, and we went."

"Was Mrs. Camarilla mentioned while you were there?"

"Ye-es, I think she was," Virginia said slowly. "Yes, Mrs. MacLaren said her friend, Mrs. Camarilla, liked living in a trailer."

"Were any other remarks made about the woman?"

Virginia regarded her hands, which were clenching and unclenching in her lap. "I don't remember the exact words," she said carefully, "but I know Mrs. Wilson made some unflattering comment, said she'd seen Mrs. Camarilla go by; and I remember now she met my eyes with a sort of— amused—or no, that wasn't it exactly—but a look that let me know she hadn't been too impressed by Mrs. MacLaren's 'dear Stella.'"

"Did you make any comment on Mrs. Camarilla?"

Virginia met his eyes and raised one hand to her cheek. "I don't know. I honestly don't know. I might have said something, but I can't remember. It was all so pointless and—and—" Her shoulders lifted in a shrug.

Granger drew some folded papers from his pocket and consulted them ostentatiously before he said, "I understand there was a cupboard of some sort next the built-in seat where you sat, a cupboard with drawers."

"Yes. That is, I guess there was."

"Were any of those drawers opened by anyone while you were in the house?"

Virginia glanced quickly at Trumbull, who was studying the captain intently.

"I—I don't know. Maybe."

Granger turned to the attorney and said blandly, "I think you'd better instruct your client to answer frankly. We know that she saw the contents of one of these drawers."

Trumbull gazed silently at the detective, a slight frown drawing his eyebrows closer together. After a moment he turned his face to the girl and said softly, "It's all right, Virginia. Did you see anything in one of the drawers?"

Her former bravado had faded entirely from her manner, and now Virginia met Trumbull's eyes with perplexity in her own. She looked back at Granger. "I saw—a gun. Mr. Wilson opened the drawer and I glanced down and—and—saw it."

"What kind of a gun?"

"A revolver, I think."

"Why didn't you tell us that last night?"

"Just a moment," Mr. Trumbull intervened. "My client will answer any questions of fact. She need not answer questions of a subjective nature, such as her reasons for speaking or failing to speak at a particular time."

"I don't mind saying why," Virginia blurted out. "I just didn't think of it."

"A woman had been shot two doors from where you saw a gun a few hours before, yet you 'didn't think of it'!" Granger whipped out.

"Was this gun," Trumbull put in suavely, "the weapon used in the murder?"

"I'm not free to give out that information," Granger retorted coldly, and to Virginia, "Did you touch the gun?"

Trumbull opened his mouth, leaning forward slightly, but Virginia spoke too quickly for him. "Never. Never. I only had a glimpse of it, and then Mr. Wilson closed the drawer. I didn't even know he knew I saw it." She halted suddenly and glowered at Granger. "I bet he didn't. I'll bet you tricked me into admitting I saw it."

"Why shouldn't you admit you saw it?"

"Virginia, don't answer that question!" Trumbull snapped. He rose and faced the officers with dignity. "I don't like the tenor of this interrogation. I fear that I shall have to advise my client not to answer any more questions at this time."

Granger raised his eyebrows slightly and let them fall. "O.K., if that's the line you're going to take. We're only doing the best we can to find out what was going on out there. And your client was there. If she'd be frank with us, we might clear this up in a hurry. But if you won't co-operate, we can't force you to."

Mr. Trumbull smiled frostily. "Please, Captain, don't threaten us."

With a shrug Granger rose, and his companion did likewise. "Who's threatening anybody?" he said with a humorous inflection.

Mr. Trumbull saw them to the door, closed it, and turned the key. "That," he said to Virginia, "is to hold off your—er—relatives for a few minutes while you and I have a confidential talk."

She regarded him suspiciously. "What do we have to talk about?"

Trumbull surveyed her oddly. "You were right, I'm afraid. Before we're through with this thing, you may have to stand trial for murder."

She swallowed, and her eyes were clear and for once candid upon him. "You think so?"

"It's a possibility." He sat on the edge of the desk with one leg and looked down at her with a softening expression. "You understand, don't you, about the relationship between an attorney and his client? No one, not even your father or your husband, will ever know what you say to me now if you don't wish them to."

She nodded. "Yes, I understand—"

The doorknob turned, and Douglas's voice was raised irascibly outside. "What is this? Open the door."

Trumbull raised his voice, crisp with authority. "We wish to be alone and uninterrupted for a time."

"Trumbull, have you lost your mind?"

"No. Will you please not disturb us?"

The door was oak and heavy, and they heard Douglas muttering in disgruntled tones, and then Bill's sharper voice; but the men apparently moved away, and the two in the study faced one another again.

Trumbull looked off through the window and stroked his chin, musing aloud to himself. "They must have found that gun, and it must be the weapon that was used." He stared at the girl absently before he asked, "Was there any chance that you could have taken the gun that day without anyone seeing you do it?"

He went on hastily, holding up his hand as she scowled mutinously, "We have to foresee the possibilities. Could you have slipped it into your clothing and walked out with it?"

She raised her clasped hands and bit one of her thumbnails. "I—don't—know," she said slowly. "I really don't know. Everybody stood up, and it was crowded. The cupboard he was talking about was opposite the door. I sort of oozed out behind that mousy little creature—Parsons was her name. And the Wilsons sort of stood to each side of the door, ushering us out, and that MacLaren woman, yakety-yakety-yak—I guess everybody was looking at her most of the time."

Trumbull stood up and with his hands in his pockets paced across the room. "This Camarilla woman—did you suspect that she was going to turn you in?"

"Absolutely not. But I was suspicious of her. I didn't think she had got wise, but I was afraid she would. They all asked questions, but I sort of instinctively felt she was going out of her way to—to—find out what she could. But I didn't think she really knew—yet." Virginia frowned reflectively. "They're right about one thing. I didn't like her. The rest of them—they were common, ignorant, but—nice. Kind, I think you would say. But somehow Mrs. Camarilla's friendliness didn't ring true. I felt as if she wasn't really as—sweet—as she pretended to be, and that made me feel that she was harder underneath than maybe she really was."

"And I suppose," Trumbull said with a faint sigh, "you revealed this antipathy to some of the others."

"Not intentionally." Virginia scrutinized the man with returning assurance. "You see now, though, don't you? It's true what I said last night. That detective thinks I did it to keep her from—exposing me."

"He seems to," the lawyer said guardedly.

"So don't you think it's smarter not to provide him with too clear-cut a—motive—by having hell raised about my marriage?"

The man regarded her quizzically. "As I mentioned before, isn't it rather a two-edged sword you have hold of there? After all, it is you, not your father, who is suspected of murder."

"The scandal and the—inconvenience of the whole thing scare my father more than the possibility of being on trial scares me. Oh, it frightens me all right; I don't kid myself about that. But I'm more afraid of being separated from Bill than of being accused of murder. I'm sure a good criminal lawyer could pull me through if it came to a trial."

"Wouldn't you consider," the man said gently, "compromising a little? If your father, for instance, could be persuaded not to have the marriage annulled, wouldn't you consent to staying on quietly at home and perhaps seeing your young man at certain intervals, say once every two weeks or so, for—well, for properly arranged—dates, until you are eighteen?"

"I would not."

"After all, Virginia," he said persuasively. "Eight or nine months, that's not so long. Then if you're still determined to be married to Bill, by law your father can't prevent it. And you do owe Douglas some consideration. He is your father."

"What do I owe him?" she asked coldly.

"Why, my dear, his protection, your home—"

"Look, where does the money come from for my home, my clothes, my car, my school? It comes from my grandfather through my mother. And she's dead. What has my father ever done for me? I'd have all these same things if he weren't even alive. A trust fund could hire the Arnolds and a yard man and a couple of maids to keep a house open for me. But I want more than that. I'm entitled to it. Anybody is. I'll admit the trailer wasn't much in the way of a home. But we don't have to hide out anymore. We can get us a couple of rooms or something now, and I can have a real home with somebody in it that cares about *me* and that I care about. And that's more important than all these rooms to wander around in."

She had risen, and she paced about flat-footed in her loafer shoes, her voice rising as she went on: "What really decided me to take off was that he told me he's going to marry Madeline next month and they're going to spend most of their time down here. That was the end. I won't be purred over and bossed around by that hypocritical bitch. I couldn't stand it. And do you know why? Because she hates me." She lifted her hand defensively as he started to speak. "I know, I know. If she hates me it's probably my fault. I resented the idea of some woman coming in here where I've always done exactly as I pleased and starting to 'manage' me. No matter who it was, I probably wouldn't have liked her. And Madeline could tell I didn't like her, and naturally nobody likes somebody that doesn't like them. At least it takes somebody who's pretty big to do it, and she's not big enough."

She halted and faced him defiantly. "So that's that. You break the news to Father. It's no go. I'll settle for nothing but the privilege of running my own life. And if he tries to interfere—well, you saw how he was about the newspapers this morning. Well, I'll really give them something to go to town on if I don't get my own way. *I'll* give interviews; you see if I don't."

"I might remind you," Mr. Trumbull said coldly, "that even though most of your father's income derives from your grandfather's estate, Douglas is not necessarily obligated to spend it as freely upon you as he has always done. And that not all of his anxiety over your behavior in the past few days was due to concern for his own comfort. He was definitely worried about your safety. But I can see that talking to you is useless. You are fundamentally, in my opinion, a neurotic, spoiled child. Nonetheless, your father and I—and at considerable further expense and distress for him—will be put to the expenditure of a great deal of time and money to save you from the gas chamber. And I assure you that those efforts will not be entirely motivated by a selfish desire to avert disgrace for the family. That will be all now. I will speak to your father, and I advise you and your husband not to leave the premises until we can advise you of the results of our conference."

Virginia stared at him mutinously, and then with a short "O.K." stalked out of the room.

When Douglas came into the study Trumbull reported the interview with Granger.

"Then it's true," Douglas said, aghast, "they do suspect her."

"It seems so. The whole situation reminds me," Trumbull went on musingly, "of a magician's act. The bright-colored handkerchiefs, the flowing gestures—all calculated to distract attention while the essential motions are accomplished unnoticed. In this case Virginia is the bright color, the flashy gesture. If it were not for her, the police would pay more attention to these people who actually owned the gun. But the good captain is obviously bemused by the coincidence of Virginia's presence at the scene of the crime, and so it is up to us to investigate these Wilsons. The private detectives who have been working on the search for Virginia must now be directed toward the Wilsons and their past and present as well as toward a survey of Mrs. Camarilla's history. It is useless for us to suggest that the police do their duty along those lines. They are much too intent on building up a case against Virginia, now that they have provided her with knowledge of the weapon and a motive. And on that score I think it best, Douglas, if we proceed softly in regard to this 'marriage' of hers. As Virginia pointed out, annulment proceedings at this time would clinch their supposed 'motive.' They are bound to dig up someone out there who will be firmly convinced that the murdered woman had recognized Virginia. People will say anything at a time like this, partly from the desire for notoriety and partly because the drama of the thing infects them and they begin to believe they actually did hear things that they didn't. So if it's at all possible, you people should put up a front of affectionate family solidarity, try to make it look like an ordinary, thoughtless elopement."

Douglas rose from his chair and took a few steps about the room. "Perhaps," he said, his voice low and thickened, "it's all for the best. This boy, we were talking together while we waited for the police to finish in here. He seemed genuinely concerned about Virginia. And somebody, I suppose, sooner or later will marry her for her money. He's impossible, of course, socially—no background, quite unpolished; but he seems—decent enough. And perhaps I have neglected the child. After all"—he put out his hand helplessly toward the attorney—"what can a man do about bringing up a little girl? I'm fond of her, and I thought I was doing my duty. She's always been in the best schools. But she *is* old for her age in some ways, and maybe"—he shrugged wearily—"maybe it's best for her to be married, to have someone of her own to—care for. It's pretty obvious now," he finished dispiritedly, "that she cares very little for me."

"I think," Mr. Trumbull said impersonally, "it would be better for me to speak to them then. I'll suggest they both stay here for a while until, amongst you, you can work out plans for the future."

When Douglas unceremoniously departed from the living room to talk to Trumbull the newlyweds were alone for the first time in hours, and Virginia went straight into Bill's arms.

"What happened, honey?" he demanded anxiously. "Did they give you a bad time?"

"Oh, Bill, it was ghastly. They've found a gun and they know I saw it and had a chance to take it."

Murmuring distractedly, he drew her down on the davenport and held her comfortingly while she poured out an incoherent account of the last half hour's developments.

When she had finished he withdrew his arms and with his elbows on his knees put his head in his hands and said unhappily, "I dunno, it seems as if we've done nothing but cause a lot of trouble. I can't help feeling it's all my fault. I never should have let you get into such a mess."

"But it's not our fault if people go and get themselves killed!"

"No, but things like this would never have happened to you if you hadn't got mixed up with me." He lifted his head and looked around the somber but luxurious room. "I didn't have any right to take you away from—all this."

"Bill! Don't talk like that!" She drew a little gasping breath and then put her face in her hands and began to cry.

He turned and drew her close again, murmuring distressed, sympathetic phrases which seemed only to increase the intensity of her sobs. Finally she became coherent enough to implore, "Don't ever leave me. I couldn't bear it if you let me down too."

"I won't, I won't. Now, don't worry. It's just that I don't want you unhappy, and I seem to have made you more so instead of less."

Her tears had subsided, and she straightened, wiping her eyes with a handkerchief from her breast pocket. She glanced at the damp shoulder of his soiled white shirt and said with a shaky laugh, "Look what I've done to your shirt." Tentatively she touched the damp cotton. "You know," she said in a low voice, "this is the first time I've ever had a shoulder to cry on—at least since my mother died—and that was so long ago."

He tightened his arms about her, and she leaned her head on his arm with a tired sigh. "I think," she said softly, "everybody needs to know that somewhere there's a shoulder they can cry on if they should ever have to. I wish you'd remember that yours is the only one I have, in case you start having qualms of conscience again."

CHAPTER 14

After Douglas and Mr. Trumbull emerged from the study Imogene announced lunch. They were joined by Madeline in a soft wool dress and what Virginia termed her "drawing-room" manner. Nothing was said about the decisions reached during the past hour, and as a result the meal was a constrained affair inadequately glossed over by a patina of casual conversation.

As they prepared to leave the table Douglas spoke to Mr. Trumbull. "I suppose you're taking off for the city now."

"Yes, immediately."

Douglas turned his head very casually toward Bill. "It would probably be a good idea for you to get your personal effects and bring them here. You would be rather—exposed—staying at the trailer park just now, curiosity seekers and reporters and so on. Perhaps it would be just as well to bring the trailer here too. It could be parked out beyond the garage—temporarily."

"If it won't be too much trouble," Bill replied deferentially. "In the meantime we can be deciding what to do—about where we're going to live and so on."

"Er—yes," Douglas said dryly.

"I'll drive over with you," Virginia said bluntly.

Douglas frowned. "Do you think that's wise? You may—er—attract attention."

"I'll look after her," Bill said quietly, and Douglas shrugged with an air of not caring to argue further.

For the trip back to the valley Virginia left on the jeans and plaid shirt she had donned in the morning, but as she faced the mirror to apply make-up she hesitated uncertainly, thinking of the people in the trailer park. She meant to see them, to say good-by if nothing else. Somehow she felt she owed it to them after circulating among them as an impostor. And somehow it seemed more fitting that she return as they had known her. Yet she shrank from the false lashes, the caricature of a mouth.

Thoughtfully she found a brown eyebrow pencil, a narrow box of cheap mascara, and went to work to bring her plucked brows and her eyes into greater harmony with her still-red hair. Using a deeper shade of lipstick than usual, but one of a more conservative hue than she had used as "Marge," she painted her mouth, exaggerating its size a little. Then she regarded herself with satisfaction. This face was an adequate compromise between the married Marge they had known and the maiden Virginia she no longer felt herself to be.

They set out in Virginia's Ford, planning to visit Shady Dell first to gather up their belongings and afterward to stop by the service station, where Bill would pick up his own car and follow the Ford back to the Forester place.

The sky had cleared to a stainless blue and the air was crisp with the promise of winter. The spirits of the two young people lifted as they followed the road downward through grassy hollows and over rustic bridges above streams rushing turbulent from the rain under their overhanging sycamores. In the freedom of being alone together with the knowledge and consent of those whom they had considered opponents, they felt as if all their problems must be dispersing just as the lowering rain clouds of yesterday had cleared away.

"You know," Bill said cautiously, "I don't think your dad is such a bad guy. Kind of high-hat and wrapped up in himself, but it looks to me as if he gave in with pretty good grace."

"What else could he do?" Virginia sniffed. "He just can't stand the thought of any more scandal, and he's afraid if we all get in a public squabble over an annulment the police will double their efforts to pin this murder on me. It would be wonderful publicity for *them*."

"I don't know," Bill said doubtfully. "I think, as far as scandal goes, your father's already had it. A little more wouldn't seem as important to him as you seem to think it would. No," he went on seriously, "I think right now, believe it or not, he's thinking about protecting you. He's more concerned about your neck than he is about more notoriety. I think he figures that if they do charge you with this—this thing, it'll look better for you if your family has sort of closed ranks around both of us than if we're all involved in a big scrap with you kicking up your heels in public about it."

"Are you," she said resentfully, "going over to their side too?"

He reached out and squeezed her leg above the knee, grinning down at her briefly. "I'm on your side, baby, first, last, and all the time. Only thing I'm saying is—maybe you haven't got it quite straight about the way your dad feels about you. Looks to me as if when the chips are down he thinks a lot more of you than maybe even he himself ever realized."

They were in the valley now, and she turned her head to look off into the quick succession of narrow avenues between the rows of leafless fruit trees that flipped past against the speed of the car.

"Well, he's been a long time showing it," she said harshly.

Tactfully Bill changed the subject. "I'll bet we'll get the old once-over from behind the window curtains when we pull into the park."

"I wonder what they thought," Virginia mused, her eyes kindling, "when they found out who I was?" She paused, and went on in a more serious tone, "You know, I feel sort of conscience-stricken over taking them in that way." Her eyes rested ingenuously on Bill's profile. "Isn't that odd? Why should I care what they think about me? But, you know, everybody was so nice to me—when I stop to think about it. Billie Grandon, for instance, going to help me get a job; and Joan and her mother, they treated me as if I was—well, just anybody. And that funny little MacLaren woman, she was so—neighborly. Even the Beans, they were—pleasant. Now that it's over, I get a warm feeling thinking about how they all just—accepted me."

"I don't see," Bill ventured in a slightly puzzled tone, "that anybody did anything unusual. That is, I can't see as anybody went out of their way to be nice to us—as you put it."

"Maybe," she said slowly, "it's that I'm not used to people being nice to me—just for no reason."

"Why, honey," he protested, glancing down at her with an uncomprehending expression. "I'd say people had always been nice to you—in that sense. Polite and—and—well, not rude or insulting or anything."

"Who wouldn't be nice," she retorted cynically, "to three million dollars? The point is, these people were nice to me when I was just—well, just me."

Bill frowned ahead at the stretch of highway between them and a truck in the distance. "You're awfully conscious of that money all the time, aren't you?"

"You're darned right I am. It's—it's—well, it's the significant thing about me, don't you see? There really aren't so many of us, you see. Wealthy people, yes. All the girls at my school come from families with money, some from richer families than ours. But I don't happen to know personally another girl who at twenty-one will be sole mistress of a fortune like mine. And when people look at me—even my family—they don't see just Virginia Forester. They see three million dollars and what it can do."

"Sometimes I'm surprised," Bill said dryly, "you didn't think that was all I saw when I looked at you."

"I knew you didn't know who I was," she said calmly, "and by the time you did," she added coyly, "I'd had ample proof you wanted *me*."

They met each other's eyes and laughed, intimately but a little self-consciously, and she moved closer and clasped her hands on his arm.

It was two-thirty when they turned in under the archway lettered "Shady Dell." Only the Skaggses' sedan and the Grandons' convertible stood in their places. The other houses were quiet, looking a little lonely and deserted without their accompanying automobiles.

Ronny Ingleborg pedaled toward them on his tricycle as Bill pulled the Ford into place beside the Morgan trailer. When Virginia climbed out of the car he sat with his elbows on the handle bars, his chin resting on his pudgy fists.

"Hi there, half pint," she said with a grin, rather surprised at her own pleasure in seeing what she had previously vaguely considered an uninteresting little nuisance. She walked toward him casually. "Glad to see me again?" she inquired flippantly.

His round eyes considered her before he spoke. "I guess so."

"How've you been?"

He put his hands back on the handle bars. "Pretty good."

"That's nice."

He turned his head and pointed back across the driveway and looked up again at Virginia. "Her," he announced confidingly, "Miz 'Rilla. She got dead. Shot." He brought his right hand up with the fingers clenched in her direction and crooked his thumb twice as he added, "Bang! Bang! Like that."

"Good heavens," Virginia muttered, and then, louder, "Little boys mustn't think about—"

Her words were interrupted by a call through the screen of a window a few feet to her left, and Virginia jerked her head around with a start as Peggy Ingleborg commanded curtly, "Ronny, you get back here. Come on now. Come in the house."

Virginia could see Peggy's head through the screen, and she opened her mouth to speak, but the metal frame of the window banged down and the head disappeared.

"I gotta go now," Ronny said, efficiently wheeling his tricycle around. When he was headed the other way he looked over his shoulder and said seriously, "Did you do it?" bringing his right hand up over his left shoulder and moving his thumb in the shooting gesture.

With a muffled gasp Virginia turned and ran around the end of the car. Bill was in the house already, and as she stumbled up the steps he said, "B-r-r, it's cold in here after being shut up like this."

She put her hand on the doorframe and decided to say nothing, since he obviously had not heard what had transpired outside. But she turned her head and glowered at the rounded edge of the top of the trailer beyond her car, and Peggy Ingleborg went off her list of people who had been "nice" to her.

They were sorting out clothes and toilet articles and stuffing them into a pair of suitcases when there was a knock on the casing of the open door.

Bill turned to see who was there, and said, "Oh. Hello, Mr. Bean."

Mr. Bean, in the tan felt slouch hat and khaki pants and shirt which he wore almost as a uniform, said, "Hello," laconically, and went on, "I was just wondering. You folks plannin' to vacate?"

"Well, in a way," Bill responded, coming to the door. "We won't be staying here. But I thought I'd leave the house till we kind of get settled. That's all right with you, ain't it? We're paid up for another week."

"Yeah, I guess that's O.K. Just thought I'd find out what the score was."

With no further ado he turned and walked away.

Bill grinned as he turned away from the door. "Not very sociable, was he?"

"Well," Virginia replied slowly, "the Beans always were sort of matter-of-fact about things."

"Yeah, but after all that's happened, you'd think he'd have something to say. From curiosity if nothing else. But it seemed to me there was a feeling in the air of 'get the hell out.'"

"Maybe," Virginia said doubtfully, "he was embarrassed. Wasn't sure about the etiquette of the situation. After all, it isn't every day he runs into tenants traveling incognito."

"May be. Anyhow, it's nothing to us." He whistled through his teeth as he wound the cord around his electric razor and stuck it down beside a heap of socks in the suitcase.

Virginia looked out through the end windows. Her eyes came to rest on the Camarilla trailer. The shade was down on the end window where she had been used to seeing the gay little potted begonia hanging from its three chains that rose like a pyramid toward a hook somewhere above. She had always been able to tell when Mr. Camarilla was at home because the trunk of the car with its white-spoked spare wheel showed beyond the end of the house when the car was parked beside it.

"I wonder," she said pensively, "where Mr. Camarilla is. The place seems deserted."

Bill came to stand beside her and poked his head down over her shoulder to peer across the driveway.

"I suppose," he said soberly, "he has things to—arrange, the funeral and all."

"Poor man," Virginia said in a strange, tentative voice.

Bill stepped back, absently rolling up the handful of neckties that he had held in his hand. "The two weeks," he said abstractedly, "when you weren't here, I talked to him sometimes in the mornings. He wasn't working, and he sort of wandered around outside when it was a nice morning."

"Was he—nice?"

"Yeah. Yeah, he was. A simple, inoffensive kind of guy. I can't say as he ever said anything that amounted to anything, but he was—well, a good guy." Bill paused, looking at the neckties in his hand. "It's too bad," he went on, shaking his head, "this had to happen to him."

Virginia turned around; her eyes had a stricken look.

"Oh, Bill, I hope it didn't have anything to do with me, her dying. I wouldn't want to be the cause of—of—" She turned back to face the window, biting her lip.

Uneasily Bill's eyes rested on her back. "It couldn't have. Couldn't have," he repeated uneasily.

"You spoke of a—funeral. Do you think we ought to go?" she said in a low voice.

"No," he answered slowly. "No, under the circumstances, I don't think we'd better." He uttered an embarrassed laugh. "I'm afraid we'd steal the show. Everybody'd be staring at us instead of thinking of her."

"I suppose so," Virginia agreed sadly, and after a moment's pause, with more spirit, "But we'll send flowers. At least then he'll know we weren't just—indifferent."

"Sure. That's a good idea."

There was a silence for a few moments and then Virginia said, "The Grandons are still home. I think I'll run over and thank her for trying to get me a job. It seems sort of rude and—and furtive to just run in and right out again without a word to anybody when I may never see any of them again."

"Sure. Go ahead. I've got more stuff here to get together than you have."

Virginia was a little nervous as she struck her knuckles against the

Grandons' metal door. It opened so quickly that she suspected her approach had been observed. But it opened only about two feet, with Billie standing so that she filled the opening. She said nothing in greeting, only stood there regarding the caller with her face closed to expression.

"I—" Virginia began uncomfortably. "We just came out to pick up some things. I may not be back again, so I thought I'd just run over and—and say good-by—" She paused.

"Yeah."

Determinedly Virginia smiled again. "I wanted to thank you for trying to get me on where you work, even though I don't need the job anymore—"

She watched Billie's face hopefully, but Billie only answered in the same toneless voice, "That's O.K. It was no trouble."

Virginia's ingratiating smile faded, leaving her face blank and cool with hauteur. "I'm glad it was no trouble," she said crisply, and turned away arrogantly. Behind her she heard the door close instantly.

She moved with mechanical steps on the gravel, and then she halted. After a moment's hesitation she set off purposefully in the direction of the highway. Billie Grandon was probably sort of a dope, anyway. But Virginia was beginning to be angry, and also curious. And she meant to find out if everybody was acting like this.

Her eyes rested sharply on the MacLaren trailer, and she saw the curtain move at one window and detected a shadow behind it. Intentionally she walked slowly, with seeming aimlessness as she came closer. She would not go in there. She would give Mrs. MacLaren opportunity to come bustling out to say hello. It was the sort of thing Josie would do. But Virginia walked clear past the end of the coach, and Josie did not do it.

The Parsons' house looked deserted, but as Virginia passed the space where the car should stand, Mrs. Parsons suddenly appeared farther down, coming out from between the Skaggses' house and their sedan. She halted abruptly at the sight of Virginia, and her eyes widened. For a moment she seemed uncertain whether to dart back out of sight or to come on. But then she moved quickly forward. They met face to face opposite the Parsons' coach.

"Hello," Virginia said, smiling naturally.

Mrs. Parsons ducked her head, uttered a breathless "'Lo," and, skirting Virginia hurriedly, scurried around the trailer and up the steps.

Virginia's face hardened and her eyes glittered, but she lifted her chin and went on. Steadily she approached the Skaggses' door and knocked, assuming a languid stance as she waited for a response.

Mrs. Skaggs looked surprised when she opened the door. "Why—why, hello," she murmured.

Virginia smiled easily. "I just thought I'd drop in and say good-by while I was here."

Mrs. Skaggs digested the word "in," and her manners got the better of her evident reluctance.

"Why—why, yes." She held the door open wider. "Yes. Come in."

Virginia surveyed her cogently and then stepped inside. She noticed the sudden worried expression that replaced the surprise and uncertainty on Mrs. Skaggs's face.

"You're afraid of me, aren't you?" she said flatly.

Mrs. Skaggs had her hand on the edge of the still-open door, and at the girl's words fear did appear unconcealed in her eyes.

"I must say," Virginia muttered, "it's a new experience, having people afraid of me."

"I'm not scared of you," Mrs. Skaggs said in a weakly defiant voice, and the words seemed to help bring about the condition they asserted, for she added with more poise, "Won't you sit down?"

Virginia did so, and looked up at the woman intently. "But you think I murdered Mrs. Camarilla, don't you? You all think so."

"Well, I—I—I'm sure I don't know. Nobody," she said with a little rush, "knows *what* to think, so much happening all at once, you turning out to be—who you are, and all."

"Everybody has been awfully quick to judge me."

"Well," the woman retorted with more spirit, "you did—well, put one over on us, pretending to be one thing while all the time you were something else."

Virginia frowned up into the woman's disapproving face. "They—you—resented my not—being what I pretended."

"What did you expect? We took you in, so to speak, as if you were one of us, and then we find out you were—fooling us."

Virginia lowered her eyes to the tiled pattern of inlaid linoleum. "I see," she said thoughtfully.

"I'm sure," Mrs. Skaggs said impulsively, "I hope you didn't do that. About Mrs. Camarilla."

Virginia's eyes were candid as she looked up into the woman's face. "I didn't," she said simply.

Mrs. Skaggs regarded her intently, and then she said slowly, "You know, I'm inclined to believe you. Having a daughter of my own, I think I can tell when a girl is lying."

"Thanks," Virginia said with a breath of relief.

Mrs. Skaggs did not sit down, however, and despite the softening of her manner it was still tinged with constraint, which Virginia could feel.

The girl rose to her feet. "Well," she said awkwardly, "I wanted to say good-by and"—she smiled wearily—"thank you for being nice to me while I was here."

"It was nothing, I'm sure," Mrs. Skaggs returned in a "company" voice. As Virginia went out of the door, she added, as if still minding her manners, "And I'm sure I wish you luck, you and—your husband."

"Thank you," Virginia said ironically.

She heard the door close behind her.

With downcast eyes and arms hanging limply at her sides Virginia walked back to her own coach. She felt lifeless, dull.

Bill was lifting a suitcase into the trunk of the car. "Finish your calls?" he inquired cheerfully.

"Yes."

She went inside and glanced around listlessly. Putting her hands in her pockets, she moved up to the end side window and stared out past the rear of the car. A window of the Ingleborg coach was directly opposite her and she found herself gazing into the face of little Ronny pressed against the glass, his nose a flat white blob on the pane. Idly she met his interested gaze for a moment, and slowly her face came to life.

That morning. Was it only yesterday morning? She had been sleepily roused by the rain's frantic beating at the walls of the trailer. Half awake, she had lifted herself and glanced across the room and out of this same window into the gray wetness outside, and she remembered now she had seen that same little face and tousled head at the window opposite. As she had crawled eagerly back into the warmth of the bed, in the gray light of the room she had noticed the alarm clock—fifteen minutes to eight. And she had almost instantly fallen asleep again.

The police would not think of questioning a child between four and five years old. But might he not have seen whoever it was who approached the Camarilla trailer that morning? He might have looked out of the end windows as well as this side one. And the Ingleborg trailer was the closest to the Camarillas', except for the Grandons'. It was not directly opposite, but the Camarilla and the Grandon coaches stood only a few feet apart, flanked on either side by their automobiles, and the Ingleborg car stood directly opposite the Camarilla house. From the end window of the Ingleborgs' one could see between the Grandon and Camarilla houses.

It was a slim chance, a very slim chance, but little Ronny must have been the only person awake and up at this end of the park between seven-thirty and eight-thirty that morning. For there had been no lights in the Ingleborg trailer, so Peggy must have been trying to sleep through the rainy morning hours after her husband went to work. The morning had been too gloomy for anyone to be up and about without lights.

Virginia stared slightly as Bill's voice penetrated her reverie. "What's the matter with you? I asked how the calls went?"

"Oh. The calls." She paused for a second. "You know, three days ago I wouldn't have believed I'd ever give a damn what anybody here thought about me, pro or con."

"Didn't get a very good reception, huh?"

"No. Believe it or not, they're afraid of me. Bill, they actually believe I did it."

"Damn, I wish the police would solve this case."

"But on top of that—their being afraid—I can feel something else." She wrinkled her forehead. "They resent me. They don't—like me."

"Well, naturally, if they think you murdered somebody."

"The funny part of it is," she said, and it sounded rather pathetic and strangely out of character for her, "I don't want them to not like me. Somehow it's important to me, their good opinion, almost as important as not being—convicted of this thing."

She had turned restlessly and was now staring out of the rear window. She knelt in the seat and gazed at the vacant place where the Wilsons' outfit had stood and down to the little porch in front of the Beans' door. Her eyes narrowed, and she was silent, not hearing whatever it was Bill was saying in reassuring tones.

She whirled suddenly. "It was the Wilsons. One of them, probably her. It has to be. Look, *I* didn't take their gun. And while we were inside there, none of the others had a chance to, because I was nearest the drawer right up to when we left. And it's not very likely that both of the Wilsons were ever out of the trailer at the same time during the time they were here. So nobody else could have got it. Yet obviously it's missing. You can tell from the way Captain Granger talked."

"I wonder why the cops can't figure that out," Bill puzzled.

"Because they're too occupied with me, and because they can't see any connection between the Wilsons and Mrs. Camarilla. But I just thought of something while I was standing here looking down the driveway. She stopped to speak to me Wednesday, Mrs. Camarilla, and she said she had an errand to do. Well, it wasn't here in the court. Because she had on a dress coat and was carrying her purse—"

"I don't see—"

"If you're just running up to the Beans' or MacLarens' or somewhere here in the court, you throw on a jacket or a sweater and you carry your cigarettes or your handkerchief in your pocket. You don't button up in a long coat and carry a handbag."

"Yes?"

"Well, I stood there, just idly looked at the car and trailer that had driven up, not paying much attention to Mrs. Camarilla; but just before I came inside I saw her pass the car. And, Bill, she stopped and took a step back, and the woman in the car leaned forward and they said something to each other. Just then the man came out on the steps, and I came on inside. I was bored and restless and I knelt on the seat, just the way I did now, and looked out and watched those people get parked, and I noticed without even thinking about it that Mrs. Camarilla was standing talking to Mrs. Bean. I was just going to turn away and start to read when Mrs. Camarilla came back down the drive, and she stopped in front of the Wilsons' car and Mrs. Wilson moved up toward her, and they talked a minute and then he came to the door of the coach; and as I turned away from the window Mrs. Camarilla was on her way back to her own house."

Bill rubbed the side of his neck. "I still don't see— That doesn't mean they *knew* each other—"

"But look, Mrs. Camarilla didn't go on with her errand after she saw and spoke to the Wilson woman. Why didn't she? It looks to me as if she changed her mind when she saw who was in the car."

"I don't understand it," Bill said slowly, "but it does look funny, when you put it all together. Did you tell Granger all this?"

"I never thought of it till now. All I told him was that Mrs. Camarilla stopped to speak to me, and then I came on inside."

"It sure looks as if they ought to look into those Wilsons a little further."

"Another thing—" And Virginia outlined her speculations concerning Ronny. "I'd like to talk to the kid," she concluded, "but I don't think Mrs. Ingleborg feels very friendly toward me either."

"It's a pretty slim chance," Bill said dubiously. "Kids will say anything to get attention. If he figures out what you want him to say he'll say it."

"I suppose so," she returned with a discouraged sigh.

"I tell you what," Bill proposed with an air of decision, "I'll go talk to 'em. I might get further than you would."

"O.K. Do that," she agreed hopefully.

Mrs. Ingleborg opened the door a good three inches and peered out sideways at Bill.

"Well, what do you want?"

"I'd like to talk to you a minute." He looked defeatedly at the three-inch aperture and smiled ruefully. "If you're afraid to be alone with me, I could ask Mrs. Bean to come down—for a witness."

Somewhat shamefacedly Peggy let the door swing wider, but she stepped into the opening instead of letting him in. "O.K. What is it?"

"About yesterday morning. Were you up in the early part of it after Mr. Ingleborg left for work?"

"I was not. I went back to bed and to sleep. At least I dozed until about nine o'clock."

"How about Ronny? Did he sleep too?"

She regarded him suspiciously while Ronny peeped around at the man from behind his mother's legs.

"Off and on," she retorted sharply. "We have him trained to look at books and color with crayons if he wakes up before we do."

"He may have been up part of the time, then?"

"Maybe; he was coloring on the floor when I got up."

"Well, that's what I'm getting at. He might have looked out of the windows. He might have seen somebody around in the yard. The police didn't ask him anything, did they?"

"No, and I don't want him brought into this mess."

"I know, but it's like this, Mrs. Ingleborg," he said earnestly. "My wife didn't do it. Honest to God, she didn't, but we've sort of gathered that some people think she did."

Peggy was regarding him curiously, some of her defensiveness relaxed; and he hurried on, "We're just clutching at straws, I guess you might say, and there's a hundred-to-one chance Ronny might have seen something. If he did and if he told us now, we wouldn't need to be bothered again. You and I are both witnesses and could vouch for it without the cops ever having to talk to him."

She eyed him uncertainly and then turned, moving aside on the narrow step. She sat down, put her arm around the child who stood on the doorsill above her, and said, "You remember yesterday morning when it rained so hard?"

He looked seriously into her face. "The wind blew—whoo-oo-whoo-oo."

"That's right. And you and Mommy went back to bed after Daddy left."

"Uh-huh."

"Did you go back to sleep?"

He shook his head. "But I was quiet," he asserted defensively.

"Yes, you were. You were a good boy to let Mommy rest. What did you do while Mommy slept?"

"I colored. And"— triumphantly—"I went toi-toi."

"Did you look out the windows?"

"Yes."

"Which ones?"

He turned to point again. "Out there. I saw her—" He turned this time to point at Bill.

Bill steeled himself, but he asked, "Did 'she' come outdoors?"

Ronny shook his head. "No."

"Did you look out of any other windows?" Bill asked.

"Uh-huh. Down there." He pointed to the end of the trailer, which was directly opposite the space between the Grandon and Camarilla houses.

"Did you see anybody out there?" his mother asked in an intentionally casual tone.

The boy thought visibly. Then he brought out triumphantly, "Mr. 'Rilla. He went to work."

"Anybody else?"

He shook his head slowly. "But—" This time he leaned forward and pointed a pudgy finger at the opposite coaches. "I saw somebody back there."

"Back where, dear?"

"Back," he repeated.

"You mean behind the trailers?"

"Yup."

"Between Mrs. 'Rilla's and Grandon's?"

"Yup. They was blue—all over." He touched the top of his head.

"They? Was it two people?"

"Huh-uh. They was running," he added reflectively, "'cause it was raining, I guess."

Bill's eyes were bright. "That's wonderful," he said to Peggy, and pleadingly, "You'll remember this, won't you?"

"Yes, I'll remember," she promised, and then, with a last flash of skepticism, "For what it's worth."

"Don't you see," he said, "if we find the right party has a blue raincoat with an attached hood, it's important. You said he likes to color with crayons, so he knows his colors. And the blue part, if a coat like that shows up, shows he wasn't imagining things."

As Bill walked away with an encouraged spring in his step, the boy doubled up his fist at Bill and worked his thumb.

"Bang," he said.

CHAPTER 15

Virginia was waiting for him tensely.

"It worked," Bill exclaimed gleefully, "it worked."

"What did he say?"

"He saw somebody in something blue running behind the Grandons' and the Camarillas'."

"Oh, Bill, not really!"

"Yep, really. And Mrs. Ingleborg questioned him herself, and she agreed she'd testify to what he said."

"It's not very much to go on," Virginia said faintly, "but it helps."

Bill ran a hand through his hair and took a step or two with the other hand in his pocket. "I've been thinking what we ought to do. Your dad had private detectives working on finding you, and Trumbull has probably put 'em to work on this thing too. We could turn over this other information and the ideas you've had to Trumbull, so if you were hauled in they could be used for defense in the trial. But what I've been thinking is, we don't want you charged at all, even if the police finally figure they've got enough on you to turn it over to the district attorney. Their main interest is to catch somebody they can hang it on. So maybe the smart thing for us to do is go straight to Captain Granger."

"I don't trust him," Virginia said mordantly. "He doesn't like me."

"Fiddlesticks," Bill retorted impatiently. "You're hipped on this idea of people not liking you. Anyhow, what difference does it make if he doesn't like you? All the cops want is the murderer."

Virginia had bridled, opening her mouth to protest, but as Bill went on she subsided.

"No, I think we'd better high-tail it right in to the sheriff's office. And listen, let me do the talking." He glanced at her judiciously. "I think you sort of—antagonize 'em."

"Well, I like that. What am I supposed to do, flutter my eyelashes at them?"

"It wouldn't do any harm," he said imperturbably. "After all, they're just men."

"Seems to me you're getting awfully bossy all of a sudden," she accused, but without much conviction.

He grinned at her. "But you don't really mind."

"N-no. From you, somehow I can take it with better grace than from anybody else."

At the courthouse they were lucky to find that Captain Granger was in his office. They were ushered in to see him immediately, and per instructions Virginia sat meekly on a straight chair and just listened while Bill recounted her interpretation of what she had witnessed on Wednesday afternoon, and her theory that if *she* had not stolen the gun, then no one else could have and hence one of the Wilsons must have used it. When he had told of interrogating Ronny, he concluded, "And if Mrs. Wilson has a blue raincoat with an attached hood, that strengthens it still more."

Granger had kept his eyes fixed alternately on the young man's face and on a ball-point pen which he turned over and over on the desk blotter.

"But why would a perfect stranger shoot the woman?"

At this Virginia could restrain herself no longer. "My father already has a firm of private detectives looking into both the Wilsons and the

Camarillas. And you policemen are going to look pretty silly if they come up with evidence that those two women were mortal enemies from 'way back."

Granger regarded her coldly. Then he ignored her, speaking to Bill, who looked as if he wished his wife would keep her mouth shut. "Just what do you suggest we do about it? We have already, you know, heard the Wilsons' statement."

"I think you ought to talk to them again," Bill said doggedly. "I guess you're in charge of this case, and I think you ought to see them personally."

Granger's lips moved in a repressed smile. Although the girl was a pain in the neck, he rather liked the young fellow, who seemed simple and earnest and didn't put on airs.

"We asked them to keep us informed of their whereabouts for a few days. They're supposed to be camped at Big Sur tonight. It's past the season there, but the state park is open. Tell you what I'll do; I'll take two of my men and drive down. It's over a hundred miles and I don't like to do it, but I'm anxious to be thorough on this thing."

"We'll go with you," Virginia spoke up promptly.

"I'm afraid that's impossible."

"For heaven's sake, why? If you don't want us to hear what you say, I suppose we can wait outside while you talk to them. But it seems to me, if you want to get the truth, you might be able to tell which one's lying if you got us face to face."

Granger regarded her speculatively. "It's very irregular, and I doubt if that lawyer of yours would approve if he knew."

"Oh—Trumbull," she sniffed, "he never approves of anything. I guess I'd better phone my father, though. Or he'll think I've run away again. May I use that telephone?"

Virginia and Bill sat in the front seat of the county car with Granger, who explained that he preferred to drive on long trips, while the two deputies sat in the rear seat, ready, Virginia suspected, to draw their guns at the first sign of any funny business.

Douglas had sputtered with disapproval when Virginia told him on the telephone where she was and where she intended to go, and had wound up with the plaintive cry, "Can't I let you out of my sight for one minute?"

The early dusk of fall shrouded the countryside as they rose through the foothills at the end of the Santa Clara Valley to drop easily into the Salinas, and it was dark when they passed through still more low ranges to reach the coast and the long, twisting trail over the cliffsides south to the mouth of the Big Sur River.

As he drove Granger talked desultorily, pointing out objects of interest in the scenery, mentioning the last time he had been at Carmel, recollecting how the expansion of Fort Ord during the war had changed the surrounding communities, until Virginia and Bill were conversing with him casually in the relaxed manner of ordinary fellow travelers.

"Some ways," the detective said, "I get around the country quite a bit in my work. Other ways it's pretty confining. I kinda envy some of those people living in trailers, always moving on. New places, new faces. They lead a kind of interesting life, I expect. I'll be interested to see what the investigations turn up about the Camarillas, for instance, and the Wilsons."

"Nothing good, I'll bet," Virginia said pessimistically.

"Funny you didn't learn something about Mrs. Camarilla's past," Granger said idly, "while you were living there at Shady Dell. Somebody must have known something that would be the key to this whole thing."

"She didn't give out with much when she talked to me," Virginia observed.

"More interested in what she could find out, I suppose," the officer said genially.

"I soon put a stop to that," Virginia rejoined smugly.

Granger chuckled. "Turned the tables on her, did you?"

"Something like that."

Bill had looked across his wife's head at the detective's seemingly indifferent profile, and he felt that he and Virginia had made a mistake. This trip, for the captain, was not a pursuit of the Wilsons. It was an opportunity to draw out his chief suspect while he had her free from Trumbull's guarding supervision. While ostensibly Granger would be probing the Wilsons, he hoped by placing Virginia face to face with them to bring out damaging admissions on her part.

"Funny thing about people," Granger was observing philosophically, "how they affect different people different. Like this Mrs. Camarilla, the way we get conflicting reports on what kind of a person she was. Sounds as if different ones was talking about different people when they mention her."

"Whatever other people told you about her," Virginia said firmly, "you can take my word for it. She was ill-bred."

Bill had furtively pushed his foot against Virginia's as a warning signal. His arm was thrown loosely over her shoulders, and now he dug his fingers into her shoulder.

"Stop it, Bill," she protested mildly, and he glared at her.

She glanced uncertainly then from him to the detective, who seemed not to have noticed the byplay.

"I'll be curious to see what your detectives turned up," he repeated amiably.

Virginia had caught on to Bill's warning, and she retorted mutinously,

"I suppose you're firmly convinced they'll find no connection between Stella and the Wilsons, which will therefore strengthen the case against me."

"Well, we shall see what we shall see," Granger said equably, while this time Bill was hitting Virginia's knee with his in an effort to silence her. She dug her elbow into his ribs irritably.

The state forest ranger directed them promptly to the parking area for trailers, where one lone but powerful overhead light stood off the seemingly primeval redwood forests of the state reserve. One other trailer with its attendant dusty sedan stood humbly at a distance from the swankier bulk of the Wilsons'. The two little houses with their brave rows of lighted windows set evenly in a band around the rectangles of their shapes were, despite the pool of electric illumination provided in the center of the area, like pioneer dwellings in the wilderness.

Granger took one of the deputies with him into the Wilson coach, leaving the other in the car with Virginia and Bill.

"I wish," Virginia fumed as, after a brief colloquy with Mr. Wilson, who had appeared in response to their knock, the door of the trailer closed behind the men, "he'd have let us go in too. I'd like to be sure he's asking the right things."

The deputy in the back seat drawled, "The captain knows what he's doing. He wouldn't have come clear down here if he didn't have something in mind."

By the dashboard clock only ten minutes had gone by when Granger opened the door again and approached the car.

"You want to come in now?" he said to Virginia.

Bill descended from the car and Virginia climbed out after him. "Can I come in too?" Bill asked.

"I guess so." To the officer in the back seat, "You better stay outside—just in case."

"O.K." The man climbed out of the car. "Feels good to stretch my legs a little."

"Did you find out anything?" Virginia demanded.

"Maybe. Maybe not. They're sticking to their story."

"I'd like to stick them," Virginia muttered vindictively as Granger pushed the door open for her.

It was warm and pleasantly lighted inside the trailer, but the looks the Wilsons directed at the girl were anything but warm and pleasant.

Virginia's face lighted with satisfaction as almost the first thing her eyes fell upon was a shiny blue slicker thrown across the table.

Granger motioned the young couple to seats. "Now," he said, "I've been telling Mr. and Mrs. Wilson that the bullet lodged in Mrs. Camarilla's brain was a .32. And they say their missing gun was a .32. We've got it pretty well narrowed down, Miss Forester—"

"Mrs. Morgan," she corrected.

"All right, Mrs. Morgan. We've got it narrowed down that nobody else had a chance to take the gun after you saw it Wednesday afternoon. One or the other or both of the Wilsons were in the trailer constantly after that. However"—he looked at Mrs. Wilson—"we have a witness that someone in a blue raincoat was seen near the rear of the trailer park after Mr. Camarilla left for work yesterday morning—"

"There's more than one blue raincoat in the world," Mrs. Wilson interrupted shortly.

"Our men are checking on that right now," Granger said calmly. "I'll get the report as soon as I get back."

"I can't see," Mr. Wilson put in aggrievedly, "why you're devoting so much attention to us. We told those men this morning all we know."

"There's an awful lot of tie-ups to you folks. The gun and now the raincoat and—other things. We have reason to think that Mrs. Wilson at least had met the murdered woman previously and has falsely denied it."

The woman's eyes fastened fearfully on the detective's unrevealing face, and it was apparent that for the first time she was uncertain of herself, wondering how far back these people could have already traced the trail of a life.

Mr. Wilson's eyes went with bewilderment from the detective to his wife.

"That's utterly ridiculous," Mrs. Wilson snapped. "I never saw her before in my life."

Virginia had listened hopefully while Granger directed his fire at Mrs. Wilson. Now she could restrain herself no longer.

"Who are you trying to fool?" she demanded angrily. "You knew her. You know you did. And it's all going to come out. You wait and see."

"What will come out?" Mrs. Wilson asked coldly.

"Something you don't want known. That's what. Something Mrs. Camarilla knew about you. And that she was going to tell—" Virginia felt her mind glowing with inventiveness. It had come to her in a flash, something about the way Mrs. Wilson looked at her, the same sort of hateful gleam in her eye that Mrs. Camarilla had had when she baited her that day in the trailer. They were both bad actors; she just felt sure of it. "You—you were both probably mixed up with a—a crime ring— something like that—"

Mrs. Wilson turned on the captain, her face white with anger. "Are you going to sit there and let that little slut talk like that to me? It's illegal, that's what it is. I could sue her for—for libel."

"Now, ladies," Granger said so mildly that the remonstrance was meaningless.

Virginia came to her feet excitedly, also addressing the officer. "You see, you heard her! Nice women don't use words like that."

"How dare you!" Mrs. Wilson was standing too. "How come if you're so nice you knew what it meant?" She turned to her unhappily watching husband. "Rupert, how can you just sit there and let people treat me like this!"

"Captain," Rupert began truculently, "are you going to let this go on? This girl—probably a murderer—and you bring her into our home to insult my wife—"

"She's the murderer, not me!" Virginia cried. "She had a gun. She was outside in a blue raincoat at the time Mrs. Camarilla was killed—"

"It's a lie! Circumstantial, that's all it is."

Bill had made a motion to restrain Virginia, but he sat back again with a frown. Perhaps this was not such a bad thing, the two women facing each other, each fighting with words for her life, the "company manners" of each of them torn away by the strain. He saw that Granger was watching impassively.

Mrs. Wilson turned on the officer. "I'll report you. The way you're handling this. Letting this little tart come into my house—"

"Who's a tart?" Virginia screamed in sudden temper. "Nobody's going to talk to me like that!"

"I'll talk to you any way I damn please," Mrs. Wilson screamed back. "You—you *chippy!*"

As she delivered the last word with concentrated venom Granger abruptly abandoned the role of spectator for that of participant. He stood up.

"That's enough," his voice whipped out. "Sit down, both of you."

He had made the long trip to Big Sur with one purpose in mind, that which Bill had suspected in the car along the way, to pump Virginia, to try to trip her up when she was faced with the respectable Wilsons. And in the last few minutes he had discovered that he must tread softly, that he must indeed hold off until reports came in from official detectives or the private eyes the Foresters had working on the case. For he saw that it was possible this Wilson woman might not be all she seemed. Her final word had crystallized his doubts. "Chippy" was never a flattering word, but in his experience no one could use it with the loathing contempt of a professional applying the term to an amateur. And Mrs. Wilson had spoken it with that extra fillip of disapprobation that he would expect from women of a certain class.

"We don't seem to be getting very far," he said calmly, "calling names back and forth. A good many more things have to be looked into yet. I will say, though, this little interview has been—enlightening."

Mrs. Wilson had seated herself, but she was breathing hard. She glared at Granger. "You'd better do your looking where it'll do some good. You can see for yourself what an ugly temper our friend here has. And if Stella made her mad—"

"She does kind of fly off the handle," Granger remarked equably.

This observation seemed to calm Mrs. Wilson a little, and she drew herself up with dignity.

"I'll admit," Granger said agreeably, "at present we're kind of weak on motive for you, Mrs. Wilson, but from our notes on this morning's interview we understand that you were out of the trailer and hence out of your husband's sight yesterday morning."

"I was not. Those men misunderstood if they said that."

Granger was watching Mr. Wilson out of the corner of his eye. He saw the man glance compulsively at the raincoat and then at his wife.

"It was Mr. Wilson who made the statement," Granger went on inexorably. "You took the garbage out." He lashed out swiftly at Wilson, "And she wore the raincoat when she went out."

Wilson opened his mouth, blinked, and closed his mouth. After these outward signs of a momentary struggle with himself, he stammered, "N-no. That is, I don't think so."

"It took her quite a while to empty that garbage, didn't it?"

"No." The man's voice was stronger. "She was just—out, and right back in."

Granger came back without a pause to Mrs. Wilson. "You spoke to the woman twice Wednesday afternoon—once as she passed while you sat in the car, again when she came back and accosted you outside."

"What's that got to do with it?" Mrs. Wilson countered shrilly. "On the road like this, strangers are always stopping to speak." Losing control again, she glared from one person to another.

"Besides what possible reason could I have for shooting Stella LaSal—"

Her voice broke on the double-*l* sound as if cut with a knife, and her eyes went wildly from the face of one officer to another.

"So her name was once LaSalle?" Granger said coldly.

"I don't know what her name was," Mrs. Wilson squeaked. "I—just—it was something foreign. I just heard those men this morning say it, and—and I didn't get it clear."

"Her name was clearly mentioned in this room Wednesday afternoon. It's been in the newspapers." He nodded at a folded paper on the chest. "And the officers mentioned it this morning. Mrs. Wilson, I arrest you as a material witness pending further investigation of the murder of Stella Camarilla."

"You can't, you can't!" she screamed. "You've got nothing on me."

"I suspect," Granger said consideringly, "we'll have a whole lot more before we're through."

The woman turned on her husband. "Rupert," she cried, "do something! Don't let them do this to me!"

He regarded her dazedly, and furtively his eyes went to the blue raincoat and back to his wife.

"I suspect," Granger observed dryly, "Mr. Wilson is recollecting that you *were* more than a minute 'emptying the garbage.'"

At this Wilson visibly straightened his spine while his wife shrilled, "No!"

"Never mind, Wanda," her husband said heavily. "I guess you'll have to go with them. I'll drive up, too, and get a lawyer."

The other officer spoke up. "I was just thinking, Captain. We'll be kind of crowded taking her in your car, having"—he nodded at the goggle-eyed Bill and Virginia—"them along. How about it if Jerry and I ride up with the Wilsons here, and you can go on ahead with the kids."

"O.K. I guess you can handle them."

Heading back up the dark highway, Virginia said thoughtfully, "So she really did do it?"

"Isn't that what you figured?" Granger said dryly.

"Ye-es, but it didn't seem—real until—until she began to screech and—and act scared. Somehow, right up till then, I didn't really believe, I guess, that things like this really happened."

"I guess now," the captain observed laconically, "you'll be satisfied to stay put behind the nice safe walls of your own class."

She looked up at Bill in the dimness of the car and moved a little closer to him. "I guess so, as long as Bill's there with me."

He tightened his hold on her shoulders, but there was an edge of irritation in his voice directed at both the detective and the girl. "I been living in my trailer over a year now, and I never had no safe wall of money between me and the world even before that, but I never ran into anything like this before. So I wouldn't say as this was typical of us kind of folks." He gazed ahead at the paved road advancing ever faster upon the darkness under the beams of the powerful headlights. "I guess," he said profoundly, "it's just life."

There was silence for a few minutes, and then Virginia spoke up diffidently. "I was wondering, could you let it sort of get out, Captain, that I—helped? To solve the case, I mean. The people there at the park, they're sort of antagonistic since this happened. And maybe, if they think I took a hand in—well, bringing the criminal to justice—they might feel—kindlier—toward me."

In the dimness of the car's interior the two young people could not detect it, but for the first time in his dealings with them there was a human, completely unofficial twinkle in the captain's eyes.

He said gravely, "That might be arranged."

And Virginia relaxed in the curve of her husband's arm.

THE END

Note on "He Got What He Deserved"

This 1959 short story, which appeared in the Mystery Writers' of America all-female anthology *The Lethal Sex*, appears to be the last piece of fiction, criminal or otherwise, which Bernice Carey ever published. Certainly Carey's crime story portrays a member of her own sex, Gloria Ericsson, as lethal indeed (or, to use a popular modern term, "toxic"). Happily it would appear that diluted Danish ancestry is the only quality which the author shared with her murderess. The story is a finely turned piece of irony, etched in the most corrosive of acids, about a daughter who only wanted to help her mother....

HE GOT WHAT HE DESERVED

BERNICE CAREY

All the ingredients for prettiness were there: lustrous blond hair; round blue eyes; full red lips; round chin; soft, plump cheeks. Neilsen wondered why they did not add up to making her a pretty girl.

Alone with her in a room at the police station, Robert Neilsen sat and listened, professionally, impassively. He had been surprised at being called. One would have thought a woman held for murder would seek a lawyer of established reputation in the community, not an inexperienced newcomer.

In the first few minutes of the interview, however, she had explained her choice, prefacing her explanation by the declaration in a high, flat voice, that Gloria Ericsson was no fool. She knew her rights. The first thing, she had demanded a lawyer. She refused to say one word to the cops until she had talked to a lawyer.

Neilsen had nodded gravely, corroborating the correctness of this procedure.

"The only lawyer we ever done business with," she had informed him, "was old Mr. Stedman, and he died a couple of months ago. So I didn't know *who* to turn to, and I just looked in the classified section of the phone book and picked a name I liked."

Her eyes grew fixed for a moment on his, and then she laughed, abruptly and briefly. In the course of their interview Neilsen became aware that she never smiled, only laughed in this sudden, disconnected way.

"Dad was Scandinavian. Norwegian," she elucidated, "and when I saw your name: Neilsen, I said to myself, that's for me. Another Scandinavian. Be kind of like one of my own folks."

Robert Neilsen smiled perfunctorily, and decided not to apprise her of the fact that although his name had come down from a Danish great-grandfather, this forefather's blood had been diluted, not to say obliterated, by typical American cross-currents all along the way: English, Irish, French, a dash of German, and a possible strain of Chippewa Indian on the side of one great-grandmother.

In school, and in his brief period of practice, Robert had learned that it is best to hold one's client firmly to essentials, suavely barring the paths to irrelevant discursiveness. But it was not easy to do with Gloria Ericsson, and after the first few minutes he quit trying.

"I killed him, of course," she said. "But the way I look at it, I was perfectly justified. All you have to do is let the judge and the jury know what was going on. Anybody would have felt just like I did. And, of course, I really did it for Mamma's sake."

"You *intended* to kill the man?" Neilsen interjected in a slightly dazed tone.

"Oh, no. That is, I hadn't *planned* to." She paused for a moment, and her pink and white countenance was entirely blank, her eyes empty.

Robert Neilsen deduced that behind this blank façade she was considering what had happened.

"I guess," Gloria resumed, "I didn't really mean to kill him even when I hit him with the vase." She pronounced it "vahze." "I was just mad, and I picked up the nearest thing and whammed him with it. You know how it is when you lose your temper."

Robert nodded feebly.

"But when I tell you what that man was up to, you'll see why it served him right, getting himself killed." Without seeming to deviate from their unseeing fixation upon his own eyes, the azure irises of hers oscillated in a sort of frantic movement from side to side, as if Gloria were unable to hold them steady in her anger at the wickedness she was recalling.

"You see, Mamma and I are all each other has. I always say parents and children are really closer than even husband and wife. Well, after Dad passed away, and I got married, I and Harold—that's my ex—we went on living in Mamma's and my home. You see, Dad left the house and his insurance and everything to Mamma. Dad was—well, a little funny that way. Not that I've got anything *against* him. But, well, you'd have thought he'd have looked after *my* interests a little. Though, of course, I was only seventeen at the time, and he counted on Mamma looking after me.

"Well, when I came of age, I had a talk with Mamma and explained to her how it was. In case she passed away, all the delay over a will, and having to pay lawyers' fees—no offense, Mr. Neilsen." She interpolated a laugh—to show there was nothing personal in the remark—and went on, reclasping her long, rounded fingers over an alligator bag, causing two diamond rings to glitter more brilliantly with the movement. "Well, I showed Mamma that the only sensible thing to do was put our property in both our names, the bank accounts, too; so they wouldn't be tied up for ages—in case anything happened. Mamma saw, of course, that it was the thing to do. My mother is devoted to me, absolutely devoted. So we fixed our home—and a little house the folks had on the other side of town that we rent out—so we have joint ownership of everything.

"And I must say, Mr. Neilsen, everything has worked out just swell. When Dad died the folks had our home fixed up lovely. Everything you could want. Electric all through. Magic Chef in the kitchen, and a Frigidaire with a deep-freeze, and a Bendix and a mangle, and a Mixmaster—"

She leaned forward a little, pushing the soft muskrat coat back on her shoulders. Her face grew intent, and although she looked straight at him, the lawyer had an uncomfortable feeling that momentarily she had forgotten his presence as she went on—lustfully was the only word he could think of—enumerating the possessions which filled her Home.

"And since I've been working—I didn't quit even when I got married—I'm an I.B.M. operator for the Sno-White Creameries—handle anything: tabulator, setter—anything you want to mention. I get a good salary—ver-ry good. Believe me, they know a valuable person when they get hold of one. Well, the money I've spent on our home! You see, me not having to pay rent, and Mamma paying for the food and utilities, I was able to get things really nice. There isn't *anything* we don't have. I guess our home can stand up against *anybody's* in this town. The living room rug alone—it's cream-colored broadloom—cost over five hundred dollars. And the bedroom sets. *Sim*ply lovely. Just last year I got a new one for my room—Swedish Modern. Blond maple, you know. And I let Mamma use my old set in her room—imitation mahogany with brass handles. It's really mine, of course. Harold's—my ex, you know—Harold's folks gave it to us for a wedding present. Cost over four hundred dollars. I managed to hang on to *that*, you bet, when him and I split up."

While she paused for breath, she settled the muskrat more securely on her shoulders and renewed her clutch on the alligator handbag. Neilsen's mind stirred with the knowledge that this was a point at which he should firmly lead the woman back to his business with her. But he was numbed by the torrent of words.

"So you can see, we were getting along fine. Had *everything*. And I never *dreamed*. She met him in church. Mamma went every Sunday, but I was usually too busy, taking care of my clothes and all. I'd only met him twice, mind you. Once at a church supper. He sat with us, but I didn't think much about it, although I remember now at the time I thought it was funny the way Mamma insisted on wearing the red dress with the white floral print that I had given her from summer before last. She said when I gave it to her she thought it was too gay; but here she was wearing it to a *church* supper after I *told* her she ought to wear the navy blue with polka dots. Mamma does dress well; she never has to buy anything for herself. I give her all my clothes when I'm tired of them."

Her eyes grew perfectly blank again. Neilsen was beginning to recognize this evidence of introspection.

"I should have known something was up," Gloria burst out. "The way she fussed over her looks these last few months. Having a new Toni every three months, and wearing the different shades of lipstick I'd given her. Honestly, it's disgusting when you stop to think of it, a woman in her *fifties*. And the *sneaky* way they went about it. That's what really gets me. Now I find out he used to call at the house evenings when I was out!"

Her eyes moved quickly, and then fastened fixedly on the attorney. "It's not," she announced virtuously, that I blame *Mamma*. Why, Mamma has always told me everything. Like sisters, people always said. It was that man. He influenced her. Had her simply eating out of his hand.

"And tonight—well, tonight they have the nerve to spring the whole thing on me out of a clear blue sky. When I got home from work, there he was, big as life, in the rose tapestry armchair in *my* living room. Mamma had invited him for supper—without even telling me. And then—" She thrust her head forward, a three-strand necklace of pearls swinging out from the sponge-soft skin above her full bosom. "They tell me they want to get married!"

In the dramatic pause which followed, Neilsen made a noncommittal noise in his throat.

"And my father dead only seven years! Why, it's indecent! And as if that wasn't enough, what do you suppose they wanted to do? *Live* in our home, both of them. He had it all planned out. He's got a chance to be head custodian in the new Farmers' Exchange Building downtown, and he was going to quit at the apartment house where he's been working, and take this job, and live in my house."

Her eyes were blank and still for a moment before she spat out, "A janitor! Imagine! But the payoff— What do you suppose he had the nerve to say to me? He said I was welcome to stay on and live with them; but I should sign over our property to Mamma—everything but stuff like the rug and the bedroom sets and my china and silver. He even had the nerve to say 'sign it back' to Mamma. And she just sat there and looked at the floor and twisted her fingers together and never said a word.

"Well, you can just bet your life I told him where to get off at. And I told Mamma just what he was up to, trying to get his hands on our home and our money. Of course, he jumped in then and said he didn't want any part of what we had. Everything would stay in Mamma's name, and she could fix a will any way she wanted, but that by God—those were his very words— he wanted Alice—that's Mamma—to be independent. She'd been dominated—imagine, dominated!—by me long enough, and he wanted her to be free to live her own life.

"Well! I tell you, I just blew up then, and did I ever tell him off! Butting into our lives and spoiling everything just when we had everything anybody could ask for. And then he started insulting me. He called me selfish and greedy—those were his very words. I will say this for Mamma; she tried to stop him.

"She said, 'Oh, Ed, she doesn't mean it. She just doesn't understand. Gloria thinks she's doing what's best for me—'

"And he butted in and said, 'All she ever thinks about is what's best for Gloria—'"

Gloria's lovely shoulders rose and fell in a shrug of righteous hopelessness. "Well, it just went from bad to worse. I could see Mamma was on his side; he'd force her to go through with this scheme, and if they went to law about it, they'd probably manage to get some of the property and things Dad left us. And I'm telling you, by that time I was so worked up I just picked up that bronze vase off the mantel and lit into him."

The eyes went still and blank again before she spoke with impersonal reflectiveness, "I guess he had a thin skull. I didn't hit him very many times. Anyway, now you see why I said any jury that knew the whole story would see I was perfectly justified. A man that was trying to break up my home, take advantage of my mother, practically rob me. He only got what he deserved."

One of the reasons Robert Neilsen had gone into law was that he had always prided himself on having a glib tongue. He had entertained youthful visions of confounding opposing counsel—not to mention judges and juries—with his rapier-like quickness in debate. But now he only sat staring stupidly into the unwinking blue eyes, bereft of words.

In an appalling psychic flash, he had a vision of Gloria Ericsson on the stand. And she would be there. Nothing on earth would stop her from "telling her own story." It made him reflect briefly as to whether he was really temperamentally suited to the practice of law.

The End

68649434R00169